# NEIGHBORS

## By Susan Carol Kent

*May all your neighbors be good ones!*

*Susan Carol Kent*

Wild Daffodil Press

*For Steve,*
*who never reads fiction but read this*

*and*

*in loving memory of Anne Bolin*

# FRIDAY
## Chapter 1

**Officer Katie Bell** was the first emergency unit to arrive at the house in the New Town subdivision of Potoma. Unlike the rest of the communities in the town, which featured gridded street plans and a chronological mix of turn-of-the-century Victorians, early 20th century bungalows and 1950s brick ramblers, New Town was developed with dead-end cul-de-sacs and European style homes. Once a summer resort for the wealthy during the late 1800s and early 1900s, a devastating hurricane followed by the Great Depression had made the quaint riverside village a near ghost town by the 1930s. Now, Potoma was a bedroom community for the large cities around it and a weekend vacation spot for families, fisherman and boaters. At 6:00 am, it was still fairly dark and Katie's siren echoed loudly in the morning quiet. Katie reported in then opened the door to her squad car. As Katie climbed from the car, the ambulance pulled in beside her and the two paramedics, jumping from the cab with emergency equipment in hand, accompanied Katie to the front door at a run. Katie knew both of them. Ben, now one of her best friends, she had graduated with from high school and dated briefly before they went off to different colleges; Allison was a few years younger but they had lived on the same street growing up. The cul-de-sac was now awash in the red and blue lights reflecting into the sky and off the surrounding houses. Katie stepped aside to let Ben and Allison enter the house in front of her then followed them as they were led up the curved staircase to a second floor bedroom. Katie saw the girl sprawled on the bed, motionless.

"She's breathing but barely," Allison announced

"Check out the needle marks," Ben observed, turning the girl's arm over.

"Oh my God!" the girl's mother screamed covering her mouth with her hands and sinking into her husband's chest.

"You think this is drug-related?" Katie asked Ben who was holding the girl's arm.

"Looks like it could be," Ben answered, without looking up.

"No. No way!" the father protested as the girl's mother began to sob.

Katie laid her hand on the father's arm. "I'm Officer Bell. Can we go out into the hall to talk?"

The father nodded and pulled his wife along with him as he followed Katie out of the room.

"They are doing everything they can," Katie assured the couple. "She's still breathing, and that's a good thing."

"I want to go back in," the mother wailed and tried to pull away from her husband who wrapped his arms around her even tighter.

"Ma'am, I know it's difficult, but it's better to let the paramedics do their job. We're just in the way in there," Katie said, positioning herself to block the woman from moving toward the bedroom door. "Can you tell me what happened, Mrs... ?

"Ashton. Ellen. And I'm Justin," the father informed Katie.

"Mr., Mrs. Ashton," Katie nodded. "Please tell me what happened."

"I...I came to wake her up for school and I...I couldn't get her to wake up," Ellen Ashton sobbed.

"When was the last time you saw your daughter?" Katie asked, flipping her pocket notebook open.

"About 11:00pm last night. That's usually when she goes to bed on school nights," Justin Ashton answered.

"Do you know if she was actually going to bed or just to her room for the night?"

"What's the difference?"

"A lot of teenagers like to stay on Facebook or texting on their cell phones late into the night," Katie suggested.

"Do you think she might have talked to someone last night after she went to bed?" Ellen Ashton asked, still weeping.

"It's a possibility. Does your daughter have her own cell phone?"

"Of course. Like every other teenager her age," Justin Ashton replied.

"Does she have her own computer in her room?"

The Ashtons both nodded.

"Do you know if she had a Facebook or My Space account?"

"Facebook," Ellen Ashton answered, wiping her cheeks with a tissue.

"We'll probably want to check her cell phone and her computer to see if she contacted anyone after 11:00pm last night. Would that be OK?" Katie asked, making notes, then flipping to a new page.

"Anything," Justin Ashton shrugged.

"OK. So the last time you spoke to your daughter...I'm sorry, what is her name?" Katie asked.

"Jessie," Ellen Ashton answered.

"You spoke to Jessie at 11:00 last night. Can you tell me about that conversation?"

"We were watching television and she came into the living room and said she was going to bed. Then she gave each of us a kiss and went upstairs," Justin Ashton replied.

"Did she seem upset or anxious? Anything out of the ordinary?"

"No. About the same as always, really," Ellen Ashton said, her eyes starting to water again. "My God, what are they doing in there? Something must be wrong!"

"Hey guys, how's everything going?" Katie called, hoping for positive feedback to calm Mrs. Ashton who looked as if she were halfway between fainting and going ballistic.

"We're bringing her out. We've got her stabilized," Ben called back.

"You can follow them out," Katie informed them.

Ellen Ashton nodded her head and her husband squeezed her shoulders. Obediently, they waited while the paramedics rolled Jessie into the hall then carried her down the staircase.

As Katie and the Ashtons followed, Katie inquired if the Ashtons had any other children.

"Our other daughter, Veronica, spent the night at her friend's house," Ellen Ashton explained.

Katie nodded. "You can go to the hospital with

Jessie but I'll have to finish questioning you later this morning. Do I have your permission to search Jessie's room?"

"Search it for what?" Justin Ashton asked, somewhat defensively.

"There seems to be physical evidence that your daughter injected herself with something. I need to ascertain if there is anything relative to that in her room. If I find anything, it could help the doctors know how to treat her."

"My daughter would never do drugs!" Ellen Ashton protested.

"I need to look," Katie replied, calmly.

"Anything you want," Justin Ashton said, hurrying after the paramedics, his wife in tow.

Katie turned around and re-entered the house, making her way back up the staircase to Jessie's bedroom. As she walked into the room, Katie noticed the dusty pink walls, the pink and black comforter on the bed, several black shag throw rugs on the wood floor. For a moment, Katie just observed the room. The comforter was in disarray, thrown back as if someone had just gotten out of bed but bunched up in spots as if they'd flopped back down on it and wiggled around. The black and white striped pillows were askew as if they had been grabbed and pulled. A few throw pillows were lying on the floor beside the bed.

Katie glanced around the room. A dresser with a large jewelry armoire on top; definitely an antique. A wardrobe with the door closed, no clothes hanging out. The desk contained a laptop computer which was shut and appeared to be turned off, a neatly stacked pile of magazines, a framed photograph of Jessie with several other girls precisely placed on one back corner. A backpack sat next to the wall on the floor beside the desk. An antique-style vanity with a tufted pink stool stood next to the window, across the room from the bed. Various boxes and fancy perfume bottles hugged the rear perimeter of the vanity. Hats in different styles and some old-fashioned beaded purses hung decoratively from the corners of the mirror. Katie focused on the nightstand beside the bed which held an alarm clock, a single book with a bookmark sticking out and a cell phone which was attached to a charger plugged into the wall. Katie was surprised to see that Jessie's room held no television.

Katie walked over to the two doors placed side-by-side in the far wall. The first opened into a closet where everything was neatly hung or stacked on shelves inside. The other door led to a tidy bathroom. Katie went back to the bed, got down on her knees and lifting the bedskirt, peered underneath. She flipped on her flashlight and pointed it this way and that. There was absolutely nothing under the bed. Not even a dust bunny. Katie rocked back on her heels and opened the drawer to the nightstand. Inside, were a box of tissues, some pens and pencils, and a drawing pad. Katie looked into the wicker wastebasket beside the desk. It contained a few gum wrappers and a short stub of a pencil.

Katie then went into the bathroom. She checked the square pink trashcan that sat between the toilet and the pedestal-style sink. She put on latex gloves and poked through the tissues lying on top. She found a flattened toothpaste tube, a used razor head, empty shampoo and conditioner bottles. At the bottom was an assortment of cotton balls and Q-Tips. Katie pulled the latex gloves off and pushed them into her trouser pocket. She opened the narrow linen closet. Several folded sets of towels and washcloths and a sheet set lay neatly on the top shelf. The middle shelf held spare bottles of various products in plastic tubs. The bottom shelf contained cleaning products, sponges and a new package of toilet paper. On the floor were a toilet plunger and a black bucket. Katie turned on her flashlight and flicked it over the items on the floor, illuminating the corners and back of the closet. Closing the closet door, Katie moved to the pink wicker clothes hamper. When she removed the top she saw that there were clothes inside. Katie put on a new pair of latex gloves and pulled each of the clothing items from the basket—a white tank top, a denim mini skirt, matching floral print bra and panties, a light green cardigan sweater. Katie felt the pockets of the skirt. They were empty. Katie shook the hamper, then turned it upside down.

Katie picked up the cell phone lying on the nightstand

beside the bed, hitting the "End" button to turn it on. The screen lit up. Katie pushed the "Send" button, bringing up recent calls. Five calls had been made or received since 6:00pm the night before. The last one had occurred at 11:35pm. Katie took out her notebook and copied down the names and phone numbers on the screen. She'd follow up on these later.

Katie opened the laptop computer on the desk, pressing the "On" button. Almost immediately, the screen lit up, rows of icons lined up on the left. Katie clicked on the "Facebook" icon. The screen went immediately to Jessie's homepage. Katie scrolled down the page to see if Jessie had posted anything last night. At 7:30, Jessie had commented on a friend's recently added photo with *"Great new pic. Love the 'do."* Katie continued to scroll down but found no additional posts. Katie clicked on "Messages". The last message Jessie had received was more than a week ago. It was from a Ruthie and included the girl's new phone number. Katie checked the other three messages. One was from the same Ruthie, confessing that she had a crush on Mark. Another was from Mark, asking Jessie if Ruthie was going out with anyone to which Jessie had replied *"No. You should ask her out"*. The third message was from a Michella and simply read, *"Call me, girl."* Katie wrote down the information in her notebook before clicking out of Facebook and closing down the computer.

Now, Katie returned her attention to looking for evidence that Jessie had injected something into her arm. She decided she should photograph the bed before she began removing the bedding so she went to her car for the camera. As she was retrieving the camera from the trunk, fellow officer, Anna Madrid, pulled up.

"Hey, you working this alone?" Anna called as she alighted.

"So far. Not sure if it's a crime scene, yet," Katie replied.

"I heard the call. It sounded like an ambulance run. What's going on?"

"Jessie Ashton's mother couldn't wake her up this morning so she called the ambulance. I was in the neighborhood so I figured I could give the paramedics a hand. You know, hysterical family members, that kind of thing. Anyway, they found needle marks on Jessie's arm. Of course, her parents are adamant that she's not into drugs."

"Typical. Do you believe them?"

"Well, from everything I've observed about Jessie so far, she doesn't look like the stereotypical drug user. But you never know," Katie replied, reflecting on the unusual tidiness and cleanliness of Jessie's bedroom suite.

"That's for sure," Anna concurred, shaking her short blond curls. "The parents have gone to the hospital with the ambulance?"

Katie nodded. "I'm doing a little investigating."

Katie had pulled the camera from the protective leather bag and hung it over her shoulder, pushing the trunk lid closed.

"Why? Do you think there *was* a crime committed?" Anna asked as she moved in beside Katie, who was walking back to the front of the house.

"I'm not sure at this point. Jessie definitely had needlemarks on her arm but so far I haven't found any paraphernalia in her bedroom or bathroom . I was just going back to take photos before I started moving anything around," Katie explained.

Anna called in, then followed Katie up to Jessie's bedroom, standing out in the hall while Katie snapped picture from several angles. Then Katie moved into the bathroom; she dumped the contents of the trashcan onto the floor, spread them it out and took more photographs. Returning to the bedroom, Katie set the camera down beside the laptop on the desk.

"I want to go through the bedding and see if a needle or vial is mixed up in it somewhere," Katie informed Anna.

"Where was Jessie found?" Anna asked.

"On her bed, lying on her back. She was under the covers," Katie replied as she reached for the edge of the comforter. "Let's just pick the comforter up and straighten it out. Maybe something is caught in the wrinkles or under this part that's flipped back."

Katie and Anna pulled the comforter flat across the

bed but found nothing. Then they removed the comforter, careful to notice if anything fell from it. Again, nothing. Gingerly, they removed the pillows one by one shaking them gently, then removing the pillowcases. Together they also pulled the sheets off the bed. After stripping the bed, they used their flashlights, on opposite sides of the bed to look underneath it again.

"There's nothing here," Katie commented.

"Did you check all the drawers? All the dark corners in the closet?" Anna asked.

"Let's double-check," Katie replied, nodding.

Katie and Anna went through every piece of furniture, pulling out each piece of clothing or other item, replacing everything in its original order. They did the same in the walk-in closet. Neither police officer could locate any type of drug paraphernalia.

Just as Katie and Anna were leaving the bedroom, Katie's cell phone rang. It was Ben.

"Hey, girl," Ben greeted. "Just wanted to touch base with you about Jessie Ashton. Those were definitely injection marks on her arm. Three of them and all fresh which is a bit strange because generally a junkie's only going to do one injection at a time. Of course, she could have been shooting up multiple drugs but only a clean freak would use separate vials for each one when it's a lot easier just to put them all together and stick the needle in once. My opinion, three fresh holes indicates someone who's probably never given themselves an injection before."

"Do you know if there's any indication of prior injections on her?" Katie asked.

"I didn't see anything. As you know she had on boxer shorts and a T-shirt but no shoes so the most common places to use a needle were exposed. I checked and didn't find injection sites anywhere," Ben answered. "Some people do inject around their belly or buttocks but that's not as common as arms, legs or feet."

"So your opinion is that she's probably not a drug user? At least not a regular user?" Katie confirmed.

"In my opinion, this was probably the first time she'd ever shot up," Ben answered. "By the way, did you find what she used?"

"That's the really strange thing. I can't find anything. No vials, no needles, no syringe, no nothing."

"Really?" Ben replied incredulously

"Yeah. Anna showed up a little while ago and we went through every inch of the bedroom, bathroom, even the closet. Nothing."

Ben signed off and Katie told Anna what Ben had said. "I need to go to the hospital and finish questioning Ellen and Justin Ashton," Katie said as she slid the camera into the trunk of her car.

"I'll follow you over," Anna offered.

When Katie and Anna arrived at the hospital they checked in with the dispatcher then made their way to the emergency room. A nurse led the two police officers to an examination room where they found Ellen and Justin Ashton flanking the bed on which Jessie lay, still unconscious and hooked up to an IV and oxygen. Ellen Ashton's face was streaked with dried tears and her short brown hair hung limply from a center part, messily pushed behind her ears. She sat on the edge of the bed holding onto Jessie's hand. Justin Ashton, in need of a shave, paced on the other side of the bed. When Katie entered the room, they both shot her a look of mixed annoyance, frustration and hope.

"I know this isn't the best time but I really need to ask you some more questions," Katie said as gently as she could.

"Do we really need to do this now?" Justin Ashton asked..

"I'm sorry," Katie answered. "Would you like to do this in here or should I find a private waiting room?"

A nurse entered the room and adjusted the IV then made notations on a clipboard.

"Is everything OK?" Ellen Ashton asked anxiously.

"Everything is stable," the nurse answered judiciously. "Can I get you anything? A soda, a glass of water?"

"No, thank you," Ellen Ashton replied and Justin

Ashton shook his head.

"I'll be back in about thirty minutes or so to check on her again", the nurse said as she left the room.

Ellen Ashton turned to Katie. "I'd rather stay here with Jessie."

"OK, that's fine," Katie said. Anna left the room, returning a few minutes later with two folding chairs. As Anna set the chairs up, Katie said, "This is Officer Madrid. She assisted me with searching Jessie's room." Anna shook hands with both of the Ashtons.

"I checked Jessie's cell phone and her computer. There were five phone calls between 6:00pm and 11:35pm. I also went on her Facebook account but I didn't find anything significant," Katie informed the Ashtons.

Katie pulled out her notebook. "Tell me if you are unfamiliar with any of these names."

The Ashtons, who were now seated next to each other in the chairs, nodded.

"Greta...Chase...Alex...Georgie...Bug," Katie read off.

"They're all friends of Jessie's. Georgie is her best friend and Bug lives next door. Jessie and Bug grew up together and he's like a brother to her," Ellen Ashton said.

"How well do you know her other friends? Greta, Chase and Alex?" Katie probed.

"Greta just moved here in the fall. We met her and her family at church. Chase is an ex-boyfriend of sorts but he and Jessie have been friends since sixth grade. I've only met Alex a few times. His family lives over in the Fairway community," Ellen Ashton replied.

"Is Alex a boyfriend or potential boyfriend?" Katie asked.

Justin Ashton shrugged.

"Are any of her friends into drugs?" Katie asked pointedly.

"No," Justin Ashton snapped. "We certainly wouldn't let Jessie hang out with someone we knew was into anything like that."

"Of course not, Mr. Ashton. I didn't mean to infer

anything," Katie apologized. After a brief pause to ease the tension, Katie continued, "You said you didn't really know Alex. What *do* you know about him?"

"He's apparently a relative newcomer to Jessie's group of friends. She first introduced him to us just a few months ago. He seems nice enough," Justin Ashton replied.

"Do you know if he's lived in Potoma long?"

"I don't think so. I think we would have met him before a few months ago if he'd been living here for a while. Jessie is pretty much friends with everyone in her high school class. I mean she has her particular group but everyone knows her and she's always friendly to everyone," Ellen Ashton said patting her daughter's hand.

"And you say he lives in the Fairway area?"

"Yes. I remember Jessie telling me that the first time I met him," Ellen answered.

"What about the others…Greta, Chase, Georgie? Where do they live?"

"Greta lives in one of the big Victorians right on the river in Riverside. Chase lives in Riverview and Georgie's a few streets over from us," Ellen Ashton replied.

Katie flipped back a few pages in her notebook. "Do you know Ruthie, Mark or Michella?"

"They're all part of Jessie's group. Jessie and Michella have been friends since elementary school and we know her parents very well," Ellen Ashton said nodding at her husband.

"Michella's father and I have worked together for fifteen years," Justin Ashton added. "The Randalls—that's Michella's family—also go to our church."

Katie read through her notes. Nothing was adding up. *Why would Jessie do drugs when it appeared that she was well-liked, well-adjusted and it didn't seem that any of her friends were into that sort of thing.*

"Has Jessie seemed unhappy lately? Has anything upset her recently?" Katie asked.

"Jessie's always upbeat. It's part of her personality. But on the odd occasion when she does get down, she always talks it out with us. We have a very close relationship,"

Ellen Ashton replied. "So the answer to all of the above is no."

Katie had exhausted all her questions. And she'd really learned nothing helpful from Jessie's parents. *Maybe Jessie's friends would know more.*

"OK," Katie said. "That's all for now. But if anything comes up, I'll get in touch with you".

The Ashtons nodded and Katie and Anna quickly took their leave.

"Hate that part of my job," Katie commented to Anna as they walked down the hospital hallway.

"Agreed," Anna nodded. "Shouldn't we try to talk to the ER doctor? Get his diagnosis?"

"That's where I was heading. I'll see if the nurse on duty can page him," Katie replied.

Just then Anna's radio buzzed and she was called away to assist another officer so Katie waited at the nurse's station alone for the doctor. When the ER doctor that had treated Jessie arrived, he told Katie they hadn't yet been able to identify what had been injected into Jessie's veins but at the moment the priority was to flush whatever it was out of her system. With more questions than answers, Katie left the hospital and headed back to the police station to file her report. She'd fill Anna in on what the doctor had said when she saw her at the end of the shift.

# CHAPTER 2

**The flashing lights** coming through the semi-sheer curtains of her bedroom had woken Grace and she got up and stepped to the window to see what was going on. She was surprised to see a police car and an ambulance in front of the Ashton house across the cul-de-sac. Designated as a golf cart town, residents and visitors alike usually opted to cruise around the streets on the open-air, socially inviting vehicles rather than their automobiles. Even the police department used golf carts for normal patrols and only employed their cruisers in high-risk emergency situations so the sight of one in the cul-de-sac made Grace all the more curious and anxious. Grace stood and watched the front of the Ashton house for several minutes but seeing no activity, climbed back into bed. Now she was annoyed; she'd had another hour before she needed to get up for work and she wouldn't be able to go back to sleep.

Grace didn't like the Ashtons. They were too perfect. Ellen Ashton was too nice and Justin Ashton was too successful. And their two daughters were just too pretty and well-behaved. She particularly disliked Jessie Ashton. Grace had always hated girls like Jessie. The popular girl, the girl most likely to succeed, the girl who got straight A's *and* got elected cheerleading captain. And Jessie was such a girly girl with all her pink clothes. She even had a pink golf cart. OK, the golf cart was really Ellen's but still… Grace wished she had a pink golf cart but all she could afford was just a plain old beige one and a used one from the golf course with the number decal still on it, at that. Grace wondered if the ambulance was there for Jessie. Grace couldn't stop from curling her lips up into a cynical smile.

**Ping walked out** of his house to his truck just in time to see the ambulance arrive. He was already going to be late for his 7:00am shift. This would be the third time in two weeks and Ping knew that he was on thin ice with his supervisor. Ping hoped he'd be able to talk his way out of it again, otherwise he might just lose his job. And if he lost his job, he'd have to sell his house and move out of Potoma. *Well,* Ping thought, *that* *might be just as well anyway.*

**Mick watched the** Ashton house nervously. Police cars and ambulances made him very anxious and he began to pace back and forth in front of the living room window. Mick had been up all night and needed some sleep. Mick wondered why the police would be there for an ambulance call. Surely, there was no need for police to be at the Ashtons. The Ashtons were the nicest, most all-American family he knew. Sure, they were nosy, especially the teenage daughter, but he couldn't imagine any reason that the police would be called to their home. Mick snorted and his eyes narrowed. Maybe, just maybe, that teenage daughter had been *too* nosy.

Mick was starting to worry. He had memory lapses sometimes. And sometimes he imagined things. Things that weren't real. He had medication for that but sometimes he forgot to take his medicine and sometimes he forgot if he had taken his medicine. Mick glanced through the window again. The paramedics were rolling the stretcher out with someone on it. A few seconds later he saw Justin Ashton and his wife, Ellen climb into his black SUV. *Was that Katie Bell?* Mick watched the petite brunette police officer walk back into the Ashtons' house. Mick really liked Katie. Unfortunately, Katie hadn't liked him very much.

**Casey watched as** the female police officer walked to her car and opened the trunk. Another police vehicle pulled up and another female officer stepped out. The two women exchanged conversation then walked together into the Ashton house. Casey bit her fingernails. She would have to wait until the police left or risk exposure. She was sure that the rest of the neighbors were watching what was going on at the Ashton house, too. Casey chewed on her thumb, counting the minutes, willing the police women to leave. Finally, they both came out of the house. After a short exchange, they both got into their cars and the leggy blonde followed the shorter one out of the cul-de-sac.

**Aster pulled up** to her house just as two police cars exited the cul-de-sac. She buttoned up her sweater and grabbed her bag from the seat beside her. She'd had a rough night. She hoped if someone was peering out the window at her they wouldn't notice the rip in her jeans or how messy her hair was. Aster glanced at the houses; most of her neighbors appeared to be gone already. She noticed that Ellen Ashton's yellow Volkswagen was still parked in the driveway. She knew that didn't necessarily mean anything. Ellen only worked part-time so she didn't work every day and sometimes she carpooled to work. Aster shrugged, put on her devil-may-care face and got out of the car. She walked to her front door pretending that she was completely oblivious to anything that might be happening in the cul-de-sac; however, she noticed Casey slip from the shadows of a large oak tree and hurry through the gate into the backyard of her house.

# CHAPTER 3

**Katie pulled her** squad car into her driveway. She lived in the Riverview section of Potoma, the post-World War I residential expansion of the town, and to her own amazement had somehow managed to buy a house that actually had a river view. It wasn't on the river, mind you, but her street dead-ended at the beach and she was just three houses back. In a plan of sheer genius the houses had all been built at an angle to the street so that each one could have a glimpse of the river. Katie's views were even more comprehensive because she had a small roof deck built over a portion of the second story of her tiny, Tudor-style brick home. Katie often climbed to the attic in the evening with her dinner on a tray in order to watch the sun go down over the water while she ate.

Ogilvie, Katie's old black Lab, bounded from the stoop to the front gate to greet Katie. Katie had had Ogilvie since her twelfth birthday and now sixteen years later he had just as much grey hair as black but was still as frisky as he'd been as a puppy. Ogilvie followed Katie into the house and up the steps to her bedroom. Katie quickly stripped out of her uniform and pulled on some sweats and a T-shirt. Padding barefoot back down to the kitchen, Katie couldn't help thinking about Jessie Ashton. Katie had called the hospital to check on Jessie just before she went off-duty. She was relieved to learn that Jessie was still stable even though she hadn't yet regained consciousness. Katie put a mug of water in the microwave oven and pulled out an Earl Grey tea bag. Ten minutes later, Katie flopped down on the sofa with her cup of tea, grabbed a magazine from the end table and punched the "On" button on the TV remote. Ogilvie was contentedly lying on the sofa next to her, curled up with his head in her lap.

Katie had lived most of her life in Potoma. When she'd gone away to college, she had never seriously considered moving back to Potoma. Katie had majored in Art and intended to be a teacher in some place far away from the little river town where she'd grown up.. But then she'd come home to stay with her parents after she'd graduated while she looked for the perfect job. And Ben had talked her into taking the part-time dispatcher position. It was just supposed be temporary—an interim job until she found something full-time. However, the more time she spent in Potoma and the more calls she dispatched, the more at home she felt—she became personally interested in the town and the people in the town. She realized that the residents—especially the ones she'd known all her life—were family and she really cared what happened to them. And so when the opportunity arose to join the police department Katie jumped on it. Even then, she didn't expect to make law enforcement her career; she envisioned an eventual teaching position at the middle school or high school. The teaching position never came along and so Katie remained a police officer, a job she wasn't sure she could give up now.

Katie mulled over the strange circumstances regarding Jessie Ashton. *If Jessie had injected drugs where was the evidence? And why would she take drugs when all signs indicated that she had no reason or desire to do so?* Katie intended to question her friends tomorrow. She knew that even though parents often thought they knew their kids, that wasn't always so. Teenagers always held back *some* things from their parents. Even the most angelic and well-adjusted ones rebelled in some way or another. Often the parents, the ones who still remembered their teenage years, were able to figure it out 90% of the time but no parent knew everything about their child. Katie knew this from personal experience.

Katie's cell phone rang and as if on cue, Ogilvie groaned in his sleep. Katie gently pushed Ogilvie's head off her lap and got up from the sofa to retrieve her phone from the kitchen counter.

"Hey, meet me at Crabby Clam for dinner tonight. Or I can pick you up," Ben said.

"Pretty presumptuous of you," Katie replied.

"You can't resist free seafood," Ben teased.

"Just as long as you know it's the seafood and not the company," Katie laughed.

"Right through the heart", Ben answered feigning disappointment.

"And remember you said "free seafood" so I'm

leaving my wallet at home," Katie said. "What time?"

"How about 7:30?"

"Pick me up?"

"Is that a come on?"

"You did say "free seafood". And I know nothing in life is free," Katie laughed again.

"I also know you pack a gun," Ben replied.

"See you then," Katie answered.

"And wear something sexy so at least people *think* I can get a date," Ben said before hanging up.

When Ben pulled up in his lifted, four-wheel drive golf cart that was painted bright blue, Katie had changed into faded jeans, a floral boho blouse with ruffles and embroidery around the neck, and cowboy boots. Ben wore cargo shorts and a retro 50s style button up shirt with boat shoes. His dark curly hair was still slightly damp. Katie loved Ben's dark blue eyes that sparkled with good humor. She had never known anyone so laid back and positive, especially given the fact that he dealt with death and serious injury so often as a volunteer rescue squad member. Katie often wondered why he hadn't become a doctor; he certainly had the ideal personality and character.

"Oh, you disappoint me. I was looking forward to four-inch stilettos and leather," Ben said shaking his head.

"And I was expecting a tux and fedora," Katie replied in kind.

Katie climbed into the golf cart beside Ben and he did a U-turn in the street. The sun had already started descending into the river and the air had turned a little cooler. Most residents had returned home from work and few autos were on the streets. By comparison, golf carts were out in droves as was common on a spring-time Friday night. As Ben turned down the main drag that led through the downtown commercial area to Riverside, the original residential portion of Potoma, they passed Anna and her husband coming from the Chinese restaurant on the corner.

"Crabby Clam?" Anna called out.

"You got it," Katie replied and waved.

The Crabby Clam was a local seafood restaurant

that had been in business since the 1950s. It had started out as a lunch café for fisherman and marina workers and was located on the harbor just a few blocks into Riverside. As usual, Ben and Katie took the "long way" to the restaurant. They turned left, then right, following Riverside Drive which ran between the beach and the river front Victorian cottages all the way to marina nestled into the point of the peninsula that jutted out into the river. The street then curved around and ran back down the peninsula along the harbor. The restaurant was near the end of the loop road and overlooked the innermost part of the harbor. Katie loved looking at the fancy homes trimmed with gingerbread and sporting all manner of porches, balconies, turrets, dormers, towers and cupolas. One of the most interesting homes had been converted to a bed & breakfast inn. The Tower House was a curious three-story home that had been built by a sea captain who lost it when he was convicted of embezzling from the U.S. Navy. Everyone in town knew the charming, petite woman named Anne that had owned it for nearly twenty years. Katie had helped her clean the house and tend to the gardens during the summers when she was in high school. Katie appreciated the fact that Ben made a point of always taking her this way when they went to Crabby Clam or were riding around in good weather together just so she could feast her eyes on something she had a passionate interest in. To Katie, Victorian architecture was pure art.

When they reached the restaurant, Ben asked to be seated on the pier which cantilevered out over the water. Ben and Katie avoided talking about work during dinner; however, by the time they had gotten back in the golf cart and were headed back toward Katie's house the conversation had turned to Jessie Ashton.

Ben was as perplexed as Katie about the lack of drug paraphernalia in Jessie's room. He suggested that she return to the Ashton house in the morning and search the ground outside of Jessie's room in case she had thrown the evidence out the window. Instead of saying goodbye immediately at Katie's house, she and Ben walked down to the beach. A couple of blocks to the north, the lights of the old steamboat moored just offshore twinkled and cast a glow over the white sand all way down to Katie's street. The steamboat had once carried tourists up and down the river; it was now a popular casino and off-track betting venue. Music and voices from the steamboat floated on the slight breeze. Ben and Katie walked down the beach in the opposite direction from the steamboat. This part of the beach was narrow and sat atop a rocky slope on the river. It was more of a low sandy levy from which to observe the water although many people did climb down the rocks and fish from the bank at the bottom.

"Remember when we were in high school? I can't even recall anyone who did drugs," Katie mused.

"Yeah…the worst we did was take beer down to The Point and skinny dip when we got drunk," Ben added.

"I remember hearing about *those* kids," Katie replied. "I didn't realize you were one of them."

"Only once or twice. And I never skinny-dipped," Ben confessed.

"Never?" Katie questioned, a mischievous grin tugging at the corners of her mouth.

"Never when I was drunk," Ben said, grinning.

"So who were you skinny-dipping with when you were sober?" Katie replied, raising her eyebrows.

"I don't skinny-dip and tell," Ben answered, pretending to zip his lips and throw away the key.

Katie turned serious. "I just don't get it. I haven't talked to any of Jessie's friends yet, but I just don't see Jessie as the kind of girl to do drugs. Especially, not the kind that you have to shoot up."

"Maybe she was depressed. People, especially teenagers, often do things that are totally out of character when they are extremely upset or even angry," Ben replied.

"But that's the thing. From all accounts, she wasn't having any problems. There doesn't seem to be any motive for her to turn to drugs," Katie persisted. "I mean, like I said, I've only spoken to her mom and dad but even the most inattentive parents can usually feel when something is different with their kid."

"Well, you might get a different story when you talk to her friends. I've found that lots of parents live in denial or they choose to ignore behavior they don't approve of or know how to deal with."

"I know, but it's not just her parents. If you had seen Jessie's room, I mean, really looked at her room like I did. Her room was in perfect order. Her bathroom was in perfect order. Even her closet was in perfect order. She is a total neatnik. But it wasn't like it was stark obsessive-compulsive neatness—it was more like it was done out of pride in doing it and it was more casual. She had photographs and knick-knacks here and there. There was clutter; it was just organized clutter. And it was comfortable, homey, like you'd be comfortable flopping down on the bed or plopping your stuff on the desk or floor and she wouldn't freak out about it. It's hard to explain. It was a feeling, you know," Katie tried to explain.

"I get what you're saying," Ben answered. "It's like the feeling of going to someone's house and walking into their living room for the first time. It can be clean and neat and look like a museum exhibit that you're afraid to touch, much less relax in or it can be clean and neat and just exude comfort and you're not afraid to sit down or put your feet on the ottoman."

"Exude? Really? Isn't that a pretty sophisticated word for you?" Katie teased.

Ben shrugged, smiling. "Well, you know, I've been reading the dictionary lately so that I can impress you with my extraordinary vocabulary."

"There you go. Another big word—extraordinary," Katie teased again, laughing.

"I learned that one yesterday," Ben replied, smugly.

After she and Ben had returned to the house and Ben had driven off, Katie climbed to the attic and went out onto her rooftop deck. Ogilvie, tail wagging, accompanied her. He laid down on the smooth wood planks beside Katie who sat in one of the two Adirondack lounges that just fit in the tiny space. She had brought up a tall glass of iced tea.

Ben's reminisces about high school brought back

memories. Because she was artistic, Katie had been somewhat of a loner back then and was considered "eclectic" because she dressed differently from the majority of the other girls and preferred to paint pictures at the beach rather than sunbathe or flirt with boys. Ben was *that guy* that everyone knew and everyone liked. Ben had played baseball and football and was good at both plus he was really, really nice. He had been voted "Class Clown" *and* "Most Likely to Succeed" their senior year.

Ben had asked Katie to the Senior Prom at the last minute—Katie suspected she had been a desperate last resort date—and then they had dated very casually that summer. After they had both gone off to different colleges they hadn't kept in touch. So it was a bit of a surprise to Katie that Ben had taken any interest in her return to Potoma four years ago and made such an effort to convince her stay there. Nevertheless, Katie was still confused about Ben's intentions toward her since their friendship had remained completely platonic for so long since. A couple of years ago, Katie stopped wondering and decided to just enjoy the relationship with Ben for what it was—steady, comfortable, totally unromantic. That, however, hadn't kept Katie from occasionally fantasizing about "what if". Tonight, Katie stopped herself before she began because if she let herself think about Ben too much, it would interfere with her budding interest in Cade Ware, the new guy in town.

Cade, a self-professed "rehab addict", had purchased several run-down vacation rental bungalows in the center of Riverside and was in the process of renovating them. The bungalows had been built California-style on a court with a common-area park and garden in the middle. Cade had moved into the first one he'd completed and was busy restoring the other six as well as the court green. Katie had met Cade when she answered a "suspicious person" call at the bungalow court. An elderly resident had seen Cade going in and out of the abandoned homes and was afraid he was "up to no good" as she had put it. Katie smiled as she remembered having pulled her revolver out and pointed it at the doorless house, demanding that whoever was inside "come out with your hands up." Katie had expected to find a weekend fisherman squatter or a bored teenager but had been pleasantly surprised, and somewhat amused, to see the well-dressed, extremely handsome man that had emerged with a frightened look on his face. Since then, Katie had made a deliberate point of stopping by the bungalows at least once a week to view Cade's progress on the renovations—partly because she was genuinely interested in seeing the bungalows brought back to their former glory and partly because she was curiously interested in Cade.

## SATURDAY
## CHAPTER 4

**The warm spring** weather had brought out the fisherman as well as some early sunbathers. Saturday promised to be busy with weekenders pouring onto the beaches and into the marina. Katie was scheduled to patrol the downtown area and Riverside Drive later in the day but first she wanted to investigate further at the Ashton house. When she pulled up on the golf cart, she noticed that both of the Ashtons' vehicles were parked in the driveway. Justin Ashton, appearing haggard and slightly annoyed, answered Katie's knock on the door.

"How is Jessie doing?" Katie inquired.

"She's still unconscious but she's stable," Justin Ashton replied. "Ellen and I just came home long enough to shower and change our clothes."

"Your other daughter?" Katie asked.

"Veronica is staying at a friend's house," Justin Ashton answered impatiently. "Is there something I can do for you, Officer Bell?"

"As you know, we were unable to find any drug evidence in Jessie's rooms. I'd like to look outside in case she may have tossed something out of her window," Katie answered.

"As I told you before, ma'am," Justin Ashton said grimacing, "my daughter did not do drugs."

"The evidence—the fact that something was injected into her arm—proves otherwise, Mr. Ashton," Katie replied.

Justin Ashton shook his head.

"Mr. Ashton, I understand that the facts are in complete contradiction to what you know about Jessie. I, myself, have a difficult time understanding why Jessie would suddenly experiment with drugs when it doesn't appear that she had any reason to do so. But the facts are the facts, and it's now my job to find out if there was a crime committed here," Katie explained.

"A crime? What crime?" Justin Ashton said, his voice rising. "Are you seriously going to charge Jessie with a crime? She's lying in a hospital bed fighting for her life! You're going to arrest her for drug use?"

Katie pressed her tongue between her lips then took a deep breath. "I don't *know* if any crime has been committed. That's what I'm trying to find out."

Justin Ashton flung his hands into the air. "The doctors haven't even figured out what's in Jessie's system. They've found traces of different substances but don't really know what triggered her reaction."

"I'm sure they'll keep digging until they can make a diagnosis," Katie tried to reassure Justin Ashton.

"At this point, I don't even care. I just want her to recover," Justin Ashton replied, rubbing the back of his head. After a moment he added, "Go ahead and search anywhere you want to on the property. Ellen and I will be leaving in a few minutes for the hospital."

Katie walked around to the rear of the house. At the center of the house, a triple set of double French doors opened from the family room and kitchen onto a large cobblestone patio. To one side was a built-in barbeque grill and bar flanked by a large table and chairs. Beyond the patio near the back fence was a big rectangular swimming pool, the winter cover still in place and covered with brown leaves. The rest of the yard was open with a few mature trees along the fence line. Katie observed the second story of the house, locating the windows of Jessie's bedroom and bathroom on the left side. A narrow french balcony with wrought iron railing connected the two windows. The cobblestone patio extended the entire length of the house under the windows and short patchy grass edged the patio. Katie could see immediately that nothing but a few stray leaves lay within the vicinity of Jessie's room. Disappointed, Katie extended her search further out. Twenty minutes later, after scouring every inch of the back yard, Katie was satisfied that nothing had been tossed from Jessie's room.

When Katie returned to the front of the house, she remembered that Justin Ashton had said that Jessie's friend, Bug, lived next door. Instinctively, Katie walked over to the house to the left of the Ashton's. After ringing the doorbell several times and receiving no answer, Katie decided that no one was at home so she walked back to her golf cart and climbed on.

As Katie pulled away from the Ashton house, she pulled her notebook from her pocket. Finding the phone number she had written down for Jessie's friend, Georgie, Katie dialed her cell phone. Since she was in the neighborhood, she decided to start with her. After obtaining Georgie's address from her, Katie headed over to her house. Georgie was much as Katie had imagined her. Slender and petite, she had auburn hair in a pixie cut and smattering of freckles across her nose. Katie sat in a plush armchair across from Georgie, her mother and her father, who were seated together on a matching sofa.

"According to Jessie's cell phone, you talked to her Thursday night around 8:00. Do you mind telling me about your conversation with her?"

"We just talked about regular stuff. You know, school and boys and what to do this weekend," Georgie replied.

"Did you make plans for the weekend?" Katie asked.

"We talked about getting together Saturday. Maybe hanging out on the boardwalk with some of our friends. Nothing definite," Georgie answered.

"Have you ever known Jessie to take drugs—experiment with anything? You need to be honest with me," Katie said, leaning forward slightly.

"Never. She's totally against it," Georgie said adamantly.

"Do you know why she might take something, then?"

"I have no idea. I can't believe she would even think about it," Georgie replied. "You really have to know Jessie…she's just not like that at all."

"Her parents told me that you're her best friend. Has she been upset or angry or anxious about anything lately?"

"No. She's a pretty happy person. I would know if anything was going on with her," Georgie said confidently.

"Think back to your conversation with Jessie. Did she say anything that might have indicated that she intended to take drugs that night?"

"Nothing. It was a normal conversation. There was

nothing unusual about it at all," Georgie replied after a slight pause.

Katie looked at the other names listed in her notebook. Jessie's parents seemed very familiar with Greta, Bug, and Chance as well as Ruthie, Mark and Michella. They'd been less sure of Jessie's newest friend, Alex.

"Do you know a boy named Alex?" Katie asked.

"I know Alex Watson," Georgie replied. "He just moved here a few months ago."

"What can you tell me about Alex?" Katie asked.

"I don't know that much about him," Georgie confessed.

"Do you know where he's from? Anything about his personal life?" Katie prompted.

"He moved here from some northern state, I think. New Jersey or Rhode Island or New Hampshire. I can't remember. I know he has a couple of older brothers that are out of school. Jessie told me that his parents are divorced and he lives here with his mom and stepdad.

"Do you know if he's into drugs?"

"I don't think so. I mean, if he is, Jessie doesn't know about it. She wouldn't hang out with him if he was a druggie," Georgie said, shrugging.

"Have you ever hung out with him?" Katie asked.

"Just when Jessie was around," Georgie replied.

"Would you say that Jessie is close with Alex?"

"I know when he first started school she sort of felt sorry for him. He sticks out like a sore thumb around here. And he's shy. He's, like, super smart but not like computer geek smart, really. He's kind of like an inventor. He likes to build stuff. Mechanical stuff. It's like he's from another world, sort of," Georgie explained. "Jessie knows if she lets him hang out with us, everyone will accept him."

Katie was impressed with Jessie's compassion. Most pretty, popular girls wouldn't risk their reputations by befriending a boy most of the kids would ostracize.

"Alex dresses kind of weird. Real old-fashioned kind of stuff," Georgie added. "I think he's a big history buff. Jessie said something about steampunk, whatever that is. She thought it was pretty cool."

Katie was familiar with that particular look and ideal. It was a combination of everything Victorian and innovative technology. It was the basis of Will Smith's "Wild, Wild, West" movie. Like Jessie, Katie thought it was cool, too, and could see why Jessie might be attracted to it. Steampunk was definitely not something she'd seen in Potoma.

"Does Jessie have good relationships with..." Katie looked at her notebook, "Greta, Chase, Bug...?"

"As far as I know," Georgie replied.

"How about Ruthie, Mark and Michella?"

"Oh, yeah. I mean she isn't really tight with Mark but they're friends. He's Ruthie's boyfriend so he gets to be part of the group by association, if you know what I mean," Georgie clarified.

Katie nodded her understanding. "Do you get along with all of them?"

"For the most part. I mean I'm not necessarily close friends with everyone Jessie is friends with," Georgie said.

"Like who?" Katie pressed.

"Like Bug. They grew up together like brother and sister. He's a year older and he doesn't really hang out with Jessie when she's with her girlfriends. Michella is also older so she has her own group of friends. Her family and Jessie's family get together a lot but they don't hang out much outside of the family things so I just don't really know Michella or see her that much," Georgie answered.

"How do you feel about Jessie's ex-boyfriend, Chase?"

"I think Jessie is crazy not to date him. He's really great and they make a perfect couple," Georgie was quick to answer. Katie got the feeling that Georgie really wished *she* could hook up with Chase.

"What about Greta?"

"We're good friends. The four of us—me, Jessie, Greta and Ruthie—are like the four musketeers," Georgie replied, giggling.

"There's no jealousy among the four of you?"

Georgie shook her head.

Katie thanked Georgie and her parents and took her leave.  Seated on her golf cart cruiser, Katie consulted her notebook again. She looked at her watch noting that she still had several hours before she had to report to the beachfront. She probably had time to question Chase in Riverview and maybe Greta in Riverside if she hurried.  Katie looked at her list of phone numbers and dialed her cell phone.

# CHAPTER 5

**Grace loved weekends.** She could sleep as late as she wanted. Thank goodness, there had been no emergency lights to wake her up this morning. She was still annoyed from yesterday. Grace pulled the curtain aside just slightly and looked across the cul-de-sac at the Ashton house. All was quiet. In fact, the whole cul-de-sac was subdued. Grace hoped it would stay that way. Grace decided she should celebrate.

As Grace slipped into the bubble bath, holding her freshly-made chocolate milkshake above the water, she felt extremely relaxed. Later she would order a pizza and eat the whole thing. Closing her eyes she began to think about her escape from Potoma. She was going to move to Florida where she could wear a bathing suit every day and spend all her free time walking miles and miles of beach turning every man's head as she passed by, tanned and toned and gorgeous. Just as gorgeous as Jessie Ashton. And best of all, Jessie Ashton wouldn't be around anymore.


**Ping had gotten** up early. He rarely slept past 5:30 AM no matter how late he had stayed up the night before. That's one reason Ping had been so mystified the day before when he'd overslept. Fortunately, Ping's boss had gotten to work later than Ping and so he didn't even know Ping was late. In a way, Ping felt disappointed. Part of him had almost hoped he'd get fired. He hated his job anyway. He hated his boss. And he hated living in this cul-de-sac.

Ping struck the dirt with all his strength, raking the soil and breaking the grass roots up into clumps he could throw into the wheelbarrow. Gardening was his stress-buster. He could take out his anger on the ground and then feel renewed as he placed the fragile plants into the earth, carefully covering the root balls with rich topsoil. No one would argue that Ping had the most beautiful property in the cul-de-sac, maybe in the entire neighborhood. His backyard was a lush paradise, even in the coldest months of winter. And his front yard contained an ever-changing collection of annuals mixed with flowering trees and evergreens. Today, Ping was preparing a flowerbed next to the picket fence for some new flowers he hoped to pick up on Monday after work.

**Mick was fidgeting**. He'd seen Katie again this morning. She looked really nice in her police woman uniform and he liked it when she wore her hair up. He wondered what she was doing in the Ashtons' back yard or why she had gone next door. It was weird that the Ashtons had left while Katie was still at their house. He'd thought about going to say hello but was afraid Katie might get mad about that when she was in her police uniform and on official business. So Mick just stayed in his house and watched.

After Katie had ridden off on her golf cart, Mick went outside and walked across the cul-de-sac. He looked around to see if anyone else was out and about. He noticed that Ping was in his backyard. Mick snickered. Ping was such a pansy always planting flowers. Ping was squatting down and didn't notice Mick. Mick reached the Ashton house and looking around one more time. Seeing no one, Mick opened the unlocked gate to the backyard. He walked around, trying to figure out what Katie had been doing back there. After a while Mick gave up and snuck back through the gate, hurrying to his front door before anyone spotted him.

**Casey was pretty** sure no one had seen her the day before. *Well, maybe that Aster creature, but she didn't really count.* Just as Casey was shutting her front door she had seen Aster walking up her front steps. But as usual, Aster was self-absorbed and seemed to be completely focused on finding her door key. It looked like Aster's skin-tight jeans were torn and her wild, thick hair seemed a little more unruly than usual but Casey couldn't be sure. Aster always kept strange hours and seemed to be gone more nights than she was home. Aster had come to the last cul-de-sac picnic but when Casey had spoken to her they hadn't gotten beyond polite greetings and mundane conversation about the weather.

**Aster looked at** herself in the mirror. Even though she looked pretty good this morning, she still didn't like what she saw. A good night's sleep last night had helped but she still felt tired and sore. The bruise on her leg was now turning blackish and the scratch across her chest still stung when her clothes pressed against it. Aster carefully applied her make-up and pulled her thick hair back into a sleek ponytail at the nape of her neck. As she stood in front of the window next to the toilet she saw Ping out in his garden, his hands almost black from plunging them into the mound of dirt on the ground.

Aster thought about what she had seen yesterday morning when she got home. It looked like Casey was sneaking into her own yard. Aster had always thought that Casey was a bit cagey but she'd always chalked it up to shyness or awkwardness. She'd tried to talk to Casey at the cul-de-sac picnic but could never get past the superficial. Not that Aster was all that outgoing herself but she tried really hard. It's just that Aster couldn't really talk about herself too much due to the particular circumstances she lived in. And now, after Thursday night, she'd have to be even more careful about what she said.

# CHAPTER 6

**Chase Jackson lived** about eight blocks from Katie's house next to the levy above the river. Chase's parents welcomed Katie into their home and led her onto a screened-in porch with a view of the river. Chase, dressed impeccably in khakis and a denim shirt over a white t-shirt, was waiting with a grim look on his face. It was obvious that he was extremely concerned about Jessie's condition and anxious to get to the hospital to visit her.

"I understand that you and Jessie dated for a while," Katie began.

"Last year for about six months," Chase replied.

"Do you mind telling me why the two of you broke up?"

Chase looked at his parents, then, looked down at the floor. "It's really personal," Chase finally replied.

"OK, maybe we'll come back to that," Katie said, realizing Chase didn't want to discuss the break-up in front of his parents. "According to Jessie's cell phone, you spoke to her a little after 6:00 on Thursday night."

"Yeah, I called her," Chase said, his eyebrows raised in interest.

"Can you tell me what your conversation was about?" Katie said, clicking her pen.

"I was talking to her about my girlfriend. We're having some problems," Chase replied.

Katie hadn't expected Chase to have a girlfriend. Katie's curiosity was piqued.

"Is that a normal thing? I mean to talk to your ex-girlfriend about your current girlfriend?" Katie asked.

"I guess so," Chase shrugged.

"How does Jessie feel about it?"

"She doesn't seem to have a problem with it," Chase replied, then, added, "Actually, I wish it did bother her."

"Do you know if Jessie has ever experimented with drugs, illegal or otherwise?" Katie asked. Katie noticed Chase's parents both jerked their heads around, obviously shocked at her question.

"Not Jessie," Chase said. "She's the biggest goody-two-shoes on the planet."

"I see," Katie replied. "When you talked to Jessie Thursday night, did she seem upset or anxious about anything?"

"No, I don't think so," Chase replied.

With no more questions to ask, Katie said goodbye to Chase. She still had enough time to run into Riverside and question Greta before relieving the officer on duty down at the beach.

After a phone call to make sure Greta was at home and to confirm her address, Katie made her way across town to Riverside Drive. The two-story Victorian painted in shades of green and blue was easy to locate. Greta was waiting on the wide front porch. When Katie walked up, she could hear hammering going on inside the house.

"Mom and Dad are working on the kitchen. They're remodeling," Greta offered.

Katie peeked through the open door into the wide paneled hall. An intricately embellished staircase stood on one side. The hall opened on both sides into large rooms, one obviously a parlor and the other a formal dining room.

Katie and Greta settled into cushioned wicker furniture on the porch. Katie felt almost as if she was staring into a mirror, looking at a slightly younger version of herself. Greta had pale creamy skin and bright green eyes fringed by long lashes. Her light brown hair had all-over blond highlights and fell halfway to her waist in wavy layers. Unlike Katie, Greta also had numerous piercings—at least a dozen small hoops in her ears, a hoop in her right eyebrow and a diamond stud in the left side of her nose. Katie suspected she probably had a pierced navel, too.

"You spoke to Jessie around 7:30 Thursday night?" Katie confirmed

"I think so," Greta replied. "That sounds about right."

"What did you talk about?"

"Girl stuff," Greta said, flicking her hair off her shoulder.

"Can you elaborate for me?" Katie said.

"Clothes, boys, this weekend. That sort of thing," Greta answered

"Did she seem upset about anything?"

"She was annoyed with her ex-boyfriend. She ranted a little bit about how naïve he was," Greta replied. "Apparently, his girlfriend is cheating on him and he's just oblivious."

"What kind of relationship does she have with her ex-boyfriend?" Katie pried.

"They're friends. I mean, it's obvious to everyone that he's still crazy about her but she's got certain standards and he just doesn't meet them," Greta revealed.

"In what way?" Katie asked. She seemed to be getting somewhere.

"He just does some stuff that Jessie doesn't approve of. Most of it is really tame...and normal for teenagers...but Jessie is pretty black-and-white on certain things," Greta replied, somewhat evasively.

"Like what?" Katie continued to push, becoming annoyed at Greta's vagueness.

"Like...lying to his parents about where he's going and what he's doing when he goes out," Greta shrugged.

Katie almost laughed but quickly caught herself and pressed her lips together to maintain her professional demeanor. "Is that all?"

"Sometimes he'll take a drag off of someone's cigarette when we're all hanging out. Like he's trying to impress somebody or act grown-up or something. Jessie hates smoking."

"Anything else?"

"I don't mean to be rude but I'm not going to betray Jessie's trust by telling you stuff she might not want anyone to know," Greta said with a sudden change of attitude.

"That's fair," Katie replied. "Other than Chase, did Jessie talk about anything else that might have been bothering her?"

"No. To be honest, after Jessie got Chase out of her system, we mostly talked about going to Fredericksburg to shop for new summer clothes. Pretty trivial stuff," Greta said.

"Have you ever known Jessie to take drugs?" Katie asked, feeling almost foolish.

"Not her. She doesn't even like to take prescription medications," Greta answered. "Why?"

"It appears that she injected herself with something Thursday night," Katie replied truthfully.

Greta snorted. "That's hilarious…I'm sorry, really…but Jessie was scared to death of needles. You should have seen her when the Red Cross came to our school to take blood from volunteer donors. She totally passed out before they even stuck her!"

Katie made a note of this.

"Is she going to be alright?" Greta said in a quiet voice, suddenly serious. "I've tried calling her parents but can't get an answer. I went to the hospital yesterday but they wouldn't let me see her. Only immediate family is allowed."

"I talked to her father this morning and he reported that she is still unconscious but stable so that's good news," Katie answered, trying to reassure Greta. "Her parents will be at the hospital all day today. You should try to go while they are there. I'm sure they'd appreciate knowing you're concerned about Jessie."

Katie noticed that Greta's initial carefree attitude had completely dissolved and now she seemed fairly fragile. She was also becoming restless, shifting constantly in her seat.

"I just need to ask you a few more questions," Katie said gently.

Greta nodded.

"How well do you know Jessie's other friends? Chase, Alex, Michella, Bug. I understand you know Ruthie pretty well."

"Ruthie is one of my best friends like Jessie and Georgie. Georgie Parker. Have you spoken to her yet?"

Katie nodded.

"I moved here last summer about two weeks before school started. So I've known Chase since school started since he hangs around Jessie a lot. He just started dating his girlfriend a couple of months ago. I don't know Michella at all.

I met her once at Jessie's house. Bug doesn't really come around much when Jessie's with her friends so I don't really know him either. He's like her big brother or something. Alex moved here after Christmas this year. He's pretty shy and when we do the group thing he doesn't talk much. Just kind of stays on the edge and absorbs everything. He's sort of weird but good weird, not bad weird." Greta explained.

"Do you know if any of Jessie's friends do drugs or have access to drugs?" Katie asked.

"I doubt it. Like I said before, Jessie has pretty high standards. She's not stuck-up about it or anything, but she just wouldn't have close friendships with anyone who did drugs. You know, she'd still be nice and friendly but she wouldn't spend time with anyone she knew was into drugs," Greta replied.

"Maybe one of her friends has friends who are into drugs?" Katie suggested.

"I guess it's possible," Greta replied.

Katie nodded as she continued to write in her notebook. Katie thought of something she hadn't asked Georgie or Chase. "One more thing. How was Jessie getting along with her parents?"

"Jessie had a great relationship with her mom and dad. Naturally, I think she was closer to her mom but they weren't having any problems I'm aware of, if that's what you're asking," Greta answered.

When Katie left Greta's house she headed toward the center of Riverside. As she made her way through the grid of streets, Katie pondered the information she had gathered about Jessie Ashton. Nothing made sense; it was all contradictions. Jessie had definitely injected some type of substance yet by all accounts she wouldn't have touched drugs and she had a serious aversion to needles. If indeed she was turning to drugs, there didn't seem to be any reason for it. It appeared that she got along well with her parents and wasn't having any major difficulties with her friends. Other than a disagreement with her ex-boyfriend regarding his relationship with his current girlfriend, so far, all of Jessie's conversations on Thursday night were normal without any major upsets. Perhaps, after she questioned Bug and Alex, she might find more clues to Jessie's uncharacteristic behavior.

As usual, Cade was working on the bungalows when Katie pulled up. He waved her over to where he was pulling rotten siding off of one of the houses.

"Am I breaking some zoning code?" he asked cheerfully.

"I'm a police officer not a zoning officer. Different laws," Katie replied with a smile. "How's it going?"

"We're just about finished with numbers two and three," Cade answered, pointing at the identical bungalows to his left. "I've just got to choose exterior paint colors and move in the appliances for the kitchen. They'll be ready to rent by the first of next week."

"Mind if I take a look?" Katie asked with enthusiasm.

"Not at all. Help yourself," Cade said sweeping his hand toward the houses.

Katie checked her watch then walked toward the restored bungalows at the entrance to the court. The first one, painted burgundy and green, was the house Cade lived in. He'd given her a tour just before he moved in. The next two bungalows were primed white waiting for individual paint schemes. Just like Cade's house, there was narrow beveled siding on the first floor with the roof dormer and second story covered in cedar shingles, replicating the original cladding. Katie climbed the steps to the broad front porch of the bungalow next to Cade's. She stopped for a moment to admire the oak-stained front door finished with wrought-iron strap hinges and a small inset leaded-glass window. Katie was equally impressed with the interiors of the two houses as she made her way through them. When she had finished her tour she complimented Cade on the restorations and the ways he'd made each house different despite their virtually identical design.

"It's amazing how you can take identical houses and make them each look so unique just by changing a few walls or varying materials and colors," Katie almost gushed.

"I have a lot of fun figuring it all out. I'd love your input if you have any ideas," Cade replied. "Got any ideas about paint schemes for those two?"

Katie was thrilled with the opportunity to give her opinions. She had ridden by this bungalow court for years wishing she had the money to purchase it and restore the houses herself.

"Actually I was thinking that it would be nice to carry through a paint scheme for each house that uses one color from the house beside it and then adds a new color. For instance, you could use the burgundy from your house on the next one and then add gray as the second color. Since the burgundy is on the second floor of your house, I would use a darker tone of the burgundy on the first level of the second house and a light gray on the top. The third house could use a darker gray on the bottom and then maybe a light gray-blue on the top and so on," Katie volunteered.

"I really like that idea. You must have already thought about this," Cade mused.

Katie then told Cade how she had always wanted to redo the bungalow court and had fantasized about what she'd do if she ever had the money to buy it.

"I wish you'd told me this before. You could have helped me from the beginning," Cade replied. "OK, you're officially in charge of the exterior paint colors for each house."

Katie laughed, unsure if he was really sincere.

As if reading her thoughts, Cade said, "I'm completely serious about this. It'll be one less thing I have to make decisions about. And I really like your way of thinking. You must have an artistic soul."

"Actually, I am an artist of sorts, although I haven't done anything earnest in that field for a very long time," Katie said.

"What kind of art do you do?" Cade asked.

"I've worked in different media but my forte is really drawing and painting," Katie responded, glad for Cade's interest.

Cade was silent for a moment and seemed to be

working something out in his head. "Would you possibly be interested in doing some artwork for me?"

"Sure. What are you thinking?" Katie answered, excited at the prospect.

"Wall murals in the dining rooms of each house. Scenes of Potoma from the time the houses were built," Cade answered. "Of course, I'd want each one to be different."

"I could use a combination of photographs from Potoma and other typical scenes from the period. Are you looking for beach scenes, town streets, people…?"

"I think I would leave it up to you. After all, you're the artist," Cade replied.

"I'd love to do it. It might take a while though. I'd have to paint around my work schedule," Katie answered.

"I can put off renting out those first two. How long do you think it would take to get the first one done?"

"Well, I'd have to compile some photos first and then compose a preliminary sketch idea. That'll take a couple of weeks given my work schedule. I'm currently working an ongoing case and I'm not sure when I'll be able to wrap it up. That might mean some overtime," Katie answered. "How many walls do you want the mural to cover?"

"All four but it's just the upper third of the wall since I've installed wainscoting on the lower part," Cade replied.

"Honestly, I don't have a clue how long it will take. I can assure you that I will work diligently and use most of my time off to get it done," Katie said.

"Good enough," Cade answered. "What do you want me to pay you?"

"Oh, I don't know. Let me think about it?" Katie replied, still somewhat off-kilter by the whole offer.

"Alright, but in the meantime let me at least buy you dinner. As a down-payment of sorts?" Cade asked, his dark brown eyes gleaming.

Katie felt a little thrill at the thought of a date with Cade.

"I'm not being inappropriate, am I?" Cade said, obviously mistaking her hesitation as a negative reaction.

"No, not at all. Dinner sounds great," Katie recovered.

She looked at her watch, realizing it was time for her to get moving in order to reach the beachfront on time. Cade said goodbye as Katie zipped off as fast as her golf cart would go. It was only when Katie reached the boardwalk in front of the huge pavilion dock where she was to relieve the officer on duty that she realized she hadn't given Cade her phone number.

# CHAPTER 7

**Grace rarely went** outside of her house except at night and when she had to go to work. She didn't like her neighbors looking at her. She had ordered her usual pizza—onions, mushrooms, ham, pepperoni, sausage, tomatoes, pineapple and extra, extra cheese—for lunch. She'd saved three pieces for dinner tonight. She'd also eaten a large bowl of cookies n' cream ice cream with hot fudge sauce and real whipped cream for dessert. Now she was sitting on her sofa trying to decide which movie she wanted to watch. She had popped some buttered popcorn in the microwave and poured a very large glass of regular soda. She couldn't stand diet drinks. The sofa faced a large bay window and she could watch the goings-on in her neighborhood without anyone seeing her.

Grace had a direct view of the Ashton house. No one had been home all day. Grace took that as a positive sign. She got tired of seeing that family flaunting their perfection. It made her almost nauseous. *Especially Little Miss I'm-all-that Jessie Ashton.* Grace noticed that Ping was back in his yard, digging. She giggled to herself when she thought *maybe he's digging to China!* Then she had an even more delightfully macabre thought: *what if he's digging a grave? A grave for that Jessie Ashton!*

**Ping had worked** all morning then taken a break for some lunch and a short nap. His goal for the day was to dig a new flowerbed the length of his front fence. He was half-way there. If he got finished by dinner time he was going to meet some friends at the Crabby Clam for seafood and then maybe he'd go to The Yacht Club and hang out at the bar. There was supposed to be a live band tonight and Ping thought he might like to lose himself in something. He hated sleeping alone in his great big king-size bed in his huge five-bedroom house. Ping wished he'd never bought this house. *What a mistake!*

**Mick watched Aster's** house. She was one strange broad and she wore too much make-up for Mick's taste. Otherwise, she was easy on the eyes with her voluptuous body and full head of hair but she kept odd hours and wasn't terribly sociable. Today, she hadn't been outside of her house until now. Mick sauntered out onto his rear deck. Aster had on shorts and a loose T-shirt and her hair was pulled back from her face. She went into the back door of her garage and returned a few minutes later pushing a lawnmower. Mick watched Aster pull the cord to start the mower, then push it back and forth across the green lawn. After a while, Mick got bored and went back inside. It was time for him to take his medicine; Mick always knew it was time to medicate when he felt his mind go dizzy. Briefly, Mick wondered what was going on with the Ashtons. Then he fell asleep.

**Casey flitted around** the kitchen, cleaning up from lunch. Her husband had gone to play golf and her son went to meet friends at the beach. She was glad to be alone. It was hard to keep up the charade. It was tiring and maddening. She really hated pretending.

Casey poured a glass of iced tea then ran upstairs to get the novel she'd been reading. Back downstairs, she slipped her sunglasses from her purse and grabbed a clean towel off the top of the washing machine in the laundry room. Out on the patio, Casey laid the towel over a padded teakwood lounger and settled in to read for a while. From where she sat she could see Ping's back yard where he was working steadily on his flowerbeds. He glanced up once and caught Casey's eye. She quickly looked back down at her book. Ping made her nervous. *Maybe we should plant a hedge on that side*, she thought to herself.

**Aster could feel** the sweat running through her hair down her face. She was also perspiring abundantly under her arms. She'd have to check her make-up soon to make sure it wasn't melting right off her face. She never let anyone see her without make-up, especially her neighbors. Aster looked over at Ping. He didn't appear to be sweating at all. *Why was she sweating profusely while he looked to be as cool as a cucumber?*

Aster turned off the mower and went inside to cool off. After pouring herself some ice water and taking a few deep gulps, Aster looked at herself in the powder room mirror. She was relieved to see that her make-up was still in place. Aster lifted up her T-shirt to check the cut on her chest. It was a little puffy and red and the sweat was making it sting. Aster ran a wash rag under the cold water, squeezed it out and pressed it to the cut. Aster saw traces of blood on the wash rag when she pulled it away. She rinsed it again and blotted at the cut, then held her T-shirt up and out so that it could air-dry. Next, Aster pulled up the fabric of her shorts. The bruise had darkened and was a little achy. Aster left the powder room after taking a last glance at her make-up and returned to the back yard to finish her mowing.

# CHAPTER 8

**Anna was already** standing on the boardwalk talking to Officer Paul Darren. Out of ten police officers, only two were female—Katie and Anna. Anna hadn't grown up in Potoma like Katie. She and her husband had fallen in love with Potoma when they spent their anniversary at The Tower House Bed & Breakfast five years ago. Anna had joined the force just a few months after Katie did and they became fast friends despite their differences. Katie was twenty-eight and never-married; Anna was ten years older, would be celebrating her fifteenth wedding anniversary in June and had two children.

As expected, the beach was lively with a crowd of weekenders. It was still a bit too cold to swim—although a few brave souls were in the water—but that hadn't stopped the fisherman, sunbathers and picnickers. So far, according to Officer Darren, there hadn't been any problems. This weekend was the precursor to the first major weekend for tourists—the annual Spring Boat Parade. Several organizations held all-day BBQs, oyster roasts and fish fryes right on the beach and the first golf cart drive-in movie was being held at Town Center.

Anna noticed Katie's peculiar glow. "Any reason you're blushing and wearing that silly grin?"

"Well, I stopped by the bungalow court on my way here…" Katie said.

"No more information needed", Anna laughed, putting her hand up.

"He's asked me to paint some murals in the houses," Katie continued.

"Are you going to do it?"

"I really couldn't turn him down," Katie said with mock exasperation.

"Yeah, I'll bet," Anna remarked.

Katie gave Anna a brief sum-up of her visit to Cade and then launched into what she had learned from Jessie's friends.

"I find it odd that not one person you've talked to has had anything remotely negative to say about Jessie Ashton. She seems just a little too good to be true, don't you think?"

"I don't know," Katie argued. "I've known a couple

of girls like Jessie. Pretty, sweet, kind, didn't do drugs or drink or get around."

"Were you one of them?" Anna teased.

"Well…yeah. I guess," Katie admitted. "But I wasn't really talking about me. I'm just saying that Jessie *could* be all that."

"Maybe we need to find someone who isn't one of Jessie's friends. You know, someone who doesn't like Jessie," Anna suggested.

"So far it doesn't sound like there is anyone in this town that fits that description," Katie scoffed.

"Maybe we just need to dig a little deeper."

"At this point, we don't even know if we should even be conducting an investigation. There's no evidence of any crime. I mean it's not as if we can even consider it an attempted suicide because we didn't find anything that could be construed as a suicide note," Katie said, shrugging in frustration.

"Well, what we know so far is that sometime on Thursday night, Jessie was injected with some sort of drug that put her into a semi-comatose state. We also know that there was no drug paraphernalia in her room so it's unknown when or how she received the injection. And if your friend, Ben, is right, only one of the needle holes is the actual injection site. The others were false starts. On the other hand, according to everyone we've talked to, Jessie Ashton never touched illicit drugs and would never, in a million years, inject herself with anything because she had a strong aversion to needles," Anna reviewed.

"Which leaves us with nothing but a big mystery," Katie finished. Anna and Katie stopped to observe a group of young men playfully pushing each other into the edge of the river. After deciding that it was just a group of friends rough-housing, they continued on along the boardwalk.

"Yo, Bug. Dude!" Katie heard from her right where a group of teenagers were playing volleyball. Katie turned to see a tall, thin, long-limbed teenage boy walking from the public parking lot toward the game.

"That's got to be Jessie Ashton's next door neighbor,"

Katie remarked to Anna. "He wasn't home this morning when I went over to try and speak to him about her."

Katie and Anna left the boardwalk and shuffled through the sand toward the volleyball game.

"Bug Bailey?" Katie asked as they approached the bleached-blond teenager.

Looking surprised and then concerned, the boy nodded.

"I'd like to ask you some questions about what happened to Jessie Ashton," Katie informed him, waving him away from the group and gesturing for him to follow her and Anna over to an isolated picnic table under an oak tree on the edge of the boardwalk.

"I don't know what happened to her," Bug said. "I wish I did."

Katie could see real anguish in Bug's eyes and she took note of him nervously opening and closing his fists.

"We've talked to some of her friends and everyone seems to be completely stunned by the fact that she apparently injected herself with drugs. It seems that you've known her longer than anyone we've spoken to…what can you tell me?" Katie asked.

"The same as everyone else. Jessie didn't do drugs. And she didn't like needles. There's no way she would have injected herself with anything," Bug replied.

"According to her cell phone, she spoke to you Thursday night. Do you mind telling me what you talked about? Did she happen to say anything out of the ordinary?" Katie questioned.

"Jessie's like a little sister. We don't really discuss stuff like friends. We just like to pick at each other. You know, joke around and stuff."

"Is that what happened when you talked to her Thursday night?"

"Yeah. We were just bantering back and forth like we always do. We made a couple of jokes about her ex-boyfriend Chase. She thinks his new girlfriend is cheating on him and he's just blind about it."

"So she didn't seem upset about him when she talked

to you about what was going on?" Katie asked.

Bug shook his head.

"Do you know why she and Chase broke up?" Katie asked.

"She and Chase didn't agree about certain parts of the relationship," Bug shrugged.

"What do you think of Chase?" Katie interjected.

"He's a pretty stand-up guy as far as I know. We don't really hang in the same circles," Bug answered.

"If you think of anything, please give me a call", Katie said, handing Bug her card. Bug pulled a wallet out of his back pocket and stuffed Katie's card into it.

"One more thing," Katie said, "Why Bug?"

Bug grinned. "When I was a little kid I wore coke bottles and so everyone called me "Bug-eyed Bailey". Then by the time I got contacts, I'd grown to 6' 5" with these long arms and legs and big feet and everyone said I looked like a praying mantis. So "Bug" just stuck. My real name is Sebastian but only my mom and dad call me that."

As Bug drifted back over to the volleyball game, Katie and Anna continued on their way. A few minutes later, Katie glanced toward the row of mobile vendors set up on an empty lot next to the boardwalk. She spotted a man in a Hawaiian-print shirt and orange and brown board shorts. His sandy-colored shoulder length hair was pulled back in a stubby ponytail and he had several days-worth of stubble around his chin. He was leaning up against the side of the Sno Kone kiosk. Involuntarily, Katie shivered. That guy always gave her a sense of the creeps. When the man saw Katie looking at him, he smiled and waved. *He looks even creepier when he smiles,* Katie thought. Katie gave him a stiff nod then averted her eyes.

"Isn't that…?" Anna said leaning her head in the direction of the Sno Kone.

"Yeah. Keep an eye on him," Katie replied in a whisper.

"Don't have to," Anna replied. "He's coming over here."

Katie groaned, then turned to watch as the man

moved toward them.

"Hi, Katie...I mean, Officer Bell," the man said brightly.

"What can I do for you, today?" Katie said, straightening her back, unable to keep her distaste for the man from creeping into her tone.

"I'm just out taking advantage of the nice weather," the man replied. "Like everybody else."

"I hope you're enjoying yourself, then," Katie answered casually.

"It's always a joy to see you, Katie," the man replied sweetly. "You look really pretty today, as always."

Katie ignored the compliment. "I'm on duty so I need to finish my patrol," Katie said, giving the man a nod as she pushed past him. Once she and Anna were well away from where they had left him, Katie took a deep breath. "I really do not like that man."

Near the Steamboat Casino was a grassy playground with swing-sets, see-saws and sliding boards. Anna's husband was pushing her two little daughters on side-by-side swings.

"Hey!" Anna called out. "What are you guys doing here?"

"We surprise you, Mommy," Anna's five year-old, Litany said. "Stop, daddy. I wanna get off."

"Yeah. I do get off, too," three-year old Echo cried.

Anna's husband, Jacques, stopped the girls in mid-flight and helped the two girls hop off the wooden seats. Anna scooped them up in both arms in huge bear hugs. As they squirmed out of her reach, Jacques greeted her with a quick kiss on the cheek. The two girls then ran toward Katie with open arms.

"Ka-tie, Ka-tie," they cried in unison as their short legs pumped through the heavy sand. After Katie had given them both hugs, they each grabbed a hand and pulled her over to Anna and Jacques.

"Mind if I take a dinner break now?" Anna asked

"No problem. I'll take mine when you get back," Katie replied, a little disappointed that she'd be eating alone instead of at one of the beachside restaurants with Anna as she had anticipated.

Leaving Anna with her family, Katie began the trek back up the boardwalk. Along the way she ran into various people she knew, stopping and chatting for a few minutes with each one. When she reached the place where her golf cart was parked she climbed aboard to make a quick ride up Riverside Drive to Point Marina where there were several beaches used mostly by the locals. There were no restaurants, shops or other vendors on that end, just pristine sand, a few scattered picnic tables and a boat launch. The boardwalk ran all the way from Riverview to Point Marina and was a popular walking stretch for residents out for a bit of exercise. Golf carts and bicycles, slow-going motorcycles and automobiles, often vied for space on Riverside Drive during weekend evenings as people watched the sun set over the river. Later in the season, horse-drawn carriages carrying tourists around the historic areas of Potoma or transporting bridal couples along the picturesque river would also contribute to the traffic on the riverfront road. However, it was still early and Katie encountered only a few golf carts as she made a leisurely ride to the marina. As always she gawked at the bounty of beautiful Victorian mansions and spattering of finely crafted bungalows that lined the opposite side of the street.

The beaches at Point Marina were sparsely occupied, mainly by young families and a few elderly couples. Dinner picnics were just being spread and the air was becoming slightly cooler prompting mothers to pull sweatshirts and jackets onto their wriggling little ones. In an hour or so, darkness would begin to descend over the sparkling water and the sailboats that could be seen in the distance would become effervescent white dots on the horizon. Katie loved evenings in Potoma, especially in the spring.

When Katie returned to the downtown area, Anna was just telling her family goodbye. They'd eaten at Freddie's Fat Bass, a restaurant right on the beach that was known for its innovative take on classic grilled sandwiches and its gourmet seafood. It also had the best sweet potato fries in the state. It was Katie's second favorite restaurant in Potoma, next to

Crabby Clam. As Katie walked up, Anna held up a paper bag.

"I felt sorry for you," Anna said.

Katie grabbed the bag and sat down at a picnic table with a clear view of the lapping water across the beach. She hadn't had anything to eat since breakfast and she was starving. She was delighted to find a grilled barbeque sandwich which combined thick sourdough bread slices dipped in garlic butter before grilling and pulled pork barbeque, thin deep-fried onion rings and crispy coleslaw topped by thick, sweet, hickory-smoked sauce. Anna had also provided Katie with a generous helping of fries and Freddie's signature BBQ grilled scallops wrapped in wilted sweet greens. Anna's daughter, Litany, handed Katie a large paper cup filled with iced root beer.

Twenty minutes later, Katie and Anna were retracing their original steps down the boardwalk toward the Steamboat Casino. The beaches were still full of activity as orange and yellow and pink began to creep across the sky, becoming more and more vibrant with every passing minute. The boat traffic along the river had slowed and the lights along Main Street were turning on automatically, one-by-one in succession. As they passed where they'd met Bug Bailey earlier, Katie noticed that the group of teenaged volleyball players had deserted the net and been replaced by several children trying to swat badminton birdies back and forth. The town custodians were making their last rounds for the day, emptying the public trashcans and spiking stray pieces of trash and soda cans that lay around them. Most of the people still on the beach and boardwalk had donned long pants and jackets. Katie and Anna walked along at a leisurely pace, smiling and nodding at passersby, their presence meant to be comforting, not menacing. Katie's mind kept returning to Jessie Ashton.

"I'm beginning to wonder if there's really any point in questioning Alex Watson," Katie said, breaking the silence. "Everyone we've talked to has said the same thing. I don't expect Alex to tell me anything different."

"Wasn't he the last one to talk to Jessie on the phone Thursday night?" Anna reminded Katie. Katie nodded.

"Well, maybe something happened after she'd talked

to her other friends but before she talked to Alex",' Anna suggested.

"That's possible," Katie acceded.

"Look, it couldn't hurt. And besides, Alex might have a completely different view on Jessie than her other friends. The others have known her for a long time. Maybe a new friend would have a fresh take," Anna said.

"True. You know, according to the time stamp on Jessie's cell phone, she talked to Alex *after* she told her parents goodnight that night," Katie replied.

"Didn't you say that Jessie last spoke to her parents around eleven? And the phone call with Alex began at 11:35? So that was enough time for something to have happened to push Jessie over the edge. It's also enough time for her to have shot up before talking to Alex. If nothing else, talking to Alex might help us determine around what time the drugs were injected," Anna theorized.

"If Jessie was already under the influence of the drugs before she talked to Alex, Alex may have been able to tell if Jessie was starting to feel the effects of whatever she injected," Katie agreed, now more energized than ever to solve the mystery.

At that moment, Katie's cell phone went off. Katie didn't recognize the number but answered it anyway. She was glad she did. It was Jessie's father, Justin Ashton. After hanging up, Katie relayed the conversation to Anna.

"About an hour ago, a group of Jessie's friends descended on the hospital so Jessie's parents decided to come home for a few hours and rest while her friends sat with her. Justin Ashton tried to get his wife, Ellen to lay down but she just couldn't sit still , much less sleep, and decided instead to gather up some things to take to Jessie in the hospital. When she saw that we had stripped Jessie's bed, she insisted that her husband help her turn the mattress before she put clean sheets on it. When they pulled the mattress up to flip it, they found a notebook between the mattress and the box spring. They don't know what to make of what's written in it but thought maybe we'd like to see it," Katie reported.

"Did Justin Ashton tell you what they found?" Anna inquired.

"He said it was some sort of list," Katie replied.

# CHAPTER 9

**Casey was bored**. She had a boring, if not very beautiful, and expensively decorated, house. She lived in a boring, though quaint and friendly, town. And she had a very boring old husband. Casey had met her husband, Ted when she was nineteen. She was smitten with his good looks, his worldly experience, and the fact that he always had plenty of money—money for dinner at the best restaurants, money for really nice jewelry, money for cruises and trips to Europe. She was also infatuated with the fact that he was so in love with her. It didn't matter to her back then that he golfed every Wednesday and Saturday afternoon and that he went bowling with his friends every Monday night or that he worked late Tuesdays and Thursdays and spent every other Sunday afternoon visiting elderly church members who were confined to the hospital or in nursing homes. Fridays he always reserved for date night with her and it was always the same—dinner and a movie, or if she was lucky, maybe a concert or a play at the local theater. Ted went to bed every night of the week at 10:00pm and was up by five. Twenty years ago, Casey liked Ted's regularity and reliability; it made her feel safe and secure and confident that her husband was a stand-up guy. But now, it just made him boring. Just like his dark suits, wire-rimmed glasses and two-tone oxfords that seemed so sexy all those years ago—now they were just plain stiff and frumpy and boring.

Casey looked at herself in the mirror. She was still attractive and looked at least ten years younger than she actually was. Short, curly brown hair, big brown eyes rimmed with long lashes, a perky little nose and high cheekbones. Her light brown skin was clear and luminescent. She was still fairly slender, maybe a little more curvy than she was at nineteen, but she considered that a good thing. Casey looked at the framed picture on the dresser. It was a family portrait that had been taken just a few months ago. Ted was still handsome but he was graying at the temples and his closely cropped moustache and beard were completely white. Crows' feet were prominent at the corners of his eyes and three faint lines creased his forehead. He was wearing his signature charcoal stripe suit with a black vest, white starched shirt and vibrant red paisley tie. Casey thought she looked more like Ted's daughter than his wife. She was now thirty-nine and Ted was fifty-eight. It had never occurred to Casey when she agreed to marry Ted at twenty that one day she'd still be young and craving adventure, and he'd be an old man and set in his ways.

**It was such** a nice day that Grace had thought about going out to the beach once the sun started going down. No one would notice her after it started to get dark. People on the beach and boardwalk would be too busy watching the sunset or grilling their steaks or gossiping among themselves. Grace hated gossips. She bet those Ashtons were huge gossips. Especially that Jessie Ashton with all her friends. After Grace had cleaned up her kitchen and cut up the pizza box into about a million little pieces and put them in four different trash bags and finally changed out of her pajamas into a long, flowy dress and stepped outside her back door, she found it had already gotten chilly. It was too cold to go out now. She'd have to stay home. Grace flopped on her sofa and turned on the TV, flipping through the pay-per-view channels searching for a decent movie. She was in the mood for a comedy or maybe an action thriller. After running through the movies three times, she settled on Steven Seagal's newest debacle. She had fifteen minutes before it started and hurried to the kitchen to prepare a snack. Just as the trailers faded out, Grace returned to the living room with a platter of cheese and crackers, half a dozen chocolate chip mini-muffins, two slices of orange pound cake, three slices of re-heated pizza and a big glass of iced coke.

**Aster had taken** a nap around four o'clock and slept too long. Now she was groggy and really not up to going out. She thought about calling and canceling her plans but Saturday was a big night and she might have to tie up some loose ends from Thursday. So, somewhat reluctantly, she took a shower, trying to wake up. It took a while to pick out her outfit and by the time she was ready to leave it was after seven. She'd have to hurry if she was going to be on time. Aster set the alarm and walked out of the house to her car. She spotted Ping backing out of his driveway. She waited until he had exited the cul-de-sac, then turned on her ignition. Lights were on in several houses but no one seemed to be outside. Aster rubbed her shoulders. It was probably a little too chilly for most folks to be in a hurry to get out the barbeque grills just yet. Aster switched on the headlights and backed up slowly. She looked around again, wondering how many people noticed her frequent night time departures. Aster knew that Grace was keeping count. Unbelievably, Grace had come up to her at the last cul-de-sac picnic and made a rather crude remark to her about it. Aster figured Grace was trying to make a light-hearted joke— something about only hookers working so much at night—and so she went along with it and laughed. Aster flinched as she turned to look out of the back windshield, making sure she wasn't backing into someone's trashcan or the basketball goal that teenage boy kept forgetting to push back up into his driveway. Aster could feel the cut on her chest rip open and the pain was searing. *Bye-bye Grace*, Aster thought as she sped away.

**Mick was still** thinking about Katie. His trip downtown had been worth it just to see her. She looked pretty sexy in her police uniform. He couldn't stop smiling. He'd seen her twice in one day. He knew he had to keep his distance especially when she was working. She had to be professional when she was on patrol, especially when other police officers were around like today on the beach. It was nice talking to Katie, even if it had only been for a minute. That definitely meant she still liked him. He'd been worried about that but now he wasn't. Mick was still wondering why Katie had been in the Ashtons' back yard this morning. The police poking around always made Mick nervous even if it was Katie. When Mick saw the headlights he peeked out of his front curtain. It was that hottie, Aster. She was always going somewhere at night. *Maybe she was a nurse on the graveyard shift. She couldn't be a street corner hooker because she looked too good to do that. She'd be skinny and hollow and obviously strung out on drugs* *if she sold herself on the street somewhere.*

**Ping's muscles ached** but he couldn't stand the thought of spending all night alone in his house. It had been a couple of months since he'd hung out with his friends and he was really looking forward to it. After Ping pulled into Crabby Clam's parking lot, he turned off his cell phone and walked toward the door. His buddies were already crowded into a booth but they squeezed together even tighter and Ping slid in on the edge. They'd already ordered him a drink and as soon as Ping sat down, the waitress hurried over to take their dinner orders. Ping relaxed as he and the guys joked and bantered and hurled good-natured insults at each other. He forgot about all the things he hated about his life and most importantly, he forgot about Thursday night. After two hours of slightly rowdy behavior with the boys, Ping and a few of them were on their way in separate vehicles to The Sandbar. It was a sports bar at the Yacht Club Restaurant at the marina that featured live bands and karaoke on the weekends. Ping pulled his phone from his pocket as he drove the short distance to the bar and turned it on. There were three missed calls, all from the same person. Ping turned the phone off again and headed into the bar behind his buddies.

# CHAPTER 10

**Anna had agreed** to continue the shift at the boardwalk while Katie went over to the Ashtons' house to pick up the notebook. Katie wished she was in her squad car instead of on the golf cart. The golf cart was just too slow when she was in a hurry. Ellen Ashton met Katie at the front door. She led Katie into the living room and offered her a seat on the sofa.

"This is it," Ellen Ashton said, pointing to an open notebook on the coffee table.

"May I?" Katie asked, reaching toward the notebook.

"Certainly. This is the way we found it. Folded back like this," Ellen Ashton replied. Justin Ashton had entered the room and sat down beside Ellen.

Katie picked up the notebook and read the writing on the page.

---

**Observations:**
Thou shall not lie
2L
Thou shall not deceive
3L
Thou shall not commit adultery
1R
Thou shall not steal
3R
Thou shall not covet thy neighbor
5R

**Sin comes with consequences.**
**How do I face them?**

---

"Do you have any idea what this list means?" Katie asked.

"Besides the obvious, no," Justin Ashton answered.

"Is Jessie particularly devout?" Katie questioned.

"No more than her friends. She's gone to church all her life. Accepted Jesus as her Savior when she was ten," Ellen

Ashton replied. "She's very active in our church, in the youth group but I wouldn't say she's overly zealous."

"Then why do you think she'd make a list like this? These are obviously quotes from the Bible," Katie remarked.

"I honestly don't know," Ellen Ashton said, shaking her head.

"Do you think she was listing her own sins?"

"That's what we thought when we found it. Especially since she wrote this," Justin Ashton intercepted, pointing to the last two sentences on the page.

"Do you think it's a suicide note?" Ellen Ashton asked, her voice breaking, threatening to diminish into weeping.

Katie swallowed then shook her head. "It could be," Katie said.

Katie knew that Ellen Ashton had wanted her to say no, that it was not possible. The loss of hope was plainly visible on the woman's face and tears flowed freely down her cheeks.

"I can't believe it," Ellen Ashton whispered as her husband wrapped his arm around her shoulders. Katie could see the tears pooling in Justin Ashton's eyes, too.

"I'm sorry," Katie muttered, not sure what her next move should be. After a few minutes, Katie stood up. "May I take this with me? If your daughter attempted suicide, I'm obligated to investigate."

"Investigate what? We already know that apparently she tried to overdose. Hasn't that already been proven?" Justin Ashton asked.

"We still don't know what substance she injected," Katie replied. "And we still haven't been able to find any trace of drug paraphernalia. At the least, there should have been a syringe and needle and a vial or container of some sort that held the substance she injected."

"What difference does it really make?" Justin Ashton said in a defeated tone.

"Well, if we knew what she injected, it would help the hospital know how to treat it," Katie replied. "The fact that there is no evidence of the injection except for the holes in your daughter's arm is problematic."

Justin Ashton sighed. Ellen Ashton had stopped crying and was dabbing at her eyes with a tissue. Katie handed her another one from the tissue box on the small table next to the sofa.

"Is there anything else in the notebook?" Katie asked.

"It's her Sunday School notebook. There are scripture references for memorizations and bible exercises—you know, questions and answers. A few doodles and such," Ellen said quietly, wiping her nose with the tissue.

"Why would she put the notebook between her mattresses?" Katie inquired.

"It wasn't actually between the mattresses like she placed it there. It was kind of stuck between the headboard of her bed, the wall, and the bottom of the box spring. Like maybe it had been lying on her pillow and accidently fell back there," Justin Ashton explained.

*Since we didn't actually move the bed when we pulled the linens off that could explain why Anna and I didn't find it,* Katie thought to herself.

"I would like to take the notebook with me if that's OK," Katie said, standing up.

"Of course," Ellen Ashton answered. "You'll let us know if you find anything?"

"Absolutely," Katie assured her. "One more thing. Do you have any idea what these notations mean below each of the sins on the list?"

"No. I can't imagine," Ellen Ashton answered.

Katie left quickly and pushed the golf cart as fast it would safely go in the dark night. She wanted to catch Anna before she left the police station. When Katie arrived at the station she was relieved to find Anna behind one of the desks at the back of the room. The tiny police station had been Potoma's original two-room schoolhouse which served the children of year-round residents, mostly laborers and servants, during the Victorian era,. The smaller front room, which had served as the upper school for older students, consisted of a counter near the door which separated the waiting area from four desks behind it that were used by the police officers to complete reports or consult with residents. The much larger back room which had been used to teach the younger children, had been divided into a conference room that doubled as an interrogation cell, a private office for the Chief of Police, two restrooms and a small area with vending machines. An addition had been built onto the back of the school that housed two holding cells and a small locker room for the police officers. The police station stood between Potoma's first bank, now the town hall, and the original fire station, now a spa called "The No-Wake Zone".

Anna waved Katie over and cleared the side of the desk. Katie laid the notebook down and updated Anna on her visit with the Ashtons. When Katie was finished, Anna perused the list written in the notebook.

"What are these notations?" Anna asked.

"No clue," Katie replied. "Got any ideas?"

"Not right off the bat," Anna replied shaking her head.

"Think this is a suicide note?" Katie suggested.

"Could be. This list could be sins she's committed. Then she writes *Sin comes with consequences. How do I face them?*" Perhaps she felt she'd done some terrible things and didn't think she could face the consequences," Anna suggested.

"I thought the same thing. But from what I've heard so far from her parents and friends, it doesn't sound like she would have committed any of the sins listed. I mean, maybe a little white lie or perhaps she was jealous of a classmate but I have a hard time believing she would steal something…or adultery? I'm pretty sure the girl is still a virgin," Katie mused.

"I agree. This whole thing is making less and less sense. I wish I knew what the notations meant," Anna replied.

"Jessie's parents were in the dark, too."

"How is Jessie doing, by the way? Has her condition improved at all?"

"She remains in stable condition. Breathing on her own and everything but she's still unconscious," Katie reported.

Anna shook her head.

"I think I'm going to try to talk with Jessie's friend, Alex tomorrow," Katie said. "Since we now have a possible suicide note and Alex was the last one to speak to her Thursday night, maybe he'll be able to shed some light."

Anna and Katie went over the case again point by point but came no closer to any conclusions and decided to call it a night. Katie was tired but she'd promised Ben she'd come by The Sandbar for a little while where his band was playing, so she headed home to shower and change. Ogilvie whined when he realized that Katie was leaving him again after a long day alone. Katie gave him a big hug and promised to spend more time with him tomorrow.

"We'll go for a walk on the levy," Katie told him as he looked at her with sad puppy-dog eyes. Ogilvie's tail wagged slightly but his head drooped and he crawled on his front legs toward her as if begging her to stay. Katie hated it when Ogilvie made her feel like a creep. She went to the freezer and scooped out two balls of vanilla icecream, placing them in Ogilvie's bowl. Suddenly, Ogilvie had forgiven her as he lapped at the sweet treat. Katie slipped out of the front door, Ogilvie too involved in his unexpected treat to even notice.

The parking area at The Sandbar was filled with trucks, cars and golf carts, and the bar was hopping. Katie checked her watch. It was almost 10:30 and Ben's band, *Local Heroes*, was already in full concert. Ben played guitar and keyboard and co-wrote many of the bands original country-style tunes. Katie moved to the front of the room, finding a seat at a table to one side of the stage. Ben, busy at the keyboard, gave her a wink and a nod. Katie ordered a Shirley Temple and small shrimp cocktail. She felt a little surprised to see Cade Ware at the bar. He seemed to be alone and was barely sipping on the umbrella drink in front of him. Occasionally, a woman would stop beside him to order a drink and flirt with him for a few minutes. He usually responded but the woman never chatted long and for the most part he seemed happy to be left alone.

Katie also noticed a small group of men at the bar who appeared to know everyone that walked their way. They were laughing and gesturing and seemed to be having a good time. One of them, a good looking dark-haired man with Asian features, seemed to be the life of the party. Katie had seen him at The Sandbar before when Ben's band was playing

At 11:15pm, the band took a break and Ben came over to Katie's table.

"How do we sound tonight?" he asked.

"Great, as always," Katie replied, sincerely.

"Thanks. And thanks for coming. I know you had a long day," Ben said. "Do you work tomorrow, too?"

"I go in at ten so I'm going to have to get going in a few minutes," Katie answered. "Sorry I can't stay for the whole gig but I don't want to get arrested for driving while asleep on my way home tonight."

Ben laughed. "Yeah, that wouldn't look too good on your police record."

"Anyway, Ogilvie is mad at me. I bribed him with some icecream but as soon as he finished it and realized I wasn't there, I know he started sulking again." Katie said with feigned concern.

"Wow! The last thing I need is Ogilvie getting mad at me, too for keeping you away." Ben teased.

Katie gave Ben a hug and pressed a one-dollar bill in his hand, an old joke. Ben grinned and walked with Katie to the bar where he stopped to order a drink as Katie headed toward the front door. As Katie was opening the door to go out she heard someone call her name. Before she even turned around she knew it was Cade.

"Hey, how long have you been here?" Cade asked as he followed Katie out onto the wood deck.

"Less than an hour. I just stopped in to listen to the band for a little while," Katie replied.

"Leaving already?" Cade questioned, looking a little disappointed.

"I worked a twelve-hour shift today and I'm wiped out. But I always try to be here when my friend's band plays," Katie explained, suddenly wanting to stay a little longer.

"Which one is your friend?" Cade asked.

"Ben. He was on keyboard," Katie answered.

"Great band. Really good original stuff, too," Cade complimented.

"Ben co-writes most of it. Words and music," Katie said, proudly.

"He's talented," Cade remarked. "I'm sorry I didn't' see you earlier. I would have bought you a drink or something."

"Thanks for the thought," Katie replied. "I hate to go but I really have to. If I don't get to bed soon, I won't be able to get up in the morning."

"You didn't give me your phone number," Cade said. Katie looked at him blankly.

"You said you'd let me buy you dinner sometime but you didn't give me your number. When you came by earlier today," Cade clarified.

"Oh, right. You know I realized that later," Katie laughed.

Katie opened the small leather bag hanging over her shoulderand pulled out one of her cards. "That's my cell phone. It's the best way to reach me."

Cade looked at the card for a moment then slipped it in his pocket. "Can I give you a ride home?"

"No. I've got my cart ," Katie said, pointing. As much as she thought she might like Cade, she wasn't all that keen on him knowing where she lived until she got to know him better

As Katie drove off, she waved at Cade who remained standing in the parking area. Even though she was beginning to feel a little sleepy and would be glad to collapse into her bed, she enjoyed driving along Riverside Drive, the cool breeze off the river blowing in her face. Across the river, lights twinkled in the distance. The night was quiet and empty except for the occasional boardwalk strollers. When Katie passed The Tower House, she glanced up at the third floor balcony that overlooked the river and saw a couple cuddled up on the tiny custom-made loveseat gazing at the stars.

The towers and turrets of the Victorian houses that lined Riverside Drive were highlighted by soft light filtering through the windows. The stained glass glowed in muted reds, burgundies, blues and greens. Downtown, Katie quickly wound through the commercial area and then passed over into Riverview. Before she knew it she was pulling up to her tiny detached garage. She pressed the automatic opener and drove her golf cart in. Katie could see Ogilvie's animated fuzzy face in the glass french doors at the rear of the house, his whip of a tail wagging furiously as she closed the garage door and walked toward the back patio.

# SUNDAY
## CHAPTER 11

**When Ping woke** up Sunday morning, he realized he's never turned his cell phone back on after leaving Crabby Clam. He'd completely forgotten about it. When he'd finally gotten home at 2:30am, he was so tired that he'd grabbed a blanket and fallen into bed fully clothed except for his shoes. Ping looked at the clock on the nightstand. It was ten o'clock. Ping couldn't remember the last time he's slept this late. Not that it mattered. He didn't have to go to work and he had no plans for the day. Stripping down to his boxers and slipping under the covers, he was asleep as soon as his head hit the pillow. He still hadn't turned on his cell phone.

**Aster had finally** returned home at four in the morning. She was exhausted and her injuries from Thursday night were still causing her pain. She gingerly removed her camisole and bra and examined the cut that sliced across the left side of her chest. It had oozed and the fabric of the camisole was stuck to it. After she pulled the fabric free, she gently pressed a cold, wet washcloth against it. Then she smeared some anti-bacterial ointment on it and taped a large bandage over it. Next, Aster removed her short skirt, grimacing at the grotesquely colored bruise on her thigh. It hurt as bad as it looked. Aster slipped on a pair of cotton pajama bottoms and a long-sleeved t-shirt. She pulled her hair back in a messy ponytail and washed off all her makeup. She'd sleep until noon then get up and do some housecleaning. Aster made sure all of the black-out curtains were completely shut, slipped a white-noise disc into her CD player and crawled into bed.

**Ted and Casey** went to the 8:00am service at church as usual. Casey wasn't at all surprised to find that Justin and Ellen Ashton were not in attendance. Pastor Snead gave a quick update on Jessie Ashton's condition, asked everyone to pray for her quick recovery and then held a special moment of silence for her, followed by a long, eloquent prayer. Casey went through the motions, looking every bit the happy homemaker and loving wife. Outwardly, she was the same person that everyone admired and envied. Inside, Casey carried the guilt from Thursday night and the worst part was that it was a pleasurable guilt. She only felt guilty because what she had done was hurtful to someone else. She had actually enjoyed what she had done. And she felt even guiltier for that.

**The first thing** Grace did when she woke up was go into the bathroom and get rid of everything she had eaten on Saturday. Then she took eight laxatives just to make sure. On her way back into the bedroom, she caught sight of herself in the full-length mirror in the dressing room. Grace turned to face the mirror, pinching the roll of fat around her belly in self-loathing. She moved her hands down to grab the excess around her hips, then turning sideways tried to smooth the front of her stomach flat, sucking it in as hard as she could. Grace quickly put on her bra and panties, sweat pants and a big sweatshirt over an oversized tank top. Grace went downstairs to the kitchen and made some diet tea, drank it down quickly and made another cup. Then she grabbed a big plastic cup, filled it with ice and turned on the spigot. She carried her ice water into the small study she had converted to a home gym. For the next three hours, she ran on the treadmill, walked on the stair climber and spun on the stationary bicycle. When she was finished, she was drenched in sweat and felt like she was going to pass out. She refilled her giant cup with ice and water and put in a Pilates DVD, then climbed back on the treadmill for another thirty minutes. After her shower, she fell asleep on the sofa in exhaustion. The painful urge to go to the bathroom woke her two hours later.

**Mick woke up** with a smile on his face and nearly skipped like a girl down the hall to the kitchen to fix breakfast. He'd been in bed by 11:30 the night before and had slept like a baby. Aster-with-the-assets had briefly roused him with the sound of her car and the glow of her headlights when she pulled into the cul-de-sac sometime early in the morning, but he had quickly fallen back to sleep. Mick's slumber had been dreamless and deep and for once in a very long time, he felt completely rested and energetic. He decided to skip his medication. After gobbling down a large plate of scrambled eggs, bacon and toast, Mick went out front to retrieve his newspaper. Not another soul seemed to be up and about at 9:00am. Mick knew some of his neighbors went to church and were already gone. Mick used to go to church but not anymore. He'd done too many bad things and visited too many bad places to sit in church with a clear conscience. He still read his Bible, though and sometimes when he was feeling particularly good he listened to Charles Stanley on the radio. Mick wondered what was going on with Jessie Ashton. *Had she recovered or was she dead?* He needed to find out. He wished he could ask Katie. Mick scoured the cul-de-sac again then retreated to his living room sofa to read the paper and sip on his coffee.

# CHAPTER 12

**Katie studied the** notations on the notebook page. Each phrase was a sin listed in the Bible. *Steal, lie, deceive, covet thy neighbor, adultery* Katie pondered. After all the interviews she had done with Jessie Ashton's friends, Katie had a hard time believing Jessie could have succumbed to any of them. However, without anything else to go on, and given the phrases "Sin comes with consequences. How do I face them?" written on the same page, Katie had to assume that Jessie was writing about herself.

Lying, deceiving someone, even coveting—being jealous of someone—were all normal things that almost all teenagers did, at least on occasion. Being a police officer, Katie also knew that some teens even resorted to petty theft like one-time shoplifting on a dare and so that could also be considered as normal for teenagers. Those actions weren't usually elevated to the level of condemnable sins, even by the most fervent of Christians. Rather, they were looked at as mistakes to learn from, bad choices or youthful impulses that would be outgrown as the individual matured. A teenager's version of committing adultery could range from simply flirting with a friend's significant other to more physical activity but rarely would a teenage girl commit adultery in the real literal sense of betraying marriage. For one thing, in Jessie's case, if it were true, it would have to mean that Jessie was having an affair with a married man and Katie was positive that that was an impossibility.

Katie wondered if the notations—a number followed by a letter—was some sort of record of how many times Jessie had sinned in a particular manner. If this were the case that would mean that Jessie had lied twice, been deceitful three times, stolen three times, coveted her neighbor five times and committed adultery once. What Katie couldn't decipher was the meaning of the letters L and R. All she could come up with were "left" and "right" and that just didn't make any sense.

As Katie continued to stew, she also concluded that if Jessie was worried about the sins she'd committed and the consequences of the sins, certainly she wouldn't have committed yet another sin. It made absolutely no sense that her solution to the guilt she felt for the sins she'd already committed would have been the even greater sin of suicide. Katie shook her head and exhaled a huge sigh. She decided she must be missing something; maybe she'd overlooked evidence that was big as life and staring her right in the face. Katie replayed in her mind her search of Jessie's room, her subsequent search of the Ashtons' backyard, the interviews with each of Jessie's friends. As she thought back, she could remember nothing of significance, nothing leaped out at her, nothing seemed to explain why Jessie would suddenly do things that were completely out of character.

Katie called to Ogilvie, who was lying near the french doors to the backyard, and put her cereal bowl on the floor for him to lick. She always saved a few drops of the sweet milk for him. Katie soon finished her cup of Earl Grey and keeping an eye on the clock, quickly finished getting ready for work. She gave Ogilvie his usual peanut butter cookie before leaving for the police station, Jessie Ashton's notebook in hand.

Katie waited until after noon to call Alex Watson in case he attended church on Sunday morning. She arrived at Alex's house in Fairway an hour later. Katie had always been impressed by the attention to detail the builders had incorporated in replicating the historic Victorian and craftsman architectural styles of the Riverside area in Fairway. She also liked the way the individual neighborhoods in Fairway were designed with gridded street patterns, brick or cobblestone sidewalks and pocket parks, reminiscent of the original historic features of Potoma. The developer had cleverly orchestrated three old-fashioned neighborhoods around three distinctly different golf courses: the old one built in 1898 called The Roller for its many hills and water traps, and two new golf courses—The Steamboat and The Monet. Alex lived on The Steamboat course, the backyard backing right up to the green. The house was a classic Queen Anne with bay windows, an octagonal turret and a wrap-around-porch that included a built-in gazebo. As Katie walked to the porch she admired the layers of gingerbread on the roof eaves, above the windows and along the veranda. A petite woman with two-tone wavy hair, wearing a tailored cinnamon-colored suit and vintage shoes answered the door. She didn't look old enough to have a teenage son. She stepped out onto the porch and directed Katie to the rear of the house. "Alex is in his workshop. He's taken over our garage," she said pleasantly.

Katie followed the driveway to the matching carriage-house-style detached garage. Katie paused, unsure of whether to knock on the entry door or just open it. Before Katie had a chance to do either, the door opened on its own. There was no one behind it. Cautiously, Katie stepped into the building calling out Alex's name.

"Come on in. I'm over here," a male voice answered.

Katie was suddenly in awe. She felt as if she'd stepped back in time to some sort of Victorian combination parlor/library/eating establishment/laboratory. To one side, behind a long wooden table, stood a teenage male dressed in a white shirt with black arm garters, a gray-striped cravat, and a black damask vest. He was peering through round-lens spectacles at some sort of machinery on the table. As Katie moved toward him, he stepped out and met Katie with a firm handshake and a gentlemanly bow. He was wearing striped gray trousers and black & white button boots. In looks, he greatly resembled Colin Firth as Mr. Darcy in BBC's "Pride & Prejudice".

"Please excuse my shirtsleeves and bare head," he said with an affected English accent. Katie was too befuddled by his unexpected mannerisms to speak at first. "Will you have a seat?" he continued, waving his arm toward a red velvet-upholstered Cleopatra sofa.

Katie followed him across the room and as they sat down together at either end of the sofa, she recovered her voice.

"Very interesting place you have here," Katie remarked, looking around, taking note of the multitude of clocks, various pulleys, strange-looking mechanical devices and plush Victorian décor.

"A compliment, I am sure," the boy answered. "May I introduce myself? I am Alex Watson. And you must surely be Officer Katie Bell."

Katie nodded. "As I explained on the phone, I am here to ask you some questions about Jessie Ashton."

Alex nodded, settling against the back of the sofa and crossing his right ankle over his left knee. "How can I help you?"

"As you probably already know, it has been confirmed that some unknown substance was injected into Jessie's arm on Thursday night or early Friday morning and most likely caused her current semi-comatose state. On Thursday night she spoke to five people on her cell phone between 6:00pm and 11:35 pm. You were the last phone call. I've already interviewed the other four people she talked to. I'm interested in your conversation with her," Katie briefed.

Alex dropped his head into his hands for a moment then looked back up at Katie. "I didn't realize I was the last person she had talked to," he said quietly.

"We believe you are. She told her parents goodnight at around 11:00pm and it doesn't appear that she talked to any of her friends after that except for you," Katie reiterated.

"I don't think I can help you," Alex replied. "Our conversation was ordinary."

"Meaning?" Katie pressed.

"We did what we normally do," Alex answered vaguely, then added, "continued our bedtime story adventure."

Katie raised her eyebrows and knew the sardonic look in her eyes was clearly apparent.

"We've created a story together. It's a running adventure that we add to each night before we go to sleep," Alex quickly explained.

"What kind of story?" Katie asked, wondering now if drugs might be part of the "adventure" Alex referred to. Katie knew very well that certain famous Victorian writers used opium and absinthe, among other things, to enhance their imaginations which supposedly resulted in their best literary works.

Alex swept his arm dramatically down his torso and out as he said "Obviously, I live in the past, or at least my own altered version of the past. My world is what some stereotype as "steampunk". I prefer "neo-Victorian" if it needs a label of some sort. In my world, people still dress with style, speak with intelligence, understand and practice proper etiquette, find value in great literature and the arts, and appreciate beguiling wit and intriguing conversation. We also crave adventure and invention, innovation and beauty. Jess has a great interest in all of these things. So we pretend we live in a society that's like that. We role play to some extent and take turns creating a new adventure for our characters each night."

Katie nodded. "And do your forays into the past include any physical enhancements?"

"You are speaking of drugs, I presume?" Alex smiled. "Absolutely not."

"So as far as you know, Jessie would not have taken any type of drug Thursday night, either before or after your conversation on the phone?"

"Jess didn't partake of drugs. Ask any of her friends," Alex replied.

"I have. They say the same thing," Katie confirmed. "And I believe them. And you."

"Why do you suppose, then, does it appear that she was injected with some type of drug?" Alex posed, shifting his body so that he was now no longer lounging against the sofa but sitting up erect with both feet on the floor.

"I can't figure that out, quite honestly," Katie admitted. "I also understand from her friends that she does not like needles. That she passes out at the sight of them."

"That is my understanding as well," Alex said, nodding. "Is it possible that someone else performed the injection?"

"There is no evidence of that, and quite simply, there is no reason to consider it. The only other people in the house Thursday night were Jessie's parents. Why would you suggest it?" Katie answered.

"Just a method of elimination, I suppose. If Jess wouldn't inject herself, yet it is certain that she was injected with something, it would seem logical that someone else must have performed the act," Alex explained. "But as you say, that would seem impractical. Certainly her parents would not do anything to hurt her."

"That's not the only reason. It looks like we may have a suicide note," Katie announced.

Alex's face contorted in shock and horror. "I can't believe it!" Alex exclaimed, his hands flying to his face. After a moment, he asked, "What did the note say, exactly, if I may be so bold?"

"I actually have it with me," Katie replied, opening the notebook she was carrying and opening it to the page she had been studying that morning. She handed the open notebook to Alex.

After looking at it for a few moments, Alex looked up and said, "Are you sure this is a suicide note? There's no salutation, no signature."

"I don't know for sure but her parents feel that it might be. The last two sentences lead us to believe that she was feeling guilty and that may have led to a suicide attempt."

"I don't believe Jess would ever attempt to cause her own demise. I'm sure I would have detected any sign of depression or overwhelming guilt. Quite the opposite. Her loving embrace of life was mesmerizing!" Alex disputed, shaking his head enthusiastically.

Katie detected that Alex's interest in Jessie extended beyond friendship or a common interest in the Neo-Victorian ideal. He also seemed to know things about Jessie that even her oldest friends might not have been aware of.

"You dress the part. Did Jessie ever express her interest in your shared...ideals, with the way she dressed? Katie asked.

"Not in real life but she designs clothes, draws them in her sketchbook, that she wants to sew. She's been particularly excited about it," Alex replied. "She's visited me here a few times and played dress up with some of the things in my wardrobe."

"Do you think she would actually wear the clothes she designs out in public as you do?"

"I think so. She wasn't shy about doing her own thing. And she didn't care a whit about what other people thought of her."

What Alex had just said about Jessie being unconcerned about others' opinions hit a chord with Katie. "Does it make any sense to you that she would be afraid others would find out about the sins she believed she had committed and she couldn't face that?

"I don't think what someone else thought about her sins would have any bearing, no," Alex answered. "Perhaps, her statement "How can I face them?" refers to her own personal inability to face the consequences of whatever sins she believed she had committed."

Katie couldn't help scoffing. "But you don't really think this is a suicide note, anyway, do you? Do you think she committed any of the sins that are listed?"

Alex shook his head. "No, I don't. Nobody is perfect, but she came very close. She would never lie or steal or be deceitful. I couldn't imagine her being jealous of anyone in any malicious way, and well, adultery…that's a very bad joke."

"I have gotten that impression from Jessie's other friends, but in truth, you haven't known Jessie for very long. Just a couple of months. What makes you so certain that Jessie didn't have a rebellious or secret side that you or her other friends just don't know about? I'll wager that Jessie's other friends don't have a clue about her involvement in this alternate world the two of you share," Katie challenged.

"It is true that I certainly haven't known Jess very long but if you met her you'd understand. There's no veil of secrecy. What you see is exactly what you get," Alex replied, looking intently at Katie.

Katie had run out of questions and she was still no further along in figuring out what had happened to Jessie Ashton. She glanced around the room again, still intrigued. "Your parents don't have a problem with all this?"

"My mother thinks it's fascinating and is quite supportive. My father thinks I have serious mental deficiencies but fortunately he doesn't live here. My mother's husband thinks I'm weird but he's nice about it," Alex answered.

"How did you manage to score the garage?" Katie

asked, still taking in the various elements.

"As I said, my mother is quite supportive of my interests. She worked it out with her husband," Alex said, his friendly smile possibly showing a trace of a smirk.

Katie stood up and slowly began to browse the room, her back to Alex who was still seated on the sofa. "Let me guess. You were less than enthusiastic about your mom's remarriage and even more resistant to the idea of moving to Potoma. So your mom made certain arrangements to entice your cooperation. Am I warm?" Katie looked over her shoulder coyly.

Alex laughed. "Something like that but don't think for a minute I can manipulate my mom with long faces and sulky ways. She truly did this for me simply because she knows how difficult it has been for me to…adapt," Alex replied.

"I can imagine," Katie murmured. "What are these things?" Katie pointed to a group of mechanical-looking devices to her left.

"I invent things, you might say. Some of them are practical and actually work, others are just what you might call art. Sculptures, I suppose," Alex answered.

"They are fascinating, really," Katie remarked with admiration. She appreciated the aesthetic quality of the functional, and non-functional, pieces that Alex had created using antique and modern materials.

"I'll show you some of my more practical things," Alex volunteered, standing and waving Katie over to what appeared to be an antique upright piano. "Watch," Alex directed as he pressed one of the keys. Suddenly the protruding section of the piano containing the ivory and ebony keys split in the middle, each section sliding to the side, to reveal a computer keyboard. Then the music stand slid downward out of sight into the piano and the middle front panel slid upward to uncover a flat panel screen. Alex then pressed one of the floor pedals and the panel to the right of the screen slid up. The compartment behind it held a laser printer. Alex pressed on the panel to the left of the screen and the hinged panel swung open. Shelves had been built inside to store printer paper, flash drives, and other computer supplies. "The rest of the equipment is stored in compartments in the bottom."

"Impressive!" Katie exclaimed. "You should think about doing this for a living. People would pay big money for these things."

"I'm not sure I want other people to have these things. As is obvious, I rather like being unusual in a crowd of sameness," Alex shrugged.

Alex demonstrated a few of his other "inventions" including a tiled shower stall enclosed in a huge French wardrobe, a bath tub disguised as an Empire style chaise lounge and a toilet hidden in an antique grandfather clock. Completely enthralled, Katie reluctantly left. She was perplexed, frustrated and even more determined to figure out what had happened to Jessie Ashton.

Hungry, and craving something sweet and something salty, Katie stopped at Ice Cream Dream, an old drive-in diner one block over from the boardwalk. She ordered French fries and a small hot fudge sundae. As she savored her snack, she idly flipped through Jessie's notebook. Just as Ellen Ashton had said, it appeared to be her Sunday School workbook with Bible quotations and scripture references, numbered phrases which appeared to be answers to questions and groups of notes about various recognizable Bible stories. The "suicide note" was near the back of the notebook. Katie abruptly had a thought. She took out her cell phone and her pocket note book and made several calls.

# CHAPTER 13

**According to Katie's** notes, at least four of Jessie's friends attended the same church as the Ashtons and were most likely in the same Sunday School class with Jessie. She had arranged to meet Greta, Michella, Bug, and Georgie at the police station. When everyone had arrived, Katie led the group into the conference room in the back of the station where they sat around a small table.

Katie laid Jessie's notebook on the table. Georgie and Greta sat close together. Bug and Michella sat next to each other with space between them and the other two girls. As Katie observed them, it was obvious that Jessie's social circle was very diverse. Georgie and Greta exemplified the typical middle-class sixteen year-old giddy teenage girl. Bug was the all-American boy-next-door from a fairly wealthy family who had the maturity of someone much older than seventeen. He was somewhat exotic-looking with dark skin and light hair. Michella typified the educated and intelligent young black woman who was destined to be successful and probably ignored racial and ethnic differences.

"As I told you on the phone, we have found some interesting information that might help us determine what happened to your friend, Jessie. I'd like you to look at it. It appears to be a notebook that Jessie used in Sunday School," Katie announced, holding the notebook up in front of her.

Without hesitation, all four nodded their heads. "That's Jessie's. We all have them. Our Sunday School teacher is also a college professor and she's a stickler about taking notes," Georgie said.

Katie nodded and opened the notebook to the page on which Jessie had written the list of sins. "Maybe you can tell me something about this. It appears to be what could be construed as some sort of suicide note."

The four teenagers looked shocked and tears welled in the eyes of Georgie and Greta. Bug held out his hand and Katie handed him the notebook.

"This is an exercise we did a couple of weeks ago," Michella said, leaning over toward Bug and looking at the notebook. "We were studying God's laws and discussing how they could be applied to today."

"It was like a homework exercise. We were supposed to observe people we knew for the next two weeks and write down any of God's laws we saw them break," added Georgie.

"We were going to discuss our observations at Sunday School next week," Bug continued.

"And you were supposed to be applying these laws to others, not to yourselves?" Katie interjected.

"Exactly. We did an oral exercise in class where we talked about what laws we, ourselves, broke on a regular basis. This homework assignment was a way to see that everyone breaks God's laws but that he forgives us for our transgressions," Bug answered.

"We were also supposed to use our observations as a way to be more conscientious of our own violations of God's laws," Michella added.

"So Jessie wouldn't have been recording her own sins but those of others around her?" Katie confirmed.

The four teenagers nodded vigorously.

"Then what do you think these two phrases mean?" Katie asked, pointing to where Jessie had written "Sin comes with consequences. How do I face them?"

"The first sentence was part of the exercise. We were supposed to list the possible consequences of the sins of others we observed," Greta explained.

"It was a way to get us to think about how breaking God's laws can affect our lives and the lives of others," Georgie added.

"What about the other sentence?" Katie urged.

"We talked about facing the consequences of sin but that wasn't something we were supposed to write down as part of the exercise. Maybe Jessie was just making notes or something," Greta suggested.

The information in the notebook now seemed logical and less like a suicide confession. Katie's initial feeling of having a break in the case now turned to disappointment.

"What are these letters and numbers?" Bug asked.

"We haven't figured that out yet. I was hoping one of you would know," Katie replied.

The four teenagers looked at each other shrugging.

"I take it these notations were not part of the exercise, then," Katie remarked.

Michella shook her head.

"Could the numbers refer to how many times Jessie saw that law broken?" Katie asked.

Michella pulled a face. "I suppose so."

"Do the letters mean anything to you? Either next to the number or even just by themselves?" Katie pressed on.

The four teenagers shook their heads in unison. "All I can think of when I look at the letters is "left" and "right". And I don't know what that would have to do with how many times Jessie observed those particular sins being committed," Georgie mused.

"That's all I came up with, too. And, like you, I can't find any sense in that," Katie concurred.

After a few more questions, Katie thanked the four teenagers and showed them out of the police station, giving them her cards and reminding them to call her if they thought of anything that might help in the investigation. Katie still wasn't sure if she should be conducting an investigation since so far there wasn't any real evidence that a crime had been committed and Jessie's parents hadn't asked for police intervention. Nevertheless, Katie sat down and began typing up her notes about Jessie Ashton.

Katie's cell phone rang. She didn't recognize the number but thinking perhaps it might be someone with additional information about the case, Katie answered on the second ring. She was wrong; it was Cade Ware.

"I know it is very last minute but I was hoping you might be free for dinner tonight," Cade said.

"I'd love to have dinner but I won't get off work until at least seven," Katie answered.

"No problem. What about meeting around 8:30?" Cade suggested.

Katie felt a little lurch in her stomach and knew that

she was probably blushing.

"Sure. Where?" Katie agreed.

"The Yacht Club?"

Katie was a little disappointed. The Yacht Club wasn't a great restaurant for a first date, or any date for that matter. The food was good but because of the bar, it was always noisy and not terribly conducive to conversation. On the other hand, if a date was going badly…

"OK," Katie said brightly. "Go ahead and get a table and I'll find you."

Cade agreed and told her that he looked forward to seeing her. Katie checked the clock. It was now almost four. Katie felt compelled to give Justin and Ellen Ashton an update on the case, especially the latest developments concerning the supposed suicide note they'd found. Katie quickly finished up on the computer and printed out the results. She added the sheets of paper to the file on Jessie Ashton that already contained the initial incident report. Katie preferred to talk to the Ashtons in person so she hopped on her golf cart and headed for their home.

It occurred to Katie on her way to the Ashtons' that one or both of them would probably be at the hospital so she stopped the cart and called Justin Ashton's cell phone number. He informed her that they were on their way home from the hospital but would be returning after a quick dinner. Katie agreed to wait for them. During the rest of her drive, Katie continued to ponder the meaning of the number-letter notations in Jessie's notebook. *What could they possibly mean?*

As Katie entered the cul-de-sac she stopped abruptly, a thought swiftly forming in her mind. The cul-de-sac was oval-shaped and contained eleven homes. The Ashton house sat directly across from the entrance to the cul-de-sac with the other homes fanning out to the left and right. Katie pulled Jessie's notebook from the glove compartment and examined the number-letter notations. "2L, 3L, 1R, 3R, 5R," Katie read out loud. *Was it possible that the notations referred to the houses in Jessie's neighborhood? Could 2L, for example, mean the second house to left of the Ashtons'?* Katie mulled the questions over trying to decide if there could be any validity to the prospect. Katie sighed with resignation. *At this point, any theory was worth looking into.*

Katie parked in front of the Ashtons' house and within ten minutes Justin and Ellen Ashton arrived. They invited Katie inside and sat down, listening intently to Katie's latest news. Katie did not reveal that she thought the number-letter notations might refer to the houses in the Ashtons' cul-de-sac. She wanted to think about it some more and discuss her speculation with Anna first.

"So you've ruled out suicide, then?" Justin Ashton questioned Katie.

"I'm not ready to completely dismiss it, given the circumstances, but it does seem to be a remote possibility now," Katie replied. "The information Jessie's friends gave me certainly indicate that what Jessie wrote was simply a Sunday School exercise."

"I'm relieved. Not that I really believed that Jessie would attempt to kill herself..." Ellen Ashton said. "Of course now, we're back to the questions."

Katie nodded in agreement. "Unfortunately, you're right."

"Where do we go from here, then?" Justin Ashton asked.

"First, we keep praying for Jessie's recovery. But until she regains consciousness and is able to tell us what happened herself, I intend to keep poking around," Katie answered.

"We would appreciate that," Ellen Ashton said, nodding.

"I'll keep you updated. Don't hesitate to call me." Katie replied standing up.

When Katie returned to her golf cart, her gaze swept the cul-de-sac as she made mental notes of which houses matched up with the notations in Jessie's notebook. While there could be some question as to what Jessie might consider "left" and "right", Katie decided that Jessie would most likely take the position of being inside her house, looking out toward the entrance to the cul-de-sac. Katie noticed that one of the houses next door to the Ashtons' was for sale and another house had a "For Rent" sign in front of it. Both houses appeared vacant.

Although most of Potoma, particularly New Town, was now inhabited by full-time residents, there were still plenty of homes that were used as weekend cottages or rented out as summer houses. The police kept a list of such houses so that they could routinely check up on them when they were vacant. Katie headed back to the station to check the list against the houses in the cul-de-sac. This could not only confirm the correct perspective for determining "left" and "right" but also help Katie determine whether her suppositions about the number-letter notations had any validity. If the houses Katie felt were signified by the notations were indeed occupied regularly such confirmation could strengthen Katie's premise that someone living in the house had committed the listed sin. How such a confirmation would help her figure out what happened to Jessie wasn't clear but Katie had a strong feeling there might be a connection.

Back at the station, Katie brought up the department's list of part-time homes. Two of the houses in the Ashtons' cul-de-sac were listed as weekend residences for homeowners that lived in D.C. Katie would have to go back to the cul-de-sac to confirm the addresses but it appeared that all of the houses that corresponded with the notations in Jessie's notebook had full-time occupants, especially if Katie had guessed correctly about Jessie's point of view. Katie checked the time. If she left now, she had just enough time to return to the cul-de-sac before her shift ended. Katie grabbed Jessie Ashton's file and headed out the door.

Sitting on her golf cart in front of the Ashtons' house Katie drew a rough diagram of the cul-de-sac, identifying each house by its numbered address. She marked the Ashtons' house with an X and then crossed out the two houses that had been listed as weekend residences as well as the house for sale and the house for rent. Just as Katie had thought, the remaining houses on her site plan matched up with the notations in Jessie's notebook. Katie was sure it was too much of a coincidence to be *just a coincidence.* She was now convinced that if nothing else, Jessie had definitely observed her neighbors breaking God's laws and had made note of exactly who was doing what.

Katie arrived at her house at 7:15pm and was, as usual, greeted enthusiastically by Ogilvie. Although she was already running late, she took the time to snap on Ogilvie's leash and jog down to the end of the street and onto the beach with him. After all, she had promised him a walk and she knew she'd be too tired later when she got home from her dinner with Cade. For fifteen minutes she played catch with Ogilvie, enjoying his utter bliss at romping through the shallow water to retrieve his ball and running at full speed to return it to her to throw into the river again. When she put the leash back on his collar, he gave her a mournful look and his tail stopped wagging, drooping until the curved tip just brushed the sand.

Katie hadn't let herself think much about her dinner with Cade. She was very good at keeping personal thoughts and feelings at bay when she was working. Now she was feeling a little anxious. At 8:15pm, Katie was standing in front of her closet still trying to figure out what to wear. In undecided desperation, she finally pulled out her old stand-bys—a pretty floral print slip dress and a tea-dyed crocheted cardigan with ruffled bell sleeves and pom-pom buttons. She also grabbed her favorite brown cowboy boots. The early spring evening had grown a little chilly so Katie decided to drive her Jeep in lieu of her golf cart.

Katie pulled up in front of restaurant at the marina at 8:40pm. The wind had picked up and the slight chill Katie had felt when she left her house was now a full-fledged one. As Katie stepped down from the Jeep she rubbed her shoulders with both hands using the friction to create a little warmth on her body. Except for the lights of the marina, the night was dark and few stars dotted the sky. Despite the savory scents coming from the restaurant, everything had a fresh, crisp smell. Katie could hear a soft hum rising from the gently rolling river slapping against its banks and the boat docks. Unbidden, Ben's face loomed in Katie's mind but Katie dismissed its appearance, convincing herself that she was just remembering being here the night before listening to Ben's band.

As agreed, Cade had arranged a table and was waiting for Katie. He greeted her warmly and they both settled into the dining booth. Katie was relieved to find that relatively few people were in the dining room and the bar seemed somewhat desolate as well, so any noise was mostly relegated to soft murmuring from other patrons and the occasional clatter of dishes and pans coming from the kitchen. Katie was pleased to observe that her choice of outfit was in keeping with the casualness of Cade's. He was wearing putty-colored pleated trousers and a red plaid shirt with rusty boat shoes. A waitress took Cade and Katie's food orders and brought them drinks and salads.

"I brought a plan for the color scheme for the houses with me," Katie said between bites of salad. She had managed to jot down paint colors before sinking into bed the night before.

"Great! I'm anxious to see that," Cade replied. "That's one aspect of what I do that I really don't enjoy. Don't ask me why. I guess I'm just not artistic in that way."

Katie pulled the list from her clutch and slid it across the table to Cade. Cade took a few minutes to look it over.

"I like the way you incorporated one color from one house into the one beside it but changed the hue depending on whether it was on the first level or second level of the house. I also like the colors you chose. I think they'll all reflect true historic colors of the period," Cade complimented.

"Well, that was my intent. I figured if you were trying to keep the bungalows as original as possible in renovating them then the paint colors needed to follow that ideal as well," Katie replied.

"I think you've definitely succeeded," Cade said. "Have you had time to think about the murals I asked you to paint?"

Katie swallowed before answering. "Not in any detail, no. Do you still want me to create collages from old photographs?"

Cade took a sip from his glass. "Absolutely. I think it would really enhance the authenticity of the renovation." After taking another sip from his glass, Cade continued, "I brought you something, too."

Cade pulled a folded piece of paper from a large

envelope. "This is the landscape plan I devised. What do you think? Will this blend with the color scheme on the houses?"

Katie studied the plan noting that Cade was planning to cluster flowering shrubs around the perimeter of the court banded by flowerbeds containing perennials and annuals.

"I think if you use plants with flowers that are in the pink, blue, purple and yellow families, this will look fantastic. I wouldn't use anything with orange flowers because depending on the hue it could clash with the colors on the houses and whites and creams would be too stark. I see your plant list includes forsythia which is the perfect yellow to coordinate with the houses, azaleas, which you can get in so many different colors and butterfly bush which comes in a great blue tone. Accenting those with daffodils, jonquils, a colorful array of tulips and violets is brilliant. I definitely think this is a great plan!" Katie commented.

"I'm so glad you think so," Cade said smiling with satisfaction. "It seems that I lucked out not knowing what color scheme for the houses you would dream up."

"Apparently, we have ESP or something," Katie joked

"Well, it's good to know that we are so like-minded," Cade commented, smiling at Katie admiringly.

Katie smiled back and after a brief lull in the conversation and a few sips of her drink, Katie asked, "Are you planning on selling any of the houses?"

"No, I don't think so. My plan is to rent them out to appreciative people who will take care of them."

"Don't you think that will be difficult? Since renters don't own the property, they're sometimes not very conscientious about their care."

"I think the fact that I'll be living next door will make my renters more responsible. Besides, I think you're being a bit unfair. I have several rental properties and I've seldom had a problem with damage or neglect by my tenants," Cade argued.

Katie shrugged. "I didn't mean that renters deliberately tear up property. I just meant that sometimes they're not as careful or attentive toward keeping rental property pristine since they know that you're going to clean, repaint, etc. when they move out. That's all."

"I will be screening my potential renters very carefully. No children, no pets and no one over the age of sixty."

"That's a bit presumptuous, don't you think. And unfair," Katie said bristling slightly at his implications toward the people he was profiling. It was one thing to make a general statement about renters that most people agreed upon, quite another to be prejudicial against specific types of people.

"Children are destructive, pets are even more destructive and old people can't maintain upkeep and tend to be hoarders, which causes even more damage. And they all tend to be dirty and messy," Cade replied, stuffing a forkful of lettuce into his mouth.

"That's just stereotyping," Katie said with disbelief at his prejudice.

"No, it's fact," Cade replied, casually wiping his mouth with his napkin. "I know. I 've been in the business long enough."

"I beg to differ," Katie contended putting down her fork and pushing her salad plate to the side. "Well-behaved children are taught to respect their homes, responsible pet owners train their animals properly and most elderly people maintain their homes even better than younger ones, whether they do the work themselves or hire someone else to do it."

Cade raised his eyebrows and studied Katie for a moment. "Wow!" he said and Katie felt like he might be mocking her. "Now I know who to call if I need someone to defend children, animals and the elderly. Next you're going to tell me that illegal aliens shouldn't be deported."

Katie was taken aback by his rudeness. She slowly took her napkin from her lap and set it on the table. She couldn't help retorting, "You're exactly right. I don't think they should be deported. Every one of us has ancestors that immigrated to this country and that's how this country was formed. Everyone just uses the excuse about paying taxes to justify their prejudices when it's a fact that not one person in the U.S. would pay taxes if they could get out of it without going to jail. And by the way, there are plenty of American citizens that have never paid taxes and never will. Should we deport them, too? Or is that out of question because they happen to have been born here?" Without waiting for an answer, Katie threw her napkin on the table and announced, "I'm going to the restroom."

When Katie entered the ladies' room she was glad to find she was its only occupant. Katie stood in front of the mirror, leaning on the sink with both hands, staring at herself, fuming. *Ben would never make such preposterous assumptions about anyone. He wouldn't stereotype people just because of their age or because they have a pet. Ben wouldn't speak to me like that, ever. He wouldn't mock me like that. Besides, Ben is the sweetest person ever and he loves children, animals and especially senior citizens! And where did he come up with the illegal aliens crack?* Katie stood up, crossed her arms and paced across the room, returning and stopping in front of the same sink and began to reproach herself. *Why do I always compare everyone to Ben? Why do I keep hoping for something with Ben? Why can't I just face the truth about me and Ben? We're just friends. If Ben had any interest in me, he'd be sitting at that table with me right now instead of that...that...mean person.* Katie's anger had turned to sadness and she felt a lump in her throat. She was disappointed in herself. Every time she tried to date someone else, she always let Ben get in the way. She thought it would be different with Cade Ware. But here she was wishing she was with Ben. Of course, Cade's behavior wasn't helping and she was seriously annoyed at Cade's attitude so naturally, she wanted the situation to be different. To be fun and casual like it always was with Ben instead of contentious as it had just become with Cade. Katie fluffed her hair and took a big breath; she just as well finish her dinner. If she was eating, she didn't have to talk. Katie was beginning to wish that the noise she usually abhorred when she dined out, was present tonight to give her one more excuse for avoiding any more conversation with Cade.

Katie could see Cade before he could see her. Katie was amused to see him sitting with his chin in his hand, downcast eyes periodically darting toward the restroom area. It was apparent Cade was worried. When Katie sat down, Cade immediately apologized.

"I'm really sorry. I honestly didn't mean to offend you," Cade sputtered. Katie decided he was sincere.

"I accept your apology. It just really bothers me when someone forms an opinion about a person based only on a generality," Katie replied.

"Can we start over?" Cade pleaded.

"OK," Katie replied, nodding. "Just so you know; I wasn't going to give up my steak anyway, even if it meant ignoring you the rest of the evening."

Cade smiled. "I had that coming."

At that moment, the waitress appeared with their plates and sat them on the table. Both Cade and Katie had ordered rib-eyes with sautéed garlic, onion and mushrooms along with loaded baked potatoes. As Katie began to cut her steak into bite-size pieces, the waitress returned to refill their glasses.

"So we were talking about the murals," Katie began, making sure to keep her voice light and even although inside she hadn't quite stopped seething from the unpleasantness of the earlier conversation. "Do you want me to ask the historical society for old photos or do you want to take care of that?"

"If you direct me to the correct person, I can do it," Cade volunteered.

"Well, it'll probably get done a lot quicker if you do it. I'm pretty busy with a case at work right now. That's actually really unusual. Potoma is generally quiet and crime-free and my busiest day usually involves writing more than two parking tickets," Katie answered.

"I didn't think there was any crime in Potoma," Cade replied.

"There isn't aside from the occasional teenage shoplifter," Katie informed him. "Usually an out-of-towner."

"So what's your case about?" Cade inquired.

"A teenage girl over in New Town. Her mother tried to wake her up one morning last week and couldn't rouse her. It appeared that she had overdosed on something but there are some odd circumstances I'm investigating," Katie answered.

"Can you elaborate?" Cade asked with interest.

"Well, first we assumed it was accidental but taking drugs was completely out of character for this particular girl. Then it appeared that it might have been a suicide attempt but that's pretty much been ruled out now, too."

"And the girl is dead?" Cade said shaking his head.

"No. She's in the hospital in a semi-comatose state," Katie corrected.

Cade's expression changed from something like sympathy to shock. "She survived?"

"Fortunately, although being in her current condition may not be much of a blessing," Katie replied, taking a sip of her iced tea.

"Is she on life support?"

"Happily, no," Katie said between bites.

"So she's basically just unconscious?"

"Basically. The doctors are not sure exactly why."

Cade chewed his steak slowly then said "Do they know what she took...to overdose?"

"That's part of the problem. They haven't been able to identify anything specific," Katie explained.

"Nothing?"

"Well, they've found traces of certain substances but haven't been able to determine what exactly might have led to her current condition."

"Do the doctors expect her to recover at some point?"

"Without knowing what was injected into her system..." Katie answered, tilting her head to one side.

"Injected?" Cade mused.

"Yes. There's evidence that something was injected," Katie confirmed.

Cade seemed to ponder the fact for a moment. Abruptly he changed the subject.

"OK, so who do I talk to at the historical society? About the photographs."

"Um...I have a list at home. Can I call you and give you the names and numbers?" Katie said, a little disoriented at Cade's sudden change in topic.

Cade nodded his agreement as he took a long drink of his soda. After finishing their dinner in relative silence, Cade offered "Are you up for dessert?".

"Are you having any?" Katie deferred.

"I'll share something. I don't think I could eat a whole dessert by myself," Cade replied rubbing his stomach.

Katie nodded and Cade asked her what she recommended. "The apple pie a la mode is delicious. So is their chocolate volcano."

"I'll go with whatever you feel like tonight," Cade conceded.

"I always go for the chocolate," Katie asserted.

"Then the chocolate volcano it is," Cade agreed waving the waitress over. A few minutes later she was back with the dessert and two spoons. Katie dug in, savoring the dark chocolate cake with its hot fudge center tempered by fudge ripple ice cream on the side. She noticed that Cade only took a few small bites and seemed preoccupied.

When the dessert was finished, Katie excused herself to wash her hands while Cade picked up the tab. When they walked out, instead of escorting Katie to her Jeep, Cade pulled her in the opposite direction toward the piers where at least a hundred boats of all shapes and sizes were moored.

"I know it's late and you want to get home but I want to show you something real quick," Cade explained as Katie hesitated.

Katie nodded and Cade led her along several connecting piers, finally stopping in front of an impressive cruiser painted red and yellow.

"This is my baby. I'd love to take you out in her sometime. I assume you enjoy being out on the water since you grew up on the river?" Cade said.

"You assume correctly. I'd love to go for a cruise. Thanks for the invitation," Katie replied with only half sincerity. She wasn't sure she really wanted to be trapped on a boat in the middle of the river with Cade. If she did go out with him, she'd have to make sure some friends, like Anna and her husband, accompanied them.

"Want me to show you around her or shall I just surprise you when we take her out?" Cade asked.

"Any other time, I'd jump right on and get the nickel tour but I've had a long weekend and I have to get up early tomorrow morning for work. So surprise me?" Katie answered. She definitely didn't want to get cornered on the boat tonight when her feelings about Cade at the moment weren't so warm and fuzzy.

Cade shrugged and nodded. He took Katie's elbow, leading her through the maze of piers back to land and then to the parking lot. Katie thanked Cade for dinner as he helped her up into the Jeep.

"I know we got off on the wrong foot but I hope you'll let me take you dinner again sometime," Cade said as Katie was inserting her key into the ignition.

In truth, Katie felt somewhat reluctant to go out with Cade again but said perkily, "I suppose I could give you a second try".

Evidently, Cade took it as a joke and smiled. "Thanks, I look forward to it!"

With that, Cade shut Katie's door and she pulled out of the parking space. As Katie drove to the entrance of the parking lot, she watched Cade in her rearview mirror. Instead of walking toward his truck, he went back into the restaurant. *Going back for a drink at the bar at this late hour on a Sunday night?* Katie mused as she turned right onto Riverside Drive and followed the street along the river.

About half-way down Riverside Drive, Katie absently glanced down the side street and perceived an unusual display of lights moving parallel along the next street. The arrangements of the lights appeared to approximate the size of a golf cart but the placement did not conform to the expected placement of regulation luminaries. Katie opened her window quickly to get a clearer view and heard a barely audible hissing sound like a kettle boiling on a stove. She thought she saw a few puffs of barely visible steam just as the vehicle disappeared from view. At the next intersection, there was no sign of the strange spectre. Briefly, Katie thought about turning down the side street and looking for the strange vehicle but her fatigue from the long day intervened and she dismissed the thought deciding that she was so tired she had just imagined that a regular golf cart was something else.

# CHAPTER 14

**Grace needed to** burn at least another 500 calories so she repeated her exercise routine from the morning and then took another eight laxatives with a tall glass of ice water. After she had taken a shower, she sank down on the sofa. She hadn't paid any attention to what her neighbors were doing all day but now, through her living room window, she noticed that female police officer sitting on her golf cart in the middle of the cul-de-sac. The police officer kept looking around the cul-de-sac, making marks in her notebook. Grace wished she had a telescope so she could see exactly what that police officer was doing.

Grace could see Mick peeking through the curtains of his house at the woman, too. Grace thought he was a pervert. She'd seen him playing Peeping Tom at her neighbor's house before they'd moved away. Grace knew one thing; she'd better never catch him looking in her windows because she'd shoot him and then call the police.

Grace also saw that weird Aster opening her curtains on the second floor of her house. Grace didn't' like Aster any more than she liked Jessie Ashton or her la-di-da mother Ellen. Grace was pretty sure Aster was a hooker or a drug dealer or a stripper, or maybe all three. Aster wore too much make-up and her clothes were always too short or too tight. Grace especially hated Aster's short skirts and Daisy Dukes because Aster had really ugly, muscular legs like a man. Grace didn't understand why Aster thought anyone would want to see her big, tree-trunk legs. Grace wondered if Mick peeked in Aster's windows. It would be really easy since they were next-door-neighbors.

Grace wished the Petersons hadn't moved away. Now the house beside her was empty and she had to worry about what kind of people might rent it next. Grace hoped they didn't have any children, especially teenagers. Grace hated teenage girls. Especially if they were like Jessie Ashton; too pretty, too goody-goody, too nice. Grace had liked Ruby Peterson who used to live beside her. Ruby was easy to get along with and she was normal. She never looked down on Grace. She always had something nice to say. Grace watched the police lady until she drove out of the cul-de-sac, then she turned on her TV in search of a movie on pay-per-view.

**Mick peered through** a tiny slit in his drapes. There was Miss Katie sitting right in the middle of the cul-de-sac on her golf cart. Her being there for the second time today was making him nervous. He'd skipped his medication that morning and was starting to feel jittery and scatter-brained. The first time she'd come, she'd gone inside the Ashton house for a while. Then she'd come back, after the Ashtons had left, and was now sitting there writing stuff in a notebook. When she looked at his house, Mick quickly stepped away from the window. Katie might be mad if she caught Mick spying on her. Mick paced back and forth across his living room. His head was bursting, wondering why Katie kept coming back to the cul-de-sac. *What was she doing? What did she know? Did she know about him?* Mick went into his bedroom to get his medicine. He was going to have to take it after all. Katie had left when he got back to the window.

**Aster felt better** after her nap but she'd slept way longer than she had intended. She quickly washed her face and re-applied her make-up. It was too late to do any baking so Aster made a sandwich and sat down at the kitchen table. Aster was glad she could stay home tonight; she was becoming weary of all the late nights and having to maintain an upside-down schedule which required her to sleep during the day. She'd be glad when her circumstances changed and she could live a normal life again.

**Ping had woken** in the early afternoon and taken a hot shower to massage the sore muscles that the ibuprofen he'd taken earlier hadn't seemed to touch. Ping had forgotten about his cell phone which was still in his pants pocket on the floor. Ping was proud of himself for going out the night before and allowing himself to enjoy it. He'd concentrated on the here and now and kept his mind from wandering. He was determined to keep his mind on other things today as well. He needed to forget about Thursday night and what happened Friday morning. For a moment, Ping felt himself returning to those events but then he shook off his brief reverie and moved to the living room, picking up the remote and quickly finding a televised ball game. Later, after successfully diverting his thoughts for almost two hours by concentrating on what was happening on the TV screen, Ping went upstairs to let some fresh air into his bedroom. As he was opening the curtains, he glimpsed a police officer on a golf cart sitting in the middle of the cul-de-sac. Suddenly Thursday night and Friday morning invaded his thoughts with such rapid speed that Ping had to sit down on the bed and take several deep breaths before he could stand up again.

At precisely 6:45, Ted returned home from his hospital and nursing home visits. Casey was in the kitchen, putting the finishing touches on a chocolate cake.

"Do you know why there's a police officer out in the cul-de-sac?" Ted called to her.

Casey's cheery mood dampened. "No, I don't. Maybe it has something to do with Jessie?" Casey suggested.

"She's sitting on her golf cart staring at what looks like a drawing of the cul-de-sac and making little notes all over it," Ted informed Casey.

"I don't know. Why don't you go ask her what she's doing," Casey replied, half-hoping Ted would question the police officer, half-hoping he wouldn't.

"I'm sure if she needs our help, she'll ask," Ted answered with disinterest as he started up the stairs.

Casey wasn't sure if she was relieved or not. Casey had noticed a police officer at the Ashton home earlier in the day but had convinced herself there was nothing to worry about. The police officer hadn't stayed long and she didn't see any long faces on anyone when she left. The fact that the police officer was back and making notes was troubling. As far as Casey had heard, Jessie had most likely overdosed on some type of drug. *That wasn't a crime was it?* Casey asked herself. As Casey placed the cake in the covered stand and set it aside on the counter, she wondered to herself why the police were still poking around.

# MONDAY
## CHAPTER 15

**Katie stretched, then** stayed in the bed for a full five minutes before she climbed out and made her way downstairs to let Ogilvie out. Katie had mixed feelings about her dinner with Cade the night before. She was still attracted to him despite their rocky beginning but once she reviewed everything that had happened, she felt that they really didn't have much in common other than a love of historic architecture. He'd also displayed an easy ability to stereotype people and a strong sense of bias. Katie considered herself very objective, something that made her good at being a police officer, and the thought of spending time with someone who appeared to have issues with objectivity wasn't a pleasant one. On the other hand, Katie admired Cade's passion for beautiful and interesting house design and historic preservation, something Katie shared. She also wanted very much to continue her involvement with Cade's renovation of the bungalows. She was especially intrigued and delighted to paint the murals in the bungalow dining rooms. She had already begun to imagine the collaboration of old photos and artistic interpretation.

Katie continued to think about Cade, but mostly about the mural projects, as she got ready for work. After feeding Ogilvie his breakfast and grabbing a bagel and an apple for herself, Katie pushed her personal life from her mind and began to concentrate on her investigation. Now that Justin and Ellen Ashton had expressed an interest in knowing what had actually happened to their daughter, Katie felt an obligation to continue to probe even if she really had no cause to officially pursue the case as a crime. Katie knew that without the permission of the Chief to look into it, she was walking a fine line at this point. If she asked for formal consent and the Chief said no, she'd have no choice but to drop it. She also knew that she had some leeway if she believed that it was possible that a crime had been committed even if there was no immediately apparent evidence. Katie decided to hang her hat on that. There was something very strange about the fact that neither she nor Anna had been able to find any evidence of drug paraphernalia in Jessie's room or outside of her windows when it had been irrefutably determined that Jessie had been injected with something and the only explanation for Jessie's current condition was a reaction to whatever was in her bloodstream.

At the station, Katie was glad to see Anna in the squad room. Katie quickly brought Anna up to speed on what had happened over the weekend. She also enlisted Anna's eager assistance in working the case with her. They decided that they needed to push Jessie's physician to try and identify what substance or substances had been injected into Jessie. And while the information contained in Jessie's notebook seemed to be irrelevant now, it wouldn't hurt to question the neighbors in the cul-de-sac. It was always possible that they had seen something Thursday night that would help with the investigation. Katie had to admit she was also curious about these neighbors who had allegedly, if Katie had interpreted the notations correctly, committed sins against God; sins that Jessie felt were noteworthy enough for her to identify the violators.

Katie was assigned to patrol the Riverside and Riverview neighborhoods. Anna had New Town and Fairway. They picked up their assigned golf cart units, agreed to meet in the Ashtons' cul-de-sac at 5:30pm, and went their separate ways. As Katie cruised along Riverside Drive she relished the cool air blowing in her face and the quiet stillness of the morning. She drove her cart slowly, as always admiring the turn-of-the-century summer cottages that were, in reality, extravagant mansions, embellished and gilded and iced with intricate details. When they had first been built, Riverside Drive didn't exist. The mansions occupied large deep lots with two-story carriage houses facing onto a back alley. Lush green front lawns swept from the wide, shady porches right down to the river's edge. Behind the grand houses were colorful summer gardens, cement swimming pools and games lawns. Gravel and sand entrance allees lined with evergreens ran from the alley along the sides of the lots, then turned and created a loop in front of the mansions. Over time, many of the driveways, still lined by the original huge oak trees, became modern paved side streets and portions of the front loops were joined together to create Riverside Drive. The alley was widened and modernized and was now called, appropriately, "Carriage Drive". Some of the large estate lots had been subdivided over time and now, here and there, miniature Victorian summer houses nestled in beside the monumental "cottages" like tiny, newborn offspring. As was the Gilded Age custom the palatial cottages bore glamorous names like Rose Garden, Pratt's Castle, Verandah, Rocky Beach and Riverhurst. Katie found it amusing that, in an attempt to mimic the grandeur of the mansions, the builders of the miniature imitations gave them momentous names also; among them, The Turrets, Greystone, Palace Gables, Grand Lawn.

Another few blocks and Katie was approaching The Tower House, one the oldest homes in Potoma, now a bed & breakfast owned and run by Katie's friend, Anne. Katie saw Anne bending over the flower bed that ringed the wide front porch of the elegant, tall house. Katie pulled off of Riverside Drive into Anne's private driveway and called to Anne. Anne looked up and greeted Katie with a warm smile as Katie walked across the green lawn toward her. Anne was petite but somehow regal with her gray page-boy coif and cultured bearing. She was wearing her usual hold-all apron with "The Tower House" emblazoned across the front, garden spade tucked in one pocket, garbage bags tucked in another. At times, Anne used her apron to carry everything from wine bottles and corkscrews for the daily afternoon wine and cheese hour on the porch to freshly cut flowers from the multitude of flowerbeds around the Inn, destincd for the breakfast tables. During the summers while she was in high school, Katie had worked part-time for Anne, helping her clean the inn and maintain the gardens. As a bonus, Anne, an incredible gourmet chef, taught Katie about culinary art. As a result, Katie now counted Anne as a wonderful and wise friend. On a lark, Katie decided to talk to Anne, always discreet as is necessary in the hospitality business, about the case.

Anne gave Katie a hug and they entered the inn together. Anne's guests had departed for the day, either having checked out or pursuing daytime activities, and the house was empty.

Anne poured ginger ale and they settled in the small front parlor dominated by a grand piano and a beautifully carved floor to ceiling fireplace mantel. The room bore its original floral Victorian wallpaper that reflected the hues of the sun-streaked jewel-toned stained glass windows. A huge china cupboard filled with exquisite porcelain, glass and silver stood in one corner. In the center of the antique oriental carpet overlaying gleaming hardwood floors was a glass top table surrounded by unmatched Victorian arm chairs upholstered in various patterned fabrics. Anne and Katie sank into adjacent chairs, sipping their drinks. Anne and Katie made small talk for a few minutes, commenting on the crowd turnout of the previous weekend and the predictions for the upcoming tourist season. Anne intuitively knew that something was on Katie's mind and soon brought the conversation around to it.

"I'm investigating a case that just doesn't make any sense from any angle," Katie began. "I'm not even sure it's a case that the police should be involved in but I just feel compelled to try and figure out what's going on."

"Do I know the person or persons involved?" Anne inquired.

"It involves the Ashtons over in New Town. The teenage daughter, Jessie, was found Friday morning by her mother, unconscious in her bedroom and is now in a semi-comatose state in the hospital," Katie answered.

Anne's expression turned from pure curiosity to genuine concern. "I know Jessie. She's a lovely girl. This is just awful!"

"Then maybe you'll have some insight...you'll be able to tell me something that I haven't heard from her friends or family," Katie replied.

Anne gestured for Katie to go on and so Katie proceeded to tell Anne the facts and events regarding Jessie Ashton, leaving out nothing. Anne listened thoughtfully as Katie described each detail and turn of affairs.

"Anna and I are meeting later this afternoon to question the neighbors in Jessie's cul-de-sac. We're hoping that something new will come to light. Maybe someone saw or heard something that didn't seem significant at the time but might at least be a clue to a lead."

"Perhaps you're not looking at this from the correct angle," Anne suggested.

"What do you mean?"

"You've assumed that the injections were self-inflicted from the beginning. Either an accidental overdose or a suicide attempt. Yet neither explanation fits the facts or maybe more importantly, the character of the girl. Everything you've learned about Jessie so far has proven exactly the opposite of your presumptions about what occurred," Anne explained in her slightly clipped accent.

"Exactly! That's why I'm so frustrated," Katie replied, emphatically.

"Have you considered the possibility that someone else was involved?" Anne asked pointedly.

"No. Well, not seriously."

"Why not?"

"The only other people in the house were Jessie's parents and I'm sure they are not involved. So that would mean that another person would have had to enter the house. While I've never suggested it to Jessie's parents, by the same token, they have never made any mention of anything that would point to a break-in of any sort," Katie replied.

"Think about the Ashton house. Is there any way someone could enter the house without leaving any sign of forced entry?" Anne prodded.

"I don't think they have an alarm system, at least, I don't remember seeing one. If someone tried to get into a locked door or window, surely there would have been broken glass or at least visible tool marks. Of course, I haven't looked for anything like that but I would think that the Justin and Ellen Ashton would have noticed something by now."

"Certainly they would have noticed a broken window. But didn't you say that Jessie's parents have spent most of the last three days at the hospital?"

Katie nodded.

"Then they may not have paid any attention to

something less obvious like scratch marks around a lock. Their minds are on their daughter; they're concentrating on her. And as you say, a break-in hasn't even been hinted at so neither of them is even thinking about that possibility," Anne clarified. "Besides, you know as well as I do that most people in Potoma don't lock their back doors. At least not in the old neighborhoods."

Katie nodded again letting Anne's implication sink in.

"Let's say someone broke in and injected Jessie with something. What would be the motive?" Katie said, looking at Anne.

Anne shrugged. "You're the investigator, but I'd start with the neighbors. Perhaps one of them wasn't too thrilled about Jessie observing their sins."

"We don't even know if any of the people on the list even knew they were on the list," Katie said dismissively.

"Even better reason to question them," Anne asserted.

"OK, I agree. But I can't see attempting to murder someone—and that is what you've been implying—over any of the sins Jessie has listed," Katie replied.

Anne chuckled. "You'd be surprised, believe me. Katie, don't allow yourself to be so naïve. I know that Potoma is quiet and virtually crime-free and living in a place like that tends to make people complacent. Everyone assumes that everybody who lives here has a perfect fairy-tale life but we both know that's not true. Everyone has vices and skeletons in their closets. Jessie's list is general at best. What was that person lying about? What was another person coveting? Being deceitful about? What did they steal? Was it a candy bar or a million dollars? And adultery? People do kill over adultery."

"You're right, Anne. I wasn't seeing the broader picture. I was just taking the point of view of a teenage girl observing things through the tunnel vision of youth," Katie owned with a sigh of self- rebuke. "I've always considered myself so objective, yet I couldn't see what was right in front of me."

"You were just following procedure and using the information you had. If you investigated every case from a thousand points of view you'd never resolve it," Anne said matter-of-factly. "I believe with a little more information you would have come to this possibility yourself. At this point it's still just a remote option. Without any evidence pointing in the direction of attempted murder, it's just one more theory of what could have happened."

"But it makes sense as the next direction to look in since it certainly doesn't seem logical that Jessie injected herself or tried to commit suicide," Katie affirmed.

"I can tell you that the Jessie I know wouldn't have any notion of trying to kill herself," Anne replied.

"How do you know Jessie, anyway?" Katie asked.

"She wrote a paper on the history of my house. We got to know each other while she was doing the research. I let her go through all of my scrapbooks," Anne answered.

"You must have really been taken with her to let her at your scrapbooks," Katie commented.

"She impressed me. And she was genuinely interested in the house," Anne remarked. "I really hope you figure out what happened. Let me know, please."

Katie promised she'd keep Anne updated then said goodbye to continue her patrol. Not long after she'd made the entire loop on Riverside Drive, Katie's cell phone rang.

"I've just had some interesting information from Jessie's doctor," Anna began. "He was reviewing her chart and found that her initial lab work turned up traces of chloroform. He said normally no one would red flag that because human exposure to chloroform can and often does occur through drinking water, where chloroform is formed as a result of the chlorination of naturally occurring organic materials found in raw water supplies. However, given the unusual circumstances in this case, he looked a little closer and felt that the amount of trace was higher than normal."

"So in other words, it's possible that the chloroform was introduced into her system in a non-naturally occurring way?" Katie replied.

"Exactly. He said exposure at a high dosage could affect the central nervous system and could cause prolonged unconsciousness. It's also been known, in rare cases, to cause death."

"Isn't chloroform usually inhaled, though? As opposed to being injected?" Katie asked.

"Yep," Anna answered.

"Which makes things even more confusing. Or not. Think about this. What if someone else administered the injection?" Katie queried.

"You're thinking this could be attempted murder?" Anna replied.

Katie filled Anna in on her conversation with Anne. "So it could be attempted murder. Or, assisted suicide."

"Another possibility except the more I learn and review the information we have, the more I doubt that Jessie had any intention of killing herself," Katie said.

"I tend to agree with you but we shouldn't rule that out just yet," Anna cautioned. "In any case, if another person is involved, it would follow that they might use chloroform to knock Jessie out before injecting her. Either because of her aversion to needles or to prevent her from struggling."

"Has the doctor identified any other substances that might have been injected into Jessie's system?" Katie said.

"When he was studying the initial blood work he discovered some indications of unusual plant derivatives. They're trying to determine the origins of those substances. He's inclined to believe that they may be naturally poisonous extracts of common flora."

"That's interesting. How long will that take?"

"Not sure. He'll call me when he knows something," Anna replied before saying goodbye.

# CHAPTER 16

**Katie's impromptu visit** with Anne had put her behind on her patrol schedule but it was still mid-morning and Katie had plenty of time to finish up in Riverside and complete her rounds in Riverview before taking a lunch break. Both neighborhoods were easy patrols with their grid-pattern layout of streets and blocks. In Riverside, Katie usually drove the Riverside Drive and Carriage Alley loops all the way around then traveled up and down the main streets that ran from Town to the marina first, followed by the side streets that crossed the peninsula from the river to the harbor. As Katie made the leisurely ride along her regular routes, she was careful to observe each and every house even though she knew that there was almost no chance she would find anything untoward or suspicious going on. Fragrant spring bulbs and shrubs had started blooming and the air swirled with sweet aromas. Yellow daffodils, pink and red tulips, golden forsythia and lavender lilacs created a profusion of color in every yard and along the perimeters of each pocket park tucked in among the residential blocks. Katie passed mothers with strollers and groups of active retirees out enjoying the beautiful spring weather. Toddlers filled the swing sets, sand boxes, and sliding boards at the parks and dogs frolicked in fenced yards, chasing butterflies and flitting birds, both real and imaginary. Katie always loved the sense of peace and serenity she experienced on mornings like this.

Cade Ware's bungalow court was located near the center of Riverside on Fifth Street between Schooner Street and Fisher Avenue. Katie felt a slight sense of apprehension as she made her way down Fifth. She was undecided whether or not she wanted to stop; partly because she was already running late and making another visit would delay her even further, and partly because she was still unsure about her feelings for Cade after last night. She could certainly write off their argument, if it could be called that, at the beginning of dinner as just an unfortunate misunderstanding, but the fact that Cade had remained at the restaurant, undoubtedly for a visit to the bar at such a late hour, bothered Katie. Katie wasn't sure just what that might mean but in her experience, hanging out at a bar on a Sunday night usually didn't have a good connotation. Of course, Katie reasoned, it could mean nothing and she was just being judgmental, and worse, she was applying a stereotype—the exact thing she had gotten angry at Cade for—without any proof. As Katie reached the court, she decided to swallow her misgivings for the moment and make a quick stop.

"I thought I might have blown it last night," Cade greeted when he saw Katie drive up.

"Well, I really want to paint your murals. Plus, I'd be disappointed if you didn't paint the houses the way I've imagined them," Katie replied in jest.

"No chance of that now. I picked up all the exterior paint this morning. Now I'm stuck with it, regardless," Cade replied. "Did you have a chance to look up the name of the person I should speak to about the old photos?"

"I'm sorry. I just didn't have time this morning before work. I'll get that information for you this evening after I get off and call you," Katie assured him.

"Great! I'm looking forward to seeing the old pictures. And seeing what you'll do with them in the murals," Cade said animatedly. "The murals will certainly be the piece de resistance of each bungalow."

"I hope my painting measures up to your expectations. I'm beginning to feel a little nervous," Katie replied.

"I've seen your paintings in the library," Cade answered. "They're fantastic!"

Katie was pleasantly surprised. "I didn't know that. When did you see them?"

"Before I purchased this property I tried to do a little research on it. I noticed your paintings right away. They're so realistic and beautiful," Cade replied.

Katie could feel herself blushing at the compliment. She quickly changed the subject. "I have to tell you that I was a bit disappointed when you suggested eating at the Yacht Club because it's normally so noisy. I had forgotten how superb their steaks are."

"I'm glad the restaurant redeemed itself. I hope I have,

too," Cade answered.

Katie gave Cade a smile and said coyly, "We'll see."

Cade invited Katie to stay for a cup of coffee but Katie declined, saying that she was already late on patrol and had to keep moving. Fifteen minutes later Katie had completed her run through Riverside and began to make her way through downtown to Riverview. Katie always had mixed feelings about patrolling her own part of Potoma. There was a certain comfort in riding through the neighborhood where she knew practically everyone but there was always the fear that she'd have to give a citation to or arrest one of her neighbors, not a task she ever relished. Fortunately, those instances were few and far between.

At 11:00am the temperature was still a pleasant seventy-five degrees and there was a gentle breeze off the river that blew along each perpendicular street. The houses in Riverview were all built between 1915 and 1960, and unlike the summer cottages of Riverside, were designed as year-round residences. Even today, only a handful were used as weekenders or vacation rentals. The neighborhood was a mish-mash of post-war Tudors, craftsman bungalows, gothic revival cottages, boxy brick ranches and Shakeresque cape cods set on small lots surrounded by picket fences. When Katie reached the street she lived on called Beach End, she made a U-turn at the end then stopped in her driveway. She planned to make a quick sandwich and grab a soda to take with her. Ogilvie was so excited at her unexpected visit that he couldn't stop wiggling and yelping. After creating a roast beef and cheddar club masterpiece, Katie chopped up some of the meat and cheese, put it in a tortilla wrap and tossed it in the microwave. Once the cheese was melted, Katie cut the wrap into half a dozen slices and placed them in a bowl which she put on the floor for Ogilvie. Katie had found that distracting Ogilvie with food was the best way to make a quick get-away.

Back on her golf cart, Katie continued on her way. The abundance of spring flowers seemed to increase in Riverview but Katie suspected that it was just an optical illusion created by the overflow from small yard to small yard. As in Riverside, residents were out in droves enjoying the delectable temperature and inviting sunshine. Just as the architecture varied greatly in Riverview, so did the residents. The neighborhood included people of all ages, races, income levels, professions, marital and family status. Katie felt like a beauty queen on a parade float as she constantly waved to those she passed, her friendly smile pasted onto her face.

When Katie passed through town on her way back to her second patrol of Riverside, she pulled up at the sole golf cart dealer and rental center in Potoma. Rivertown Transport had been established by Ben's father fifteen years ago and was now run by Ben. Although Ben's father had been the public driving force behind the ordinance allowing golf carts to share the streets with automobiles, what most people didn't know was that the idea had actually been 14-year old Ben's brainchild. It had been a positive change that actually made getting around Potoma safer, quicker and more economical. Potoma's unique designation as a golf cart town also increased tourism which, in turn, greatly improved town revenue and created a growth spurt in small businesses that catered to residents and visitors alike. A town that had once struggled to keep its restaurants afloat in the off-season and offered no basic services other than a grocery store, a pharmacy and a couple of banks now had dry cleaning services, three florists, a jeweler, several maid services, bakeries and delis, insurance agents, and accountants as well as a number of boutiques, antiques stores, and gourmet food shops. Golf carts of every description and brand lined the sidewalk in front of the store. More golf carts were displayed inside, easily visible through the large glass windows. Katie could see Ben seated at a desk at the rear of the showroom.

"Hey, girl! What's shakin'?" Ben said, leaning back in his desk chair, arms resting behind his head.

"Not out saving lives today?" Katie retorted with a smile.

"Looks like you are, Miss Policewoman," Ben replied. "How many today so far?"

"You'll be happy to hear not a one. I'm saving them all for you, hero," Katie answered.

"I'll remember your generosity in my will."

"Should I murder you now then?"

"Nah, I'm not worth enough, yet. Wait a few years," Ben said, shifting forward and picking up a pen, flipping it through his fingers. "Got anything good to tell me?"

"I thought you might be interested in what's going on with Jessie Ashton," Katie replied.

"How's she doing?"

"She's still unconscious," Katie replied, sitting down in the chair across from Ben. "But we've had some interesting things turn up concerning the circumstances of her condition."

Ben tapped the pencil against the desk blotter repeatedly. "Go on."

Katie told Ben about her interviews with Jessie's friends as well as Jessie's notebook and its possible connection to Jessie's neighbors. She also told him about her conversation with Anne and Anne's suggestions concerning the case.

"So now you're looking at the possibility of attempted murder? Seems a little far-fetched in this town," Ben replied, shaking his head in disbelief.

"Normally, I'd agree with you but no other scenarios we've tried seem to fit," Katie said. "Plus the toxicology report the hospital ran when Jessie was brought in showed traces of chloroform."

"But chloroform can be released into the air from a large number of sources related to its manufacture and use, as well as its formation in the chlorination of drinking water, wastewater, and swimming pools. It's not an unusual find," Ben argued.

"I know but Jessie's doctor feels that the numbers are a little high indicating that the chloroform might not have been introduced in a random natural way," Katie countered.

"Do you have any other evidence to support the idea that someone else was involved?"

"Well, there's the fact that we haven't been able to find any drug paraphernalia. I mean how did Jessie inject herself without a needle or syringe and at least some sort of vial to hold the substance?"

"Good question. Is there any evidence that someone

else was in Jessie's room?"

"Unfortunately, Anna and I weren't looking in that direction when we searched Jessie's room. I can say that we didn't find anything like footprints or something that appeared to be a disturbance of Jessie's room. On the other hand we didn't dust for fingerprints or anything like that."

"Is it too late to do that? Dust for fingerprints."

"Possibly. Jessie's mother has cleaned up the room since we searched it. That's how she came across Jessie's notebook."

"How about outside of her room? Isn't there a balcony?"

"If someone else was involved and didn't come in through the front door then it is possible they used the balcony."

"I'm skeptical, I have to admit but accidental overdose or attempted suicide seems just as illogical given what we know about Jessie," Ben shrugged.

"So I have your permission to pursue the murder theory?" Katie asked sarcastically, raising an eyebrow impishly.

"Proceed with my blessing," Ben answered, giving Katie a salute.

Katie saluted back with a "See ya" as she exited the store.

Returning to Riverside, Katie was deep in thought. It was clear that she and Anna needed to check for fingerprints. That meant they would have to inform Ellen and Justin Ashton that what had happened to their daughter could have been an attempt on her life. Katie didn't want to think about their reaction to that news. Before Katie started her route around Riverside, she called Anna on her cell phone and briefed her about her meeting with Ben. Anna agreed to pick up a fingerprint kit from the police station before meeting Katie later.

Katie's stop at Ben's store hadn't helped her schedule and so she sped along as fast as she could. Katie struggled to be observant as she passed each house, her mind on the possibilities that were emerging in the case. Absentmindedly, she waved and smiled at passersby and residents outside their homes. So far today, Katie hadn't come across any law-breakers; generally, that meant cars parked illegally or people fishing in the posted "No Fishing" areas of the beaches. Just as Katie passed the entrance to the marina, the ringing of her cell phone interrupted her reverie.

"Heard back from Jessie Ashton's doctor," Anna announced. "They're running tests on particular natural substances that have been determined to be plant materials. The doctor thinks they will end up being toxic. In other words, naturally poisonous stuff extracted from common plants."

"You think someone injected Jessie with plant poison?" Katie asked incredulously.

"Starting to look that way," Anna replied. "Weird, huh?"

"Totally," Katie answered. "When does the doctor think they'll have the results?"

"Most likely later this afternoon. I'll call you," Anna replied before hanging up.

*Maybe the use of plant poisons would provide a clue to the perpetrator, if in fact this was a case of attempted murder,* Katie mused.

An hour later, Anna called Katie again.

"Azaleas and daffodils," Anna said.

"You're kidding!" Katie said. "They're poisonous?"

"In the case of the azalea, yes, every part of the plant is poisonous. Roots, branches, leaves, flowers...but rarely fatally. Mostly the poisons in azaleas cause nausea, diarrhea, headaches. However, daffodils are another story. The bulbs are poisonous and can definitely cause death," Anna explained.

"Wow! I wonder how many people know that," Katie exclaimed. "I'll never look at a daffodil or azalea bush the same way again!"

"Me neither. My yard is full of both."

"So my guess would be that normally the poisons would be ingested somehow and accidentally," Katie suggested.

"Yes. Most cases have been a very young child putting the plant part in his or her mouth and chewing on it or a pet doing the same thing. Extracting the poison from the plant and injecting it is very unusual," Anna said.

"Which would indicate deliberateness. I imagine it would be a somewhat complicated operation and would require someone with specific knowledge about the plants as well as chemical processes," Katie surmised.

"Exactly."

"And the doctor is sure that this is what was injected into Jessie. She couldn't have swallowed it?"

"They've been monitoring Jessie's waste and there's been no indication that those substances passed through her stomach, bladder or colon," Anna replied. "They've only been found in her bloodstream."

"Then I would say that we're definitely looking at attempted murder. Nothing I've learned about Jessie would indicate that she would have had the necessary knowledge or know-how to extract natural poisons and manufacture them into a suicide cocktail," Katie asserted.

"And because we didn't find any drug paraphernalia, we have to assume that whoever injected Jessie simply took the evidence with them," Anna concluded.

"Agreed," Katie affirmed. "At this point my theory would be that someone entered Jessie's bedroom, maybe from the balcony, subdued her with chloroform, then injected her with the poison concoction, leaving her for dead and escaping back out through the balcony."

"And the use of chloroform could indicate that the perp knew about Jessie's aversion to needles or it might have just been a simple way to keep her from alerting her parents to what was going on upstairs," Anna said. "The doctor said that in large doses, chloroform can be fatal. It can also cause unconsciousness and coma so it could have contributed to Jessie's current condition if it was administered by someone who was inexperienced in anesthesia."

"In any case, it seems that my original instinct was correct. There's a lot more to this than what it appeared to be Friday morning," Katie remarked

Katie checked the time. She still had half of her

Riverside patrol to complete and another full sweep of Riverview before meeting Anna in New Town. Katie knew she'd have to hurry and avoid any more delays to be on time. Katie hoped everyone was obeying the law to the letter today.

# CHAPTER 17

As usual, **Grace** waited until the garage door had come all the way down before she got out of her car. The police were here again; two of them were parked in the middle of the cul-de-sac. It must be that Jessie Ashton again, Grace thought. *She was dead, wasn't she?* She'd looked pretty dead when Grace had last seen her Friday morning on the stretcher. Then Grace panicked. *Don't they usually cover people's faces up when they're dead? Jessie's face wasn't covered up.* It hadn't occurred to Grace until just now that Jessie hadn't been dead. Quickly, Grace got out of her car, grabbed her purse and the bouquet of daffodils lying on the front seat and hurried into her house.

Just as Grace finished arranging the flowers in a vase, her doorbell rang. Grace froze for a moment. She didn't usually answer her door. Grace set the vase of flowers on the dining room table, then went into the living room to peek through the curtains. The two female police officers, the same ones that had been at the Ashtons' on Friday, were at the door. Grace knew instantly that she was trapped; she'd have to open the door because the police officers had seen her drive into her garage. Her palms began to sweat and she started shaking. It always happened when she had to be around attractive women, women that made Grace feel like a frumpy beanbag chair. Grace dried her hands on her skirt and took a few deep, slow breaths before moving to the front door.

"Grace Garfield?"

Grace nodded.

"I'm Officer Bell, this is Officer Madrid. We'd like to ask you some questions. May we come in?"

"What's this about?" Grace asked, reluctant to invite the police officers in.

"Are you acquainted with the Ashton family?"

"Not really," Grace replied, shrugging.

"May we come in, please? It would be better to talk about this inside."

"I really don't think I can be of any help," Grace said in an unusually high voice. Grace's nervousness was showing and she knew it.

"Let us be the judge of that, please. Let's just sit down for a few minutes and talk."

Grace was angry. These woman—these thin, pretty women—were forcing her to let them in her only haven. The only place she had to get away from women like them. Grace spun around and walked toward the entrance to her living room. The two police officers followed her, one of them pausing to close her front door.

Grace sat down in her favorite chair, the two police officers sat on the matching sofa.

"We're investigating what happened to Jessie Ashton. You are probably aware that she was found unconscious in her bedroom Friday morning?"

*Unconscious? Not dead?* Grace thought, her heart pounding. Grace nodded at the police officer.

"Were you at home Thursday night?"

"Yes," Grace answered, wondering if she should admit to it.

"And what time did you go to bed Thursday night?"

"I always go to bed at 11:00pm," Grace replied.

"And you went to bed at 11:00 on Thursday night?"

"Like I said, I always go to bed at 11:00pm, seven days a week," Grace reiterated.

The blond police officer seemed to be annoyed. *Good,* thought Grace.

"And where is your bedroom located? At the front or rear of your house?"

"It's in the back", Grace replied. *What difference did that make?*

Grace was trying to maintain eye contact; she knew if she didn't she would look suspicious. Grace wished her hair was curly like Officer Madrid's. It wasn't fair how some women had what Grace so desperately wanted. Grace hated her stick-straight hair that looked like straw and made her look like a scarecrow—at least from the neck up. Grace wondered how Officer Madrid kept her bright pink nail polish from chipping or how her natural-looking make-up stayed perfect all day like that. By noon, Grace's face was shiny and half of her make-up had faded away. Grace wanted to ask Officer Madrid what brand she used. *Maybe that was the secret.*

"Did you notice anything unusual Thursday night? People you didn't recognize or unusual activity, particularly around the Ashtons' house?"

Grace shook her head. "No, everything was normal," Grace replied.

"I notice that you have this big window here and your house is almost directly across the cul-de-sac from the Ashtons' house. It looks like you have a perfect view."

Grace wondered where Officer Madrid was going. *What was she implicating?*

"Are you sure you didn't see anything Thursday night?"

Grace shook her head vigorously. "I don't spy on my neighbors for one thing," Grace said indignantly. This blondie was really ticking her off.

"I'm sure that Officer Madrid was not suggesting that you do. It's just with such a clear view, with your curtains open, it would be almost impossible for you to not to see what was going on at the Ashtons'"

"I usually keep my curtains closed," Grace protested, pouting ever so slightly.

The two police officers exchanged a glance. Grace didn't like it that they were talking about her even if they weren't using words.

"Do you live here by yourself?"

"Yes," Grace replied. *Was that some sort of insult?* Grace wondered.

"Do you own the house or rent?"

"It's my house," Grace replied defensively.

Another glance between the officers.

"Where do you work, Miss Garfield?"

"Why do you need to know that?" Grace asked, folding her arms across her chest.

"Just trying to get a feel for the neighborhood. What's your normal work schedule?"

I work from 8:30 in the morning to 5:00 in the

evening," Grace replied.

"Monday through Friday?"

Grace nodded.

"Do you ever work weekends?"

"No," Grace answered.

"So you're generally here every evening and most weekends, then?"

"Why?" Grace was getting impatient and it was becoming more difficult to control her shaking. It was none of their business where she spent her evenings and weekends, Grace thought. Of course, they would assume that Grace never went out anywhere just because she wasn't as pretty and perfect as them.

They ignored her question. "So you would know if someone was in the cul-de-sac that isn't normally here?"

Grace shrugged feigning ignorance. "I guess so," Grace said.

Again the police officers exchanged a look. These silent conversations between them were really getting on Grace's nerves. *They think they're so smart,* Grace smirked. *I'll show them smart,* Grace decided.

"I would recognize an unfamiliar car or person, if that's what you're asking," Grace volunteered. "I don't recall seeing either on Thursday night."

"You said that you don't really know the Ashtons. Have you ever spoken to any of them?"

"You know, just small talk at the cul-de-sac picnics," Grace answered.

"Have you ever spoken with Jessie Ashton?"

"No, just Ellen Ashton," Grace answered. "She's very nice."

Grace almost choked on the compliment but she knew it would sound good to the police officers for her to seem friendly toward her neighbor.

"I know you said you didn't know the Ashtons very well but can you think of any reason why someone might want to hurt Jessie Ashton?"

"Jessie Ashton seems to be the all-American girl. I've

never heard anything bad about her," Grace replied. Inside Grace was fuming. Grace really wanted to say that anybody normal would want to hurt Jessie Ashton just for being so perfect and thin and beautiful and nice.

The police officers nodded at each other and stood up. Then the dark-haired one looked down at her notebook. "One more thing, Miss Garfield. Do you think anyone would ever say that you covet your neighbor?"

"I don't even know what that means," Grace said, taken aback and raging inside. She actually did know what it meant but they were obviously accusing her of something and playing ignorant seemed to be the best course of action at the moment.

"It means being jealous or envious of someone. Wishing you had what they have."

"I don't think anyone would have a reason to say that about me," Grace replied. "Why do you ask?"

The police officers ignored her question.

"Beautiful daffodils you have there. Are they from your garden?"

"No. I just bought them from the florist today," Grace replied.

The two officers thanked Grace for her time and left. Grace shut the door, then ran into the living room and sank down on the sofa. *If those two had been normal women instead of magazine models I might have told them the truth,* Grace thought to herself.

# CHAPTER 18

**Ping had seen** the police golf carts in the cul-de-sac when he pulled in but was taken by surprise when he opened his front door to see two police officers standing there. When they asked to come in, Ping led them into the kitchen where he had just put a kettle on for tea. The police officers sat down at the small kitchen table and pulled notepads from their breast pockets. Ping was surprised that they didn't use electronic devices to record information. Ping also sat down at the table.

"We're investigating what happened at the Ashton house Thursday night. Are you aware that the teenage daughter, Jessie Ashton, was found unconscious Friday morning?"

"No," Ping replied. "I mean I saw the ambulance there when I left for work but I didn't know what had happened."

"And none of your neighbors have spoken to you about it?"

"I'm not really friendly with any of my neighbors," Ping answered.

"Is that by choice?"

"I don't know. I work a lot of hours," Ping shrugged. Ping wondered how these questions related to what had apparently happened to Jessie Ashton.

"How long have you lived here?"

"A little over a year," Ping answered.

"Do you live alone?"

"Yes...now I do," Ping stammered.

"And before...?"

"I used to have a fiancee," Ping explained. "She moved out six months ago."

"What do you do for a living, sir?"

"I'm a landscaper...landscape architect, actually," Ping replied. The kettle had begun to whistle and Ping rose and went to the stove. "Would you like some tea?" Ping asked the officers. They both declined and waited while Ping prepared a cup for himself. When Ping had returned to the table with his tea, they continued the interview.

"Were you home this past Thursday night?"

"Yes. I got home about six," Ping answered.

"And what time did you go to bed Thursday night?"

Ping hesitated. He wasn't really sure how to answer the question. *Did they mean what time he got into bed or what time he fell asleep?* He decided to go with the latter.

"I went to sleep around 2:00am," Ping said, taking a sip of his tea.

"Where is your bedroom located?"

"Over the living room," Ping said.

"So it faces onto the cul-de-sac?"

Ping nodded, mid-sip.

"Did you notice any activity at the Ashton house Thursday night at any time after you went to bed?"

"No," Ping said. *Not that I would have noticed anyway,* Ping thought to himself.

"Did you see any strange persons or vehicles in the neighborhood Thursday evening?"

Ping shook his head. "Honestly, a lot of traffic goes in and out of this place. I probably wouldn't know if someone was supposed to be here or not, if you know what I mean."

"Which houses get the most traffic?"

"Mainly the Ashtons and the Baileys. Then there are the three weekend houses. They often bring guests with them," Ping answered.

"As a landscaper I assume you are very well educated in botany. And assuming that is true, I would also assume that you are familiar with which plants are poisonous and which are not?"

"Of course," Ping declared. "You'd be surprised how many common plants that most people plant in their gardens and yards can cause illness."

"Are you friendly with the Ashtons?"

"I've had a few conversations with Justin Ashton, and Ellen Ashton hired me to do her landscaping in the front yard last fall," Ping revealed. "So of course, I spent some time discussing that with her."

"Have you ever had any interaction with their daughter, Jessie?"

"No, not really. Just in passing. Hi,-how-are-you

kind of stuff," Ping said, putting his cup down on the saucer and wiping his mouth with a cloth.

"Would there be any reason someone might call you a thief?"

Ping swallowed hard. He was glad he had finished his tea or he probably would have choked on it.

"Has someone accused me?" Ping asked.

"Not specifically."

After the police officers left, Ping poured another cup of tea. His stomach was churning. *Did the police officers sense that he had been lying?* Ping wondered.

# CHAPTER 19

**Frankly, Casey was** amazed that the police hadn't come to her house days ago. She knew they'd spoken to her son because he was one of Jessie's best friends but as usual, he hadn't given her any details of the conversation. Unfortunately, Casey and her son were pretty much estranged these days.

When the two police officers appeared on Casey's doorstep she was just beginning preparations for dinner. After seating the officers in her front sitting room, Casey excused herself to put the chicken breasts and raw vegetables back in the refrigerator. Casey sighed, knowing that Ted would not be happy about dinner being late, police officers or not. Casey was pretty sure Ted would probably arrive in the middle of her meeting with the police and he wouldn't be very excited to see them in his home. First, because Mondays were bowling nights and he would want to eat and leave as quickly as possible to make his seven o'clock game. And secondly, for all his mild-mannered characteristics, Ted had an almost paranoid fervor against government intrusion into a person's private life. He became so enraged by police forcing their way into people's homes on television, search warrant or not, that Casey had learned long ago not to watch those types of shows when Ted was around. Casey knew that Ted would view this occasion with the same disgruntlement.

"You live here with your husband and son, is that correct?"

"Yes. I also have another son but he's away at college," Casey replied.

"And your family is well acquainted with the Ashtons?"

"Oh, yes. We've been neighbors for years," Casey said. "As you already know, my son, Sebastian, and Jessie are very close friends."

"Does your family interact regularly with the Ashton family?"

"I suppose. I mean we usually speak several times a week and have dinner together at least once a month," Casey replied.

"So it could be assumed that you know Jessie

Ashton pretty well?"

"Well, you know teenagers. How well does a parent ever know their child once they become a teenager, much less their friends?" Casey shrugged.

"How would you describe Jessie?"

"She's a really lovely girl. Inside and out," Casey replied. *Well, for the most part when she's minding her own business instead of everyone else's,* Casey added silently.

"Do you know of anyone who might want to hurt her?"

Casey could think of at least two but then that would lead to more questions that Casey didn't want to answer. Casey shook her head.

"Were you at home Thursday night?"

Casey nodded, shifting uneasily in her chair. *It depends on what you mean by home,* Casey thought.

"Did you notice anything unusual going on at the Ashtons' or in the cul-de-sac in general?"

"I was rather preoccupied," Casey said, then immediately regretted it. "I was busy and didn't pay attention to what may have been happening outside my house."

"Was your husband home Thursday night?"

"He always works late on Thursdays. He got home around 8:45pm," Casey informed them.

"When do expect him home tonight?"

"He should arrive any minute but he plays on a bowling league on Mondays and he'll want to eat and run," Casey warned them. She didn't know if she should say something about the decidedly negative reaction he'd have to finding police officers sitting in the front room interrogating his wife.

"Did he mention seeing or hearing anything abnormal on Thursday night?'

Casey shook her head. "When he works late he's exhausted by the time he gets home. He just gulps down his dinner, takes a sleeping pill and is in bed by 10:00pm."

"And that's what he did Thursday night?"

Casey nodded.

"What time did you go to bed, Miss Bailey?"

"I don't really remember," Casey replied. *It was*

*late; really late,* Casey thought to herself.

"Was it after your husband went to bed?"

Casey nodded.

"Do you think it was after 11:00pm that night?"

"Yes," Casey answered.

"And where is your bedroom located?"

"Upstairs, over the kitchen," Casey replied.

"On the opposite side of the house from the Ashton's property, then?"

Casey nodded.

"Tell us about the nature of your son's relationship with Jessie Ashton."

"I'm not sure what you mean," Casey said, wondering if she was now going to have to defend Sebastian for some reason.

"Their relationship has been described by several people who know them as a sibling-type relationship."

"I would agree with that," Casey replied nodding vigorously. "They have been friends and pretty much inseparable since they were small children."

"So there has never been a romantic interest on either side?"

"Not that I'm aware of," Casey confirmed.

"Would your son talk to you about it if there was?"

"I don't know," Casey shrugged. *No, not now,* Casey knew.

"Do you have a good relationship with your husband?"

"Yes," Casey replied, perplexed at the question.

"Have there been any problems in your relationship lately?"

"No," Casey answered, now bristling.

"Have you or your husband ever had an affair?"

"I don't think that's any of your business. And what does that have to do with what happened to Jessie, anyway?" Casey retorted angrily.

At that moment, Ted walked through the front door and for once, Casey was glad that he didn't like police invading his private space.

"What's going on here?" Ted asked suspiciously.

"We're investigating what happened to Jessie Ashton. We're interviewing all the residents in the cul-de-sac."

"Did you let them in here?" Ted asked Casey, his face already becoming red with irritation.

Casey shrugged. "I didn't really have any choice."

"They don't have the right to come into our house unless we want them here," Ted protested.

"Mr. Bailey, we're simply trying to find out if anyone in the neighborhood noticed anything out-of-the-ordinary on Thursday evening."

"I'm sure my wife has assured you that we did not," Ted replied, walking toward the two police officers and gesturing for them to stand up. "I would appreciate it if you would leave now."

"Your wife informed us that you arrived home at about 8:45 pm on Thursday night and went to bed around 10:00, aided by a sleeping pill. Is this correct?"

"It is," Ted replied, again gesturing for the police officers to rise and follow him to the front door. The two police officers acquiesced, moving slowly behind Ted. Ted opened the door and swept his arm in front of him, a movement that had the effect of seeming to sweep the two officers right out onto the front stoop. They turned to face Ted before he had a chance to shut the door.

"Mr. Bailey, do you know of any reason why anyone would want to do harm to Jessie?"

"No, I do not," Ted replied sternly before firmly closing the door. Then he turned to Casey. Casey knew she was going to be reprimanded for allowing the police to enter their home. Then Ted would blow up about the fact that dinner wasn't ready and he would storm out complaining that he'd have to pick up some fast food on the way to his game. Casey wasn't that worried about Ted; by the time he came back home he'd be back to the same old laid-back Ted. Casey was worried about what the police officers might have gleaned from their interrogation.

## CHAPTER 20

**When Aster saw** the two police officers going from house to house she became annoyed and anxious. The last thing she wanted to do was talk to the police. Aster walked from room to room listening for the doorbell to ring. She wondered how long she'd have to wait. It didn't occur to her not to answer the door or pretend she wasn't home. She knew that her neighbors had probably already told the officers that she stayed home during the day and was gone at night. She knew that the police would wonder what she did at night, where she went. Aster knew she'd have to stick to the story and make it believable.

When Aster finally saw the police officers approaching her house she suddenly felt a sense of relief, even though she was still nervous about their visit. At least she'd get it over with instead of continuing this nerve-wracking waiting game. The two officers were casual and non-threatening as they introduced themselves and followed Aster inside the house. Despite their physical attractiveness and soft-spoken politeness, Aster knew that most women policemen were equally as tough as their male counterparts and could be even more forceful. She didn't expect that these officers were any different.

"Are you aware of what occurred at the Ashton house last week?"

"I saw an ambulance there Friday morning," Aster replied, feeling safe with that answer.

"So you're not aware that Jessie Ashton was found unconscious Friday morning?"

"No," Aster answered.

"Do you know the Ashtons?"

"I met them at a cul-de-sac picnic," Aster replied. "I had just moved into the neighborhood."

"How long have you lived here?"

"Almost two months," Aster said.

"And that picnic was when?"

"About six weeks ago," Aster replied. "It was actually a covered dish supper at the Ashtons' house. Obviously, the weather was a little chilly for a picnic at that time."

"Did you meet Jessie Ashton at that supper?"

"Yes," Aster affirmed.

"Did you have any conversation with her?"

"Just introductions. And she complimented me on the dress I was wearing," Aster explained. "Most of the time she and the boy who lives next door sat off by themselves."

"And did everyone stay in one particular area of the house during the supper?"

"Everyone gathered in the kitchen and adjacent dining room but there was something wrong with the plumbing in the powder room downstairs so they told us to use the upstairs hall bath," Aster answered, feeling like she'd just said too much.

"Did you use the upstairs bathroom?"

"I don't remember," Aster replied.

"Can you tell us who else was at the Ashtons' house that night?"

"I think everyone who lives here full-time was there. I know the Baileys were there, and my next door neighbor Mick was there. The guy who lives across the court from me, I think his name is Wing or Ching or something like that, was there. And Grace who lives on the corner and her next door neighbors, the Petersons. It was a sort of welcome supper for me, actually and a goodbye dinner for them. The Petersons, I mean. They moved out a month or so ago," Aster listed, trying not to forget anyone.

"Anyone else?"

"Not that I can remember. There could have been. At the time I didn't know anyone in the neighborhood. I had only been living here a couple of weeks so until that evening I hadn't met anyone but Ellen Ashton who came over with a cake the day after I moved in and then came back a week later to invite me to the supper," Aster explained.

Aster watched the two police officers carefully. It was obvious to Aster that they believed something nefarious had happened to Jessie Ashton and they were trying to figure it out. They obviously suspected that someone in the cul-de-sac could be involved. Aster knew it was better to appear cooperative; she would be less likely to become a person of interest. Aster certainly didn't want the two officers to think she was hiding anything even though she was.

"Were you at home this past Thursday night?"

"No. I didn't get home until Friday morning," Aster admitted.

"Where were you?"

"I was working," Aster answered.

"What do you do for a living?"

"I'm a waitress. I work nights," Aster said. She let out a silent sigh. She'd said it convincingly. The officers hadn't shown any sign of questioning it.

"You must work at one of the casinos across the state line."

Aster nodded. She wasn't going to elaborate if she didn't have to.

"When did you leave for work on Thursday?"

"Around 4:00pm," Aster answered.

"And you got home Friday morning at …?"

"Around six-thirty or seven," Aster said. "I pulled in just before the ambulance left."

"I imagine that's a tough schedule to work. I notice you have a bandage on your chest. Did you have an accident?"

Aster hesitated. She didn't realize the bandage was visible. *Be cooperative, volunteer information,* Aster said to herself.

"There was a bar fight a few nights ago. Unfortunately, I accidentally got cut by a broken beer bottle," Aster explained.

"Are you a deceitful person, Miss Bancroft?"

Aster was speechless for a moment. *Were they questioning her answers? Did they think she was lying? Was her secret that apparent?*

"I wouldn't consider myself as such, no," Aster finally answered.

The two police officers exchanged an indecipherable look and thanked Aster for her cooperation. After they had left, Aster hurried to the mirror. She was relieved to see that she didn't look any different than she had before they had arrived. She assured herself that despite that last question they had no reason to believe she wasn't telling the truth. Police liked to leave people a little nervous.

# CHAPTER 21

**Mick wondered if** Katie was going to come to his house, too. *Wouldn't she be surprised when he opened the door?* Mick grinned, preening in the mirror of the powder room. Mick was glad that he'd remembered to take his medicine; he'd be able to act normal around Katie if she did come. And that cute blond that was following her around. Mick wondered why Katie was going to everyone's house. *It must have something to do with the Ashtons,* Mick decided.

Mick loved the look of surprise that crossed Katie's face when he answered the door. She'd asked him to wait a minute and stepped out of earshot with her pretty sidekick. They'd spoken in low tones for a few minutes, then come back and asked to come in. Mick noticed the way they both looked around his house as he led them to the back where his den overlooked the backyard.

Mick was disappointed when the blond began to question him instead of Katie. Katie just wrote stuff down in her notebook and avoided eye contact with Mick. Mick tried not to get upset; he concentrated on giving the blond the correct answers to her questions.

"How long have you lived here, Mr. Wilson?"

"Ten years," Mick replied.

"And you live here alone?"

"Sometimes," Mick said in a flirtatious tone, trying to arouse Katie's jealousy.

"How about lately? Say in the last year."

"I have lived here by myself for the last year," Mick answered, sneaking a look at Katie to see her reaction. She continued to write with her head down and Mick couldn't see her face.

"How well do you know the Ashtons?"

"Well, I've known 'em for the ten years I've lived here," Mick said, unsure of the question.

"Would you say you know them well? That you're friends, acquaintances, or just neighbors that speak on occasion?"

"Um…we talk on occasion. We talk more when

we have the cul-de-sac picnics," Mick replied.

"How often do you have these picnics?"

"About once a month but in the summer we do a couple of extra barbeques out in the middle of the court, too," Mick explained.

"And does everyone take turns having these picnics?"

"Ellen Ashton always schedules 'em and organizes 'em but we all take turns havin' 'em at our houses," Mick answered, not bothering to mention that he'd never been asked to have a picnic at his house.

"Do you know Jessie Ashton?"

"I guess so. I mean I've watched her grow up," Mick said remembering Jessie as a little girl riding her bike in the cul-de-sac.

"Have you spoken with her lately?"

"No, not in a while," Mick said shaking his head.

"Have you ever known anyone who particularly didn't like Jessie or might have wanted to hurt Jessie for some reason?"

"I can't imagine. She's the sweetest little girl I've ever met," Mick replied, looking at Katie. *Except for Miss Katie over there.*

"Were you at home last Thursday night?"

"I believe so, yes," Mick nodded.

"Can you recall anything that might have happened that night that you would call strange or atypical?"

Mick tried to think back that far. He had a hard time remembering things sometimes, especially if he forgot to take his pills.

"I don't think so," Mick finally said.

"Do you remember what time you went to bed that night?"

"Can't say," Mick answered.

"Can you see the Ashtons' house from your bedroom, Mr. Wilson?"

"No. My bedroom's back there," Mick replied pointing to the hall that opened to the den.

"Have you ever told a lie, Mr. Wilson?"

"Of course. Hasn't everyone once in a while?" Mick admitted.

"Have you told one lately? A big one?"

"Maybe. I guess it depends on what you consider a *big lie*, you know," Mick said, grinning, trying to flirt again. Katie was still busy writing in her notebook, ignoring him.

"Mr. Wilson, what do you know about flowers?"

"I know women love 'em," Mick quipped giving her what he perceived to be his million dollar smile. "I got some pretty daffodils out front you might've seen on your way in. I'd be happy to cut you and Miss Katie a whole bunch of 'em if you'd like."

"I notice you have a lot of azaleas blooming in your front yard, too. Are you partial to azaleas?"

"They was here when I moved in. You like azaleas better?" Mick asked.

"Your flowers and bushes are lovely but I think it's best we leave them in your yard for now."

Katie glanced up at the blond who'd been asking all the questions and nodded sharply.

"I think that's all the questions we have for you, Mr. Wilson."

Katie and the blond stood up and the blond extended her hand to Mick.

"Can I get you ladies a drink or somethin' before you go?" Mick asked, desperate for Katie to stay.

"Thank you for your hospitality but we have other business to attend to," the blond said as she and Katie continued toward Mick's front door. Mick stood in the doorway and watched Katie and her partner walk to their golf carts. They spent several minutes in conversation that Mick couldn't hear, then the blond removed a large gray case from the back of one of the carts and the two of them proceeded to the Ashtons' house. Mick watched as they exchanged a few words with Justin Ashton, then disappeared into the house.

Mick was elated. Katie had been at his house, sat in his den. He could still smell the faint scent of her and it smelled like roses. The blond had smelled spicy. Mick sat down in the exact spot Katie had been sitting on the couch; it was still slightly warm. Mick closed his eyes and breathed in slowly, reveling in Katie's sweet perfume and replaying the picture of her on his couch over and over again in his mind.

# CHAPTER 22

**When Katie and** Anna had reached the area where they had parked their golf carts, they pulled out their respective notebooks to compare notes.

"I think they're all hiding something," Katie commented immediately.

"I agree. I got the sense that each one of them was being evasive about something," Anna nodded. "And I see what you mean about Mick Wilson. He is definitely a little creepy."

"Grace Garfield is a strange one, too. I wonder what her deal is?" Katie remarked.

"What about Aster Bancroft? Something was a little off about her, too and I'm not just talking about the way she looks," Anna observed.

"Danny Ping is an interesting person. He seemed so nervous and kind of sad, you know, which is really weird because I saw him at The Sandbar Saturday night and he looked to be the life of the party," Katie said, shaking her head. "He's a good suspect since he knows so much about plants but compared to the others, he seems the least likely."

"What about Casey Bailey? Soccer mom extraordinaire don't you think?"

"I noticed that her husband appears to be a lot older than her. They look like an odd couple, you know, like they don't really go together. I wonder if it was about the money for her and the arm candy for him," Katie mused.

Anna shrugged. "After seeing the situation, I can certainly believe that a little adultery could be going on."

"Me, too," Katie concurred. Anna was already lifting the fingerprint kit from her golf cart and so Katie pushed her notebook back into her breast pocket and followed Anna toward the Ashtons' house.

Justin Ashton had agreed to meet Katie and Anna but he had not been apprised of their mission yet. After perfunctory greetings, Katie and Anna stepped into the entry foyer.

"The reason we are here again is that we have reason to believe that someone may have somehow entered the house

Thursday night and injected Jessie. Has her doctor explained to you what substances they found in the toxicology?" Katie began

"I am aware that they were tentatively identified as natural, possibly plant, materials," Justin Ashton replied.

Katie explained what they had learned earlier.

"So now you think someone deliberately poisoned my daughter?" Justin Ashton said, realization slowly transforming his curious expression.

"Yes, that is the theory. We don't have conclusive evidence yet, though. That's why we are here. We're hoping that if this is actually the case, we might be able to find fingerprints that will lead to a suspect," Anna answered.

"My wife had our housekeeping service clean Jessie's room on Saturday," Justin Ashton said apologetically.

"We're aware that any fingerprints may have already been obliterated but we think it's worth the long shot. Actually, fingerprints are a lot more difficult to remove than you would think. Often, standard cleaning and dusting products fail to remove skin residues even if it looks like it to the naked eye," Katie said.

"Well, you're more than welcome to try to find something," Justin Ashton replied.

"Of course, if we find any fingerprints, we'll need to fingerprint you, your wife, and both of your daughters in order to discern family from possible suspects," Katie instructed.

"That's no problem. My wife's fingerprints should already be on file because she worked for the Census Bureau in 2010. And Jessie's and Veronica's should be in your police files from the Child Find program," Justin Ashton volunteered.

"Perfect. I'll call the officer on duty at the station and get him to confirm that we already have everyone else's fingerprints, then," Anna replied.

Anna pulled out her cell phone and stepped into the living room. Katie asked Justin Ashton for permission to use his dining room table to fingerprint him and proceeded to set up the kit. Katie took each of Justin Ashton's fingers and lightly rolled them on the ink pad before gently rolling them over the fingerprint card. Then she did the same with each of Justin

Ashton's thumbs. Next she instructed Justin Ashton to lay his fingers flat on the ink pad, then pressed them gently onto the bottom of the card, followed by his thumbs, making sure to capture not only his fingertips but also the first joint of each finger. After reviewing the card, Katie was satisfied she'd produced "classifiable" prints. By the time the ink had dried, Anna had rejoined Katie and Justin Ashton.

While Justin Ashton walked to the kitchen to wash the ink from his hands, Katie and Anna climbed the staircase to Jessie's room. For forty-five minutes, they both worked in silence, dusting every surface in the bedroom and adjoining bath from which they might be able to lift fingerprints. Then they did the same thing outside on the balconies. When they had finished, they had lifted eleven complete fingerprints and four partials. After re-checking the documentation for each print, identifying where it had been found, Katie and Anna placed everything in the gray case and went back downstairs.

When they reached the bottom step, Anna's phone rang. When she hung up thirty seconds later she announced to Katie and Justin Ashton that the police department did indeed have fingerprint records for Ellen, Jessie and Veronica. After thanking Justin Ashton for his cooperation, Katie and Anna climbed onto their golf carts and left the cul-de-sac. In order to discuss the case while driving their individual units back to the station, Katie and Anna connected their cell phones to hands-free receivers.

"Let's start at the beginning. OK, Grace Garfield," Katie said, adjusting the volume. "She lives alone and doesn't seem very friendly toward her neighbors, particularly the Ashtons."

"She wasn't friendly toward us either, at first," Anna added. "She was very defensive in the beginning."

"Perhaps she was just nervous about being questioned by the police. That's a pretty normal reaction," Katie replied.

"True," Anna agreed.

"So the next question is: does she covet her neighbor?" Katie posed.

"I got that impression. Definitely," Anna answered

with conviction.

"Then the next question is: enough to kill her?" Katie continued.

"Why would Grace want to kill Jessie Ashton? Grace is a grown woman, Jessie is a teenager," Anna countered.

"Jealousy can be a powerful emotion. In reality, Grace is only a few years older than Jessie. Maybe Grace thinks she's competing with her in some twisted way," Katie replied thoughtfully.

"Maybe," Anna considered. "

"Next: Danny Ping," Katie ticked off.

"Very good looking," Anna said.

Katie laughed. "Agreed, but besides that..."

"He has an amazing yard—all the flowers and trees. Beautiful!" Anna gushed. Anna loved gorgeous gardens but pretty much lacked a green thumb.

"Agreed, again but besides that...," Katie replied. "He was pretty straightforward in answering our questions but I had the feeling he was holding something back."

"I think you're right. Did you get the feeling he was any kind of thief?" Anna asked.

"He might steal a heart but anything else...," Katie answered.

"Of all of the neighbors, he was the one who had the knowledge about plants. I would bet he would know enough to extract poisons from them," Anna reminded Katie.

"There is that. But what reason would he have to kill Jessie?" Katie raised.

"Let's say he actually did steal something and he knew that Jessie had seen him do it," Anna proposed.

"Then he might have had a reason to eliminate her depending on what he stole," Katie concluded.

"Alright. Casey Bailey. At least twenty years younger than her husband, beautiful, wealthy. Nothing obvious but there did seem to be some tension when we mentioned her son," Anna remarked.

"I noticed that, too. And she got very defensive when we asked if she or her husband had ever been unfaithful,"

Katie reminded her.

"I'd get pretty upset if I felt someone was accusing me or my husband of adultery, too," Anna admitted. "I think that was a fairly natural response."

"Admitted. But her reaction is precisely why I can't discount her as a suspect. What if Jessie made the same accusation about her or her husband? And speaking of, her husband was an unpleasant fellow, wasn't he?" Katie replied.

"He definitely didn't like police in his house, that's for sure," Anna laughed. "I'm not sure if it was us or guilt."

"I guess we're not going to find out either unless we can find a way to detain him for questioning," Katie answered. "It's obvious he's not going to speak to us voluntarily."

"OK, moving on to Aster Bancroft."

"Incredibly weird. It was almost as if she was playing a part. I felt like she was giving us the answers and reactions she thought would make her seem normal or innocent or something," Katie offered.

"I got the same feeling. She seemed really fake. Did you notice how much make-up she was wearing? I got the impression she could be a transvestite or transsexual who isn't completely comfortable with her identity yet," Anna replied.

"I'm not sure how much of what she said I actually believed," Katie said. "Did you notice her reaction when I asked her about the bandage? I could almost see her forming the story about the beer bottle in her mind before answering."

"That's exactly the way I saw that, too. And she seemed really uncomfortable, like way more uncomfortable than most people are when they are questioned by the police," Anna added.

"I found it interesting that she hesitated for a moment before answering when we asked her if she was a deceitful person. Like she had to think about it," Katie said.

"So if she is being deceitful in some way…let's say that our hunches are correct and she's not what she is portraying herself to be, is that a reason to kill Jessie Ashton?" Anna asked.

"I would say that depends on what she's trying to

hide," Katie answered bluntly.

"I agree. Now we come to Mick Wilson," Anna declared.

"Yes, Mick Wilson. Creepy to say the least," Katie said.

"And apparently obsessed with you," Anna teased.

"Unfortunately," Katie conceded. "He really didn't give us much information we could use."

"No, he didn't. He was too busy trying to impress you with his prowess," Anna teased again.

"Seriously, although he's odd, he seems harmless, at least in terms of carrying out a murder," Katie said. "I could see him peeking in windows or spying on his neighbors though."

"I wouldn't think he'd be a very popular neighbor. He's probably invited to the cul-de-sac picnics out of good manners rather than the desire to actually have him there," Anna pronounced.

"That would be my guess. As for him being a suspect, he does have a yard full of azaleas and daffodils. We don't know that he's not aware that they contain natural poisons or that he wouldn't know how to extract those poisons if he wanted, too," Katie said.

"It's obvious that he has some mental problems or deficiencies. Why would he have any reason to kill Jessie?" Anna challenged.

"People with mental issues don't always have to have a reason for doing the things they do. They just do them because they're compelled to," Katie argued.

"That is true," Anna granted. "What do you think he lied about?"

"Anything. Everything. He admitted to it," Katie sighed.

"Well, one thing we know for sure," Anna asserted. "According to Danny Ping, everyone we interviewed had access to the Ashton house a month ago. They all had the perfect opportunity to locate Jessie's room, check it out, and develop a plan for getting into the house and administering the poison."

"Now, we just have to figure out if any of them had

enough motive to do it," Katie replied as she and Anna pulled up in front of the station. As they disconnected their cell phones from their ear buds, they agreed that Katie would call the high school principal in the morning and make arrangements to gather Jessie's friends together to take their fingerprints. Anna would go to the school with Katie and assist her with the process.

It was after 8:00pm when Katie finally reached home. Ogilvie made sure she knew she was overdue by whining and yelping and continuously jumping on her even though he'd been trained to stay down.

"I know I've been neglecting you a little bit lately," Katie admitted, stopping to sit down on the floor and rough-house with Ogilvie for a few minutes.

Once she had placated her faithful companion, Katie went directly to the bathroom and began to run a shower. After she had adjusted the water temperature, Katie stepped in and spent ten minutes just standing under the hot, pulsating water that massaged her tired muscles. Katie put on soft, fluffy pajamas and curled up on her couch with Ogilvie to watch TV for a couple of hours before turning in for the night.

# TUESDAY
## CHAPTER 23

**The next morning**, after a quick phone call to the very amenable Potoma High School principal, Katie drove to the station. Just after Anna arrived, the principal called Katie back, confirming that he had obtained the required parental consents and Katie and Anna set out for the high school.

When Katie and Anna arrived at the school they were ushered into a small meeting room adjacent to the school office. By the time the students reported to the room, the fingerprinting kit had been set up and Katie and Anna had worked out an efficient process. They greeted each of the teens and quickly took them through the fingerprint process.

"We are doing this mainly to eliminate you from being a suspect in the case," Katie informed the group. "At this time we believe that someone other than Jessie injected poison into her system in a possible attempt to murder her."

It was obvious that the group of teens were dumbfounded. "Why do you think that? I thought the police believed Jessie did it to herself," Michella asked.

"We've received some toxicology reports that lead us to believe otherwise," Anna answered, intentionally neglecting to elaborate.

"What did you find?" Georgie and Greta inquired excitedly in unison.

"Unfortunately, we can't release that information right now," Katie deferred.

"I assume that you have lifted some fingerprints from Jessie's house," Bug said, crossing his arms over his chest.

"We have," Katie nodded.

"How long will it take to identify them?" Bug asked.

"At least a couple of days. We don't have the equipment here so we had to send them off to the district lab," Katie replied.

"Do you have any suspects?" Bug asked.

"Yes and no. You might say we've identified some persons of interest," Anna answered cautiously.

"Why would someone try to kill Jessie?" Ruthie blurted.

"Do any of you have any ideas?" Katie threw out.

Katie noticed that several of the teens exchanged glances and nods but no one spoke. A few of them shook their heads at Katie and Anna.

"Is there anyone you might consider Jessie's enemy?" Anna said trying another tact.

"Like we told you before. Everyone likes Jessie," Georgie replied while the other girls in the group nodded in agreement.

"Certainly, there are a few people who are jealous or envious of her," Katie replied.

"Not that we know of," Ruthie answered, looking at Greta and Georgie who shook their heads in confirmation.

"How about you four?" Anna asked, gesturing toward Bug, Chase, Alex, and Michella.

"I'm sure there are some girls in town who are jealous of Jessie. I mean she's pretty, smart, super-nice. She can afford nice clothes and lots of guys like her," Michella said.

"Is there anyone you know that has been in direct competition with her, like for the attentions of a guy maybe they both liked?"

"No. Her last boyfriend was Chase," Michella said pointing at him, "and I don't really know of anyone she's been interested in since they broke up."

The other four girls in the room nodded, murmuring in agreement. Bug and Chase shrugged. Alex made no gesture at all and Katie made a mental note to interview him alone later about his feelings for Jessie. It was obvious he was the newcomer to the group and wasn't going to spill anything in front of the others. Having achieved their objective, Katie and Anna dismissed all of the teenagers except for Bug and Alex. Asking Bug to wait in the lobby of the office, Katie began to question Alex while Anna collected the fingerprint cards and organized everything back in the kit.

Katie sat down in a chair and gestured for Alex to do the same. "I noticed that you didn't want to elaborate earlier with Jessie's other friends in the room."

Katie supposed she had expected Alex to be

embarrassed or reluctant to discuss any romantic notions he had about Jessie so she was a little stunned when he admitted that his interest in Jessie was more than platonic.

"She had me from hello, as they say," Alex admitted in his charming effected European way of speech.

"Does Jessie know that?" Katie asked, more than curious.

"It's mutual," Alex replied.

"But none of Jessie's friends know? Why is that?" Katie inquired.

"It's complicated," Alex answered.

Katie raised her eyebrows, waiting for Alex to expound on the subject.

"Jessie wanted me to be accepted by her friends before she introduced me as her boyfriend. I know to an adult that sounds silly but when you live in a small town and go to a small high school, it's important. Especially since I have a reputation as, and I admit to being, a bit eccentric," Alex explained. "I'm already on the "don't" list of all her friends."

Katie nodded in understanding. "Is her close relationship with Bug a problem for you?"

Alex shook his head.

"What about her continued friendship with Chase?" Katie prodded.

"I don't have any right to tell Jessie who she can be friends with. And I trust her," Alex answered.

After sending Alex back to class, Katie asked Bug to come into the meeting room.

"Are you aware that we have questioned several of the residents of your cul-de-sac including your parents?" Katie inquired.

"Yeah, I found out last night after I got home from work. My dad was pretty riled about it," Bug replied.

"Why would your father have that reaction?" Anna asked.

"My dad has a thing about police or government agents being able to invade someone's privacy or come on someone's private property without that individual's permission. He believes it's against the Constitution," Bug explained.

"I see," Anna said slowly nodding her head. "Is there anyone who lives in your court that would have any reason to hurt Jessie?"

"Not that I know of. I mean we have some characters there, you know. Mick Wilson is totally whacked and that lady that lives beside him is just too weird. She's always coming and going at odd hours and something about the way she looks just isn't right. Miss Garfield is a little...funny, too," Bug laughed.

"What about Danny Ping? Do you know him?" Katie said.

A shadow crossed Bug's face and Katie thought she could detect the slightest trace of distaste in Bug's expression. "Nope."

"What's your impression of him?" Anna pressed.

"I don't have one. He's just a guy who lives in my neighborhood. He does a lot of gardening," Bug said, somewhat evasively in Katie's opinion.

"Did you notice anything the least bit out of sorts Thursday night? Any activity in the cul-de-sac that wasn't normal?" Katie asked.

Bug hesitated, then said, "No. Nothing.".

"You were in attendance at the last cul-de-sac picnic...the covered-dish supper held at Jessie's house about six weeks ago?" Anna attempted to confirm.

Bug nodded.

"Can you tell me who else was there?" Katie asked.

Bug thought for a moment, closing his eyes. Then he said, "All of the Ashtons, my mom and dad and me. Creepy Mick and Astra, Aster, whatever her name is. Asian dude. Miss Garfield. The Petersons. They moved away. That's it."

"According to one of your neighbors who was at the dinner, the Ashtons' first floor powder room was out of order so you had to use a bathroom on the second floor. Is that true?" Katie confirmed.

"Yeah, I do remember that," Bug replied.

"Is that bathroom connected to any bedrooms?"

Anna asked.

"It's actually one of those "Jack-and-Jill" type bathrooms that connects Veronica's room and a guest room. It also has a door to the hall so when someone's in the media room up there they can use it, too," Bug answered.

"I take it you know your way around the Ashtons' house pretty well?" Katie commented.

"Of course." Bug replied.

Katie told Bug that he could return to class as she and Anna gathered up their things. They made a quick stop at the principal's office to thank him for his cooperation and then made a beeline for the station so that they could transfer all of the fingerprint information they had collected to a courier for transport to the district lab.

After dispatching the fingerprints, Katie and Anna typed up their notes, adding them to the growing file on Jessie. Confident that they had enough to officially open an investigation, they were ready to let their Chief in on the details of the case. The Chief met with them in the conference room and listened thoughtfully to the information they had accumulated. After a few perfunctory questions, he approved the investigation and authorized Katie, as lead, with Anna, as back-up, to continue with their inquiry, formally labeling it "attempted murder".

After their meeting with the Chief, Katie and Anna remained in the conference room to discuss their next move. Working from their notes, Katie and Anna began to develop charts and profiles to help them identify possibilities.

"It looks like we have a lot of potential suspects with motives but not enough evidence to point to any one as the likely perpetrator," Katie said, a little frustrated.

"At least we have suspects. I think you were right about the notations in Jessie's notebook corresponding to Jessie's neighbors. So we have a good place to start," Anna encouraged.

"Assuming Jessie's notebook does identify the sinners in her neighborhood, we need to determine specifically what those sins were. If we do that, we may be able figure out who sinned badly enough to warrant murder to try and cover it up," Katie replied.

"That means we have to directly confront the neighbors about what was in Jessie's notebook," Anna contemplated.

"The fingerprints could be very helpful but it'll be at least Wednesday before we get any results," Katie sighed.

"It's too bad we don't have any strong suspects yet. It would have been better if we could have fingerprinted Jessie's neighbors, too," Anna added.

"I suppose we could check the system to see if any of them are in it," Katie suggested. "If they are, we can have the lab cross-reference those first and call us if they are a match. That way we won't have to wait until the official results come back to start investigating those persons as suspects."

"Good idea," Anna replied. "I can get on that right away."

Anna left the conference room to access a computer and Katie gathered up all of their paperwork. She placed everything in particular order in Jessie's file and quickly created a list of the various items included in the file which she stapled inside the front cover.

In the squad room, Anna was still seated in front of the computer. When Katie walked up behind her, Anna said, "I just finished searching and I got a few hits."

The two women slapped a high-five with a little squeal. Officer Darren, the Officer on Duty, looked up from his computer, smiling and shaking his head.

"Grace Garfield and Mick Wilson," Anna said proudly, pulling several sheets of paper off the printer next to her.

"Interesting," Katie replied.

"I've already called the lab. They're going to run them against the ones we sent in as soon as they receive them and let us know if they match," Anna informed Katie. "Unfortunately, that probably won't be until tomorrow."

"Well, whether or not the fingerprints match, we need to re-question the neighbors so I think we should go back out this evening and do that. At least talk to Miss Garfield and Mr. Wilson," Katie replied.

"I agree," Anna concurred. "What do we do until then?"

Looking at her watch, Katie said "I'm thinking that we should call Miss Garfield and Mr. Wilson and have them come in to the station this afternoon."

# CHAPTER 24

**Mick was excited**. He was seeing Katie twice in two days. He especially liked it when she wore her police uniform and talked to him in her police officer voice. He was a little annoyed that she wanted to talk about Jessie Ashton some more. *Jessie Ashton has caused me enough trouble,* Mick thought. He was also disappointed that Katie's blond partner had called him instead of Katie but he knew Katie was an important police officer and that meant she was busy.

He could have come right over to the police station and been there in less than five minutes if he drove his car but he wanted to make sure he looked his best for Katie. He needed time to take a shower and dress carefully. He also needed time for his pills to work so that he would act normal.

When Mick arrived at the police station, Katie's blond partner met him at the front and escorted him back to a conference room. Mick could smell Katie's rosy perfume before he even stepped into the room. Katie was seated with a notebook and pen lying on the table in front of her. She gave Mick a curt nod of the head. *She has to appear professional at her job*, Mick reminded himself so he wouldn't be disappointed that she didn't smile at him. The blonde indicated to Mick to sit in the lone chair on the opposite side of the table from Katie.

"Mr. Wilson, we have concluded that someone tried to kill Jessie Ashton. Would you know anything about that?"

Mick could feel himself start to sweat. He shook his head vigorously.

"Mr. Wilson, why are your fingerprints in the police database?"

"I…I don't know," Mick stammered.

"You don't remember having your fingerprints taken?"

"Yes. I remember," Mick said. *Why were they looking at his fingerprints?*

"And when was that?"

"I don't know," Mick answered, struggling to remember the last time.

"Does this refresh your memory?"

The blonde slid a print-out over to Mick. Mick tried

to read the words on the page but they blurred together. He looked up at the blond blankly. From the corner of his eye he could see Katie looking at him.

"You don't remember being arrested twelve years ago?"

"Maybe," Mick replied slowly. "That was a long time ago."

"It says here you were accused of being a Peeping Tom."

Mick shrugged. He looked over at Katie. He could see the disgust on her face. Mick felt his stomach drop. *Now Katie would stop liking him. And it's all because of that dumb blonde!*

"Who were you peeping at, Mick?"

Mick was feeling sick. His head was spinning and he could feel the anger rising in his belly. He needed to concentrate on remaining calm, controlling his rage.

"It says here, you were looking at a teenage girl."

Mick remained silent. He wasn't in the mood to talk to this mean blond monster that was turning his sweet Katie against him.

"You like looking at teenage girls, Mick? Maybe you peeped on Jessie Ashton. Did she catch you, Mick? Is that why you tried to kill her? So she couldn't tell anyone?"

Mick began to quiver and he felt soaking wet from perspiration. He shook his head in great big arcs. "I didn't try to kill her!" he shouted.

"Are you sure, Mick?"

"I didn't do it!" Mick shouted again. He looked at Katie but she was busy writing on her pad of paper.

"Are we going to find your fingerprints in Jessie's room?"

"No. I never been in her room," Mick replied angrily. *How dare she accuse him of something he didn't do!* Mick's anger was being replaced with composure of a sort. It was Mick's way of taking control of an uncontrollable situation.

"When you went to Ms. Ashton's party last month, did you go upstairs to use the bathroom?"

"What?" Mick asked, unable to switch his mind to

the new line of questioning that fast.

"Did you go upstairs to use the bathroom when you were at the Ashtons' house?"

"No. I don't use other people's bathrooms. I don't use public bathrooms. I pee in the bushes if I have to go when I'm not at home," Mick said in an even tone. The blond almost laughed but caught herself in mid-smile and returned to her stern expression.

"So you pee in the bushes when you're spying on young girls?"

Mick wasn't going to answer that one. He shrugged his shoulders dramatically, instead. *Let that ugly blond witch think what she wanted. She was turning Katie against him.* He could see Katie looking at him; she had no expression on her face at all.

"Did you go to college, Mick?"

"Yes," Mick replied, again confused at the rapid-fire change in questions.

"And did you obtain a degree?"

"A Masters degree in bio-chemistry," Mick answered. Mick saw a look of shock register on both the blond's face and Katie's.

"Do you work in that field?"

"No, not anymore," Mick said, looking down at his feet. He was ashamed of the fact. He'd had a great career but he'd blown it. It wasn't all his fault but that didn't really matter now. When Mick looked up, he saw a curious expression on Katie's face. *At least she knew he was educated; maybe she'd like him again since she knew that.*

The blond told Mick to sit tight and she and Katie left the room together. Mick wondered what was next. He was really feeling depressed now. They had figured out that someone had tried to kill Jessie Ashton. They had figured out that he'd gone to jail for something involving a teenage girl. They knew he used to have a career in bio-chemistry. They were putting things together. Mick wondered if he should start panicking. Right now he was too depressed to panic. He just wanted to go home and take more of his medicine.

After a few minutes, the blond came back.

"I'm going to assume that no one can confirm that you were in your house all night Thursday night. Am I right?"

"I live alone, like I told you before," Mick replied

"So you have no alibi. Just your word. And since you're a criminal, that's not saying much, huh?"

"I was at home all night," Mick asserted. *What else did they expect him to say?* He wasn't stupid. There was no way he was going to break down and confess to what they were accusing him of.

"So you say, Mick. Well, we're going to cut you loose. We don't have any choice at the moment but if we find your fingerprints at the Ashton house...well, that's another story. Don't plan to leave Potoma any time soon."

The blond walked to the door, opened it, and gestured to Mick. Mick ducked his head and grinned. Then he looked back up, the smile erased and replaced by a feigned expression of humility. When he stepped out of the station into the bright sunshine, he breathed a big breath of relief.

# CHAPTER 25

As **Grace pulled** up to the station, she noticed Crazy Mick from the neighborhood walking to his car. Grace looked in the rear-view mirror and applied a fresh coat of rose-hued lipstick. She pulled out her compact and brushed the pad over her face to dull down any shiny spots. She was glad she'd worn a straight skirt and tunic to work today. She almost looked slim. The three-inch heels on her pumps helped with the illusion, too. Grace checked her hair to make sure there were no pieces sticking straight out from her chignon.

Grace alighted from her car and walked confidently into the police station. She always walked like she was a thin model on a catwalk, imagining all the men and women turning their heads to admire her. She wondered why Mick Wilson had been at the station. *Were they questioning him, too?* The male officer at the counter smiled at her and Grace smiled back. She read his name tag: it said "P. Darren". She'd have to remember that. Before she had a chance to talk to him, that blond female police officer walked up to her and told her to "come on back."

The other female police officer that had come to her house was seated at a table in the conference room. Grace sat down across from her. The blond sat down, too. The blond wrote something on a pad of paper. Grace looked around the room. There was a window or a mirror—Grace couldn't tell which from her vantage point—on the wall. Grace figured it was one of those one-way things you see on TV where people stand on the other side and watch everything that goes on. She wondered if someone was looking through the glass at her. Grace looked at the blond. *Maybe if she was nice to her today, she'd ask the blond what kind of make-up she wore.*

"Miss Garfield, we asked you to come down because we're now investigating what happened to Jessie Ashton as an attempted murder."

Grace gulped in a big breath of air.

"Last night after we interviewed you, we were able to lift some fingerprints from Jessie's room. They are at the lab right now being identified."

Grace was dying to know whose fingerprints they'd

found. Her curiosity was outweighing her sudden growing fear.

"Have you ever been in Jessie Ashton's room?"

Grace felt a sharp pain in her chest. It swiftly dawned on Grace that she might be a suspect. *But they hadn't identified any fingerprints yet, had they? Isn't that what she just said? She said they were in the process, right?*

"I told you already that I'm not part of the Ashtons' clique," Grace replied, avoiding a direct answer to the question.

"But you have been in the Ashtons' house, haven't you? About a month ago, at a cul-de-sac picnic?"

*Oh, yeah, that's right,* Grace thought. It had been too cold to really have a picnic so they'd done the old covered dish supper thing. Grace had been assigned dessert and she'd brought her most scrumptious strawberry swirl lemon pound cake. Everyone had swooned over it. Mick had brought some weird spinach dish that tasted like seaweed and looked like— well, Grace didn't want to think about that.

"I was at the picnic, yes," Grace admitted.

"And do you recall that the powder room was out-of-order so everyone had to use the hall bath upstairs?"

"I don't remember," Grace replied. "I must not have had to use it." Grace did remember. She didn't have to use the bathroom but she pretended she did so she could see more of the Ashton house.

"We have your fingerprints on file on our database. Can you tell us why?"

"I had my fingerprints taken a long time ago when I was a substitute teacher," Grace volunteered. It was true.

"How long ago?"

"Two or three years ago," Grace replied. "I worked as a substitute for about six months after I graduated from college."

"So that makes you, what, twenty-two, twenty-three?"

"I'm twenty-three." Grace said indignantly. *What difference does it make how old I am?* Grace thought.

"I'm curious, Miss Garfield. How do you own a home at twenty-three?"

"I inherited my house when my parents died," Grace replied.

"How much money do you make per year Miss Garfield?"

"None of...." Grace thought better of her answer and said "about $60,000 plus I have investments that pay another $20,000 or so in dividends." Grace smiled smugly. *See how smart I am? Way smarter than you two Barbie dolls! You thought I had a sugar daddy, huh? Cause that's the only way I could be doing as well as I am, huh? Surprised aren't you?*

"You are quite successful, Miss Garfield. And obviously a whiz with finances. I'm impressed. I don't understand why you are jealous of Jessie Ashton."

"Who said I was jealous of Jessie Ashton?" Grace asked, now on the defensive.

"Aren't you?"

"Why would I be jealous of a sixteen-year old girl?" Grace scoffed.

"My question exactly."

"I wouldn't be. I'm not," Grace denied. *What did they know? They didn't have to live across from the Perfect family. Especially that perky Jessie with a zillion adoring friends.*

"You know the décor in your house looks a lot like the Ashtons'. Did you do that on purpose? Or is it just a coincidence?"

Grace knew the police officers were just taunting her, hoping she'd admit to something. "I guess we just have similar taste," Grace answered dismissively.

"You know, people often commit murder out of sheer jealousy."

Grace pressed her lips together. She was not going to respond to that. *They thought they were clever; they were just a really bad cop duo act in a B movie.*

"Could you be jealous enough to hurt Jessie Ashton?"

"I'm not jealous. And I don't even know Jessie Ashton," Grace retorted. "I'm beginning to think I need an attorney." *There, let them chew on that!* Grace knew from the cop shows and action movies that the last thing a police officer wants is for their suspect to lawyer up.

"You might want to hire one if your fingerprints

come back as a match to the ones in Jessie's room."

At that, the police officers told Grace they were finished with their questions for the moment and told her she was free to leave. Grace walked out with her head held high. When she passed the front counter she smiled at Officer Darren. He returned the expression and Grace could feel him watching her as she opened the door and walked out.

When Grace reached her car she was trembling. She collapsed into the front seat, taking deep breaths. After Grace had calmed herself, she started the car and drove toward home.

# CHAPTER 26

**Katie and Anna** went over their notes from the two interviews. "We still have nothing solid. Until we get the fingerprint results, we're still just grasping at straws."

"I imagine Mr. Wilson's arrest wasn't the first or last time he peeped at someone," Katie replied. "But it seems it was the only time he was caught. If Jessie caught him peeping on her, would he have been scared enough about going to jail again to kill her so she couldn't tell?"

"Good question," Anna said, raising her eyebrows. "What I find very interesting—and unexpected—is his professional credentials. A bio-chemist would definitely know how to extract poison substances from plants. The two facts together make Mr. Wilson a prime suspect in my opinion."

"I agree. I think we need to move him to the top of the list for now," Katie concurred. "On the other hand, I'm wavering a little on Grace Garfield. There's no doubt that she's harboring a lot of envy for the Ashtons but she doesn't seem to have a lot to gain by killing Jessie."

"Jealousy turns people inside out and messes with their minds, often causing them to do things they wouldn't even think about otherwise," Anna cautioned.

"True enough, but we have no indication that Miss Garfield has any idea how to use poisonous plant toxins," Katie reminded her.

"Well, we know she likes daffodils. Remember how huge that bouquet was? Must have cost her $60 or $70. I know it's weak evidence but it might signify," Anna replied.

Anna tapped her pencil on the table. "This would be so much simpler if Jessie would just regain consciousness and tell us what happened."

"Even if she wakes up, she may not have a clue what happened to her. Especially if, as we have surmised, someone knocked her out with chloroform and then injected her with the poison," Katie replied.

As if on cue, Anna's cell phone rang. As Anna listened to the call she wrote "hospital" on a piece of paper and slid it in front of Katie. After Anna had hung up she said, "Jessie is beginning to stir. Apparently she has opened her eyes several times today. According to the doctor, she appears to recognize her parents and be listening when they or the doctors speak to her but she hasn't responded in any perceptible way. These eye-opening instances only last a few minutes at a time and the doctor warns that it might not mean anything; it could just be some sort of automatic nerve or brain activity."

"But it could also mean she's coming out of the coma?" Katie asked hopefully.

"Definitely. Her brain may be trying to assimilate and just doing so slowly. Sometimes it just takes time for the brain to organize all the information to heal itself. Of course, she could have suffered brain damage, too," Anna answered.

"Well, we'll just have to hope for the best and pray," Katie resolved. "I'm going to call Ben. He'll be interested in the latest development."

Katie picked up her cell phone and stepped from the room. Ben answered on the first ring and Katie filled him in on the interviews with Mick Wilson and Grace Garfield as well as Jessie's medical progress. Katie was well aware that discussing the case with non-enforcement personnel was generally against the rules but Ben was a good sounding-board and would never reveal confidential information to anyone else. Ben agreed that Mick Wilson was the best suspect for the moment but that Grace Garfield still wasn't above suspicion. He cautioned Katie against getting her hopes up about Jessie's possible improvement. He explained to Katie that even if Jessie regained full consciousness she might suffer from amnesia or other memory problems. He also warned Katie that it was equally possible that Jessie could relapse.

"You're such an optimist!" Katie exclaimed sarcastically.

"I can't help it. I work in the medical field," Ben defended himself. "Sometimes when you're too optimistic, you just end up heartbroken."

"Optimism works the other way, too, you know," Katie countered. "Sometimes being optimistic can actually will something good to happen."

"I'll keep that in mind," Ben said. "You think that will help my personal life, too?"

"Didn't know you needed any help in that area. Care to elaborate?" Katie laughed.

"Well, there is this one girl but I think she just wants to be friends," Ben replied somewhat soberly.

"Do I know her?" Katie asked, half curious, half afraid of the answer.

"Very well, as a matter of fact," Ben answered, then abruptly asked Katie to hang on while he took another call. When he came back on the line a minute later, he told Katie he needed to hang up so Katie said goodbye.

Katie was now frustrated. She wondered who this "girl" could be. Supposedly, she knew her "very well". "That's all I need," Katie said out loud. Then she began to chide herself. After all, she had dated other men occasionally in the last two years. She'd just been out to dinner with Cade Ware two nights ago. *What business was it of hers if Ben was interested in dating someone? He had every right.* Self-reproach aside, Katie still felt an empty feeling of loss when she considered the fact that Ben might have an interest in a relationship with another woman. Katie took a few deep breaths and shook her hands out as if she was preparing to free-lift a heavy barbell. She knew she needed to shake off her emotion so she could concentrate on the case at hand. In a few minutes she felt calmer and went back into the station house

Anna was sitting at a desk, typing up the notes from the two interviews. She finished up quickly and printed them out.

"Looks like we have about an hour before we need to be at the cul-de-sac to interview our other suspects again," Anna said tapping her watch. "What do you want to do until then?"

"Honestly, I feel like taking a ride. Interested?" Katie answered.

"Why not? You can never have too much police presence," Anna shrugged.

Katie and Anna climbed aboard one of the police golf cart units and took off in the direction of Fairway. Katie had decided to show Anna where Alex Watson lived since he was a witness of sorts in the case. As they drove through the tree-lined streets, Katie described her previous visit with Alex, detailing the amazing ingenuity of Alex's "inventions" and "innovations". Anna was as equally intrigued as Katie had been and suggested they stop at Alex's house and see if he was at home. Anna was anxious to see Alex's machinations for herself.

Katie stopped the golf cart in front of the Watson residence and rang the bell. When no one answered after a few minutes, she led Anna around back to the garage-turned-Neo-Victorian paradisio. Katie turned the old-fashioned key bell and could hear the distant sound of church bells inside the building. Alex did not come to the door and so Katie and Anna cupped their hands and peered through the small windows of the carriage-style doors into the interior. An object, mostly covered by a tarp, caught Katie's attention. It appeared to have the shape of a golf cart but certain contours and protrusions under the tarp interrupted the regular lines of such a vehicle. The object had not been there when she'd interviewed Alex on Sunday.

It was obvious that Alex was not inside, so, disappointed, Katie and Anna climbed back on the golf cart and headed back downtown. Katie wondered about the strange vehicle—she was sure it was some sort of vehicle—she had seen in Alex's workshop. Something niggled at the back of her mind about it. She was sure it was another of Alex's adaptations and Katie was extremely curious about just what it was. His alternate universe intrigued her with its fantastical possibilities and practical aesthetics. Katie knew it was an appeal to her artistic and creative character, a side of her that she'd had few opportunities to explore in the past four years since she'd become a police officer. If the opportunity to create color schemes for Cade's houses and paint murals on every dining room wall had awakened her mostly dormant passion for art, her introduction to Alex's world had only served to make that passion burn hotter. Katie had gone to sleep the last few nights devising her own "steampunk" machines and machinations in vivid detail in her mind.

When Anna entered the cul-de-sac she asked, "Who first?"

"How about Aster Bancroft? I'd like to catch her before she leaves for work," Katie suggested.

"I was thinking the same thing," Anna replied as she guided the golf cart into the driveway of Aster Bancroft's house.

# CHAPTER 27

**Aster had just** finished touching up her make-up when the door bell sounded. She walked into the upstairs foyer and looked through the window. *The police again,* Aster thought with an audible groan. Adjusting her top and skirt, Aster slipped her feet into her house moccasins and made her way downstairs.

"We're sorry to bother you again, Miss Bancroft, but we've made some new discoveries in the case of Jessie Ashton and we need to ask you a few more questions."

"What new discoveries?" Aster inquired, genuinely interested.

"We've learned that Jessie Ashton was poisoned. We've also lifted a number of fingerprints from her house."

Aster studied the two police officers. They hadn't brought a fingerprint kit with them so they probably didn't have fingerprint analysis back yet. It was obvious, though, that she was on their list as a person of interest. Despite her chagrin at being considered a suspect, Aster was interested in knowing exactly how these two officers were connecting her to Jessie Ashton.

"You told us last time we interviewed you that you were at the Ashtons' house about a month or so ago for a cul-de-sac supper and that guests had to use the upstairs hall bath. Did you go upstairs to use the bathroom during the evening?"

Now Aster got the connection. If she had gone upstairs to use the bathroom, she might have explored a bit and she might have left some fingerprints somewhere.

"I believe I did," Aster replied. *Why not admit to it?* Aster thought. *In case they do find my prints somewhere.*

"Did you enter any other rooms upstairs?"

"I may have peeked into a room if the door was open," Aster answered.

"Maybe you *peeked* in Jessie Ashton's room?"

"Maybe," Aster said. Aster knew being non-committal made her less suspicious. *What if they found her fingerprints somewhere besides the bathroom? Admitting it was a possibility rather than flat-out denial made her look less guilty of whatever crime they were suggesting she might have been suspected of committing. If nothing else.*

"Would you be surprised if we found your fingerprints in Jessie Ashton's room?"

Aster remained calm. She was sure they didn't know whose fingerprints they'd found yet. They would have already asked to fingerprint her. "Did you?" Aster said trying not to sound cocky.

"We haven't gotten the results back yet but we should know something by tomorrow."

Aster was a little surprised that the officers were showing their hands. She wouldn't have admitted to having nothing yet if she were them. Aster looked at the clock on the mantelpiece. She needed to leave soon.

"I have to go to work," Aster said.

"Then we won't keep you much longer. Just a few more questions."

Aster shifted in her chair and nodded, smoothing her skirt down and re-crossing her legs.

"Do you know why anyone would accuse you of being deceitful?'

Aster was surprised at the question. She was sure she had covered all her tracks. She was always so careful. "I wasn't aware that someone had accused me of that," Aster said, buying time.

"We have a document that we believe does just that."

"A document that says I am deceitful?" Aster questioned.

"Something to that effect. What could that be referring to, Miss Bancroft?"

"I have no idea," Aster replied shrugging. *Did they really expect her to confess all her sins?*

"I'm sure you do. I'm also sure that you're going to continue to deny whatever it is."

Aster didn't reply, silently listing her recent deceptions in her mind. One of the officers stood up and walked around the room as if making an inspection.

"Houses in this neighborhood start at about a half

million dollars. How does someone on a waitress' pay afford it?"

Aster wondered why they hadn't asked her that before. She already had her story ready, rehearsed and believable.

"I make really good tips," Aster quipped, unable to resist, then explained, "Actually, the owners of the house bought it at a foreclosure auction for about half its value. It's my understanding they plan to retire here in about five years and so it's just an investment for them. I lease it through an agency and got it for a reduced rent in exchange for keeping up all maintenance on it at my own expense."

The police officers had grinned at Aster's joke. They asked for the name and phone number of the agency that had rented the house to Aster. Aster went to the desk in the hall to retrieve the information, which the dark-haired officer copied into her notebook.

"You won't mind if we call your rental agency to confirm your story?"

"Not at all," Aster said knowing her story would check out.

"We may need to come back and take your fingerprints. Do you have any objection to that?"

"No," Aster replied, knowing she'd have to avoid it if at all possible.

"Have you ever been fingerprinted? Maybe under another name?"

Aster hated lying to the two officers but it was necessary. "No," Aster replied.

"We'll need your social security number to confirm that."

Aster recited the number to them without hesitation. The dark-haired officer wrote it down, repeating it back to Aster.

"Thank you for your cooperation. We'll let you get to work now."

Aster stood up to show the officers out.

"Almost forgot. What is your regular work schedule?"

"I usually have to be at work at 6:00pm. I get off

anywhere from two to four in the morning depending on the day and when all the customers go home," Aster replied. "The days vary from week to week."

Aster shut the door and watched through the sidelites as the officers backed out of her driveway. She looked at her watch and rushed upstairs to finish getting ready for work. She didn't have time right now to ponder the implications of the turn of events regarding Jessie Ashton.

# CHAPTER 28

**Ping had gotten** off work a little late and was still in his car when the two police officers pulled up behind him. He noticed Casey Bailey standing in her dining room window watching. He looked in his rear view mirror and saw that the police officers were walking toward his car. Ping was too tired to stand up; he'd been bending over garden beds all day and his back and legs were sore and achy. The two officers greeted him and seemed content to stand in front of him while he remained in the car, his door ajar.

"We've had some new developments concerning Jessie Ashton. We'd like to ask you a few more questions if we may."

Ping shrugged and held out his hands.

"Jessie Ashton was poisoned. We thought you'd be interested in what was used."

Ping shrugged again.

"Toxins from azaleas and daffodils."

Ping could tell they were gauging his reaction. Ping stared at them blankly for a moment.

"Do you know how someone could extract those poisons?"

Ping knew that they thought he would know since he worked with plants as a profession.

"If it were me, I would try grinding up the poisonous parts of the plants."

"And how would you create a liquid to inject?"

Ping shrugged. He felt very defeated today and at the moment could care less if they thought he was involved with poisoning Jessie Ashton. "Maybe make a tea out of them. You know, put the ground up plant material into boiling water, then strain it through cheesecloth."

"That's interesting information. Have you ever done that with plant material?"

"I've made tea from several types of plants. To drink. I've never tried to make poison before," Ping said, annoyed at their obviousness.

"We've also lifted several fingerprints from Jessie Ashton's bedroom suite. Would there be any reason any of them would be yours?"

Ping sighed. "Could be."

The two officers looked at each other with raised brows. "Why is that?"

"When I designed the landscape for the Ashton's I did go out on the balcony of Jessie's room to get an idea of the aerial view of the gardens. So I may have touched the handle to the balcony door," Ping replied, then added, "Ellen Ashton was with me when I was in Jessie's room."

"Ms. Ashton will be able to confirm this?"

"Well, it was a year ago," Ping replied, raising his hands with palms up.

"Did you steal anything from the Ashtons when you were working on their landscaping?"

"What?" Ping cried. He'd been taken off guard.

"We have a document that implies that you are a thief."

"What document?" Ping demanded.

"We really can't elaborate. Would there be any validity to that claim?"

Despite his feelings of despair, Ping's reflex to defend himself ignited. "I am not a thief!" Ping asserted. "And if I was, I certainly wouldn't steal from my neighbor."

"Why not?"

Ping just shook his head without answering. He was a thief but not the kind they were looking for. *There, he had admitted the awful truth.*

"Will you willingly submit to fingerprinting?"

Ping nodded. He just wanted the interview to be over so he could go in and get a hot shower. He didn't look forward to his empty house but he figured he'd fall asleep from exhaustion soon enough and wouldn't have to endure the loneliness for very long.

"Well, Mr. Ping, we may be back. We should have the results of the fingerprint analysis sometime tomorrow."

Although he was angry at the officers for their cruel insinuations, Ping stood and shook hands with both officers before they walked back toward their golf cart and he moved slowly in the opposite direction toward his front door.

# CHAPTER 29

**Casey watched the** police officers as they talked with Ping. She was too far away to even attempt to read their lips but she suspected something significant had happened with Jessie. After they left Ping's, they pulled their golf cart into her driveway and walked up to the house. Almost on automatic pilot—that's the way she lived most of her life these days—Casey moved from the window to the front door, opening it before the officers could ring the doorbell.

"I assume there's been some development in the case," Casey said, her arms crossed across her chest. She was standing in the doorway and had not made any move to ask the police officers into the house.

"Yes. Jessie Ashton was poisoned."

Casey raised her eyebrow and eyed the police officers. "How do you know?"

"We have a toxicology report that confirms it."

"May I ask what she was poisoned with?" Casey said, changing her stance, jutting her hip to one side.

"Toxic—potentially fatal—substances from plants. Azaleas and daffodils to be exact."

Casey felt her stomach flip and the pang stayed behind. It was obvious now why they were questioning Ping. A feeling like fear washed over Casey and she hoped it didn't show on her face. Instinctively, Casey felt compelled to defend Ping but she wasn't sure how to do that without throwing suspicion on herself. Uselessly, she remarked, "I don't understand why anyone would want to hurt Jessie."

"That's exactly what we're trying to figure out. When will your husband be home, ma'am?"

"He always works late on Tuesdays. Just like Thursdays. He'll be home around 8:45," Casey answered. "Why?"

"We would like to ask him some questions. When is a good time to talk to him?"

"He's usually home on Friday evening unless we go out together," Casey replied, flippantly.

"It appears that your husband doesn't spend much

time at home. Is there a particular reason for that?"

"He's works hard and has several hobbies," Casey threw out, inspecting her fingernails.

"You seem a little bitter about that."

"I'm not bitter," Casey lied.

"Ms. Bailey, do you think your husband is having an affair?"

Casey couldn't control the spontaneous noise that escaped from her throat. *As if!* "No, I don't," Casey said, half-chuckling.

"Why not?"

*Were these officers serious?* Casey struggled to keep from laughing out loud. "My husband just wouldn't."

"And you are sure of this?"

"Absolutely," Casey said with resolute confidence.

"Are you the one having an affair, then?"

Casey looked incredulously at the officers. She wondered what evidence they might have that would lead them to that question. They'd implied the same thing just a few days ago. "It appears that you think either me or my husband are having some sort of illicit relationship. Why?"

"We have a document that seems to indicate that."

"What document?" Casey asked insistently.

"We can't reveal that."

Casey could feel her body shaking but when she looked down at her hands, they remained still. *Damn that Jessie!* Casey thought. "What does Jessie being poisoned have to do with whether or not one of us is having an affair?" Casey asked, feeling indignant.

"We believe the document we have may be connected to the poisoning."

Casey connected the dots. "And this document, does it indicate anything else besides the possibility that my husband or I might be having some sort of affair?"

"In fact, it does. We're following up on all leads."

Casey wondered what other "leads" they had gleaned from this mysterious document.

"We may need to take your fingerprints later. Your

husband's, too."

Casey nodded her assent. *She really couldn't refuse without looking suspicious, could she?*

After the police officers left, Casey paced around her house for a while. She wandered aimlessly from room to room, upstairs and down. She'd laughed at the notion of Ted having a lover but now she wasn't so sure. She began to question his deliberate weekly routine. *Was he really working late on Tuesday and Thursday? Did he actually go bowling on Mondays and golfing with his buddies on Wednesdays and Saturdays? And Sundays...was he really visiting the sick and shut-in?* Casey didn't know any of those things for sure. She didn't like to bowl or golf and on Sunday, she liked to stay in pursuing nothing. She used to spend Sundays with her son, doing whatever he wanted to do, but nowadays he spent very little time at home and even less time with her. She'd never checked up on Ted when he said he was working late. She trusted him. She'd never had any reason not to. But now...now a seed had been planted and Casey was fertilizing it and watering it and letting it grow. Casey tried to rationalize that her sudden suspicions were just a product of her own guilt but it was futile. That seed had a stalk and leaves and buds and Casey was suddenly burning to find out if indeed her husband was having an affair like the officers had suggested. Like some document they had insinuated.

Casey dialed Ted's cell phone..

"The police came to the house again," Casey said.

"What for?" Ted asked..

"They now have evidence that someone tried to poison Jessie," Casey answered.

"And..."Ted said.

"They had more questions. But I couldn't really offer them much help," Casey replied then took a deep breath, knowing her next sentence was going hit Ted like a ton of bricks. "They also asked if one of us was having an affair."

"Why would they ask such a ridiculous question?" Ted roared.

"Apparently, they have some document," Casey

answered.

She hung up a few minutes later still wondering whether or not Ted was indeed involved with someone else.

# CHAPTER 30

"**So what do** you think now?" Anna asked as she maneuvered the golf cart through New Town.

"I think everybody in that cul-de-sac is guilty of something. Maybe not poisoning Jessie Ashton, but *something*," Katie replied

Anna grinned. "I agree. Casey Bailey is a piece of work, huh?"

"Tell me about it. And somebody in that house is cheating. That much was obvious," Katie replied.

"Aster Bancroft was certainly a very cool customer," Anna remarked.

"Almost too cool, if you ask me. I still get the feeling she's playing a role, putting on a show. She seemed to anticipate our questions and have an answer or reaction ready, practiced," Katie concurred.

"She's definitely being deceptive. I just wish we could figure out what it's all about," Anna mused, pushing her thick curls behind her right ear.

"Despite the fact that Jessie's notes in her notebook seem to be spot-on, I'm not convinced that Aster Bancroft or the Baileys have the know-how to make a poison cocktail out of plants," Katie asserted.

"Well, we didn't have a clue about Mick Wilson so you never know," Anna replied waving her hand.

"True," Katie nodded. "Danny Ping's a good candidate. He didn't hesitate when we asked him how to make poison from azaleas and daffodil bulbs."

"He was talking tea, not poison. Besides, if he did the poisoning, do you think he'd so readily admit to knowing how?" Anna countered.

"I know you're in love with his gardens but that's no reason to leave him off the list," Katie teased, laughing lightly. "Besides, if he is the villain, maybe he was being cooperative to try and throw us off. You know, making it so easy to suspect him that we think it's too easy and so we don't."

"There is that," Anna conceded. "What do you think he stole? Plants?"

"There are a lot of plants. Thousands of dollars-worth, I'm sure. But I don't think taking some plants is worth killing over," Katie replied.

"Make up your mind, Miss Wishy-Washy," Anna exclaimed. "Is he a suspect or not?"

"I still consider him a suspect. He does have the know-how to make the poison," Katie confirmed.

"Well, if I had to pick one right now, my money would be on Mick Wilson," Anna said.

"He's probably just creepy enough but we don't have much evidence other than his degree in bio-chemistry," Katie replied.

"Unless his fingerprints come back," Anna reminded Katie.

"That still won't make it open-and-shut. Unfortunately, all of our suspects, including Mick Wilson, could have left fingerprints in Jessie's room and be perfectly innocent of everything except curiosity," Katie said as they pulled up to the station.

After typing up notes on the interviews and placing paper copies in Jessie's file, Katie and Anna headed home in opposite directions. As Katie whizzed along she realized that she was both hungry and tired. Usually, after a day of writing a few parking tickets and patrolling the neighborhoods, she felt more like a couch potato than someone who had just finished a triathlon. Katie's mind was spinning and she felt as if she was putting together a jigsaw puzzle, trying to fit all of the evidence together in a coherent way. It seemed to her that some of the puzzle pieces were missing or maybe she was just overlooking them. Katie hoped that the fingerprint evidence she received the next day would give them some strong leads and help fill in the empty spaces.

As Katie pulled into the driveway, Ogilvie came flying around the house, barking and bouncing wildly. Katie knew that she had been neglecting him since getting involved with the Jessie Ashton case and couldn't bring herself to scold him when he jumped up on her, tail wagging furiously. Despite the growling of her stomach and her fatigue, as soon as Katie had changed out of her uniform into shorts and a sweatshirt, she clipped Ogilvie's leash on and took him down to the beach. The water lapped the beach with gentle waves and as soon as Katie unhooked his tether, Ogilvie rushed into the water, swimming in circles. Bounding out, Ogilvie shook glistening, cold droplets all over Katie then crouched down, back end high in the air, begging to be chased. Too worn out to comply, Katie found a small piece of driftwood and threw it for Ogilvie to fetch.

"Hey, I was hoping I'd find you down here," Ben's familiar voice called out.

Katie turned around to find Ben, barefoot, sauntering toward her on the beach. For a moment, Katie was swept away by his rugged good looks and the sexy smile on his face. She noticed that he hadn't shaved in a day or two and the scruff on his face gave him a movie-star kind of appeal. Ben was wearing faded blue jeans and his retro western shirt was half unbuttoned. *All he needs is a cowboy hat*, Katie thought. For a moment, Katie felt like she was watching a Levis ad come to life.

"I knew I was being stalked," Katie replied lightly, pulling herself out of the slight fog of romantic folly.

"Better call the police," Ben warned with a grin as he grabbed Katie in a bear hug and pretended to accost her.

Katie felt the familiar tingle at Ben's touch and relished the warmth of his arms around her. Too soon, Ben released her as Ogilvie barked excitedly, dropping his stick at Ben's feet. Ben picked up the stick, throwing it into the water, laughing, "Great security system you have there." Ogilvie dashed into the river, searching for his toy. Within a few seconds he had retrieved it and flopped down on the sand to chew it.

"To what do I owe the honor of your presence?" Katie asked, bending down to pet an exhausted Ogilvie.

"I happened to be in the neighborhood?" Ben replied with a sultry grin.

"Methinks the gentleman speaks an untruth," Katie challenged, her eyes gleaming.

"My lady, you wound me deeply!" Ben cried in

mock horror, pressing his hands to his heart dramatically.

"Perchance the gentleman should speak an honest word," Katie continued with a quick curtsy, looking up at Ben through her lashes and fighting the impulse to laugh.

"Alas, the lady has won the game," Ben said hanging his head and bowing deeply. Katie could no longer suppress a wide smile and neither could Ben who grinned broadly. "I actually do have an agenda but that doesn't mean I wouldn't stop by without one."

Kate looked at Ben quizzically, waiting for him to explain. Ben sank down onto the beach and Katie followed suit so that they were both sitting beside Ogilvie, looking out at the river.

"What do you know about Cade Ware?" Ben asked, his hands laced around his drawn-up knees.

"What do you mean?" Katie queried, surprised by Ben's question.

"How well do you know him?" Ben replied, turning to look at Katie.

"Not well. I stop by the bungalow court he's restoring once in a while when I'm on patrol to see his progress so we've become acquainted. And he recently asked me my opinion about the exterior color schemes for the bungalows. He also asked me to paint murals in the dining rooms of the houses but I haven't started on anything. Why?" Katie answered.

"You left something out," Ben said, looking out at the river again. "You had dinner with him Sunday night."

"Are you spying on me?" Katie asked, half joking.

"I don't have to. You know that," Ben replied, referring to the fact that practically everyone in Potoma knew him and his family.

"OK, but why are you concerned about it?" Katie inquired, feeling a little annoyed.

"Did you know that he's bought up quite a few of the old houses over in Riverside and several in Riverview?" Ben answered.

"No. So what? He's interested in preserving the architecture of the town," Katie said, feeling defensive.

"Maybe," Ben replied. "Are you aware that he's planning to rent out the bungalows?"

"Yes. We talked about it at dinner the other night," Katie confirmed.

"Did he happen to mention how much he was going to be renting them for?"

"No. I don't think so," Katie answered, thinking back to the quarrel that occurred over his seeming biases toward particular types of tenants.

"Katie, those bungalows were built as affordable housing for the people who provided services for Potoma. Although Potoma was originally a playground for the rich it hasn't been that way for a hundred years. The income level of most of those who live in Riverside and Riverview, too, is middle class. The rents that are going to be demanded by Ware are going to make affordable housing in those areas obsolete. With Fairway and New Town housing prices way above most of those in the older neighborhoods, a lot of desirable residents are going to be squeezed out because they aren't going to be able to afford to live here anymore," Ben explained.

"The families that live in the big houses on Riverside Drive are definitely not middle-class. I know most of those houses went for upwards of six or seven hundred thousand and a couple of them sold recently for more than a million," Katie countered. In a way, she resented the fact that she would probably never make enough money in her lifetime to ever buy one of her beloved riverside Victorians.

"But those houses are the exception and anyway, most of those homes have been passed down from generation to generation. Only about twenty percent of them have ever been sold out of the family that built them or acquired them at the turn of the century," Ben argued.

"What's your point?" Katie asked

"If Ware keeps buying up real estate in Potoma, pretty soon he'll own and control a good chunk of the town," Ben surmised.

"And you assume that he will either rent or sell that real estate for exorbitant prices?" Katie replied.

"Exactly," Ben said.

"Well, he'd have to find a way to attract people who are willing to pay that much. Potoma is not exactly close to any major cities," Katie mused.

"It's close enough for those who live in Fairway and New Town. And it's close enough for the weekenders who already own property here," Ben contended.

"You might also notice that a lot of the property in those areas has frequent turnover," Katie reasoned.

"Doesn't matter about turnover. With such high rents and sales prices, middle class residents will be priced out of the market quickly," Ben disputed. "And not just residents but tourists, too. We have always been the affordable alternative for middle-class and even lower income families for vacations. As soon as real estate prices start to climb so will the prices at restaurants, boutiques, all the beach vendors."

"I understand your concern but there's no way to prevent Cade from buying property. If he has the financing, he has every right. And I don't think there's any law that prevents him from charging whatever he wants to for rent or if he sells his property," Katie said, reaching over to rub Ogilvie's nose.

"Do you really want to be involved with someone who could literally force you out of Potoma because you can no longer afford to live here?" Ben said, looking at Katie, an unreadable expression in his eyes.

"Well, that's not fair," Katie said, now scratching Ogilvie's ears. "And I wouldn't say I'm "involved" with him. We had one dinner together, not some full-blown passionate affair."

"But you did agree to help him with the bungalows..." Ben said.

"I agreed to paint murals. How could I turn down the opportunity to do something I really love?" Katie replied, her eyes pleading with Ben for understanding.

"You couldn't," Ben answered, a soft look in his eyes. He squeezed Katie's hand briefly, then stood up. After he had helped Katie up and she had clipped the leash onto Ogilvie's collar, Ben and Katie walked off the beach and up the street to Katie's house.

Ben took a seat on Katie's sofa while she went into the kitchen to get some sodas out of the refrigerator along with a bag of corn chips and dip. Plopping down beside him, after handing him a can, Katie asked Ben, "Do you have a plan for stopping Cade from taking over Potoma?"

"Unfortunately, you're right. If he wants to buy and someone is willing to sell to him, there's nothing anyone can do," Ben replied shaking his head slowly. "All I can do is make people aware of what the consequences could be."

"Have you thought about the other side of the coin?" Katie suggested munching on chips. "He could be doing cheap vinyl siding makeovers and asking low rents thus drastically reducing the property values in Potoma. That could be a much worse scenario."

"Very true but I'd rather my property be valued at less than be forced to sell and move away because of astronomical mark-ups on everything from groceries to business taxes to town services," Ben remarked.

"Well, if Cade has his way, I should get a pretty good pay raise," Katie teased.

"You might have a lot more than parking tickets and trespassing citations to deal with, too," Ben answered ruefully. "Where wealth is conspicuous, opportunity for crime is that much more enticing."

Katie nodded in agreement. "Well, if I solve this Jessie Ashton case, at least I'll finally have some solid practice in real crime. I never imagined I'd be investigating a case of attempted murder when I took this job."

"Me, neither. I thought being a police officer in Potoma would be fairly safe and I wouldn't have to worry about you coming home at night," Ben replied. Katie was dying to ask Ben what connotation his statement might have but she kept silent. He couldn't possibly mean what it sounded like he did. After all, he was interested in pursuing a relationship with some mystery woman.

"By the way, anything new on that?" Ben said interrupting her thoughts, reaching for dip.

"We have two good suspects. At least they both have the knowledge to concoct a poison out of plants. I'm hoping that when the fingerprint IDs come back tomorrow we'll get some direction," Katie reported.

"I don't suppose Jessie Ashton has fully regained consciousness yet?" Ben inquired.

"Not that I've heard. We were assured by the doctor that the police would be informed if and when she did," Katie replied.

Katie was sure she had proof of ESP when her cell phone rang thirty seconds later and the police officer on the other end informed her that the hospital had called to report that Jessie Ashton was awake and lucid. Katie quickly apprised Ben of the news, then called Anna. They agreed to meet at the hospital immediately. With a word of caution about lowering her expectations as to what Jessie might remember or be able to tell them, Ben bade Katie a quick goodbye and left on his golf cart. Katie climbed into her Jeep and hastily headed toward the hospital.

# CHAPTER 31

**Katie and Anna** arrived in the hospital parking lot simultaneously and walked in together. Jessie's hospital room was filled to capacity with family and friends, all talking excitedly as Jessie, looking slightly bewildered and sitting up in bed, smiled at them all. When Justin Ashton saw the police officers standing in the door, he quickly quieted the crowd and ushered them out.

"Hi, Jessie. I'm Officer Bell and this Officer Madrid," Katie said as she moved to the side of Jessie's hospital bed. "I know you're probably still trying to comprehend everything but we really need to ask you some questions about what happened to you."

Jessie nodded with a sweet smile.

"Has anyone told you anything about how you got here?" Katie asked.

"My parents told me that they found me unconscious on my bed Friday morning and called the ambulance," Jessie replied.

"We haven't told her anything else," Ellen Ashton quickly added.

Katie nodded at her then continued questioning Jessie. "Do you remember what happened?"

"It's a little foggy. I remember I had turned out my light and I think I had just fallen asleep when a noise woke me up. It sounded like a door creaking, like when you open it real slow," Jessie replied. "I saw someone come in but I thought it was just Veronica. Sometimes she sneaks in at night and crawls into my bed when she's had a bad dream. But then I remembered that Veronica was at her friend's house so then I figured it must be mom or dad so I just laid there and watched them come in the room. I guess I was just watching them to figure out which parent it was. I supposed they thought I was asleep and were trying to be quiet and not wake me up. I was wondering why mom or dad was in my room, not in a bad way or anything, you know, just watching to see why they were there. I remember the person just kind of stood there for a few moments but I assumed they were just trying to adjust their eyes to the darkness so they didn't run into furniture or whatever. Then the person started coming over to my bed and I realized it didn't look like mom or dad. I mean I couldn't see their face but just something about them, like the way they walked and their shape didn't look like either of my parents. So then I started getting a scared feeling in my stomach. At first I was too scared to move but the person kept coming toward me so I tried to get out of the bed. I sort of got up but the person grabbed me and put something over my face. I was fighting with the person and pulling at their clothes and they let go of me. So I tried to crawl over my bed away from the person but they grabbed me and put their hand over my face again and pushed me down on the bed and I felt like I was suffocating. I don't remember anything after that."

"That's really good, Jessie," Katie encouraged. "Can you remember what the person was wearing?"

"I don't know. Dark clothes I think," Jessie answered.

"Great," Katie said. "Can you describe the person's height or maybe how thin or fat they were?"

"Taller than my mom or dad. Not fat," Jessie said after closing her eyes for a moment.

"Could you tell if it was a man or woman?" Anna inserted.

"I don't know," Jessie replied, grimacing.

"That's OK," Katie consoled, patting Jessie's hand. When Katie glanced at Jessie's parents, she noticed the pain showing on their faces.

"Did the person say anything?" Anna prodded.

"They whispered *I'm sorry, you saw too much* to me just before I passed out," Jessie said, nodding. "I'll never forget that."

"Do you have any idea what they meant by *you saw too much*?" Katie asked.

"No," Jessie replied, shaking her head.

Katie exchanged a quizzical look with Anna, then looked over at Justin and Ellen Ashton. Justin Ashton nodded his assent.

"Jessie, we found a notebook under your mattress. In

it you had made a list of God's Laws with some abbreviated notations. Your friends looked at that particular page and suggested that it was part of a Sunday School assignment. Do you remember the item to which I am referring?" Katie began.

Jessie nodded.

"Will you tell me what the notations meant?" Katie continued.

"They referred to my neighbors," Jessie replied.

Katie smiled, flashing a triumphant look at Anna. "That's what we thought. Do you think the person that came into your bedroom was one of your neighbors?"

A horrified look crossed Jessie's face and she covered her face with her hands. Looking back up and smoothing her hair back behind her ears she said, "Do you?"

"It's possible," Katie admitted. "Maybe one of them knew you were watching them. Maybe saw you write something in your notebook?"

"I wrote everything in my notebook at my desk in my room. I didn't carry it around or anything," Jessie explained.

Just as Katie opened her mouth to continue her line of questioning, the doctor, followed by several interns and a nurse, entered the room.

"I'm going to have to ask you to leave, Officers. I need to examine Miss Ashton and run some tests. And she's had enough excitement for today," the doctor announced. "She really needs to rest, now."

"Understood," Katie nodded. "When can we return to finish our investigation?"

"Soonest would be tomorrow morning," the doctor instructed then added "I'm sorry but it's really very necessary for us to run the tests now."

Frustrated that she wasn't able to complete the interview, Katie nevertheless pasted on a gracious smile and shook hands with the Ashtons and Jessie. Anna followed suit and they both exited Jessie's room.

# CHAPTER 32

**Aster looked into** the dirty, cracked mirror, checking her make-up. Tonight was the night and she had to look perfect. The cut on her chest had finally begun to heal and for once it didn't sting when she touched it. After straightening her tight purple leather skirt so that the slit on one side opened at the right angle, Aster pushed through the door and stepped out into the hall.

When Aster walked back into the bar, she scanned the room, finding the man she was seeking sitting at a table in a dark corner, shoveling pasta into his mouth. Several other men sat at the table as well, all of them busy with heaped platters of food. Aster asked the bartender for beers which she balanced expertly on a tray and lifted above her shoulder.

"On the house, boys," Aster said huskily as she served the men their frothy mugs. Aster made sure that she showed just enough leg to pique their interest and remain in their thick-headed memories.

"Thanks, sweetie," the pasta shoveler said, leering at Aster. "Does that include you, too?"

"No, big boy, I'm extra," Aster teased. "And I'm expensive."

"I'm sure you're worth every penny, baby," Pasta Shoveler replied, giving Aster the once-over. "Come back when I'm finished eating and we'll make a deal."

Aster gave him a sultry smile and another healthy portion of thigh before turning and walking back to the bar, gyrating her hips in what she hoped was a highly erotic way. At the bar, Aster looked back toward the table, satisfied she'd hooked the man she was after when she saw that he was still staring after her.

Aster kept an eye on the table as she went about her business serving drinks, wiping tables and making deposits into the cash register. When she was sure her man was finished with his plate she waited a few more minutes, then sashayed over to the table.

"Can I get you anything else?" Aster purred.

"Right now, another beer. When I'm finished with that

…well…let's just say I'm still interested in making a deal," the man said.

"Sure thing, big guy. Coming right up," Aster replied. A minute later, Aster returned to the table with the beer. She noticed that her man's companions had scattered and he was now sitting alone. As Aster casually scanned the room, she noticed that the men who had been eating with her man were now stationed at various places along the bar and wall, surreptitiously eyeing them.

"Have a seat, sweetie," the man said, sweeping his hand toward the chair to his right.

"Sorry, baby. I'm on the clock right now," Aster said, cocking her leg out to expose as much thigh as possible.

"When do you get off, then?" the man asked.

"Another hour. What you got in mind, baby?" Aster said coyly.

"How'd you like to spend the night in a mansion?" the man offered.

"Ooh, sounds exciting! You got a mansion, big guy?" Aster squealed.

"A big one. Thirty-four rooms," the man said proudly.

"That is big, baby. You gonna show me all thirty-four rooms if I come home with you?" Aster replied, bending down with both hands on the table.

"You got it, sweetie. You like swimming pools and hot tubs?" the man asked ogling Aster's chest.

"Oh, I love water. Especially hot water," Aster said, putting on her best dumb-blonde act.

"I'll definitely get you into some hot water, sweetie," the man replied, tiny sweat beads forming on his forehead.

"I can't wait," Aster breathed as she quickly turned, grinding her hips hard as she walked away.

Aster passed the bar and turned down the hallway, slipping into an office where several men and women were seated at a table. On the table was electronic equipment and a couple of computers.

"Good job. We got it," a woman with long blond hair complimented.

"I had no idea what a good actor you were," a skinny balding man quipped. "You're so good, I wanted to take you home myself."

Aster shook her head grinning. "I'm sure your wife and mother-in-law would be excited about that."

"Given a choice between you and Don here, the wife and mother-in-law would probably be jumping for joy," the fat man sitting beside the blond woman remarked.

"So we've got one hour. This is it," the blond woman said. "You ready for this to be over?"

"So ready!" Aster sighed.

"Not enjoying the life of a sleazy waitress?" Baldy teased good-naturedly.

"I don't mind the sleazy part. But my feet are killing me," Aster grinned, pulling one of her four-inch heels off and massaging her toes.

An hour later, Aster followed the Pasta Shoveler named Bobbo, out to a black Jaguar and climbed in beside him. Bobbo's entourage followed behind in a black Cadillac SUV. Within ten minutes, the Jaguar was pulling through tall iron gates, rolling down an allee, the tall trees like looming warriors in the early dawn light. During the ride, Bobbo had surprisingly been a gentleman, keeping his hands to himself. The car came to a stop in front of a brick monstrosity that had very little style and was, in Aster's opinion, one of the ugliest houses she'd ever seen. *Pseudo mediterranean spanish french gargantuan crap,* Aster thought.

As Aster walked slowly from the car to the front door, she pretended awe as she looked everywhere, mentally taking pictures of everything she saw. Bobbo, somewhat inebriated, chattered incessantly as he had done in the car. His entourage had pulled up behind them but none of the men followed Bobbo and Aster inside.

Aster took out her cell phone. "Can I take pictures? Your house is fabulous, baby!"

Before Bobbo could answer, Aster swung the camera around and clicked off several frames. She was sure to include the front door, entrances to several rooms off the front foyer and the double staircase that swept up each side of the foyer wall, meeting at a landing in the center. Unknown to Bobbo, Aster also hit a button on the phone to send the pictures to the group at the bar.

"You can take all the pictures you like in my bedroom, sweetie. I even got a video camera if you want," Bobbo replied swaying slightly and grabbing Aster around her waist.

"Ooh, a video camera. That's sexy, baby," Aster cooed. "But show me around first. I never been in such a big house before."

"No problem, sweetie. Look around all you want," Bobbo said. "I'm gonna get a drink. You want one?"

"You got stuff for a martini?" Aster asked as she followed Bobbo into an expansive living room separated by thick fluted marble columns from an equally large dining room. Bobbo walked to the far wall to a cherry wood bar and slipped in behind it. Aster continued to take pictures.

"Bobbo baby, where's the little girls' room?" Aster asked as she surveyed the living and dining rooms.

"Go back out in the hall and through the arch under the stairs," Bobbo directed as he pulled down glasses from a rack.

Aster gave Bobbo a seductive smile and walked provocatively out of the room. Aster quickly found the powder room and texted the group at the bar to confirm that they were receiving the pictures she was transferring to them. Aster looked into the mirror to check her make-up and hair and seeing that all was in place she quickly went back to the living room where Bobbo was still standing behind the bar, downing his drink.

"Got your martini all ready for you, sweetie," Bobbo announced with a slur as Aster entered the room.

"Oh, thank you, baby. You gonna show me around now?" Aster stalled, picking up the drink and pretending to take a sip.

"I'm a little too wobbly to walk around. I'm gonna stay right here. Why don't you take yourself around?" Bobbo said, pouring something strong into his highball glass.

*This is just too perfect,* Aster thought to herself. *Free reign over the house? What's his game? He cannot be this stupid!*

"You sure, baby? I mean most men don't like the women they bring home nosing in their stuff," Aster remarked.

"I ain't got a thing to hide from you," Bobbo said with a silly grin on his face. "Anyway, you ain't nothing but a bar maid from Potoma."

*So he did check me out,* Aster thought. "That's right, baby," Aster said, pretending to take another sip.

"I checked you out. I got my boys to follow you home the other night," Bobbo confessed. "You live in a nice place but not as nice as this, huh?"

"Why you following me, baby? You could have just asked," Aster replied, running her tongue along her top lip slowly.

"Got to make sure you ain't no 'thority," Bobbo answered, slumping against the bar heavily.

"Why you worried about that?" Aster asked, hedging.

"I ain't worried. What I got they can't find nohow," Bobbo replied, his façade of sophistication slipping.

"Well, I'm not looking for nothing but you, big boy," Aster assured him, giving him her best Marilyn Monroe voice. "I just got to see this beautiful house! I'll be back in a few minutes, OK?"

"Take your time, sweetie. Bobbo's got all night for you," Bobbo replied, gulping down the rest of the liquid in the cup.

Aster, struggling to keep from running, left Bobbo holding onto the bar and swaying. She'd deposited the full martini glass on an end table on her way out. Opposite the entrance to the living room and dining room was a short hall. Off the hall was a restaurant-style kitchen, a separate breakfast room and an office. At the end of the hall was a huge paneled library with floor-to-ceiling bookshelves on all four walls. Aster quickly snapped pictures from all angles then returned to the foyer. She retraced her steps into the short hall beyond the arch under the stair landing and found herself in what could only be described as a ballroom which appeared to stretch the entire length of the house and had a dozen double french doors which opened onto a large patio with a pool in the center. Next to the patio was a wide lawn that merged with the darkness beyond.

Back in the foyer, Aster took the staircase to the left up to the landing where it doubled back for three steps before becoming a hallway that ran a semi-circle around the two-story foyer. Six doors opened off the hallway, all bedrooms with luxurious attached baths and all empty of occupants or any sign of such. From the staircase landing, another U-shaped staircase led up to the third floor of the house. The first door Aster opened led to what was obviously the Master Bedroom. The walls were richly paneled in cherry wood and the triple cove ceiling was painted with a mural of the night sky filled with stars and constellations. A king-sized bed with a mirror fitted into the canopy top dominated one side of the room. An immense fireplace with a marble surround was opposite. Half a dozen closets opened off the hallway to the Master Bath where every inch was covered in the same marble as the fireplace of the bedroom. Aster had to admit she was impressed.

Three smaller bedrooms were also on the third floor; each obviously vacant. To the right of the Master Suite was a small enclosed staircase. Aster followed it up into the darkness, her eyes gradually adjusting to the lack of light. At the top of the steps was a door. Aster turned the knob but found that it was locked. Aster opened the small purse she had flung across her body and found a fake credit card. After several minutes of trying to slide the lock in vain, Aster gave up. At the bottom of the steps she took a picture then descended back down both flights of stairs into the foyer.

To Aster's dismay, Bobbo was stumbling out of the living room. "OK, sweetie, you seen enough. It's time to get down to business with ole Bobbo," he announced.

"But I haven't seen the bottom floor yet," Aster protested.

"There ain't nothing down there you gonna be interested in, honey," Bobbo replied, reaching for the banister and missing. To Aster's relief, it was obvious that Bobbo wasn't going to be able to climb two flights of stairs, not by himself anyway, much less perform in the bedroom.

"Oh, baby, just let me take a peek real quick," Aster pleaded, sidling up to Bobbo and caressing his shoulder. "It'll only take a minute, I promise."

"You can do that tomorrow. Right now we're going upstairs and your gonna make a movie with me," Bobbo insisted still trying to reach the banister.

"OK, then," Aster said, giving him her best pout.

"You gonna have to help me up," Bobbo said reaching out to Aster. Bobbo's alcoholic stench was almost enough to make Aster sway from the fumes but she managed to take his arm and pull him over to the stair rail so that he could pull himself up the stairs. Slowly, with his arm around Aster's shoulders, Bobbo made his way up the curving staircase to the landing.

"You sure you can make it, baby?" Aster asked looking doubtfully at the next set of stairs.

"I know you gonna get me there," Bobbo replied, almost incoherently.

Aster tugged at Bobbo, all 350 pounds of him, and somehow managed to thrust his body up each step to the third floor. When they reached the bedroom, Bobbo burst through the door and would have fallen flat on his face if Aster hadn't managed to pull him back. Aster mentally crossed her fingers and helped Bobbo over to the bed.

"You just lie back and let me get a little more comfortable," Aster said giving Bobbo a sly wink.

Bobbo tried to wink back but passed out instead. Quickly, Aster pulled off Bobbo's shoes and pants. After unbuttoning his shirt she was unable to get it off of him, so she left it on. For fifteen minutes, Aster pushed and pulled and finally managed to get Bobbo under the covers. For a moment she contemplated turning out the lights but decided to leave them on in case darkness was some sort of sign to Bobbo's men to come into the house. Then Aster ran out of the room and down the stairs to the foyer. An open stair to the basement lay beneath the right-side staircase and Aster found herself in a small vestibule. Large double doors revealed an enormous garage which housed numerous sports cars. Aster would have loved to check them all out but she didn't have time; a quick walk through the inventory taking pictures would have to do. Opposite the garage was a hallway with doors off of both sides. Aster found that all of the doors were locked and guarded by some sort of security system. Not wanting to set off any alarms, Aster made no attempt to gain access to whatever lay behind the steel. Satisfied that she'd photographed everything of importance, Aster returned to the third floor Master bedroom.

Aster thoroughly searched the bedroom but found no security cameras. She found Bobbo's video camera hidden in the overmantel of the fireplace. It hadn't been turned on. Aster checked the clock on the nightstand. It was just after 2:00 am. She'd been there long enough and it was time to go. Aster turned off the light in the bedroom and casually walked down the stairs. Just as she'd presumed, she found a couple of Bobbo's men loitering in the foyer.

"Can I get a ride back to the bar?" Aster asked one of the men.

"Bobbo done with you already?" the man asked, winking at the other one.

Aster nodded. "If I don't get my car out of the parking lot, it'll get towed."

"OK, then," the man said. "Let's go."

Aster followed Bobbo's musclehead out the front door and climbed into the SUV that had followed Bobbo's Jaguar to the house just a few hours ago. After the men had driven away from the bar, Aster slipped inside.

"Excellent job," the blonde at the table said when Aster entered the office. "We've got everything we need to nail him."

"Can I go home now?" Aster asked, yawning.

"Not yet," the blonde replied. "But very soon, I suspect."

## CHAPTER 33

**When Katie got** home from the hospital she was feeling anxious. She and Anna had sat in Anna's car for a while and discussed what Jessie had revealed to them about last Thursday night. It was very unsettling to think that one of Jessie's neighbors might have tried to kill her. And over a relatively innocent list that had been part of a Sunday School assignment. At least Jessie had been able to confirm that she was sedated with chloroform. It seemed she had no memory whatsoever of being injected.

Katie and Anna had been very intrigued by the fact that Jessie had described the doer as coming into her bedroom through the bedroom door. They'd both assumed that the killer had gained access from one of the balconies. This had certainly cast a new light on who the killer could be. *Who could have come through the house without anyone noticing? Who would have been that bold?* Katie and Anna had run through the suspects. *Danny Ping and Mick Wilson seemed to have the knowledge to concoct the poison. But what could Ping have stolen that would justify killing a teenage girl? And according to Wilson's modus operandi, he liked to peek in windows not invade houses. Grace Garfield obviously had issues with the Ashtons but killing Jessie didn't seem to have any practical logic in resolving those issues. Although it was plausible that Casey or Ted Bailey might be able to come and go from the Ashton house without suspicion because of the long-standing friendship between the families, certainly there would be some awkwardness if they were caught doing it in the middle of the night.* Besides, Katie and Anna couldn't quite believe that Casey Bailey would try to kill Jessie, even if Jessie had caught her in a compromising position. *Ted Bailey was a mystery since they'd been unable to question him to any extent at this point. Aster Bancroft was just weird but that didn't make her a killer. However, Jessie did say she'd fought with the killer. And Aster Bancroft did have a nasty cut on her chest. But what deep, dark secret was Aster Bancroft hiding? Just because she was supposedly being deceitful didn't mean she could or would attempt to murder someone.*

Katie paced around her living room. Ogilvie had followed her back and forth for the first five minutes but then, confused, had just curled up on the sofa to watch her with soulful eyes. *What did Jessie see?* Katie pondered. While Jessie's information had established a better picture of what had happened that night, it had also raised more questions and really brought Katie and Anna no closer to identifying the would-be killer. If only the doctor had let them finish questioning Jessie, Katie thought, they might have more to go on!

Katie was wearing a path into her wooden floor and decided she needed some fresh air. To Ogilvie's delight, she clipped on his leash and led him out to the golf cart. Some dogs love to ride in a car but Ogilvie's wheels of choice had always been the golf cart. He could sit up on the seat with Katie and see everything as it whizzed by, the air blowing in his face and his nose working overtime to acquire, separate and react to all the scents they encountered along the way. As they sped along the residential streets, Ogilvie leaned into Katie, savoring his doggy heaven.

It was after 8:00pm and most people were settled in for the night. As Katie passed house after house she could see through their windows the flicker of television screens, kids at counters bent over books, and adults staring at computers. Noises blared and ebbed, music, words, vacuum cleaners and the hum of dryers filled the air. Katie breathed in the cool, but not cold, evening air and tried to empty her mind of all thought. Finally, the rapid fire questions about Jessie Ashton faded away but were soon replaced with re-plays of her visit with Ben. Over and over she pictured him coming toward her on the beach, his curls lifted by the wind, his dark blue eyes, intense, yet mischievous at the same time. She wondered what he saw when he looked at her. *Did he think she was beautiful or ordinary? Did he like her curves or think she'd look better if she lost ten pounds? Did he see her as a potential lover or did he always just look at her as his "girl buddy"?*

Katie had been disturbed by what Ben had said about Cade. Like Ben, she didn't want her safe, quaint, little town to turn into some ritzy, crowded resort, that was for sure. But what bothered her even more was the possibility that after convincing Katie that he was only interested in preserving the town for historical reasons, that Cade might actually have ulterior motives that had nothing to do with preservation at all. Katie had loved the idea that she and Cade had a passion for history and architecture in common. She had thought that it could make for a strong basis for an eventual relationship. It was disheartening, to say the least, that Cade's interest in those things might be superficial or even non-existent. Just a way to lure Katie in; *to or for what Katie wasn't quite sure.*

Katie took her time, driving through the different residential neighborhoods and the commercial area. She knew this was a rare treat for Ogilvie and she also knew she'd neglected him lately. Katie tried not to think about Ben and Cade anymore. Now she wanted to distract her thoughts of the two men by thinking about the Jessie Ashton case but her mind kept wandering. Katie turned onto the street that ran beside the beautiful brick Victorian elementary school where all ages had been taught at the turn-of-the-century. Three blocks down, in the gathering dusk, Katie glimpsed an odd-looking vehicle running along the cross-street that seemed to puff smoke from a stack on the back. She couldn't quite process what she saw and pressed the pedal on the golf cart to full speed. Katie wanted a closer look. When Katie got to the intersection and scanned the street, whatever she had seen was gone. Nevertheless, Katie turned in the direction the vehicle had been heading, traveling as fast as the golf cart would go, scrutinizing each street she passed. It was as if the strange-looking vehicle had just disappeared into thin air.

Katie was intrigued. She knew that her eyes had not deceived her. Something kept niggling at Katie but she just couldn't put her finger on it. It was as if she should know something but couldn't quite remember it. Giving up on her fruitless search for the unlikely apparition, Katie gave Ogilvie a good rub which resulted in frantic tail thumping, and steered the golf cart back toward town. On the way, Katie called Ben, inviting herself over so that she could update him on the latest news about Jessie Ashton.

Ben lived in Riverside in one of the riverfront Victorians. Like most of the ornate mansions on the water, the house had been passed down through Ben's family for generations. Technically, the house still belonged to Ben's parents but they preferred to live on one of the golf courses now in a Victorian replication that came with all the latest conveniences and none of the upkeep and problems of the real thing. Ben's house was a typical Queen-Anne with decorative verge boards and gingerbread, a three-story turret and multiple bay windows. It was painted in shades of yellow, black, gray, green and plum with unusual wrought-iron railings on the porch and balcony. It had long been one of Katie's favorite houses, even before she ever met Ben.

Ogilvie bounded up the front steps of Ben's house ahead of Katie. She and Ben both believed that Ogilvie had a thing for Ben's mixed hound, Betsy. At the door, Ogilvie and Betsy exchanged sloppy kisses, then Ogilvie took off to the kitchen to check out Betsy's food bowl. Betsy followed closely behind, baying loudly, no doubt hoping that a game of chase would soon ensue.

Ben led Katie past the formal parlor filled with original antiques to a room in the rear of the house that he used as his living room. It was really the rear parlor and would have been used as a family room during the Victorian era. It contained comfortable leather furniture with vintage silhouettes that provided plush modern comfort but still evoked the spirit of the century-old home. Katie knew Ben had furnished and decorated the room himself and she was impressed with his sense of style.

"Okay, what's new?" Ben inquired.

Katie gave Ben a detailed report of the information Jessie Ashton had related at the hospital. She went on to describe the follow-up discussion about Jessie's neighbors that she and Anna had held in the parking lot.

"So even more questions, now," Ben remarked.

"It seems that way," Katie replied. "I wish we'd been able to find out exactly how Jessie's neighbors had committed the sins listed in Jessie's notebook. Then we might be able to pick out a strong suspect."

"You're convinced it's one of the neighbors?" Ben questioned.

"The person came into the house, went up the stairs and entered Jessie's room from inside. It just seems the most reasonable answer," Katie replied. "It was obviously someone who knew the layout of the house and felt comfortable entering the house. That points to one of the neighbors."

"When can you talk to Jessie again?" Ben asked.

"Sometime tomorrow morning. I'll have to get the OK from the doctor first," Katie said. "The fingerprints should come back sometime tomorrow, too."

"Well, between those two things, you might just be able to wrap up this case by the end of the day," Ben answered encouragingly, slapping Katie lightly on the thigh. "You want something to drink?"

Katie looked at her watch. "Actually, it's getting late. I'd better be going," Katie replied.

Ben and Betsy walked Katie and Ogilvie to the door. Before Katie pulled away from the house, she looked back up at Ben standing on the porch, backlit by the interior house lights. He struck her as god-like with a halo of light outlining his physique and highlighting the chiseled features of his face.

# CHAPTER 34

**Mick crept up** the metal stairs trying not to make them clang with each footstep. He hoped he wouldn't meet anyone but he knew the chance was fairly remote since most people used the elevators. They used the elevators because they were lazy and because they were afraid someone might accost them in the empty, cavernous cinderblock shafts where no one could hear you scream. Only the security guards traveled these out-of-the-way passages and only on occasion. In Mick's case, that was a good thing. He didn't want to be seen.

When he reached the third floor, Mick peered through the small glass window in the heavy metal door. There was no one in the hall near the stairwell and Mick eased the door open just a crack. The hall was empty, at least to the closed double doors at the other end. Mick stepped back and eyed the floor plan on the fire escape notice taped to the wall. The room Mick was looking for was through the double doors and about halfway down the hall to the left. Mick cracked the door to the stairwell again, listening for movement, voices. All was quiet and the hall was dimly lit. It was late and the bright, harsh lights had been turned down so that the occupants could sleep. Mick tentatively stepped out of the stairwell, stopping and listening intently. Mick walked slowly, furtively toward the double doors. The sound of rolling wheels made Mick stop and flatten himself against the hall wall. As the noise faded away, Mick began moving toward the double doors again, pausing before pushing the swinging door silently outward and slipping through.

Mick looked left and right, his head twitching like a nervous bird perched too near active humans. The corridor he was now in appeared to be abandoned. Low lights created dark areas along the walls, punctuated by small spotlights above each room entrance illuminating the doors and numbers pasted on them. Patterned carpet muffled Mick's steps and he was able to move along in silence. Always on the lookout for any activity, Mick walked quickly but nervously. When he reached his objective, he surveyed the corridor again, then pressed his ear to the door. After he was sure that the coast was clear, Mick stole into the room.

Except for the tiny pinpoints of colored lights on the machines along the wall, the room was dark. Mick stood still while his eyes adjusted to the blackness around him. After a few minutes, he could make out a lumpy horizontal figure transposed against the vague shapes of the apparatus surrounding it. Mick remained where he was, afraid to disrupt the scene before him. For the moment, he was content to watch and create visions in his imagination. Mick was feeling really guilty and it was interfering with his thoughts. He'd made a promise and broken his promise. He'd lied knowing he was lying and knowing he couldn't stop doing what he was doing. He'd been a disappointment, a big disappointment. And he was a liar. That word pounded against his head, over and over, causing the backs of his eyes to spark with bursts of shooting pain that made him unwillingly tear up. Unable to control his emotions, Mick wiped his eyes with the backs of his hands and turned slowly toward the door. He reached for the shiny silver doorknob that glowed eerily from the light seeping in through the crack beneath the door.

# CHAPTER 35

**Grace walked through** her house admiring each room. If only the other people in the cul-de-sac could see what she'd done. Her house looked like theirs, only better. She'd copied their high-end hired-decorator interiors but she'd done it on her own without spending the thousands they'd wasted.

Grace's living room was virtually a carbon copy of the snooty Ashtons' except Grace's antique fainting couch looked so much more elegant sitting in the bay window than the Ashtons' did relegated to an unused corner. Grace had found the same designer drape fabric at a discount store and sewed her own; Grace was sure she'd spent a quarter of what that talentless Ellen Ashton had. And even though Grace's area rug was different from the Ashtons', it had the same color way and coordinated just as well with the upholstered furniture. Grace had precisely mimicked the Baileys' Master Bedroom in one of her spares, custom matching the paint colors and hand-painting the furniture to match the Baileys' French Country bedroom set. Even though the layout of Grace's kitchen was slightly different, the room sported the same cabinetry, countertops and stainless steel appliances as weird Aster's. Grace had even laid the same marble tile on the floor and backsplash. Grace had also duplicated the design in Ping's bathrooms for her own right down to the faucets and lighting fixtures. Now they both had guest baths done in black & white with gray accents, an art deco powder room in pink and green and another full bath with a multi-blue hued theme. Grace had also copied bedrooms from two of the weekend houses and had replicated the Baileys' sun porch, furniture and all.

Grace had left the best rooms for last—her master suite. She was copying Jessie Ashton's bedroom and bathroom with its pink and black color scheme and mix of antique and PB Teen furniture and accessories. The last time Grace had snuck into the Ashton house it had been a miserable fiasco. She'd almost gotten caught but she'd resolved the problem with her preparedness and fast thinking. Grace always carried certain "tools" on her when she broke into the houses just in case someone was there that she didn't know about. However, she'd never used them until that night at the Ashton house. She'd felt terrible about it afterward but everything had turned out alright so Grace was feeling pretty remorseless now. She hadn't dared go back to the Ashtons' since then but she was beginning to feel antsy and she wanted to take a few more pictures so she could hurry up and finish the rooms. She couldn't wait to complete her beautiful house that was so much more elegant and refined and better than her neighbors. Finally, she'd have exactly what they all had.

Grace revisited all her rooms, ending up her self-tour in the in-progress master suite. She'd been using the "Bailey Bedroom" as she called it but couldn't wait to occupy her proper place in her magnificent home. She'd finished painting the walls of the master bedroom the perfect shade of pink and several items of furniture sat in the middle of the room, covered by pristine white sheets. The paint in the bathroom was also completed as was the tiling and the installation of the various bathroom fixtures. Mainly, she was just waiting on the accoutrements like her towels and hamper and decorating items to arrive. As Grace walked round and round the suite, she wondered if it was too soon to make another visit to the Ashtons' house. Certainly, she needed to go again before Little Miss Perfect Jessie came home from the hospital. Grace really didn't want to have to repeat what had happened before; with those nosy policewomen around, surely she'd get caught if the same thing happened a second time.

# CHAPTER 35

**Ping was miserable.** He'd hoped his phone would ring but it had been silent for days. He knew he shouldn't have turned it off over the weekend but he'd been angry and wanted to make a point. Unfortunately, it seemed, it had all backfired. It was true; he had genuinely enjoyed himself when he went out with his friends and it had been a relief not to think about anything but having a good time. He'd kept his mind occupied with jokes and age-old fish tales he and his friends had been telling for years and he hadn't felt lonely or sad or even angry the whole night. For once, he'd lived in the present, in the real world, not in a fantasy of what would or could be if he just waited a little longer. But the weekend was over, his friends and the bar were a memory, and now the real world was one of loss and loneliness and despair.

Ping sat in the chair in front of the wide-screen TV, absent-mindedly flipping through the channels with the remote. One of his favorite shows, a detective drama, would be coming on in an hour and he tried to look forward to it. At least it would distract him from his sadness, from feeling utterly and completely alone. When Ping heard the door to his back porch squeak, he ignored it. Just wishful thinking, he chided himself. Even the faint slap-slap of flip-flops didn't completely register until suddenly he saw the shadow in the hall. Without a thought, Ping stood up and ran toward the door, toward the filmy silhouette whose source was just out of sight.

When he saw her, unbidden tears of joy welled in his eyes and raced down his cheeks. In the gathering darkness of the hall, only the outline of her beauty was visible but Ping didn't need to see her clearly, he knew every curve and straight line by heart. Her sweet smell, like vanilla and gardenias, wafted around him and he couldn't help but breathe in the intoxicating elixir. All of a sudden he was afraid to reach out to her, afraid to touch her, afraid he had fallen asleep in his chair and was simply dreaming. He was afraid she wasn't really there but an apparition created by a deranged man crazy in love with a woman he couldn't have. Ping stared at the exquisite creature in front of him willing himself to wrap his arms around her, draw her to him, feel her flesh and bone and warm breath against him. Frightened that she would simply fade away, all Ping could manage was to brush his fingers against the soft skin of her cheek. And then he knew she was really there and he caressed her face again and he could feel the wetness of her tears against his fingertips. He slid his hands down her shoulders and arms, taking both of her hands in his, and he sunk down on his knees kissing her hands again and again. She knelt down too, then and with his hands still grasping hers, she held his face in her hands and kissed his lips ever so lightly and tenderly, like the brush of a cat's whisker.

Ping wrapped his arms around her, embracing her gently, his chin resting on her shoulder and her face pressed against his chest. "I'm so sorry," she whispered, to which Ping replied, "I'm sorry, too."

# WEDNESDAY
# CHAPTER 36

**Katie was awakened** at 5:00am from a deep sleep and reached for her jingling cell phone, looking at the number flashing on the screen. It was the police station. Immediately, Katie scooted up in the bed to a sitting position and pressed the "send" button. She was simultaneously shocked and intrigued by the news she received. Jessie Ashton had disappeared from the hospital.

After hanging up, Katie hurried to take a shower and get dressed, then ran out to her Jeep and took off for the hospital. On the way, she phoned Anna, who was also en route. Just as the night before, they both arrived at the same time and went to Jessie's hospital room together. Jessie's parents had not yet arrived and the nurse who had discovered the empty room met them in the hall.

"I came in about 4:30 this morning to check on Miss Ashton, take her vitals, and found that she wasn't in her bed. I knocked on the bathroom door but when she didn't answer I opened it and saw she wasn't in there either. I called the nurse's station to see if anyone had seen Miss Ashton in the hall or one of the waiting rooms. We searched the building for her for about fifteen minutes before we called 911," the nurse explained.

"Is there anything missing besides Jessie? Clothes, medication, personal items, anything like that?" Katie questioned.

"I don't think so. It's like she just vanished. In fact, she left the hospital gown she was wearing last night in the bed," the nurse replied.

"She what?" Katie asked, thinking she had heard the nurse incorrectly.

"She left everything. Even her hospital gown," the nurse confirmed.

"So you're saying she walked out of here in her panties or worse, completely nude?" Katie inquired.

"It looks that way," the nurse nodded. "You need to see something, though."

The nurse led Katie and Anna into Jessie's hospital room and pointed toward the bed. The blanket was pulled back and most of it rested on the floor, only a corner still remained tucked under the mattress. Four pillows were arranged in an S down the length of the mattress and a hospital gown lay on top of them.

"Apparently someone wanted it to look like Jessie was still in the bed. Did you pull the blanket off like this?" Anna asked the nurse.

"Yes. I thought it was strange that the pillows were in the bed like that but it didn't dawn on me until after I checked the bathroom that whoever put them there might have been trying to make it look like Miss Ashton was still in the bed," the nurse answered, her lip quivering.

Anna had brought a camera and began taking pictures from different angles. "Have you or anyone else touched the bed otherwise or moved anything on it?"

The nurse shook her head.

"When was the last time someone checked on Jessie before you came in?" Katie asked.

"I worked the night shift and I came in at..." the nurse said checking the chart "...at 1:45."

"And how long did it take you to complete your rounds?" Anna questioned as she continued to snap photos.

"I was back at the nurse's station by 2:15," the nurse answered. "I know this because I got a phone call right after I got there and I remember looking at the digital clock on the wall."

"And from the nurse's station you can't see down this hall because it's around the corner", Katie confirmed.

"That's correct. I always thought it was a poor design for this wing but..." the nurse remarked.

"Did you see anyone other than medical personnel in this area after, say, midnight last night?" Katie continued.

"No. Everything quiets down after visitors hours are over at 10:00pm and no one but medical staff is allowed on this floor after that time," the nurse answered.

"How do you keep someone from coming up here?"

Katie asked.

"We have security guards posted at the elevators to let outsiders know that guests aren't allowed after ten," the nurse informed Katie.

"What about the stairs?"

"Very few people, including employees ever use the stairs so the hospital doesn't bother to secure those," the nurse shrugged.

"So someone could have come up here using the stairs?" Katie suggested.

The nurse shrugged again and said "Sure but it's very unlikely. Most people don't even know where the stairs are located. And if they find them they are reluctant to use them because they are so out of the way. I myself find them kind of scary and prison-like."

"Can you show me where they are?" Katie asked.

"This way," the nurse said gesturing for Katie and Anna to follow her down the long corridor. At the half-way point on the right was a pair of swinging doors. The nurse led Katie and Anna through the doors and pointed to the end of the short hall.

"The door to the stairs is on your right," the nurse said. "Are you finished with me? It's time for me to get off."

"Give me your phone number, in case we have any more questions," Katie replied. "And one more thing. Do you recall Jessie or anyone who was here last night saying anything that might relate to Jessie's sudden disappearance?"

"I really didn't talk to anyone and I try not to listen to private conversations when I'm making my rounds. I just do my job as quickly as possible and get out of the way," the nurse replied.

At that moment, Jessie's parents arrived, in a panic. Katie led them to a private waiting room across from the nurse's station and explained the situation. Despite Katie's attempts at reassurance, Justin and Ellen Ashton seemed more disturbed than when they arrived.

"Why don't you look through Jessie's things and see if there is anything missing," Katie suggested as the three of them returned to the hospital room.

After carefully and gingerly inventorying Jessie's belongings, Ellen Ashton announced that everything was still intact.

"What do we do now?" Ellen Ashton pleaded.

"Just go home. There's really nothing you can do here," Katie answered. "We will let you know anything we find out."

The Ashtons nodded and stood up. "Should we gather up Jessie's things?"

"Right now they may be evidence so we'll need to take them down to the station," Katie replied.

Ellen Ashton nodded, completely broken and exhausted. "Will you call when we can have them back?"

"Of course," Katie replied. "I promise. We will call you as soon as we have a lead."

After the Ashtons left, Katie began to pack Jessie's clothes and other personal items in the travel bag she found in the wardrobe closet. She wondered how a naked sixteen-year old girl could have been spirited out of her hospital room, even in the middle of the night, without being seen or heard. *Of course, someone could have drugged her to keep her quiet but how did they get her out? Carry her? Put her in a laundry cart like she'd seen in the movies? Or on a gurney, covered up like a dead person? Wouldn't any of those things seem strange in the middle of the night? Or did the person who took her just have the incredible luck not to pass anyone on the way out? And where was Jessie now? Was she still alive? Or had someone come back to finish the job they'd started on Thursday night? And if that person wanted to kill her, why didn't they just leave her in the hospital? Why remove her body?* All of these questions assaulted Katie's mind and she was eager to find Anna so they could brainstorm together.

# CHAPTER 37

"**Hey, Bastian,**" **Casey** greeted her son when he bounced downstairs on his way to school. "Aren't you going to have some breakfast?"

"No time," Sebastian replied, brushing by her.

"I'll drive you if you want," Casey suggested hopefully, following behind him.

"I'm taking the golf cart," Sebastian called over his shoulder as he opened the front door.

Casey sighed and slumped down on the sofa. Things were so tense between her and Sebastian lately. They used to be so close and it pained Casey to watch their relationship unravel. It also made Casey angry. Ted was never around, never involved himself much with his family but somehow when things turned upside down, Casey was the villain and Ted was just an innocent bystander. Casey had begun a countdown. Her oldest son was already gone and likely not coming back. At the end of the summer, Sebastian would be leaving, too. Then she could change her life, start over. She just had to get through a few more months, just bide her time and try to keep everything as peaceful and even as possible for just a little while longer.

Casey got up and walked back to the kitchen where she mindlessly loaded the dishwasher with breakfast dishes and leftover snack bowls from last night. She pushed the buttons on the machine, then automatically picked up the disinfectant spray to clean off the counters. As Casey tidied up the room, moving to the living room and then to her bedroom, she fantasized about what her life would be like once she was free from daily routine. She'd always wanted to be an actress; maybe she'd go to Los Angeles and try to break into the movies. She'd also wanted to go back to college, perhaps earn a graduate degree in communications or journalism. Then she could work her way up to an anchor position on the local news or maybe even co-host one of the news programs like *60 Minutes.*

As Casey finished plumping the bed pillows and straightening the nightstands, she realized that what she really wanted above everything else—and she really did want to make a new start with a fabulous career—was to be with a man who was her one true love, the one she would want to grow old with. If she stayed with Ted, he'd be old and rickety long before she was. She was already watching him grow old and grumpy and set in his ways while she was still young and full of hope and dreams.

Most of the time, Casey didn't think Ted would even notice if she left or even care. Most of the time, Casey felt like she was just a babysitter and housekeeper for Ted. And once Sebastian had left home, Ted wouldn't need someone to take care of the children and he could easily hire a new housekeeper. Casey realized that she had spent so much time feeling guilty for being unappreciative of all the things Ted had given her—a big, beautiful house, designer clothes and furnishings, lavish jewelry, exotic trips and freedom from having to work a nine-to-five job—that she'd forgotten about all the things she had given up. Her youth, her career aspirations, her independence, real enduring heart-wrenching unforgettable love.

In the last few weeks Casey had finally faced the truth: she was a trophy wife, the ultimate symbol of Ted's financial success. Of course, Ted wasn't the only one guilty of ulterior motives. Casey knew deep down inside that she'd married Ted because he had money. She was attracted to him, yes, and yes, she'd grown to love him but she never would have considered marriage to someone so much older than herself if it didn't come with the enticement of wealth and privilege. And loving someone and being in love with someone were two entirely different things, especially for women. Most men didn't seem to differentiate the two very much and so Casey didn't really know which was the case with Ted. But Casey had known from the very beginning that she was never, even for a moment, in love with Ted. At the time it didn't seem to matter, but now that she was older, more mature, so unhappy in her situation…well, she wanted to be with someone she was in love with. She wanted to wake up beside someone she could never tire of seeing first thing in the morning, excited that that person was still there and not just the fleeting ghost of someone she had dreamed about and wished was real.

Casey opened the door to Sebastian's room. As usual it was messy and cluttered. *Why were boys so careless?* Casey thought to herself. Sebastian's clothes lay in piles on the floor with no clue as to which were dirty and which were clean but too much trouble to put into the dresser drawers. Apparently Sebastian had a system but he'd not shared it with Casey. Mounds of books also dotted the room in no particular pattern and half a dozen bath towels were balled up in one corner. Sebastian hadn't made his bed and it was littered with empty Coke bottles, candy bar wrappers and scraps of paper. Casey wondered if Sebastian actually slept in his bed with all that trash. Without entering, Casey shut the door again, making a mental note to herself to get on him about cleaning it up when he got home today.

Casey knew she had to shake her thoughts of a future without a chaotic and uncommunicative teenage son and a cold and monotonous husband or she'd sink into depression and just sit around watching *Jerry Springer* and reruns of *Law & Order* all day. She picked up the phone and dialed Ellen Ashton. She and Ellen had been very close for many years but recently, they'd grown apart. Casey knew it was her fault; she'd been less social since determining that she was going to move away and change her life once Sebastian graduated from high school. It was preservation reflex; cut ties so that you don't back out, so you don't change your mind.

When Ellen answered the phone in tears, Casey felt terrible. Sebastian had already informed her that Jessie was missing; somehow that fact had made the rounds of the teen network long before the adults had started phoning and spreading the news. Casey offered to come over and sit with Ellen but Ellen declined saying she just needed to be alone, and besides, Justin was there. Casey felt a pang of jealousy; Ellen and Justin were in love and always had been. They'd ridden the waves of life together, through good times and bad, and she knew they'd grow old together just as much in love as always. Ellen would never refer to Justin as her ex-husband and Justin would never speak about his first wife or the mother of his children in the past tense. They were solid.

Casey, in need of some fresh air but too exhausted by sheer unhappiness to go anywhere, grabbed some as-yet unread magazines from the perfectly upholstered ottoman in the sun room and went outside to the deck. As she settled into the chaise, she was glad that Ping was at work. Whenever he was in his back yard, it made her uneasy. Once again she considered planting a hedge on that side that would block the view.

# CHAPTER 38

**Katie received the** fingerprint packet before she had a chance to return the early morning phone call from the lab that had come in while she was at the hospital. The results showed that fingerprints matched those of Mick Wilson and Grace Garfield as well as the Ashton family members. There were also several unidentifiable prints. That meant she and Anna would have to fingerprint the other neighbors. A few days ago, Katie would have considered the fingerprints a lead in finding a suspect; now, the lack or presence of them didn't mean much. And besides, Jessie's disappearance and the fact that she might be in grave danger was much more pressing..

"Do you really think someone snuck into the hospital and kidnapped Jessie Ashton?" Anna asked, interrupting Katie's thoughts.

"Do you have another theory?" Katie replied,

"Well, there's always the chance that she left on her own," Anna suggested.

"According to her parents and the nurse, there were no clothes missing and as we saw, even her hospital gown was still there. Do you really think a sixteen-year old girl would walk out completely naked?" Katie eschewed.

"Maybe she had help," Anna shrugged.

"So you're saying someone did get into her room undetected and then she and this person also got out of the hospital without being seen?" Katie answered, thumping her pen against the desk.

"Does the hospital have cameras?" Anna asked picking up the phone receiver.

"Maybe in the halls. Don't you think they would have offered up that information already, though?" Katie said scooting her chair back from the desk and sticking her feet out, slouching down and putting her arms behind her head.

"Don't you ever watch cop shows on TV?" Anna laughed. "People forget about the cameras all the time."

"All we can do is ask," Katie sighed, gesturing for Anna to dial the phone.

When Anna hung up from her brief conversation,

there was a smile on her face.

"They have cameras in every hallway," Anna reported, giving herself pat on the back. "And they're pulling the videos right now."

Katie and Anna rose together and walked quickly toward the door to the station. As they passed the front desk, Katie asked the Officer-on-Duty to phone the Baileys, Aster Bancroft, and Danny Ping, requesting that they come in immediately to have their fingerprints taken. She then instructed him to compare those fingerprints with the mystery prints in the packet and report to her immediately with the results.

When Katie and Anna arrived at the hospital, they went directly to the Administrator's office to view the tapes from the night before. Although the Administrator's office was spacious, it was cluttered with file cabinets. Jammed closely together in one corner by a window were two upholstered chairs with a battered end table between them, all facing a small television. The Administrator graciously offered them coffee which they both declined, then without further ado, loaded one of three videotapes arranged in chronological order beginning at 12:00 am. Katie fast-forwarded through the footage as she and Anna scanned the faces of the people appearing and disappearing in camera view. For several hours, the only people recorded appeared to all be hospital personnel and after twenty minutes, Anna ejected the first tape and loaded the second. A little more than half-way through, Katie froze the frame. Coming through the double doors that led to the stairwell hall, was a figure that was unmistakably male even though a hood hid his face.

Katie pushed the play button and she an Anna watched the man, dressed all in black, walk furtively down the hall and enter Jessie Ashton's hospital room. For approximately ten minutes there was no activity, then the man slipped back out, and hugging the wall, retraced his steps back to through the double doors. Katie stopped the tape and rewound it and she and Anna watched the scene again, straining to pick up any clues as to who the person could be.

"What do you make of that?" Katie asked, looking

curiously at Anna.

"Well, Black Hood, didn't take Jessie. That much is clear," Anna replied. "But what the hell was he doing in there all that time?"

Katie was at a loss. "Let's see if he comes back?"

"Really? What do you think he was doing? Casing Jessie's room?" Anna laughed.

Katie knew it sounded stupid but she really had no explanation for what they'd just observed. Katie shrugged, then pushed the "Play" button. The rest of the tape proved to be uneventful. Somewhat reluctantly, Anna agreed to sit through the last one "just in case".

"There!" Katie exclaimed, jamming her finger against the "Stop" button on the remote.

The still-frame showed a scene almost identical to the one on the second tape: a figure clad in dark clothing pushing through the double doors from stairwell hall. When Katie resumed the tape, the figure moved down the corridor quickly, disappearing into Jessie Ashton's room. Again, about ten minutes elapsed before the figure left the room.

"And you laughed at me," Katie picked at Anna, raising her eyebrows in victory.

"OK, but I still didn't see Jessie Ashton come out of that room," Anna replied. "Keep rolling."

Katie and Anna continued to view the tape. About an hour after the second figure had appeared on the tape, several nurses and orderlies passed in and out of Jessie's room, followed closely by Katie and Anna's own visit. When the tape ended, Katie and Anna were stumped—Jessie had never left the room.

"Let's go back to the first appearance of Black Hood," Katie said. "I think I might have seen something."

Anna pulled the last tape from the machine and inserted Tape 2. Katie hit the button on the remote to rewind it. When she reached the figure emerging through the double doors, she slowed it down.

"Just what I thought," Katie said nodding excitedly. "That's Mick Wilson."

"How do you know?" Anna inquired, looking perplexed.

"See his hand, right there on the door. You can just see that ridiculous tattoo on his wrist", Katie replied, stopping the tape and walking over to the screen to point out the visible portion of the 1970s Playboy symbol.

"Excellent eye, girl!" Anna almost screamed. "We've got him!"

Katie fumbled with her cell phone, calling the 911 operator and ordering an all-points-bulletin for Mick.

"Let's head to Mr. Wilson's house. I'd love to be the one to pick him up," Katie said as she and Anna climbed into the police car. Once they'd pulled out of the hospital parking lot, Anna flipped on the roof lights and floored it.

# CHAPTER 39

**When Ping walked** into the Potoma police station he wasn't surprised to see Casey and Aster there, too. He wondered why Mick and Grace weren't there as well. Ping wasn't thrilled about having his fingerprints taken; in fact, he was terrified. He'd always had an irrational fear that if his fingerprints were on file that somehow he'd be mistakenly identified as a criminal and be sent to jail for the rest of his life. Three upholstered wooden chairs were placed along the front wall. Casey and Aster had taken the seats on each end, leaving the one in the middle vacant, and having no other choice, Ping sat there.

"Hey," Casey greeted. "You here for fingerprints, I guess?"

Ping nodded. "You, too?"

"Not looking forward to this at all," Casey remarked in reply.

Ping noticed that Aster looked particularly uncomfortable. "Guess you're here for the same thing," Ping directed to Aster as a means of greeting.

Aster nodded but remained silent. A moment later, Ping noticed that Aster's eyes were closed and she seemed to have dozed off. Ping remembered that Aster often left her house around dinner time and didn't come home until the wee hours of the morning. *Last night must have been one of those nights,* Ping thought to himself.

When Ping looked back over at Casey he noticed that her hand, which was resting on the arm of the chair, was trembling. Without thinking, Ping placed his hand over Casey's and said in a low voice "It's going to be fine." A look of surprise registered in Casey's eyes and panicked, Ping quickly removed his hand from hers.

"Thanks," Casey whispered, ducking her head and averting her gaze.

A few minutes later, a tall, portly police officer came to stand in front of them. "OK, who's first?"

Casey continued to stare at the floor and although Ping wanted to make his exit as quickly as possible he said "Why don't you go first, Aster? You look like you need to get home and get some sleep."

Aster tipped her head at Ping, then rose and followed the police officer to the back of the room. Alone with Casey, Ping studied her from the corner of his eye. He'd always thought she was a beauty with her dark curly hair and animated eyes. She had high cheekbones and thin wide lips that hid perfectly straight, white teeth. Casey always seemed to be smiling or laughing and when she spoke, her hands did also. Ping felt awkward sitting so close to her and he wondered if he should move over into Aster's vacated seat. Then thought better of it. He didn't want her or anyone else to think he didn't want to sit next to her. Ping began to wonder why Casey's husband, Ted wasn't present or if he would show up any minute. Ping didn't know what to say to Casey, especially after such an intimate gesture earlier, so they sat in silence for what seemed like forever. Just as Ping was about to stand up, Casey raised her head and swiveled her body ever so slightly toward him.

"Did you know that Jessie is missing from the hospital?" Casey said, looking at Ping sideways.

"I hadn't heard," Ping replied. "Is that why we're being fingerprinted, then?"

"Maybe. The officer over there also told me that some of the fingerprints they lifted from Jessie's house couldn't be identified from police and FBI records," Casey said.

"Do the police really think one of us has something to do with what happened to Jessie?" Ping muttered under his breath.

Casey shrugged. "I don't know."

Ping couldn't think of a way to keep the conversation going and so he sat forward in his chair and put his chin between his hands, his elbows resting on his knees. Casey uncrossed her legs, then re-crossed them and adjusted her skirt. Ping could feel his heart beating faster each minute he waited. He really wanted to stand up, move around, work off some of his nervous energy. When he thought he couldn't stand it any longer, he saw Aster walking toward him, followed by the police officer.

"You go next," Casey said. "I know you need to get back to work and I'm just going back home when I'm done here."

"Thanks. If you're sure," Ping replied, standing and smoothing his hands down his thighs to wipe away the sweat.

Casey nodded, then looked away.

"Ms. Bailey, when do you expect your husband to arrive?" the police officer asked Casey.

"I'm not sure. I haven't spoken to him," Casey replied. Ping thought he could detect a look of disdain on her face for just a moment. He could tell from her body language that she was hoping he wouldn't show up, at least not while she was there.

"You sure you don't want to go ahead and get this over with?" Ping asked Casey.

"I'm fine. I'm sure you need to get back to work," Casey replied. "Anyway, I need to go to the rest room right now."

Casey stood up, grabbed her purse and walked away toward the door at the end of the hall.

The police officer gestured Ping to the follow him, then lead him to a table set up at the back of the room where he'd taken Aster previously. While the police officer manipulated his fingers, rolling them in ink and making marks with them on white cards, Ping concentrated on not giving any indication that inside he was shaking with fear. It seemed to Ping that the whole process only took a few minutes; it had appeared to take so much longer when he was waiting on Aster.

Ping didn't consciously decide to avoid Casey but opting to wash his hands in the Men's Room prevented him from running into her again. By the time he came out, she was already being fingerprinted. Ping noticed that her husband still hadn't shown up and he wondered why. Surely he would have known that she was nervous about it all and would be compassionate enough to make sure he was there to calm her. Almost immediately, Ping changed his mind, knowing that Casey's husband was hardly ever home and even when he was he'd never seen them spend any time together. Ping had always been amazed at the neglect that Casey's husband inflicted on his lovely, sweet wife. *If she were mine*...Ping said silently in his head, but he stopped himself before completing his thought.

# Chapter 40

**Mick noticed the** flashing blue lights and immediately knew he'd been caught. He had reprimanded himself continuously since last night for sneaking into the hospital. Mick didn't want to go to jail, he wouldn't survive. He knew that. But he also knew he was trapped and had no escape. He could see police officers swarming his house and the rotating beams of red and blue were already making him dizzy. He stumbled around his living room, utterly confused and frightened. Finally, he threw himself into his favorite chair and grasped the arms as tightly as he could. He could hear a female voice demanding that he open his front door. But Mick couldn't move and his head was spinning. Mick kept trying to push back the blackness he knew was coming by replaying in his mind exactly what he had done last night when he arrived at the hospital. The blackness kept obscuring his inner picture and every now and then Mick lifted a hand and smacked himself on the side of the head, desperately attempting to knock the shadows forming over his memory back out of the way.

Mick heard his front door slam open and heard shouting but he couldn't discern what was being said. He sat in his chair with his hands gripping the soft, velvet upholstery, unable to will himself to move. The voices came closer and through a fog he saw the outline of people advancing toward him. He didn't see the guns but he was sure they were there, held out in front of the police officers like on the cop shows on TV. Mick could hear his breathing, the great gulping gasps he made as he tried to take in enough air to keep him from fainting dead away. Mick looked down at his shoes and began to concentrate on counting how many X's his laces made.

Mick felt his arms being pulled on, then jerked away from the safety of the chair. He felt himself being lifted and nearly flung across the ottoman, his arms being wrenched behind him and cold, metal being clamped down on his wrists. Then once again he was lifted and Mick managed to get his feet underneath him. Still, he stared at his shoes, counting the X's over and over. He became aware of being pushed and prodded and saw his feet moving beneath him. The police officers were shouting at him. *Where is she? Where are you keeping her?*

The blackness came swiftly and Mick felt himself falling forward, then his knees buckled and he felt a hard thud against his shoulder. He kept hearing the same thing, ringing over and over in his head. *Where is she?* And Mick kept answering "Who?"

When Mick opened his eyes, the room was hazy but he could pick out the furniture and knew that he was still in his living room. He was sitting up against a wall, the hard surface pressing painfully against his spine. Slowly the haze lifted and Mick saw a police officer standing just a few feet away, watching him.

"Where is she, Mr. Wilson?" the police officer demanded in an angry voice. "We've searched your house and she's not here. Where are you hiding her?"

Mick opened his mouth but for some reason he couldn't make any words come out. The police officer scowled at him, and tipping his head to someone out in the hall, he moved forward, roughly grabbing Mick's arm. Mick felt a hand on his other arm and he was pulled up to a standing position.

"You gonna faint again, peeking pervert?" the police officer behind him goaded, jabbing Mick in the back.

"Just get him in a car," a female voice intervened. Mick recognized that it was Katie.

As the two police officers escorted Mick none-too-gently to the squad car parked on the street in front of Mick's house, Mick tried to wrench around to see Katie. The police officers, obviously mistaking his wriggling for an attempt to escape, grabbed his arms more tightly and increased their pace. When they reached the police car, they pushed Mick inside and slammed the door quickly. Mick stared through the window, frantically searching for Katie in the throng of uniforms standing outside of his house. He thought he caught a glimpse of her, just as the two police officers that had put him in the car, climbed inside and quickly pulled out.

When they arrived at the station, Mick was taken from the car, up the front steps into the station and into the same room where he'd been questioned by Katie and her partner the day before. On the way in, he passed Casey Bailey who was just leaving. She gave Mick a panicked look, then ducked her head and rapidly walked by him. Mick wondered what she was doing at the station.

The police officers left Mick's handcuffs on when they pushed him into the room and Mick heard the metal click of the lock when the door was shut behind him. The same table and chairs stood in the room just as before and Mick sat down in one. His arms were beginning to hurt from being stretched behind him and he attempted to alleviate the discomfort by moving his shoulders back and forth. Mick tried to remember the last time he'd taken his pills.

A few minutes later, one of the police officers came back into the room, followed by Katie and the blonde female officer. Mick couldn't remember her name. The police officer unlocked the handcuff on one hand and ordered Mick to put his hands in front of him where he secured it again. The pain in Mick's shoulders soon began to subside. Almost immediately, Katie began to fire questions at Mick.

"Where is she?"

"Who?" Mick asked. "I don't know who you are talking about."

"Don't try my patience, Mr. Wilson. Tell me where she is."

"Where who is?" Mick said, cocking his head to one side like a dog when it's trying to figure out the source of a strange sound.

"OK, I'll bite. Jessie Ashton."

"Jessie Ashton?" Mick parroted.

"Look, we know you were at the hospital last night. We have you on tape sneaking in from the stairwell. So don't deny it."

"I don't deny it," Mick replied matter-of-factly.

"What did you do with Jessie? She's not at your house. We've looked."

"I don't know where she is. Isn't she still at the hospital?" Mick answered, cocking his head the opposite way.

"Obviously not, Mr. Wilson , if we're here questioning you about her whereabouts."

"The last time I saw her she was sound asleep in her hospital bed. That's the truth," Mick protested, placing his hands over his heart.

"Don't lie to me, Mr. Wilson. We saw you on the tape. You snuck in twice last night. Once at around 2:30 am and then again around 4:00am."

"Whoa-oa-oa!"Mick exclaimed, putting his arms up as if to shield himself from a physical attack. "I was only at the hospital once."

"Then explain how we saw you at two different times."

"I can't but I can tell you I was only there once. I was in my bed asleep by 3:30 this morning," Mick informed the two women.

"Can you prove it?"

Mick was silent for a moment trying to shake something from his memory he knew he should remember. Then a smile began to spread across his face as he realized he actually might have an alibi.

"Maybe," Mick replied. "Aster, the weird chick that lives next door, got home the same time I did. She must have seen my car."

Katie and the other one looked pissed or confused; Mick couldn't really tell which.

"You're admitting to being at the hospital in Jessie Ashton's room at 2:30 this morning?"

Mick nodded. "More like two or two-fifteen."

"What were you doing there?"

"I wanted to see if she was OK," Mick replied, weakly.

"Did you know she'd just regained consciousness a few hours before that?"

"She did? No, I didn't know," Mick said, happier than he should have been sitting in a police interrogation and clearly being accused of a crime.

The two women looked stumped. They turned their backs to Mick and held a whispered conversation that Mick couldn't hear. When they turned back around, Mick could see aggravation written all over Katie's face. The blonde's expression was unreadable.

"What were you planning to do to Jessie Ashton at two o'clock in the morning?"

"Nothing. I just wanted to see her," Mick insisted.

"Why?"

Mick didn't answer.

Katie's face twisted in anger. Mick's heart skipped a beat.

"You've been peeping at her?"

Mick felt his face flush and his stomach flipped and sank. He knew Katie would never like him now. He'd blown it. She'd never be his girlfriend. Mick didn't reply and Katie didn't seem to care. She gestured to the glass on the wall and the police officer that had left a few minutes earlier walked back into the room. Katie told him to put Mick in a holding cell. Mick was surprised she hadn't also told the police officer to throw away the key.

# Chapter 41

**Aster arrived just** as the police cars were parading out of the cul-de-sac. She thought she glimpsed Mick Wilson in the back of the lead car. *They must have called out the entire Potoma police force!* Aster thought to herself. Aster was sure the police mob had something to do with Jessie Ashton. Aster glanced in the direction of Grace Garfield's house and saw her peering through a crack in the drapes. As she looked away and entered her house, Aster was unable to suppress a yawn. Her late night was telling on her and Aster, too sleepy to climb the stairs to her bedroom, dropped her purse on the coffee table and collapsed on the sofa.

Aster was awakened by the doorbell and it took her a few seconds to orient herself. She'd been in a deep sleep and was jolted to consciousness by the loud *ding-dong*. Aster roused herself and once standing, moved quickly to the powder room to assess her appearance. Satisfied that everything was in place, she hurried to the door. Through the peephole, she saw the two female police officers that had questioned her about Jessie Ashton's disappearance. Aster opened the door and looked at the two uniforms expectedly.

"Miss Bancroft, we have a few questions for you."

"In regard to Jessie Ashton, I presume," Aster replied.

"Yes and no. We have a suspect who claims that you may be able to provide an alibi for him."

"Mick Wilson?" Aster blurted, then tried to explain. "I thought I saw him in the police car earlier."

"What time did you arrive at home last night…or this morning, to be more precise?"

Aster looked from one officer to the other. There was no reason not to tell the truth. Aster just hoped that it wouldn't lead to more questions about her activities last night.

"Probably around 3:00am, give or take," Aster replied.

"Did you see Mick Wilson at the time you arrived at home?"

Aster immediately understood the gravity of her answer. Personally, she'd love to see that creep, Mick, go to jail for a very long time, especially after the things she'd witnessed. It had been extremely difficult for Aster to just stand by and do nothing but above all she had to protect her job. Aster quickly evaluated whether or not admitting to having seen Mick would have any bearing on what had happened last night. She decided it did not.

"Yes, I did. We pulled into the cul-de-sac about the same time," Aster answered.

"Are you sure about the time?"

"Not specifically," Aster replied.

"Could it have been later? Say, after 4:30 am?"

"No. It was around three. Three-thirty at the latest," Aster confirmed.

"Did you see Mr. Wilson leave his house later?"

"After I got home, I went straight to bed," Aster said, trying to stifle a yawn but failing. She put her hand over her gaping mouth.

"How long did it take you to fall asleep, do you think?"

"Maybe five minutes. Maybe less," Aster replied, shifting her weight and leaning heavily against the door frame.

"And you slept until when?"

"Until the phone rang and woke me up at 8 o'clock this morning," Aster answered pointedly. "You guys summoning me to the police station to take my fingerprints."

"And you don't remember hearing Mr. Wilson's car leaving his house or any other noise that might indicate his departure?"

"No. But I was dead to the world and I sleep pretty heavy so he could have left without me waking up," Aster volunteered.

"Did you see Mr. Wilson get out of his car when you got home early this morning?"

"No. I really didn't pay attention. I was dead on my feet and just wanted to get into my house and my bed. Mick probably pulled into his garage and shut the door before he got out anyway. That's what he usually does," Aster explained.

"OK, Miss Bancroft. You've been very helpful."

The police officers turned and walked to their squad car and Aster returned to her place on the sofa. Within a few minutes, she'd fallen asleep again.

# CHAPTER 42

**Grace watched the** two female police officers as they questioned Aster in her front doorway. She wondered what had happened. She'd been leaving for work when she saw all the police vehicles file into the court. She'd seen them drag Mick Wilson out of his house and put him in the back of a police car. *Why had they arrested Mick? What had he done? And why were they questioning his next-door-neighbor?* Grace couldn't miss what was happening so she'd called into work and told them a story about her car not starting and having to call a tow truck to take it to the shop and so she'd either be late or not there at all but after an hour had passed with no more action she'd decided the big event was over and she could go to work. Just as she had been about to walk through her front door, the police had shown up again—this time at Aster's house.

Grace peeked through the window again. The police car was gone. Grace went to the kitchen and poured herself half a glass of milk. She sat at the breakfast bar and drank the milk slowly. Grace thought about the foolish thing she had done the night before. She didn't even know why she'd done it. It wasn't like she was even friends with the Ashton family; the raw truth was that she pretty much hated the Ashton family. They were perfect and Grace knew she would never be perfect. She'd never be as rich as them. She'd never be part of an ideal family. *Who would marry her? Who would be able to overlook her thick thighs and the inch of fat on her belly and her chubby cheeks and her ugly feet?* She would never be as nice and pretty as Ellen Ashton or Jessie Ashton. She'd never have designer clothes. And she'd never be popular nor have umpteen friends. She'd always be who she was. Fat, plain-looking, anti-social, unpopular, and middle-class. No matter how hard she tried to be like Ellen or Jessie Ashton she'd always just be Grace Garfield.

## Chapter 43

**Katie's phone rang** and she saw from her caller ID that it was Cade. She hesitated before answering. She really wasn't sure she wanted to talk to him right now. After their pretty much awkward, if not disastrous, first date and then the information Ben had related to her about Cade, Katie was cautious about getting further involved. However, her good manners won out and Katie pressed the "Send" button.

"Hello, Cade," Katie greeted in a voice sweeter than she felt by a long shot.

"Hope I'm not catching you at a bad time..." Cade began.

"Actually, you are," Katie interrupted more abruptly than she meant to. "I mean I'm working a case right now and my partner and I really need to discuss our next move. Things are crazy. We're trying to figure out what happened...well, I really can't talk about it..."

"OK," Cade replied. Katie could hear a slight annoyance in his tone but he was hiding it well.

"Can I call you back later, when things have calmed down a bit?" Katie offered, not really sure that she any intention of doing so.

"Uh, sure. But I just wanted to see if you were free for dinner tonight. Nothing fancy or anything.. We could just grab a sandwich and eat it on the Boardwalk, if you want," Cade said quickly.

"I don't know...you know it depends on this thing I'm working on right now. I'll have to call you later. OK?" Katie answered.

"You'll call, though?" Cade said, sounding like an awkward fifteen-year old who'd just asked a girl out on his first date.

"I'll let you know," Katie replied impatient to be off the phone.

After she'd ended the call, Katie looked over at Anna and rolled her eyes.

"What's with the cold shoulder to Cade Ware all the sudden? I thought you were into him," Anna commented.

"I don't know if I am or not. Well, as you know, our first date wasn't exactly stellar. And after the conversation I had about him with Ben last night..." Katie shrugged.

"What conversation?" Anna inquired, her eyes widening.

"Oh, Ben came over last night about an hour before I got the call about Jessie waking up. He'd heard—through the Potoma grapevine, of course, since everyone and their brother knows him—that I was dating Cade and he was concerned because he thinks Cade is out to ruin the charm of little ole Potoma," Katie replied.

"Meaning?" Anna prompted.

"He says that Cade's not really interested in preserving Potoma's old houses for the sake of history. He's really only interested in making a lot of money from renting them and maybe selling them for huge profits," Katie explained.

"There's no crime in free enterprise," Anna pshawed.

"No, but Ben's point was that if rents go up and house prices go up then property taxes will follow. Potoma will become a rich man's resort and costs for everything will increase to a point that the average middle-class person can no longer afford to live here or vacation here," Katie continued.

"Hmmm..." Anna mused for a moment, nodding her understanding. "How does Ben know Cade's intentions?"

"Same grapevine that notified him that I had dinner with Cade, apparently," Katie smirked.

"I can understand Ben's concern but really, what can anyone do about it if Cade does do all of that and incite a price increase and the destruction of Potoma as we know it?" Anna surmised.

"Nothing. Ben knows that," Katie replied. "He said he wanted to warn me because he was concerned about me having an association with someone who might ultimately become an enemy of the town, so to speak."

"Mighty chivalrous of him," Anna laughed. "Maybe he just doesn't want you to be involved with him for ulterior reasons."

"I've told you. Ben's not interested. Not in that way,"

Katie protested. "If he was, we'd be dating already."

"Some guys are just slow on the upswing," Anna teased.

"Whatever!" Katie said shaking her head and smiling.

After a moment of good natured grinning between girlfriends, Anna slapped both palms on the steering wheel. "OK, enough personal stuff. We've got a teenage girl to find."

Katie and Anna had pulled up in front of the station. "What's our next move?" Anna asked. "Looks like Mick Wilson may have an alibi after all."

"Is it a reliable alibi, though? I mean, Mick and Aster are neighbors and they may even be friends," Katie cautioned.

"I think Aster is believable. I think if she were trying to cover for Mick she wouldn't have admitted that he could have gone back out after she went to sleep," Anna said. "I think the real question is: Did Mick go back to the hospital after he got home from his two o'clock visit?"

"Doesn't really seem logical that he would come all the way home for what, an hour or so, and then drive back to the hospital, does it?" Katie questioned.

"No, not for your normal average person, it doesn't," Anna concurred. "But Mick Wilson isn't really too normal is he?"

"I guess that depends on your definition of normal. But I just have a hard time seeing any logic in sneaking into Jessie's room at two in the morning just to leave her sleeping if you are planning to kidnap her. Was it some sort of recognizance mission? I mean that's the only explanation I can think of. But then, when he saw that no one was around and he hadn't been detected by anyone, why wouldn't he have gone ahead and taken her? Why would he risk being seen by going back a second time. That just really doesn't make any sense at all," Katie reasoned.

"When you put it that way, I can see your point. He was all clear to kidnap her on the first visit. There is no obvious reason for him to leave, come home, and then go back and take her," Anna agreed.

"So the next question is: How come the video camera shows him there twice, several hours apart?" Katie pondered, rubbing her temples as if she were expecting a genie to pop out of her head and give her the answer.

"Is it possible that he is telling the truth and he was only at the hospital once? Let's say that's what happened. Did Mick have an accomplice? Was Mick just doing the surveillance to size up the situation and someone else actually took Jessie somehow?" Anna said, her eyes becoming wider and more animated with the possibility.

"If that's the case and there is an accomplice, why would the accomplice wait two hours to go to the hospital? Why chance it? In two hours the entire set-up could have changed. That doesn't really make much sense," Katie critiqued.

"You're right. The smart plan would have been for the accomplice to immediately follow in Mick's footsteps. Waiting until four thirty would have been foolish!" Anna concluded.

"So we're back to Mick making two trips even though from a strategic point of view it seems ridiculous," Katie sighed. "Maybe we should go back to the hospital and look at the tapes again. Maybe we missed something."

# CHAPTER 44

**Casey was startled** by the slam of the front door. Surely, Ted hadn't come home early; he just never did that. Casey used an old grocery list to mark her place in the book she'd been reading and stood up.

"Mom!" Casey heard her son call out. Casey hurried down the hall toward the living room.

"What are you doing home?" Casey asked, bewildered and concerned at the same time. "Are you sick?"

"I'm not sick. I just can't sit in class listening to the teacher drone on and on when Jess is missing," Sebastian replied. "I need to be looking for her."

"We're all worried, honey, but as far as I know there's no clue as to where she is," Casey said trying to somehow be soothing.

"She can't have just disappeared!" Sebastian insisted. "Obviously the police are incompetent. I mean after all, they're just small-town traffic cops. Barney Fifes."

"That's not fair, Bastian. They are doing everything they can," Casey defended, though she didn't know exactly why. She paused then hesitantly added, "They dragged me into the police station just a few hours ago to take my fingerprints."

Sebastian looked shocked for a moment. "What the hell for?" he asked angrily in an accusing tone.

"First, watch your language," Casey scolded, then explained. "As you know, they lifted fingerprints from Jessie's room. Since we are frequent visitors to the Ashton house and particularly since we were present at the last cul-de-sac get-together there and had access to the upstairs because of the bathroom situation, they assumed that I might have been in Jessie's room. Your dad had to get his taken, too, as well as everyone else that was at that party."

"Why would you be in Jessie's room?" Sebastian questioned, eyebrows drawn up.

"I didn't say I was," Casey retorted. "The police assumed that anyone who went upstairs to use the bathroom that night may have taken an impromptu house tour, Jessie's room being a stop on the tour."

"Why would someone just go into Jessie's room?" Sebastian asked.

"Plenty of people are curious about other people's houses and want to know how they're laid out or decorated or whatever," Casey replied.

"That would be a total invasion of privacy," Sebastian said, obviously outraged at the thought. "Do you let people go into my room without my permission when I'm not here?"

"You're really blowing this out of proportion, honey," Casey answered, trying to calm her son down. "But yes, on occasion, I have shown first-time visitors your room. We don't go in or anything. I just open the door, they peek in, I apologize for the mess and then I close the door and we move on."

"I can't believe you would let some total stranger invade my privacy that way!" Sebastian yelled, making Casey jump slightly with surprise at his anger.

"Bastian, calm down. I know you're upset about Jessie but you're really overreacting to this," Casey said, touching her son's arm. "I won't do it anymore if it bothers you that much."

"You'd better not ever do it again!" Sebastian yelled again. Casey could see that his eyes were watering up but he was trying his best to blink black the tears.

"OK, OK," Casey replied, wishing Sebastian was still just a small boy and she could take him in her arms and rock him and sing him songs until he cried out all his tears.

Sebastian brushed past Casey, heading for his bedroom. Casey stood still trying to decide what she should do now. Ted would ground Sebastian for leaving school without permission and then put him in the car and take him back there. Ted would tell Sebastian to suck it up. And if Ted found out that Casey hadn't done those things, Ted would be angry at Casey and give her the silent treatment for the rest of the week. Casey couldn't help the smile that wound its way through her lips no matter how hard she tried to suppress it. Ironically, Ted gave her the silent treatment most of the time anyway no matter if he was angry with her or not. He was just more verbal about giving her the silent treatment when he was mad at her. And that irony made her lips twitch into an even bigger smile.

Casey walked to Sebastian's room and knocked on the door.

"Just go away!" Sebastian yelled through the closed door.

"Look, I'm not going to even get angry at you for leaving school but we need to talk," Casey yelled back.

"I don't want to talk to you," Sebastian replied. "About anything."

Casey was silent. She knew Sebastian's anger was about more than her letting people look into his room without his permission. And it was about more than the fact that Jessie was missing and he was worried sick about her. Things had been boiling between them for a while now ever since Sebastian had overheard a conversation she'd had with their neighbor, Danny Ping. Sebastian hadn't liked some of the things he'd heard and he'd been deeply hurt by them. At the time, and even now, Casey didn't know whether she owed Sebastian an apology or not. Sometimes she felt like she did and sometimes she felt like the things that Sebastian had overheard were none of Sebastian's business so she had no reason to say she was sorry to him.

After going back and forth about it in her mind for several minutes, Casey decided to leave Sebastian alone for the time being. Casey walked back to the living room and picked up her cell phone, dialing the local number for the Potoma police department. Maybe they had some news about Jessie. Maybe by now they'd stumbled upon some clues they'd missed before about Jessie's current whereabouts.

"I'm sorry, Ms. Bailey. We really can't give out any specific information to anyone except Miss Ashton's parents," the friendly police officer on the other end of the line said apologetically.

"Can you at least tell me if the police have any new information on what happened to Jessie or where she might be?" Casey cajoled.

"I can say that Officers Bell and Madrid are actively working on the case as we speak and have questioned a person of interest in case," the police officer replied.

"So you have a suspect?" Casey replied excited by the prospect.

"I didn't say that, Ms. Bailey. I said the officers talked with a person of interest. That doesn't necessarily mean they think that particular person has committed a crime, only that they may have information about the case," the police officer explained in a cheery voice.

"Is that all the information you can give me?" Casey asked, deflated at the lack of intelligence she was privy to.

"I'm afraid so at this time," the police officer answered.

Casey hung up. She had been hoping that the police would tell her that they'd stumbled on to some new leads or even better, had arrested someone already and had found Jessie safe and sound.

Casey went back to Sebastian's closed bedroom door. "I called the police. I have some news that might be good," Casey called out.

Casey heard Sebastian's bed creak and then heard his bare feet padding across the wood floor. He opened the door and leaned on the door frame. "What?" Sebastian said, a mixture of hope and defeat showing clearly in his shining eyes.

"They questioned someone. They say it's "a person of interest" which means at this point it could be someone they suspect had something to do with Jessie's disappearance or someone who at least knows something about it," Casey informed him.

"Who is it?" Sebastian asked warily.

"They wouldn't tell me," Casey conceded. "Innocent until proven guilty and all that, I'm sure."

"OK, so that's the news?" Sebastian said scoffing. "That's it?"

"That's all I've got, honey," Casey shrugged. "You know, stewing in your room isn't going to change anything."

Casey knew she'd said the wrong thing as soon as it was out of her mouth.

"Yeah, I guess you know about that firsthand, don't you?" Sebastian shot back at her.

"What's that supposed to mean?" Casey replied, noticing the vehemence in Sebastian's expression.

"You know exactly what I mean," Sebastian retorted. "You didn't sit around stewing about things did you?"

"As opposed to what, Sebastian?" Casey replied crossing her arms over her chest, anger simmering just below the surface at the continuous disrespect he had shown her since he arrived at the house.

"As opposed to what? Really, Mom? Seriously?" Sebastian said, flinging his arms about him with sarcasm apparent in every gesture.

"What exactly are you so bitter about? Because this attitude of yours is not about supposed invasion of your privacy and it's not even about Jessie right now," Casey let loose.

"I don't believe you. I really don't believe you. How can you stand there and ask me what I'm so bitter about?" Sebastian replied putting both hands on the back of his head and shaking it viciously.

"Why don't you just put it to me so we can have it out?" Casey answered, her head bobbing slightly on its own. She could feel what she called her "homegirl ancestry" coming out.

"I heard you and the Asian dude," Sebastian groaned, stepping back a few inches. "I heard what you said!"

"What you overheard Danny Ping and I talking about is absolutely none of your business!" Casey asserted.

"None of my business?" Sebastian replied in a loud voice, his arms flailing. "Anything that affects my family is my business!"

"Exactly how has your family been affected? Tell me that. Has anything changed?" Casey challenged.

"My brain has changed after hearing what I heard. I know stuff. Maybe stuff I wasn't supposed to know but now I know and I can't un-know it," Sebastian replied, clearly tongue-tangled.

"You haven't answered my question," Casey said evenly.

"Yeah, Mom. I will never think of you the same way again. And now I feel like I have to take sides,"

Sebastian replied, his voice a little hoarse with the tears Casey could hear forming in his throat.

"Have I asked you take sides? Nothing in this family, in this household has changed," Casey remarked.

"Yeah? Not yet. But it will. Do you really think that waiting until I graduate and move to Wyoming in the fall to go to college will make it any easier for me to live with those changes?" Sebastian replied, anger still flaring in his eyes even though his normally upright posture had deteriorated to slumping shoulders and slouching legs. "Just because I'm not actually living here with you and Dad doesn't mean I won't be living with the changes."

Casey was amazed at the mature insight her son was exhibiting at that moment. And he had left her somewhat speechless but she knew that she couldn't let the conversation drop at that critical juncture.

"I guess I hadn't looked at it that way," Casey began tentatively. "I think in my own mind I had just assumed "out of sight, out of mind". So I will apologize to you for that. But I'm not going to apologize to you for wanting to be happy in my life. And you also need to understand and realize that I didn't get unhappy all by myself. Your dad had a part in that, too."

"Oh, now you're blaming Dad for what you've done?" Sebastian went on the defensive again.

"I take responsibility, full responsibility for my actions. But a marriage is made up of two people who both have to give one-hundred percent and when one or both doesn't, the marriage isn't happy and it doesn't work," Casey said gently. "So yes, I am blaming your dad—for not giving me one-hundred percent."

Sebastian sat down on his bed and was quiet, looking up through his long eyelashes at Casey. Casey kept glancing down, watching her foot as she circled her big toe on the floor, waiting for some sort of reply from Sebastian. The ball was in his court now. After what seemed like a very long time, Sebastian walked over to Casey, bending his tall frame down at least six inches to wrap his big strong arms around his petite mother. It was a quick hug but it was enough for Casey.

"I'm not going to pretend to understand all that about your marriage and Dad or why you did what you did but I accept your apology and I'm sorry for being so disrespectful. I can't say that I'm not still angry with you, though," Sebastian said after he'd released Casey from his embrace. "I am still angry about what I heard you and Asian dude talking about and I don't know how to get over it."

"Fair enough," Casey said quietly, staring at her son.

"Can we change the subject now?" Sebastian asked, rubbing his jaw thoughtfully.

"Sure," Casey replied.

"What do we do about Jessie? I'm so worried about her," Sebastian said so plaintively that Casey was afraid he would burst into tears.

"We pray, honey," Casey answered giving Sebastian a one arm hug around his waist and rubbing the small of his back. She tried to sound encouraging but she knew that at this point there was a good chance that Jessie could be in real, serious danger.

## Chapter 45

"**I don't get** it. Those tapes ran from 2:00am to 8:00am this morning and not once did we see even a trace of Jessie or any type of vehicle—laundry cart, gurney, nothing—that could have hidden her, come out of the room," Katie said, tossing the remote on the end table.

"I still don't understand the two Black Hoods going in and out of her room in the middle of the night. Was it the same person or two different people?" Anna replied, throwing up her hands.

"Maybe we should look at those two portions again. We might be able to at least ascertain if the same person made both visits. I mean Mick Wilson is adamant that he only made one visit—the first one and although he's not the most credible person in the world, our interview with Aster Bancroft seems to back up that claim. At least from a logical point of view, anyway," Katie suggested, picking the remote back up to rewind.

"We need a dual screen to do that," Anna stopped her. "We'll have to take these back to the station."

After receiving clearance from the administrator to remove the tapes from the hospital, Katie and Anna headed to the station. With help from the IT specialist, they set up to watch Tapes 2 and 3 simultaneously. Anna forwarded each tape to the portion containing the dark figure in the hall. They watched one sequence, then the other, rewinding them and freezing them both as the man in black pushed his way through the tall silver doors.

"Not the same person," Katie determined after studying the dual images for a few minutes. "First guy is broader, shorter and I'd say probably older. See, he doesn't stand as straight. That's definitely Mick Wilson. Look at that swagger."

Anna rolled her eyes at Katie and they both burst into laughter.

"You're right. And if you look closely, they're not actually wearing the exact same thing either. I think the first guy is wearing a navy jacket or maybe charcoal. I don't think it's black. And he has on black jeans or dark blue," Anna pointed out. "Second guy is definitely in black and he's wearing trousers."

"Shoes are different, too. First guy has on tennis shoes. Second guy's wearing some kind of boot," Katie added.

Anna played the tapes simultaneously in slow motion. At first they saw nothing out of the ordinary but then something on the second tape caught Katie's eye.

"Back up second guy," Katie ordered. "Something isn't right."

Anna began to rewind the tape in slow motion.

"Stop, there," Katie said pointing at the screen. On the tape the figure had just emerged from Jessie's room and was moving briskly up the hall to the double doors. "Look at the clothes. What do you see?"

"Bingo!" Anna cried, her eyes wide. "Now the trousers on second guy are too long and the coat is definitely too big. That's got to be Jessie!"

Katie and Annie high-fived. "OK, so what happened to second guy? How'd he get out without being seen?" Katie mused.

"Easy," Anna replied. "Remember the orderlies and nurses? He could have just disguised himself as a hospital worker and slipped out."

"Then we need to find him. Fast-forward to that part," Katie urged, excited by their discovery.

Within a few minutes, Katie and Anna had spotted a tall male orderly coming out of Jessie's hospital room. Unfortunately, he had turned his head and looked down just before he came into view of the camera so Katie and Anna couldn't tell what he looked like.

"What do we do now?" Anna said, deflated by their failure to identify the supposed hospital worker.

"Well, we know one thing for sure now. Jessie left the hospital room willingly and on her own two feet. No one was coercing her, at least not physically," Katie replied carefully laying out what they had observed so far. "So that would mean that whoever switched clothes with her was someone she knew and more than likely was trying to help her."

"Agreed. So what males that are a part of Jessie's life are tall and fitfully thin?" Anna continued the thread of thought.

"Fitfully thin? Is that some new P.C. term for guys who have nice physiques?" Katie scoffed with a grin.

"Whatever," Anna grinned back, shrugging good-naturedly.

"Two of her male friends spring to mind immediately," Katie replied. "Big brother Bug Bailey—say that three times fast—and the dapper, Alex Watson, inventor extraordinaire." Katie had adopted an English accent when naming Alex.

"What did you put in your tea this morning?" Anna teased, then got serious. "That's who I'm thinking about, too. If Bug's really as sibling-like as everyone says he is he's going to do whatever it takes to protect her like any big brother would," Anna said.

"So we've got Bug on the list," Katie answered, ignoring Anna's quip. "I definitely think Alex would participate in this kind of scheme, too. It's obvious that he's head-over-heels for Jessie."

"Well, then, first step is to see if Bug and Alex are at school today," Anna suggested. "I'll call."

A few short minutes later, Anna reported that neither teenager was in class. When the resource officer checked the parking lot, neither Bug's car or the golf cart he drove to school was present. At that, Katie and Anna agreed that the next step was to visit the boys' homes and see if they were there.

# CHAPTER 46

**Mick Wilson stared** at the cinderblock wall that was painted a light pea-green. He wondered why all the holding cells in local jails were painted that same color. Was it literally to make you sick? He much preferred the slightly off-white coloration found in prisons. Not that he wished he were in a prison instead of here in the Potoma police station. To be honest, he was a little mystified at exactly why he was being "detained" as Katie had put it. He admitted that he had gone to the hospital to see Jessie after visiting hours were over and that was against hospital rules but it wasn't actually against the law was it? It's not like he did anything bad to her. He'd simply pulled the covers away from her face. That was it. Then he'd left. He hadn't been there more than a few minutes.

Mick's back was beginning to get stiff sitting on the cinderblock bench against the cinderblock wall. He was also chilled to the bone in his shorts and thin short-sleeved cotton shirt. They'd taken his tennis shoes and given him a pair of flimsy plastic flip-flips for his feet and his toes were like little blocks of ice. *Why did they keep jail cells so cold?* Mick mused. *This place is going to freeze my brain if I stay in here much longer!*

Mick thought about lying down but then he'd have to start all over again creating a warm spot against the cold surface with the little bit of body heat he had left. Maybe he should get up and walk around, get his juices flowing. Surely that would warm him up a little bit and stretch out his sore back muscles. Mick rubbed his arms frantically with his hands as if he were rubbing two sticks together to produce fire. His brain was starting to cloud over like it did when he forgot to take his medicine or when he took too much. Mick was sure he was getting brain freeze and not the kind you get momentarily when you eat ice cream too fast.

Mick decided to concentrate on what he had done so he wouldn't forget the facts. He was going to tell Katie the whole story when she questioned him again so that she would know that he didn't do anything to Jessie. He would tell her how a long time ago he used to look into his female neighbors' windows and watch them. He especially liked to watch Grace Garfield. She was so pretty and had such a nice curvy figure, like Marilyn Monroe or Rita Hayworth. Grace had this tiny little waist and long slender legs and arms. Grace had always liked to soak in the bathtub and before Grace remodeled the inside of her house, Mick could hide in the thick, leafy tree outside of the bathroom window and watch Grace without her even knowing he was there. He also liked to watch Grace cook; she looked like one of those professional chefs on TV and she always wore a spotless white apron that accented her figure the way it tied in the back and pinched in her stomach.

Grace did everything on a schedule so Mick always knew exactly what nights she took a bath and what time she prepared her meals. Before Grace's parents died, he had to be more careful about watching her because he didn't want her father to catch him looking at her. After that day at the cul-de-sac cookout when he couldn't take his eyes off of her and her father had noticed and made it clear to Mick to stay away from his teenage daughter, Mick had been terrified of Grace's dad. So from then on, he'd been very cautious about watching Grace. Even so, a few times he'd been looking through the window at Grace in the bathtub, Grace's father had come outside and almost caught him in the tree.

Jessie wasn't really Mick's type. She was too thin, for one. She looked like a magazine model with tiny breasts and small hips and muscular arms and legs. Mick liked girls like Katie and Grace that had hourglass figures and reminded him of the pin-up girls from the 50s. Jessie's mother, Ellen, was shaped just like Jessie and so Mick had never been tempted to peep into their house, much less pay much attention to their comings and goings. Suffice it to say, he really never noticed Jessie unless she was standing right in front of him.

Six months ago, he had been watching Grace, no longer afraid of getting caught since Grace's dad wasn't around anymore. He was only looking in through the French doors watching her cook dinner and he thought he was well-hidden in the dark. Suddenly, right there in front of him was Jessie. She had demanded to know why he was hiding in Grace's side-yard and obviously spying on her. Mick had been so flustered at being caught without warning that at first he couldn't even speak. Jessie had threatened to tell Grace what he was doing and started walking away when Mick finally found his voice and begged her not to.

"Give me one good reason why I shouldn't tell Miss Garfield what you're doing!" Jessie had demanded.

"Because I'll never do it again. I swear!" Mick had promised, panicked at the thought of going back to jail.

"Why should I believe you?" Jessie had replied, raising her eyebrow.

"Because I know you will tell her if I do it again and then I could get into some real bad trouble," Mick had said weakly.

"I really don't believe you. Who else do you play "Peeping Tom" to?" Jessie had questioned. "Do you do this to all the women in this neighborhood?"

Mick had hesitated. The truth was that he'd peeped at most of the women in New Town at one time or another but most of them weren't to his liking and the only one he'd been looking at lately, really for the last two years, was Grace. He decided to tell the half-truth.

"I only look at Grace. I really like her but I'm too shy to tell her," Mick had said, trying to look pitiful.

Jessie had studied him for a few moments, clearly trying to make up her mind as to whether or not he was being truthful. Finally she had said "OK, you *were* only watching her cook dinner. It's not like I caught you watching her get undressed or take a shower or something. But you have to promise me you won't ever do this again."

Mick had promised and even done the "cross-my-heart-and-hope-to-die" thing to emphasize his commitment. And at the time he really had meant to live up to his promise. Something about Jessie Ashton had made him want to do the right thing and fight his bad impulses. Something about her innocent goodness made him want desperately to be good and live up to her expectations.

Mick *had* been good until a few weeks ago. He hadn't

gone to Grace's house once. Sometimes he'd peek out of his own window to watch her weeding her flowerbeds or getting her mail but that was different from skulking around her house at night, peeking in her windows when she didn't know he was there. Then one night, Mick had forgotten to take his pills and he just lost control. He couldn't help it. He'd sneaked over to Grace's house to watch her in the kitchen. She was making her own bread and he liked the way she kneaded the dough and got sprinkled with flour in the process. When everything was cooked and ready to eat and Grace had taken her plate to the living room to watch TV, Mick had left, feeling guilty already for breaking his promise to Jessie.

Just as he was stepping out of Grace's yard onto the pavement of the street leading into the cul-de-sac, Jessie and her neighbor, the Bailey boy, had come whizzing in on his golf-cart. They'd almost run right over Mick. When the boy had stopped to apologize, Mick had glanced at Jessie and he had known right away that she knew what he'd been up to. The look on her face made Mick feel so ashamed that he couldn't look her in the eye and he had immediately dropped his head to stare at the ground. Jessie hadn't said one word to him but he knew exactly what she was thinking. He was a liar and he'd disappointed her tremendously.

Mick's heart raced for hours that night, afraid Jessie was going to tell Grace what he had been doing and afraid that Grace was going to call the police. He paced, stopping every few minutes to look out of the window to see if police cars were barreling into the cul-de-sac to arrest him. When he finally went to bed at midnight without being arrested, he began to breathe a little easier and when several days past without incident, he eventually realized that Jessie hadn't told anyone what she undoubtedly knew he had done.

Mick had wanted to tell Jessie that he'd kept his promise to her up until that night and the only reason he'd messed up was because he'd forgotten to take his medication but he could never seem to find a time to get her alone when no one would notice him talking to her. Then, just as Mick had decided that no matter what he was going to have to find a way to talk to

Jessie because he was just feeling so horrible about betraying her trust, she was found unconscious and he couldn't tell her all those things.

That's why he'd gone to the hospital in the middle of the night. After he found out she was alive and well, he'd wanted to tell Jessie what had happened and beg her to forgive him. He wanted to be able to talk to her without anyone else around because he didn't want anyone else to know what he'd done and maybe call the police on him. He wanted to assure Jessie that he would try as hard as he could to keep his promise to her from now on. But then when he saw her, she'd been sleeping so peacefully in her hospital bed, he just hadn't had the heart to wake her up.

# CHAPTER 47

**Aster was so** glad that her assignment was almost over. She missed her family and she was tired of wearing the uncomfortable sleazy waitress clothing the assignment demanded. She especially hated the high-heeled shoes that made her feet feel like sardines in a can. She only had to sit tight for a few more days until things were wrapped up and then she'd be on her way back home. When Aster reflected on the past few months, it was hard to believe that she had pulled off this deception so well and for so long. Her neighbors hadn't had a clue. Sure, she knew that they all thought she was a little strange and she didn't really fit in with the rest of them but she was positive that none of them had guessed the truth about her.

On the other hand, those two female police officers were exceptionally bright and it was entirely possible, were she to hang around much longer, that they might become suspicious. They'd already given her peculiar looks when they'd questioned her as if they were aware that something odd was going on but they just couldn't quite nail it down. Aster wished she could just come clean with them instead of continuing the charade but for the sake of the operation she just couldn't take the risk of blowing her cover. All she had to worry about right now was the fingerprints they'd taken. Hopefully, her boss had been successful in quashing that problem and the results would come back clean, belonging to a thirty-something waitress named Aster Bancroft.

Aster was lying on the sofa flipping through the TV channels with the remote. After all the interruptions, she'd given up on actually getting anymore deep sleep but was hoping that if she found something monotonous enough on TV, she might at least doze off for a little while. Settling on a documentary about African insects, Aster let her eyelids fall closed as she listened to the British-accented narrator. Aster had just settled into a light nap when her phone rang.

Startled, Aster felt for the cell phone on the table next to the couch without sitting up.

"Look, we've got a problem", the voice on the other end announced. "We thought you'd gotten away clean last night but now it appears that your friend has been talking to his friend. This friend is going to be at your bar tonight and I don't have to tell you what's going to happen if the friend recognizes you...which is a sure thing."

Aster had been brought to her full senses. "So what do you suggest?"

"We'll have to sweep up tonight instead of waiting as we'd planned," the voice replied.

"How do you suggest we do that? Have you even had time to review the photos I took?" Aster asked.

"We're working on it. We should have a plan of action in a few hours. You'll know what to do by the time you leave for work tonight," the voice answered.

"What about the girl?" Aster inquired. "What do we do about her now?"

"Nothing."

Aster sighed with relief. She really didn't want anything bad to happen to Jessie Ashton. After all, Jessie had just accidently stumbled into the operation and truth be told, didn't have a clue what she really knew.

# CHAPTER 48

**Katie answered the** cell phone on the second ring without bothering to look at the caller ID. When she heard the voice on the other end, she immediately regretted not screening first.

"Hello, Cade," Katie began. "I'm sorry I haven't called you back but I've just been extremely busy and I don't know how my evening is going to go yet."

"No problem. I was just checking. I've been using some pretty loud equipment and thought I might have missed my phone ringing," Cade replied, a little edge to his voice although it was obvious to Katie he was trying to sound casual.

"I would have left a message if I'd called," Katie replied, deliberately repressing the annoyance she felt.

"Well, you never know. Sometimes cell phones lose messages or delay them for hours," Cade suggested.

"True. I'll call you as soon as I know if I'm free tonight. OK?" Katie said, anxious to hang up.

"Sure. I'll be waiting," Cade replied, forced cheerfulness apparent in his tone.

"Cade, again?" Anna questioned.

Katie nodded. "He seems desperate to have dinner with me tonight. Weird."

"Maybe he just really likes you and thinks he screwed up big- time on your last date so he wants the chance to change your mind," Anna remarked, shrugging.

"Maybe, but bad date aside, after spending some time pondering what Ben told me about him, I'm beginning to wonder myself if he's all he's represented himself to be. Or was all that talk about preservation and art just a come on to get me to go out with him?" Katie commented, slipping her phone into her pocket.

"Going out on a second date might help you figure that out. Why don't you just ask him straight up if what Ben said about him is true? I mean you wouldn't have to say it came from Ben. You could just say it's a rumor you've heard," Anna suggested as they paused at a stop sign.

"I suppose I could do that. But I'm inclined to believe

what Ben says without even checking it out. I mean, Cade's attitude alone toward certain groups of people is enough to convince me that he's only interested in money, not saving historic architecture or even providing a service for someone," Katie said.

"You've got to remember that for some people, business is business, and not everyone is civic-minded. I mean, let's say what Ben says is true…that he's only interested in making a lot of money on these properties he's buying up and restoring. That doesn't mean he doesn't genuinely care about preserving them. If he's as flush as Ben says, he could just as easily tear the old ones down and put up new ones for probably about the same price. And if you haven't noticed, he doesn't have contractors in doing all the work—he's actually being very hands-on and getting dirty, too," Anna reminded Katie.

"What makes you so pro-Cade all of a sudden? A few hours ago you were cheering for Ben," Katie remarked, her eyes narrowing at Anna.

"I'm still cheering for Ben. I think he's the one for you and I think he's a lot more interested in you than you recognize. But if he's not going to make the move, I don't see any reason you can't have fun with Cade for a while. He seems like a decent guy," Anna replied.

"Ben's not going to make a move on me. He told me so a couple of days ago," Katie said quietly.

"How do you know that? What do you mean he told you so?" Anna replied while simultaneously pulling over on the side of the road under a shady tree.

"He admitted to me that he was interested in some other woman," Katie answered shrugging.

"Who?" Anna said, turning to face Katie full-on.

"He didn't say. He said I knew her, though," Katie said, sighing.

"So someone in Potoma?" Anna asked.

"I guess," Katie replied shrugging her shoulders slightly and wrinkling her forehead.

"I don't believe it. Why haven't we ever seen him out with her? Why haven't we ever seen her hanging around his business? Was there a woman he was particularly friendly with at his gig Saturday night?" Anna rattled off.

"Maybe he's been dating her just occasionally up until now. And no, I didn't see anyone I thought he was with Saturday night but that doesn't necessarily mean anything. I'm sure she has a life and maybe she just couldn't make it to his gig," Katie answered.

"You know, you shouldn't have told me about this because now I have to investigate," Anna threatened.

"No, you don't. Besides, we have a much more important case for you keep your attention on," Katie scoffed.

"Don't worry, I'm fully committed to finding Jessie Ashton and figuring out what happened to her and who is responsible for her poisoning," Anna assured Katie. "But that doesn't mean I can't nose around a little and find out who Ben's new spark is, too."

Katie knew better than to argue with Anna once she set her mind to something so she just rolled her eyes at her and said in an already trounced tone-of-voice "Leave it alone. I don't even think I want to know."

"Well, I do," Anna said, as she whipped into Versailles Court, driving straight for the Bailey house.

## Chapter 49

**When Casey answered** the door she groaned audibly. She was in no mood to talk to the police again. She was still reeling from her argument with Sebastian and the reminder of what he had overheard her say to Danny Ping. Her long-time indifference to Ted had suddenly become anger and suspicion. And she was worried about Jessie—worried about what she might tell the police if she suddenly turned up.

"What is it this time?" Casey asked without attempting to disguise her displeasure.

"Is your son at home?"

"Which one?" Casey replied. She knew they were referring to Sebastian but she was feeling confrontational at the moment.

"Bug—Sebastian. Is he at home today?"

"Yes, he is. Why?" Casey demanded, wondering what on earth they could want to talk to Sebastian about. They'd already questioned him and taken his fingerprints. What more could they want from him?

"We need to talk with him."

"About what?" Casey replied. "Haven't you upset him enough? I assume this is about Jessie?"

"We believe he may know something about Jessie's disappearance from the hospital."

"I can assure you that Sebastian doesn't know anything," Casey answered, stepping toward Officers Bell and Madrid.

"We need to ascertain that for ourselves, ma'am."

"Why would you think that Sebastian knows anything?" Casey asked, her voice rising. "He came home from school today because he's so upset about her disappearance he couldn't concentrate on his classes."

"We really need to talk to him, Ms. Bailey. Please have him come to the door."

Casey crossed her arms and leaned up against the door frame. "Look, he's very upset right now. I don't want you to upset him any further."

'I'm only going to ask you politely one more time to

get your son. Otherwise we will have to retrieve him ourselves."

Casey glared at the two police officers, quickly working out the pros and cons of refusing to let the police officers question her son. She realized she really had no choice.

"I'll go get him," Casey said resignedly, turning her back to the police.

Casey took her time walking to Sebastian's bedroom. He wasn't going to be happy about having to talk to the police. Even though they had called a truce, Casey knew her son was still extremely bitter about what he knew, about what he'd overheard, and he wasn't even close to forgiving her or forgetting about it. On top of that, he was genuinely worried about Jessie and the last thing he would want to do is be harassed by the police right now with his emotions in such high gear.

"Bastian, the police are here and want to talk to you about Jessie's disappearance," Casey said after she had knocked on Sebastian's closed door.

"Tell them I have nothing to say," Sebastian called back.

"I already did. They're not taking no for an answer," Casey replied.

A moment later, Sebastian's door opened and he stood in front of her bleary-eyed with tousled hair and no shirt. "Why do they want to talk to me?" Sebastian asked.

"They think you might have information about Jessie's disappearance. They wouldn't tell me why they think that," Casey replied.

After Sebastian had put on a T-shirt and run a brush through his unruly hair, he followed Casey to the front door.

"Hi, Bug. Or would you rather me call you Sebastian?"

"Bug's fine," Sebastian replied.

"Where were you this morning between about two and six?"

"I was here, asleep," Sebastian answered. "Why?"

"Can you prove that?"

"Sebastian was here. Where else would he be, especially on a school night and at that time?" Casey interjected.

"How do you know he was here, Ms. Bailey? Kids sneak out all the time. Were you awake and monitoring him during that time?"

"No, I was not awake. I was sleeping, too," Casey lied. "But my son would not go anywhere at two o'clock in the morning without telling me about it."

"Are you sure about that, Ms. Bailey?"

"Yes, I am," Casey insisted.

"And you were here during that time, Ms. Bailey. From two until six this morning?"

"I said so already," Casey retorted, her temper erupting. "Are you accusing me of lying?"

"Any mother would lie for her son. Especially if he were a person of interest in the disappearance of a young girl."

"I'm not lying for my son and my son is not lying," Casey replied with a twinge of guilt. She was lying but not for the reasons the police officers had in mind.

"Bug, did you visit Jessie in the hospital last night?"

"You saw me there when you came to question Jessie. You know I was," Sebastian answered matter-of-factly.

"And when did you leave?"

"Right after the two of you did. The nurse came out to the waiting room and told us that Jessie wasn't going to be allowed any more visitors for the night. So we all went home," Sebastian replied. Casey wondered where this was going.

"And you didn't return to the hospital later? Say around 4:30 this morning?"

"Like I told you I was in my bed asleep. I went to bed around 11:30 last night and I woke up at 6:30 this morning as usual," Sebastian informed the two police officers.

"What would you say if I told you that we have videotape of someone your height and build sneaking into Jessie's room at about 4:30 this morning?"

"I'd say you ought to be out finding that person instead of standing here questioning me," Sebastian retorted, the tips of his ears red, a sure sign of the anger and outrage building inside of him.

"The videotape suggests that you, or someone that resembles you, went into Jessie's room and switched clothing with her so that she could leave the hospital undetected. Then you, or the person that resembles you, walked out later disguised as an orderly. Now, do you know anything about this?"

"You're saying that someone snuck into the hospital and helped Jessie disappear? She wasn't kidnapped?" Sebastian said with a perceptible sense of relief.

"That is how it appears. Or perhaps you already knew about it and this show of anguish was just a big act to cover up that knowledge?"

"I swear, I don't know anything about what you're telling me," Sebastian answered. "I have to admit, it was an ingenious plan, though. You know, Jessie was probably scared that the person that tried to kill her would come back and try again once they knew she was out of danger and conscious again."

"Did Jessie tell you she was scared?"

"No, but when we—all of her friends—were out in the waiting room, we were talking about it. We were all scared that might happen. When we were told we had to leave the hospital, no one wanted to go and some of us did mention trying to sneak back in. You know, just to watch over Jessie and make sure no one tried to hurt her."

"Who was talking about coming back?"

"We all were. I didn't think anyone was really serious, though. It was just an idea because we were all nervous about leaving her alone. You see that kind of stuff on TV where someone sneaks in to a hospital room and puts something in someone's IV or shoots them with a silencer," Sebastian explained.

"Was Alex Watson at the hospital with everyone else last night?"

"I think so. There were a lot of Jessie's friends there and as you know we don't all run in the same circles so we were kind of split off into different groups. Alex isn't part of my gang so I can't say for sure. Why?" Sebastian questioned.

The two police officers exchanged meaningful glances that apparently signified that it was time to wrap it up. Abruptly, they thanked Sebastian and Casey for their cooperation and left.

As soon as the police had disappeared from the cul-de-sac, Sebastian turned toward Casey, anger flashing anew in his eyes. "Just so you know, I lied to the police and I did it for you".

Casey narrowed her eyes at her son. "You lied about being here all night?"

Sebastian glared at Casey and said, "I only lied about being asleep. I was wide awake all night and I saw you leave. And I know exactly where you were going!"

# Chapter 50

**A police officer** had brought Mick a blanket and cup of coffee. The blanket was thin and had a few holes in it and the coffee was almost too strong for Mick to drink but both of them warmed him up enough to allow him to curl up on the bench and take a nap.

A few hours later, the same police officer had shaken Mick awake. Mick had been disoriented at first but quickly found his senses when the police officer informed him that he would be released after he made a written statement about his hospital visit. Mick was glad that he had thought it all through ahead of time so that he could write it all down. Mick was relieved he could finally confess. He hoped it wouldn't mean he had to go back to jail for peeping but he certainly didn't want to go to jail for kidnapping Jessie Ashton, either. He'd have to be in prison for a long time for that. Mick didn't stop to think about how anyone would prove that he'd kidnapped her when he hadn't. He just knew that jail time for peeping was a lot shorter than jail time for kidnapping.

The police officer took Mick to the same room where Katie and her partner had questioned him earlier. The same room where they had accused him of doing something bad to Jessie Ashton. The police officer told Mick to sit down at the table and then he gave him a form and a pen. It took a while for Mick to write everything down but he was pleased he had done it when he was finished. Now Katie would read it and know the truth and maybe she'd like him again. And Katie would know that there was no way Mick would have hurt Jessie and that he wasn't involved in her disappearance. Mick read what he'd written all the way through three times before he signed it at the bottom. When he handed it to the police officer, he smiled.

The police officer told Mick to wait and he left the room with Mick's confession. Mick hoped he wouldn't have to sit in that room much longer. He hated being in places that had no windows. It made him a little claustrophobic and depressed him. Mick wondered how long he had been at the police station and looked around for a clock. When he couldn't locate one, he made a note to himself to ask the police officer what time it was when he came back.

Mick thought about Grace Garfield and wondered if anyone was going to tell her that he'd been watching her all these years. He knew she'd be really mad if she found out. She didn't like people to bother her. On the other hand, she didn't mind sneaking in to other people's houses when they weren't home. At first Mick thought she was stealing stuff but then one time he decided to spy on her. He was flabbergasted when he saw that all she was doing was taking pictures and making measurements and writing things down in a notebook. That made Mick like her even more. He thought they were kind of like kindred spirits except he liked to look at people and apparently, she liked to look at people's stuff. Then over the past few years, he noticed that the inside of Grace's house was beginning to look just like the insides of their neighbors' houses. Mick thought that was really weird. *Why would anybody want to copy someone else's stuff?*

Despite Mick's obsessive proclivities, he was extremely intelligent. He had, after all, once been a highly regarded and well-paid chemist. Drugs and jail had addled his brain a bit in the past fifteen years but when he put his mind to it, he could still think intellectually. Mick realized that Grace was extremely jealous of her neighbors and all the things they had that she didn't. He noticed that Grace tended to dress like Casey Bailey and Ellen Ashton who often wore designer labels but Grace wore knock-offs from a department store and added her own details to make them appear to be the real thing. It also became apparent to him that Grace copied the interiors of her neighbors' houses so that she could feel like she was living as high as they did even though Grace couldn't afford the high-end furniture and accessories they could. Instead, Grace bought similar things and made or altered items to resemble one-of-a-kind and expensive pieces they had. Mick often wished he could tell Grace that she didn't have to feel that way or do those things. He was sure no one in their cul-de-sac looked down on her. In fact, during the course of his peeping, he heard occasional comments from the women in particular that were very complimentary toward Grace. They especially remarked on how attractive and talented she was and how they wished she'd join in more.

Mick wondered if he should screw up the courage and just go to Grace and admit to her what he'd been doing before anyone else told her. Maybe if he did that she wouldn't press charges against him. Maybe she'd even like him a little. But Mick soon put that thought away. No woman that he'd peeped on would ever like him because in their eyes he'd always be some sort of social deviant, a pervert that they couldn't trust. And when Mick thought about it, he knew they were at least partially right. He'd been watching women since he was fifteen years old and it would take some sort of miracle to cure him of his obsession. He was going to try really hard for Jessie's sake, he still intended to make every effort to keep his promise to her but he also knew it would be an incredible uphill battle.

After what seemed like forever, the police officer entered the room again. He told Mick that everything was in order and that as soon as another police officer was free, he'd be given a ride back to his house. Mick told the police officer that he appreciated the free ride but he'd rather walk. He also asked the police officer to bring him back his tennis shoes; his toes were still freezing in the ugly plastic flip flops.

# Chapter 51

**Katie was ready** to turn her cell phone off and throw it in a ditch. So far, after leaving the Bailey house, two salespersons had called wanting to sell her replacement windows and carpet cleaning, and someone had mistakenly called her number to order a pizza. So when her phone rang again, she almost didn't answer it.

"Officer Katie Bell speaking," Katie said into the phone, irritation apparent in her voice.

"Well, hello, Officer Katie Bell. This is CEO Ben Keller, of Rivertown Transport, or you might also know me as Paramedic Keller of the Potoma Volunteer Rescue Squad or possibly just Ben the lead guitarist for an awesome up-and-coming band, *Local Heroes*," the voice on the other end mocked.

"Actually I prefer the guy that buys me free seafood," Katie answered, relieved to hear Ben's voice.

"Is that a hint?" Ben asked.

"Might be. I just realized I haven't had any lunch today," Katie replied.

"Then I'll take the hint. Meet me at Freddie's and I'll buy you a shrimp croissant with a side of oysters-and-angel hair," Ben said eagerly.

Katie looked at Anna. "I just got an offer I can't refuse. Can you take me to Freddie's Fat Bass?"

Anna rolled her eyes. "Do I get a free lunch, too?"

"I don't think the offer was a two-for-one," Katie grinned. "But you're more than welcome to join Ben and me."

"Actually, I'll drop you off. I brought my lunch to the station so I'll go there to eat, then pick you back up," Anna replied.

"Thanks. I won't take too long. I'm anxious to keep moving with our investigation," Katie promised. "Maybe we should try calling Alex Watson's house."

"Good idea. You do it while we're on the way," Anna agreed.

Katie called the police station to get Alex's phone number. When Katie dialed it, there was no answer. "I'll try again in a little while but if we still don't get him, let's just go over there. He could be out in his shop."

Katie spotted Ben walking up the sidewalk just as she and Anna pulled into the small parking area beside Freddie's. She hopped off the cart, waving to him as Anna pulled off. "Give me twenty minutes," Katie called after Anna and she nodded as she turned the corner.

"Hey, Officer Katie Bell," Ben said when he reached Katie.

"Hey Mr. Free Seafood," Katie greeted.

Ben opened the door of the seafood-and-sandwich shop for Katie and followed her in. After placing their orders at the counter they found a table beside a large window that overlooked the river. While they waited for their lunch to be delivered to their table, Katie filled Ben in on the latest developments in the Jessie Ashton investigation. She wasn't surprised to learn that he and apparently most everyone in town now knew what had happened to Jessie and the fact that she had mysteriously disappeared from the hospital.

"You're sure that Bailey kid was being truthful?" Ben questioned when Katie revealed that they had questioned Bug and were now trying to find Alex Watson.

"I'm pretty sure I believe him. I mean, if he had helped her escape, so to speak, why wouldn't he just bring her back to his house and tell us she was there. We don't have the authority to force her to go back to the hospital. That would be up to her parents," Katie replied. "Besides, I think if Jessie was at Bug's house, his mother would have known about it and being a mother, and Ellen Ashton's good friend, she would have undoubtedly let Jessie's parents know about it."

"But what if he didn't bring her back to the house? What if she went to the house of one of her friends?" Ben suggested.

"Judging from the parents that I've met and the kids that are Jessie's friends, I'm almost positive that any of those parents would notify Ellen and Justin Ashton if Jessie was staying with them," Katie argued. "I mean, I don't think Jessie was running away from her parents. I think she was just genuinely frightened to stay at the hospital. Just like Bug said, they've all seen what happens to witnesses in hospitals on TV."

"Well, if the Bailey boy didn't have anything to do with it, Alex Watson is probably a good guess. From what you've said, it seems like he and Jessie Ashton might have a close relationship," Ben concurred.

"I just hope we can find him," Katie replied, between bites of her shrimp-laden croissant flavored with sautéed onions, tomatoes and herbed cream cheese. "Remind me to try his number again when we're finished with lunch."

"You said he hasn't lived here long, so he probably wouldn't know too many places to go," Ben said, then changed his mind. "Although, Jessie's lived here most of her life so she'd most likely know every nook and cranny."

"That's what we're afraid of. Potoma's a relatively small town—it's not like we're in New York City—but there are still plenty of places to hide. At least for a little while," Katie replied. "I probably shouldn't admit this, but when I was a kid, me and my friends used to make a point of knowing which boats down at the marina were renting slip space year-round and we'd sneak onto them when no one was watching and play inside them for hours. No one ever knew we were there and we could probably have stayed on them for days without anyone ever being any the wiser."

"You--Miss Upstanding Citizen-- breaking and entering?" Ben exclaimed, truly surprised.

"Yeah, well, don't tell anyone. I could lose my job," Katie answered, looking around furtively as if worried that someone had overheard.

Ben laughed. "Don't worry your secret is safe with me."

Katie had started on her oysters, the lightly seasoned shellfish combined with angel hair pasta and melted cheeses. After a few bites she said, "Cade Ware has called me twice today. He wants me to have dinner with him tonight."

"And you're telling me this why?" Ben asked, putting down the salmon-and-swiss-on-rye he was half-way through.

"He seems awful urgent about it. Almost pushy.

I guess I just wanted a guy's point of view," Katie answered. She secretly wondered if it bothered Ben at all that she was considering another date with Cade, Cade's supposed plan to take over Potoma notwithstanding.

"On what? Being pushy or the fact that you're considering it?" Ben asked, his blue eyes seeming to bore into Katie.

"Both, I guess," Katie said, dropping her eyes to her plate to avoid Ben's intense stare.

"Well, if he's intent on having dinner tonight, he must have a reason for it to be tonight," Ben suggested, shrugging. "Have you considered what that reason might be?"

"Honestly, our first date didn't really go all that well. He seemed concerned about that. Very concerned," Katie admitted.

"Is there anything special about tonight that would make him so anxious to see you?" Ben asked.

"Not that I can think of," Katie replied. Katie put the last forkful of pasta in her mouth before adding, "I like him and I'd really like to have the chance to paint the murals for him but I'm not sure I really want to be involved with him."

"Really?" Ben said, seemingly genuinely taken aback. "Why not?"

Katie wanted to tell Ben that it was because she wanted to be involved with *him* but given the fact that Ben had admitted to her he was interested in pursuing a relationship with another woman, Katie's pride wouldn't let her make a fool of herself. "I'm not so sure we have enough in common," Katie answered weakly.

Ben's face seemed to fall into something like disappointment but that expression was quickly replaced with his usual mischievous grin. "So what are you looking for in the perfect date mate?"

*You,* Katie thought. "Are you serious?" Katie replied.

"Why not? I've got a few single friends. I might be able to hook you up…" Ben said, wiping his mouth with his napkin and placing it on the table next to his empty plate.

"OK, I'll play as long as you do, too," Katie replied,

raising an eyebrow.

"Agreed. But you go first," Ben nodded.

"Most important, an impeccable sense of humor," Katie began. She was dead serious about that. "And he has to be good-looking, no average guys for me."

"Gotcha. What else?" Ben played along.

"I don't know, all the usual things a girl looks for. Compassionate, kind, a real gentleman who opens doors and brings me flowers for no reason and likes to take long walks on the beach…" Katie continued, giggling.

"And…" Ben urged.

"Must love dogs," Katie added, thinking of Ogilvie. "Big, spoiled dogs."

Ben nodded, smiling.

"And he has to have a job. No job, no date, 'cause I expect free seafood whenever I want it," Katie finished in a fit of laughter.

"You know, I might just fit the bill, if you're interested. Especially the part about free seafood," Ben joked.

Katie wished he wasn't joking. She also wondered if he'd realized that she'd just given him a partial description of himself. For a moment, she watched him laugh, just taking in his handsome face, the sexy smile, the hair that she would love to run her fingers through.

"You done?" Ben said. "Or is there more?"

"Done for now. It's your turn," Katie replied.

"OK, here goes," Ben began, looking somewhat serious. "She's got to have the potential to be my best friend."

Katie waited for Ben to say more but he didn't. "That's all, that's it?" Katie asked.

"Yep," Ben replied.

"So if she's ugly, boring and unemployed that's OK with you?" Katie questioned, unbelieving.

Ben grinned. "I only surround myself with very attractive, interesting friends, so ugly and boring would never happen." Then Ben's expression became serious. "And I make more than enough money from my business to support someone else so a job is of no consequence."

"I'm speechless, I have to say," Katie answered.

"So you thought I was one of those shallow guys that pick their dates based on beauty or their fondness for partying?" Ben asked pointedly. Katie couldn't tell if he was disappointed or happy that he had surprised her with his answer.

"I honestly don't know what I thought," Katie answered awkwardly. She thought back to their prom date all those years ago, the one she was sure only happened because Ben's first choice had probably backed out at the last minute. She'd always questioned why he'd asked her of all the girls he could have invited. They hadn't really known each other well at the time, just had some classes together where they'd built up a kind of friendship through sarcasm and a few running private jokes.

At that moment, Anna knocked on the window, waving Katie out. Katie gave her the "just a minute" finger sign and Anna walked back to the golf cart.

"Looks like my ride is here," Katie said. "You never gave me an opinion on Cade's seemingly urgent need to have dinner with me tonight."

"He probably just wants to scoop you up before someone else does. There aren't that many single ladies in Potoma on a full-time basis, you know," Ben offered.

"Seriously? That's your answer?" Katie moaned. "You're a lot of help."

Ben shrugged, standing up and gathering their paper plates, napkins and Styrofoam cups. After disposing of them in the nearby trashcan, Ben gestured for Katie to go ahead of him down the aisle between booths and out the front door of the restaurant.

"Thanks for lunch, Mr. Keller, CEO," Katie said as she hopped on the golf cart with Anna.

Ben pretended to tip a non-existent hat on his head to Katie before turning to walk down the street toward his store.

# Chapter 52

**Katie tried calling** Alex Watson again and got no answer at his house.

"Let's just head on over there. Chances are he's in his workshop," Katie suggested.

"From what you have described, it would be easy for him to hide Jessie there. Apparently, his mother and stepfather don't step foot inside," Anna mused.

"My thought exactly," Katie concurred. "The question is, if he's there and he is hiding her there, will he admit it?"

"You seem to have established a good rapport with him. What are the chances that he'll come clean with you?" Anna posed.

"I guess that depends on what Jessie wants him to reveal or not reveal, as the case may be," Katie replied. "He's going to do whatever Jessie wants and whatever he feels protects her the most. Of that I am sure."

"So what do we do if he denies that he knows anything about her disappearance?" Anna questioned. "Threaten to take him down to the station for questioning or detainment? Would that shake him up enough to make him tell the truth?"

"I guess that depends on whether or not he is involved, whether or not he's hiding Jessie or knows where she's hiding, and whether or not he thinks she's safe wherever she is," Katie counted off, using her fingers for emphasis.

"And what if he's not at home? Where do we go from there?" Anna queried.

"The thing is, we still have an attempted murder to solve and so we keep working on that, regardless of whether we find Jessie or not," Katie reminded Anna.

Anna nodded in agreement then changed the subject. "You and Ben looked pretty intense when I pulled up. Lovers quarrel?" Anna teased.

"Actually, we were playing a game called *Who's Your Perfect Date Mate?* He'd just revealed to me his one and only requirement. I was taken a little off-guard," Katie answered, shaking her head.

"Well, don't keep me in suspense?" Anna urged.

"She has to have the potential to be his best friend," Katie revealed.

"Well, then bingo, you've got that, girl! Lately, the two of you have been practically attached at the hip," Anna whooped.

"I already told you. He's let me know he's dating someone," Katie protested.

"Even if he is, that doesn't mean she's his 'perfect date mate'. Maybe he was giving you one big hint," Anna contended. "For goodness sakes, he takes you out to eat at least twice a week almost every week and how many times have the two of you seen each other in the last week alone?"

"You're exaggerating big time. It's not that much," Katie disputed.

"Look, count them down. You went out to dinner Friday night, you went to hear his band play Saturday night, you went to his place a few nights ago and he showed up at your place last night, not to mention lunch today," Anna said in a victorious tone. "And don't forget the numerous phone calls in that much time, too."

"Well, first, I really like his band so I didn't just go to see him Saturday night. And lunch today was just a spur-of-the-moment thing. I don't even know if he was planning to take me to eat. I mean I sort of invited myself and he's such a nice guy that he just went along with it," Katie continued to debate.

Anna looked at Katie wide-eyed then shook her head. "It's plain as day to everyone but you. Why are you such a non-believer?"

"Like I said before, if Ben wanted to be in a relationship with me, he'd have already let me know. I mean, we've both been here in town for the last four years," Katie said almost smugly.

"Did you ever stop to think that he's been trying to let you know and you're just so dense, you're not picking it up? Seriously, what guy, who could have his pick, would spend so much time on a woman he wasn't interested in. He not only spends money on you every time you get an appetite for seafood, he spends an awful lot of time on you, too," Anna asserted.

"We're friends. I never denied that we have become good friends. Just because he likes to hang out with me doesn't mean he wants to pursue a relationship with me," Katie insisted. "If he wanted to date me, why would he be dating someone else and telling me about it to make sure I was clear about it?"

"You're impossible!" Anna said, flinging her hands in the air then quickly returning them to the wheel of the golf cart after realizing she was still driving.

As Katie and Anna pulled into the driveway of Alex Watson's house they could tell that Alex's mother and step-father were gone as no vehicles were in the driveway. They alighted from the golf cart and went to the front door of the house to ring the bell. After several pushes on the button with no response from inside the house, Katie and Anna made their way to the garage.

"Alex, it's Officer Katie Bell. If you're in there, please answer," Katie shouted as she knocked on the entry door to the converted garage. Alex did not answer and neither Katie nor Anna could detect any sound or sign of movement inside the structure.

Katie waited a minute then tried knocking and calling out again. When she received no response a second time, Katie and Anna peered in the windows. Katie noticed that the golf cart-like contraption she'd seen inside Alex's workshop before partially hidden under a tarp was missing.

"He's not here. I'm sure of it," Katie announced. "His machine is gone."

"You mean the weird golf cart you discovered before?" Anna confirmed.

"Exactly. I'm pretty sure if it's not here, he's not here," Katie affirmed.

"Then there's no point in sticking around. We'll just have to keep trying to call the house. Maybe after his parents arrive home from work, they'll be able to tell us where he is," Anna suggested.

Katie nodded and they walked back to the front of the driveway. After they had climbed back on the golf cart, Katie taking a turn at the wheel, Katie said, "Like I said, we've still got to try and figure out who attempted to poison Jessie, so we just as well work on that right now."

Anna nodded her head. "By now, Mick Wilson has been released. I'm beginning to doubt that he had anything to do with the attempted murder. I don't really buy his supposed reason for sneaking into the hospital last night but I'm pegging him for just being a weird dude and fairly harmless."

"I agree, although, I'm not sure being a Peeping Tom is harmless. Not if you're the one being peeped," Katie said. "I am curious to read his confession, though."

"So then there is Grace Garfield. I'd take her off the suspect list, too. It's obvious she has some issues concerning the Ashtons but I don't think being jealous of their million-dollar interior design scheme would drive her to attempted murder," Anna clicked off.

Katie nodded. "So that leaves us with the Baileys, Aster Bancroft, and Danny Ping. The Baileys are debatable and we don't know which Bailey Jessie was referring to in her notebook. I wish I'd thought to ask last night."

"True, so that's a problem. And she could have been referring to both," Anna added. "There is something very mysterious about Aster Bancroft. I get the feeling she's not who she says she is, that she's hiding something."

"Whatever she's hiding, she's hiding it well. I'm hoping the fingerprints we took this morning will shed some light on her," Katie continued. "And then there's Ping. We already know he has the knowledge to concoct a poison from azaleas and daffodils but where's his motive? I mean, according to Jessie's notebook, he stole something but for all we know it could have been somebody's morning paper."

"Without Jessie to explain her notations, we've really got nothing to go on," Anna surmised.

After Katie and Anna arrived at the police station, Katie checked in with the fingerprint lab.

"I've got interesting news," Katie announced as she hung up. "First, the mystery fingerprints in Jessie's room are still a mystery. They don't match anything we've submitted.

So whoever they belong to is not in our databank."

"Terrific!" Anna exclaimed. "But realistically, they probably belong to some friend that we didn't fingerprint."

"I think so, too," Katie agreed

# Chapter 53

"**What's next, boss**?" Anna asked, grinning.

"We should take a look at Mick Wilson's statement. Make sure that it matches what he told us during questioning," Katie suggested.

"Why don't you do that while I go over the fingerprint info again? I just noticed that the official documents from the lab have been delivered," Anna replied, pulling a large white envelope off the corner of the desk.

Katie located Mick Wilson's paperwork and she and Anna, sitting on opposite sides of the heavy rectangular desk, settled in to read through their respective information. Anna finished quickly and began typing into the computer. Although Katie was absorbed in the somewhat shocking information contained in Mick Wilson's statement, she was aware that Anna was checking various police and government databases. After Katie finished reading Mick's entire statement she looked up.

"Who goes first?" Katie asked , knowing that Anna had undoubtedly found something interesting in the fingerprint information she'd been reviewing and was using the databases to follow up.

"Go ahead. I can tell your dying to," Anna conceded.

"We probably could have avoided questioning Grace Garfield if we'd taken a look at Mick Wilson's statement first," Katie enticed.

"Well, don't leave me hanging..."Anna urged.

"OK, but let me enlighten you about the Mick/Jessie connection first. I'll get to Miss Garfield in a minute," Katie replied.

"I can't wait to hear this," Anna said, her eyes wide with anticipation.

"Mick wasn't peeping at Jessie. In fact, according to his statement, Jessie isn't his type so he's never "watched" her, as he puts it. However, Grace Garfield is another story. Apparently, he has peeped at Grace since she was fifteen or sixteen years old. Anyway, about six months ago, Jessie caught him looking in Grace's window and confronted him about it. He claims that he promised her he wouldn't peep at Grace anymore if she didn't tell Grace or call the police, and he claims that he kept his promise until a couple of weeks ago. He says he forgot to take his medication, which I assume curbs his impulses to some extent, and he lost control. Jessie caught him coming out of Grace's yard and he knows that Jessie knew what he was doing," Katie explained.

"So he was afraid that she was going to go to Grace or the police?" Anna interrupted.

"Exactly," Katie answered. "But apparently she didn't. In his statement, Mick says that he kept trying to find a good time to talk to Jessie when no one else was around because he wanted her to know that he'd only broken his promise to her that one time because he forgot to take his pills. He wanted to let her know that he wasn't going to do it again. He says he didn't want her to be mad at him. Anyway, he could never find a good time and so he had decided he'd just go to her front door, no matter what the consequences and talk to her. Unfortunately, someone poisoned Jessie before he could get up the courage to do so."

"And he's claiming it wasn't him?" Anna filled in.

"Yes. He swears he had nothing to do with it," Katie replied.

"So if that's true, why was he sneaking into the hospital at two o'clock in the morning?" Anna inquired.

"He knew she'd regained consciousness and knew that most likely no one would be around at that time. He claims he just wanted to talk to her and reaffirm his promise to stay away from Grace," Katie answered. "But once he got there and saw how soundly she was sleeping, he changed his mind."

"Do you believe what he says?" Anna asked.

"I believe he was peeping at Grace Garfield. Wait until I tell you what he said about her!" Katie answered.

Anna gestured for Katie to continue.

"According to Mick, Grace has been breaking into her neighbors' homes when they're not at home," Katie announced.

"She's a thief?" Anna exclaimed.

"Not exactly. At least not in the traditional way," Katie continued. "She steals decorating and fashion ideas."

"What?" Anna said, wrinkling her brow.

"Mick says that when he spied on her in other people's houses she was taking pictures, measuring things and making notes. That's all. He never saw her take anything from the houses," Katie explained. "It's weird but on the other hand, we've never had any reports of any burglaries in that neighborhood, that I can recall."

"I think you're right about that," Anna concurred. "So let me get this straight. Grace was breaking into her neighbors' houses so she could replicate their interior decorating?"

"According to Mick Wilson," Katie replied, nodding. "That certainly meshes with Jessie's notation about Grace "coveting her neighbor". Do you think Jessie caught Grace in the act?"

"Let's ask her," Katie said quickly.

# CHAPTER 54

**Grace had thought** she was off the hook, only to be accosted by the police again. Now she was back in the interrogation room with the gaping two-sided window where she was sure she was being ogled. Grace sat in the chair waiting for questions to once again be hurled at her. Grace was shaking, mostly from anxiety, and her stomach was doing leaps and bounds, making her feel vaguely nauseous.

The same two female police officers, Bell and Madrid, entered the room and sat down across from her. They were both very pretty, in different ways. Women police officers weren't supposed to be attractive; they were supposed to be hard and masculine. Grace was sure they were both looking at her, thinking about how fat she was, how she needed to lose at least twenty pounds.

"We've just received some new evidence in the Jessie Ashton case. Has Jessie Ashton ever been inside your house, Miss Garfield?"

"I don't know. Maybe," Grace replied. "I and my parents, when they were alive, have hosted several of the cul-de-sac cookouts."

"When was the last time you hosted one?"

"About a year ago. I think it was in the fall," Grace answered, wondering where this line of questioning was going.

"You know, I noticed that your living room looks a lot like the Ashtons' living room. Same kind of furniture, similar rug and curtains, that sort of thing. Did you copy the Ashtons interior design for that room?"

Grace was elated. "In fact, I did. But I didn't have to pay the outrageous prices they did for their stuff. I'm quite handy when it comes to re-upholstering, shopping for bargains and making my own stuff like curtains and pillows. I'm really good with paint, too. Everything from basic walls to faux finishes," Grace replied proudly.

The two police officers had clearly not expected her to admit to making her living room resemble the Ashtons' and Grace was frankly confused by that reaction.

"How did you know exactly what furniture to buy

and how to decorate?"

"Well, I've been in the Ashtons' house several times. You already know this," Grace replied, wondering if the officers were somehow trying to trick her.

"What other houses in the cul-de-sac have you been in?"

"All of them at one time or another," Grace said, looking cautiously at the police officers.

"By invitation? Or did you break in?"

"Are you accusing me of breaking into other people's houses, now?" Grace asked making sure she sounded incredulous.

"Let's just say that you've been accused of doing just that. Did Jessie Ashton catch you in the act?"

"Since I'm not going to admit to breaking into someone's house, obviously, I'm going to deny that Jessie Ashton ever caught me doing such a thing," Grace replied making herself sound outraged at the very thought.

"If you've never broken into anyone's house, can you explain to me, then, why your kitchen, which you just finished re-doing, looks almost identical to Aster Bancroft's?"

Grace began to panic but managed to remain outwardly calm. "I've been inside Aster's house."

"We know that Ms. Bancroft has not hosted any neighborhood get-togethers since she moved in just a few months ago. We know you do not socialize with your neighbors, other than the cookouts. So how did you know what Ms. Bancroft's kitchen looks like?"

Grace remained silent. She wasn't going to admit that she had, indeed, forced her way into her neighbors' houses to see what the interiors looked like.

"Nothing to say, Miss Garfield? Well, you don't have to admit to it but we know it's true. So let's move on. How about telling us why you really visited Jessie at midnight last night? I'm pretty sure you knew she was conscious when you went to the hospital. I think Jessie knew you were breaking into the neighborhood houses or she had at least noticed that you were copying your neighbors and she confronted you about it. And I think once you knew she was awake, you went to the hospital to make sure she didn't spill the beans about what you had been doing."

Grace wasn't about to admit she'd committed a crime even if she had by breaking into her neighbors' houses. She hadn't stolen anything or damaged any property and she'd barely even touched anything. And most of her neighbors didn't lock the doors on the backs of their houses, so technically, she hadn't even broken in. She'd simply opened the door and walked in. Grace wasn't a criminal and she wasn't going to let these uppity police women accuse her of being one.

"It's not a crime to steal decorating ideas! Do you really think I would hurt Jessie Ashton because she knows I stole her mothers' interior designer's decorating scheme? I could just as easily have gotten it from a magazine," Grace spat out.

"Actually, we don't. So we're not going to arrest you or even detain you any longer. However, be forewarned that if we even have a hint that you've entered someone else's home without permission, we will open an investigation and charge you with trespassing, breaking and entering, burglary…or anything else that is applicable. Is that understood? Go buy a decorating magazine, Miss Garfield."

Grace glared at the blond police officer that had been speaking. *Talk about belligerent and rude!* Grace thought to herself. Grace would just bet that that police officer's house was a hovel without an ounce of sophisticated décor or style. *Go buy a decorating magazine my rear end*, Grace shouted inside her head. *I'll buy one, roll it up and hit you over the head with it, you stuck-up dumb blonde,* Grace vowed. But she kept it to herself and instead, gave the police officers a compliant nod and a weak smile, hoping that they would be placated enough to get her out of there as quickly as possible.

# CHAPTER 55

**"You never had** a chance to fill me in on your news," Katie said as soon as she and Anna had returned to the desk. Out of the corner of her eye, Katie watched Grace Garfield being led out the front door by one the other police officers.

"Better late than never," Anna quipped, then got down to business. "I had an odd feeling about Aster Bancroft's fingerprints. They came back perfectly clean and they didn't match up to any of the fingerprints we lifted in the Ashton house, or as you know, the stairwell at the hospital."

"Then why are they in question?" Katie asked.

"I spread the fingerprint sheets out that we took yesterday. The ones of Casey Bailey, Aster and Danny Ping. If you recall, Mr. Ping is an average-sized guy, about six-one or two, maybe 130 pounds. Casey Bailey is an averaged-sized woman although on the slightly petite size. I'd say she's about five-foot three, no more than 115 pounds. I didn't notice anything unusual about either one of them, you know, proportionately, as far as body parts, hands, feet, whatever", Anna explained.

"OK...?" Katie shrugged.

"When I compared Bancroft's fingerprints to Bailey's and Ping's guess what I noticed?" Anna replied.

"What?" Katie played along.

"Bancroft's flat prints were almost the same size as Ping's. Being a woman, you would expect them to be smaller than a man's prints, closer to the size of Bailey's prints. But they weren't," Anna revealed. "Remember how we said there was something odd about her, how even though she definitely looked like a woman she seemed to have a masculine edge about her?"

Katie nodded. "You think because she has big fingers, she's a man?"

"Well, the thought did occur to me but it was only just a seed that got me suspicious. We've always said that we thought she was hiding something," Anna answered.

"So you went digging in the computer files and what did you find out?" Katie asked, excitement flaring inside of her.

"I found a legitimate social security number for Aster Bancroft that led to a legitimate birth certificate. However, when I checked IRS records on the social security number, I found something very interesting. Current tax returns list Aster Bancroft as a waitress for the past five years but when I pulled up records going back further, her occupation is listed as "teacher-secondary education.""

"And all teachers have to be fingerprinted when they are employed by any school system. So Aster Bancroft's fingerprints should have already been in the system but they weren't", Katie quickly surmised.

"Bingo, so we could be looking at some sort of deliberate cover-up or identity theft," Anna replied. "If it's a legitimate cover-up, it's probably witness protection or she's an undercover agent. On the other hand if it's identity theft, we need to arrest her immediately to protect the real Aster Bancroft."

"I say we bring her back in for questioning, then," Katie suggested. "If it looks like identity theft, we can get a warrant for her arrest."

"And if it's a legitimate cover-up, the Calvary will ride in and spirit her away and everything will get swept under the rug. We'll get a stiff talking-to for looks by the Chief but at least we'll be able to mark Ms. Bancroft off our suspect list," Anna remarked. "It's a win-win in my book."

While Anna went on the radio to get a patrol car to pick up Aster Bancroft from her house, Katie continued to ponder the possible whereabouts of Jessie Ashton. It was clear to Katie that Jessie had walked out of the hospital of her own free will. And Katie was certain that the figure leaving in the dark, oversized clothing was indeed Jessie. They'd ruled Bug Bailey out as her accomplice and so the likely perp was Alex Watson. Everything pointed to him—the accomplice had been tall and thin and decidedly male, he was someone that Jessie trusted implicitly and he was someone that could easily adapt the persona of a medical professional comfortable in an adult environment. Alex was all of those things; perhaps the most important part being the fact that Alex's unusual maturity and extreme intelligence made him believable as an adult who worked at the hospital. Orderlies, interns and medical assistants were plentiful at any hospital and as long as Alex could play the part, no one would question his presence. There was also the fact that Alex had not reported to school today and his golf-cart contraption was missing from his workshop. Katie just hoped that meant that both of them were safe and just holed up somewhere for the moment. Katie also hoped they hadn't left the Potoma area.

Katie switched gears slightly, as she opened Jessie Ashton's file and began to review the notes she and Anna had continuously added to in the thickening folder. With frustration, Katie admitted that she was no closer to finding the person or persons who had tried to poison Jessie almost a week ago. They'd pretty much ruled out Mick Wilson, a former chemist who would have had the knowledge to concoct the poison, and Grace Garfield, whose greatest crimes it seemed were trespassing and stealing decorating ideas. There was a possibility that Aster Bancroft might become a strong contender, especially if they found she was impersonating someone else for financial benefit but she might also have a legitimate excuse for her deception. Katie still had a difficult time believing that the Baileys or Danny Ping could have been involved. The Baileys had been close friends with the Ashtons for years and their children had grown up together. Other than the vague accusation of "adultery" by Jessie, there didn't seem to be any motive. And Katie had to remember that in Jessie's eyes, if Casey or Ted Bailey even flirted with someone else, she might consider that cheating. Danny Ping, too, seemed to be a long shot, because although he clearly knew how to make a poisonous tea from plants, there just didn't seem to be any connection between him and Jessie. Who knew what Jessie was accusing him of stealing? And since there hadn't been any reports of a theft or burglary in Potoma in the past six months it was likely that whatever Jessie was referring to was something trivial and not worth risking a murder rap for.

"They're en route with Aster Bancroft right now. She was pretty irate about it as she was just leaving for work.

Apparently, she's got her lawyer on the way, too," Anna announced, interrupting Katie's thoughts.

"Questioning people with their lawyers in tow is always so pleasant," Katie said, rolling her eyes.

"Yes, always a joy," Anna agreed then changed the subject. "I forgot to mention that Ted Bailey never showed up to have his fingerprints taken. I noticed they weren't included in the packet and when I questioned Woody up there about it, he said he tried to call Bailey a few times but couldn't ever reach him. He knew we were anxious to get results back today so he went ahead and sent over what we had."

"Well, depending on what happens with Ms. Bancroft, we might not need Ted Bailey's prints anyway," Katie replied. "By the way, how did you know that Grace had never been to Aster Bancroft's house?"

"I didn't. I just figured if she'd been there when someone else was living there, she'd say so," Anna answered. "It was a risk."

"Not much of one it turns out, though," Katie complimented. "I wonder if she really did copy Aster's kitchen. She didn't deny it. And she was some kind of proud of the fact that her living room looked just like Ellen Ashton's expensive designer one."

"Keeping up with the Jones' and all that," Anna laughed. "I have enough trouble keeping up with Litany and Echo! I couldn't imagine trying to work in fake designer interiors!"

"I hear you," Katie joined in. "Anyway, I don't think Ogilvie would really appreciate 18th century English antiques, real or faked!"

Anna's cell phone rang a moment later and she retreated to a quiet corner to answer it, leaving Katie to continue reviewing the Jessie Ashton file. The more she read, the more unclear a motive for killing Jessie became. For Pete's sake, all Katie could see that Jessie had done was keep a list of the sins her neighbors had committed. Grace Garfield coveted her neighbors, that was plain as day. Mick Wilson had lied; he'd lied to Jessie about never peeping at Grace again. One of the

Baileys had committed adultery, at least in Jessie's eyes. Danny Ping was a thief but what had he stolen? And Aster Bancroft had committed the sin of deceit. *Had Jessie figured out somehow that Aster wasn't who she claimed to be? Was it Aster that had tried to kill Jessie to cover up her deception? Well,* Katie thought to herself, *we're just about to get the answer to that. Just as soon as Ms. Bancroft and her lawyer arrive.*

## CHAPTER 56

**Ping walked out** of the real estate office with a smile on his face. The signs would go up tomorrow and with any luck, he'd be out of Potoma within a few months. He'd already instructed the agent to begin advertising for renters, in case the house didn't sell quickly. He was giving it until the end of August at the outset and then no matter what, he was leaving. And the best part was that she'd agreed to go with him.

Ping imagined his new life with her. They would be married as soon as possible and then she would help him start his own landscape architecture business. He would work while she went back to school to pursue the education she had given up all those years ago. And when she had achieved her educational goals, she would have her own career. They would build their dream home on a lake or maybe even on a beach somewhere up the coast and spend their vacations traveling in Europe.

Ping had listed his house for quite a bit below the market value just to get rid of it as quickly as possible. He would still make a profit, one that would be big enough to use as seed money for his own business with enough left over to live on for at least a year if he was frugal. She had assured him that she didn't mind living lean for a while as long as they were together.

Ping climbed into his truck and turned it on. It was only then that he noticed the folded note stuck under his windshield wiper. Ping opened the window and leaning forward reached out and around to pull the piece of paper from the glass. Ping could detect lettering through the paper. He slowly opened the note and couldn't believe what he read. In bold capital letters were the words:

## YOU CAN HAVE HER.
## I WAS DONE WITH HER A LONG TIME AGO

Ping's heart raced. He picked up his cell phone and dialed her number. She didn't answer and so he hit the "Send" button again to re-dial. She answered on the fourth ring.

"I can't talk right now," she said breathlessly.

"We have to. Something has happened," Ping insisted.

"I'll call you back when it's safe," she replied, disconnecting immediately.

Ping sat in his truck, looking in every direction. He didn't know what he was looking for. He didn't really think her husband was hanging around, watching him find the note. Ping tried to take slow, even breaths to calm down. He began to wonder why he was anxious. If the cat was out of the bag and her husband already knew and didn't care, there was really nothing to be nervous about. *But why would he be so compliant?* Most rich and powerful men like her husband wouldn't give up their wives to another man so easily, even if they didn't want them anymore. It was a possession thing. Ping wished he could talk to her. *Did she already know her husband knew? Is that why she couldn't talk? Was he there right now, confronting her, threatening her even?* He didn't think her husband was ordinarily a violent man but adultery could bring out the worst in even the most passive individual. Should Ping go to her house and check on her? *Or would that just be playing into her husband's hands and make things worse for her?* Ping sat in his truck in miserable indecision. The wonderful bliss he'd found just a few minutes ago had suddenly been replaced by worry and fear.

# CHAPTER 57

**Aster noticed that** the two female police officers that had been making her life difficult remained at their desk as she was escorted through the station to the interrogation room in the back. Aster was left alone in the room and she heard the lock on the other side of the door click once it was closed. Aster just hoped her lawyer got there soon. If not, their operation tonight was in danger of falling apart. Aster sat down in a chair and crossed her legs, bobbing the one on top impatiently. She continued to check her wristwatch, noting the minutes just ticking away. The police officer that had picked her up had refused to tell her why she was being taken to the station other than the need to question her further in relation to the Jessie Ashton case and some new developments recently discovered. Aster was sure she'd lose her cool and betray her cover if she had to sit and wait much longer. She closed her eyes and concentrated on breathing slowly.

Fifteen minutes later, the door opened and several people filed in. In the lead was the same police officer that had brought Aster in. He was followed by Aster's lawyer and her associate. Bringing up the rear were Officers Bell and Madrid. Everyone but the male police officer took a seat; he left, closing the door behind him.

"We're going to get right to the point. Your fingerprints didn't check out, Ms. Bancroft."

Aster looked inquiringly at the frosty blond playing her lawyer, who was in truth, her commanding officer, Janice. Janice raised an eyebrow in answer, her eyes revealing her surprise.

"What exactly do you mean by that, Officer?" Janice asked.

"It appears that at one time, Ms. Bancroft worked as a school teacher."

Janice looked at Aster then averted her eyes back to the police officers. "So?" Janice said.

"Well, that's a problem. Because, you see, Ms. Bancroft's fingerprints weren't in our database or any fingerprint database for that matter. And every teacher has to be fingerprinted before they can begin employment. Do you see what our problem is now?"

"Why don't you explain it to me so I'm clear, Officer?" Janice replied.

"It's very simple. It appears that this woman is impersonating the real Aster Bancroft."

"I see," Janice mused. It was obvious to Aster that Janice was just stalling for time, probably trying to decide how much to share with the police officers.

"It appears that your client may be guilty of identity theft. We're going to have to detain her until we can investigate further…unless you can clear this up somehow."

Janice exchanged looks with her assistant. Aster knew him as George. "What proof do you have of this, other than information that indicates my client at one time worked as a teacher?"

"Quite frankly, that's it. But it's enough to keep her here while we dig deeper. I'm sure it wouldn't take very long find the real Aster Bancroft or at least ascertain who she is but then who knows how long it might take to set up a meeting with her and obtain all the facts."

Aster watched Janice. She knew Janice was thinking the same thing she was. Aster had to be released tonight or the operation could be compromised. And after over a year of hard work, they just couldn't risk it.

"Is identity theft your only guess?" Janice asked coyly.

"Well, we did consider some sort of undercover operation or witness protection. Care to comment on those theories?"

Janice looked at George again and George nodded. Janice appeared indecisive. Aster knew she was still weighing her options. After a few minutes of silence, Janice blew out an indignant breath. Janice leaned forward and said "This is not identity theft in the criminal sense."

"So what is it?"

"I'm not at liberty to say anymore," Janice replied, tight-lipped.

"Let me brief you then about the situation we have right

here. A teenage girl was poisoned in her own bed and left for dead. Miraculously she survived, even though she was comatose for several days. Then, as soon as she regained consciousness, she disappeared without a trace from her hospital bed. We believe she left the hospital with an accomplice but now she and her accomplice are missing. Ms. Bancroft is our strongest suspect at the moment. So even if we believe Ms. Bancroft hasn't perpetrated criminal identity theft, we still have plenty of reason to think that she might have been involved in the attempted murder of the girl. Are you following?"

"I'm afraid not," Janice answered. "Why would my client be a suspect?"

"The girl made a list of the sins her neighbors had committed. According to the girl, your client broke a commandment that says "Thou shalt not deceive." That leads us to believe that somehow, the girl figured out that your client is not who she claims to be. Depending on what your client is involved in, that could be a perfect motive for killing her. To keep her quiet in order to protect your client or whatever activities your client is carrying out."

Janice's face softened slightly. "I see," Janice said. "However, I can assure you that this is not the case. My client has absolutely nothing to do with the attempted murder of your teenage girl."

"I'm afraid I can't take your word for it. We need a little more than that before we can release Ms. Bancroft."

Janice bit her lip and took a deep breath. Aster could tell that Janice's resolve was wavering. "Just tell her. If we don't get out of here soon, it'll be too late," Aster said.

Janice flashed a look of irritation at Aster. Then she looked at George again. George shrugged but Aster could tell it was in resignation.

"My client and my associate appear to be in agreement—that I should give you more information. I disagree but it seems that I am out-numbered and as time is of the essence right now, it's imperative that you release Ms. Bancroft as soon as possible. So I'll tell you what you want to know," Janice said. "However, what I tell you is confidential and can go no farther than this room. You'll need to turn off the recorder and the intercom, first. There can be no written record of what I am about to reveal. Agreed?"

"Understood."

"Ms. Bancroft is an undercover agent involved in the investigation of a major drug dealer. I am not, in fact, her lawyer but her handler and George, here, is also an agent. Ms. Bancroft has been posing as a waitress at the club casino frequented by the drug dealer and just recently gained access to his personal residence where she was able to obtain important information that will enable us to shut down his operation and put him away for a very long time," Janice explained.

"That explains quite a bit. Does Jessie Ashton know about your operation? Is that her reason for noting that Ms. Bancroft was guilty of deception?"

"No, Miss Ashton knows absolutely nothing about the investigation. Unfortunately, she discovered something more personal about my client," Janice answered, nodding at Aster. Aster knew that lying while telling the truth was just a part of the undercover game and it worked out better to reveal the lesser of two evils when given the choice.

"I'm not a waitress," Aster said, abandoning the usual husky Demi Moore-like voice and grinning like a Cheshire cat. "My real name is Charles."

The two female police officers didn't seem to be too shocked by the revelation although they shook their heads.

"You almost had us fooled. Have you ever considered working in the movies as a make-up artist?"

"Whenever I was at the house in New Town, I always wore my disguise except for once. The one time I washed off all my make-up and didn't immediately put a fresh coat back on, Jessie saw me. At the time, I was also topless so there was no question that I was a male, not a female. It was late at night and I thought I was safe to step outside onto my back porch for a quick breath of fresh air. Jessie picked that moment to walk across my back yard. I thought she was going to faint from surprise," Aster, now known to be Charles, continued.

"Weren't you afraid she'd tell someone?"

"Actually, when I told her I was a cross-dresser and really worked as a female impersonator at a club across the river, she seemed to think it was really cool. I told her that I didn't want anyone to know because I didn't want people to discriminate against me. I told her that's why I'd moved to New Town. That when people in my old neighborhood had found out that I liked to dress up like a woman, they'd plastered my house with toilet paper and rotten food and sprayed graffiti across my porch. That pretty much got her to keep it to herself. She's a really sweet, caring girl. I did feel badly for lying to her about it all," Charles explained. "I have a teenage daughter myself, you see."

After a lengthy pause while Officers Bell and Madrid digested the information they'd just been given, they nodded at each other. "I think we know all we need to know. You are free to go, Ms. Bancroft...or should I say, Charles. Good luck and much success tonight."

"Thank you, Officers," Janice said as everyone stood up. "I do hope you find Miss Ashton. And you find her alive and well."

Charles echoed Janice's last statement in his head. What they hadn't revealed to the police officers was the specific reason, Charles had been installed in that particular cul-de-sac. One of Jessie Ashton's neighbors was tied to the drug operation and Charles had been doing double-duty and keeping an eye on that person. Unfortunately, contrary to what Janice had told the officers, Jessie had been at the wrong place, at the wrong time and unwittingly become a witness to that connection as well as seen evidence of a few other unsavory operations her neighbor was involved in.

# CHAPTER 58

"Well, that was interesting. Not exactly what I expected, though," Anna commented after Aster (a.k.a. Charles) had left and she and Katie had returned to their station desk.

"I knew there was something really off about Aster Bancroft. Now at least, I know my intuition was correct," Katie replied. "I wonder why they didn't just use a female agent?"

"Who knows?" Anna said, shrugging, then picked up Jessie Ashton's file. "So now we've ruled out Aster Bancroft, too. Where does that leave us?"

"The Baileys and Danny Ping," Katie stated the obvious.

"What do we know about Ping?" Anna began. "He's single and he's only lived in the neighborhood a couple of years. He works as a landscaper for a company based about a half hour out of Potoma. He doesn't seem to socialize much although I did notice him at the Sand Bar last weekend and he was with several other guys who I assume to be friends or co-workers. He appears to be in his late thirties and has never mentioned any kind of love interest or steady relationship other than his ex-fiancee. My impression of him is that he is relatively quiet, and gardening is obviously a pretty passionate hobby of his from the looks of his property."

"And his connection to the Ashtons is the fact he lives in the same cul-de-sac and Ellen Ashton hired him to do some landscaping for them a year ago," Katie added. "The only apparent connection to Jessie is some possible interaction at cul-de-sac get-togethers a few times a year; however, I doubt, given the generation gap, that that interaction was much more than polite conversation, if that much."

"I'm inclined to agree with you," Anna nodded. "Given what we know about Jessie's social scene and her dating life, I don't see even the remotest possibility that there was any secret relationship between them, platonic or otherwise. So unless Ping stole something pretty significant and knew Jessie had knowledge about the theft and therefore wanted to keep her quiet, I can't see him being involved in her attempted murder. I just can't find any other motive."

"So that leaves Ted and/or Casey Bailey," Katie said.

"They've obviously been married for quite some time as their youngest son is eighteen. It's pretty apparent just by looking at them that Ted is at least twenty years older than Casey. Not that it matters, necessarily. They've been neighbors and friends with the Ashtons since the children were small so at least fifteen years or so, and the kids interact like siblings."

"Ted owns an accounting firm and Casey is a stay-at-home mom. They have plenty of money and despite what's written in Jessie's notebook, they appear to be a stable couple. We know that Ted doesn't like police much if he thinks they are intruding on his rights and we also know that when Ted doesn't like something, he has somewhat of a temper. Casey seems to be the more laid back one although, as we saw earlier today, she can be a little bit of a Mama Bear when she's protecting her children," Anna picked up.

"According to Jessie's notebook, someone in that house is guilty of adultery. I wonder what the consequences of that would be if the spouse found out?" Katie mused. "Do you think, if for example, it was Casey who was cheating, that Ted would be able to leave her with absolutely nothing in the divorce? Or if it were Ted, Casey could walk away with everything?"

"Those are possibilities and good reasons why one of them might try to silence Jessie," Anna answered. "But in reality, the injured spouse would have to be able to prove adultery in court and that's not usually very easy unless there are photographs or videotapes..."

"You're right. And I'm not so sure either of them would be able to bring themselves to put Jessie on the stand or involve her in a nasty divorce proceeding," Katie said. "I mean, would you put your daughters in that position just to show what a horrible cheater your husband was? Would it really be worth the emotional anguish it would cause them just to get back at their father for hurting you?"

"Absolutely not. No parent who truly loves their child would make them do harm to the other parent, regardless of the circumstances," Anna replied passionately.

"So, then again, we have no real motive," Katie

concluded. "Or should I say, the only motive we do have is weak at best."

"If the perp is Ted or Casey Bailey, there is definitely another motive for wanting Jessie out of the way. One we don't have any idea about," Anna concurred.

"So now we have to look elsewhere. Cast our nets farther afield, as you said earlier," Katie said, bouncing her pen on the table.

"If she was not a victim of her friends, family members or neighbors, who's left?" Anna replied.

Katie threw her pen down in frustration. "The whole town of Potoma, it seems!" Katie cried.

# CHAPTER 59

**Katie was glad** to be on her way home. It had been a long a day and Katie yearned to soak in a bubble bath for a while, then lose herself in a good movie before going to bed early. At least part of her was glad to be going home finally; the other part of her was hoping to get a call from the station with new information about Jessie Ashton that would at least lead to her recovery. So when Katie's cell phone rang, she answered it immediately.

"Katie, I don't mean to be a bother but it's getting to be evening and I just hadn't heard from you about dinner tonight," Cade said.

Katie had been so wrapped up in the case she had forgotten all about Cade's invitation.

"I'm just on my way home, actually," Katie began, then realized she shouldn't have revealed that information. "I would have called you as soon as I got there. I don't like to dial and drive."

"No problem. So…it looks like you're free for dinner then?" Cade said hopefully.

"Well…" Katie's plans for a quiet, relaxing evening fading away. "I guess so."

"Great!" Cade replied. "Can I pick you up?"

"Let me just meet you somewhere," Katie interjected quickly. She wasn't about to give Cade the go sign for showing up at her house uninvited in the future.

"OK," Cade answered in a clearly disappointed tone. "Where would you like to go? I know you're not terribly fond of The Yacht Club."

"You're paying for dinner so it's really your choice," Katie said, realizing her phrasing sounded extremely rude and presumptuous but not really caring since she didn't like feeling as if she was being cornered into dinner with Cade.

"Then how about the Chinese place tonight?" Cade suggested non-plussed.

*Wrong again*, Katie thought to herself. *We're clearly not compatible!* "Actually, I love Chinese food but it doesn't love me," Katie declined.

"Not a problem. Why don't you just meet me at the main entrance to the boardwalk? It looks like most of the regular beach vendors are open so you'll have your pick of a dozen different kinds of food. We can just make it a picnic of sorts," Cade said.

"That's a good idea," Katie answered. "Give me about an hour or so." Katie was relieved. Since it wasn't a real formal date they could eat quickly and she wouldn't have to stick around indefinitely waiting to be served each course. She'd hang out for a little while for some polite conversation so as not to be rude but at least she wouldn't be shanghaied for half the night. She'd have to forget about her movie but she still might get in her bubble bath!

Before Katie even pulled into her driveway, she could hear Ogilvie's yelps of joy. He ran in and out of his doggie door, circling the yard and leaping up and down on the fence. When Katie entered the back yard, he nearly knocked her down as he bounded up against her. Katie sat down on the ground and gave him a good belly rub and lots of kisses before hauling herself back onto her feet.

After Katie had taken a quick shower and dressed casually in cut-off denim shorts and a cute embroidered cotton top, she dried her hair, braiding it into two long plaits that hung behind her ears. She always thought she looked about twelve years old with her hair styled like that but tonight she didn't really care. She wasn't trying to impress anyone and she suspected that subconsciously she might even be trying to deter Cade from pursuing her. Slipping on some comfortable flip-flops, she gave Ogilvie a small bowl of doggie icecream to distract him, then slipped out the door and onto her golf cart.

Katie was in no hurry to meet Cade and so she drove slowly, stopping a few times to exchange greetings with her Riverview neighbors. When she finally arrived at the golf cart parking lot next to the boardwalk entrance she noted it had been over an hour and a half since she'd spoken to Cade on the phone. Technically, she was late for their date.

Cade was standing out on the pier, leaning against the railing and watching the sailboats and cruisers glide up and down the water that was beginning to glitter as the sun started to set. He didn't see Katie until she'd walked up beside him. Katie thought she caught a glimmer of irritation in his expression when he greeted her but his tone of voice was cheerful.

"I figured we'd just walk until we found something that made us hungry," Cade suggested. "It probably won't take me long since I'm starving."

Katie could definitely hear accusation in his tone then. "I ate a very late lunch so it might take a bit longer for me," Katie said lightly.

After a few minutes, they reached a pizza-by-the-slice truck. After receiving their giant savory slices of thick pie and some drinks, they sat down at a nearby picnic table.

"How is your case coming?" Cade inquired between bites.

"Quite frankly, we seem to be at a dead end. None of our original suspects, or at least their motives seem to have panned out," Katie revealed.

"You know it's all in the news now. I heard this morning that the girl disappeared from the hospital. Is that the truth?" Cade asked.

Katie nodded, her mouth full of warm, chewy cheese.

"Do you know how she disappeared or have any clue as to where she is now?" Cade said.

"It appears she had help leaving the hospital and no, there's been no sign of her," Katie answered.

"What will you do now that the trail has gone cold, as you law enforcement types say?" Cade asked, tipping up his cup and taking a long swig.

"Keep looking, of course," Katie replied pertly. "We think we know who she's with and so we think we have some clues as to where they might go."

"Really?" Cade looked surprised.

"The police never release all of the information to the public," Katie explained. "We always keep something back to help us better identify suspects and ultimately, we hope, the perpetrator."

"Clever. Does it usually work?" Cade said looking at Katie with what appeared to be challenge in his eyes.

"If we question the right suspect," Katie answered. She didn't add that she only knew this through Anna. As a Potoma police officer her entire four-year career, she'd never even seen a case involving attempted murder or a missing person, much less been in charge of one.

"Why do you think someone tried to kill that girl, anyway?" Cade probed.

"We don't really know. We assume she saw or overheard or somehow stumbled upon something that she shouldn't have and someone wanted to make sure she didn't talk," Katie replied.

"Here, in quiet, quaint, safe little Potoma? Isn't that a bit dramatic for an unassuming place like this?" Cade laughed. *There it went,* Katie thought. *That condescending attitude, again.*

"It's a bit hard to believe that something major enough to warrant attempted murder could happen here but it seems that may be case," Katie shrugged, suddenly wanting to finish her dinner and cut the date short.

"Or maybe she really did try to kill herself just like everyone thought at first," Cade interjected.

"We've definitely ruled that out. It was undoubtedly attempted homicide, not suicide," Katie corrected, irritated at his know-it-all attitude.

Apparently, Cade had sensed Katie's growing annoyance with him because he immediately switched gears and tone of voice.

"Have you been by the bungalows in the last day or two? I've finished all the exterior paint and they look amazing! Your color schemes were perfect," Cade complimented.

"I've been too busy to get over there but I'll definitely come take a look as soon as I get the chance," Katie replied.

"I'm also looking forward to seeing your murals. I've just finished the renovations on houses two and three and number four is in fairly good condition so it should only take a week or two to make the cosmetic changes to that one.

Basically, you've got three bungalows, not counting the one I'm currently living in, ready for your paint brush," Cade announced.

"Well, as soon as I can find some time to make preliminary design outlines, I'll let you know when I can get started. Have you received the photos from the Society archives yet?" Katie answered.

"According to the Archivist, they are still being assembled but I should have something in hand within the next few days," Cade replied.

Katie already had some designs in mind but she wanted the photographs in order to flesh out those ideas and get all the details accurate. One mural would focus on the riverfront resort amenities during the Victorian era, another, the casinos and amusements of 1950. She also intended to make one mural a collage of the most interesting Victorian cottages lining Riverside Drive. Other murals would include scenes of the The Point Marina at different time periods, the commercial district of Potoma and the original Victorian era golf course community now part of the Fairway section.

Katie was so busy conjuring the planned murals in her head that she had unintentionally tuned Cade out. "I'm sorry. I kind of zoned out there for a minute and I didn't hear what you said," Katie apologized.

"No problem. I was just commenting on how beautiful the sunset was. Like you tonight." Cade said.

Katie felt herself blush. "I'm flattered," Katie replied, not sure she really believed him given the fact that she'd done absolutely nothing to make herself look particularly attractive for him.

Cade slipped around to Katie's side of the picnic table and sat down close to her, his arm and shoulder pitched firmly against her. "The sunsets over the river are just spectacular here, aren't they? The ideal backdrop for romance, don't you think?" Cade said in a low voice as he leaned his head lightly against Katie's.

At that moment, Katie saw movement out of the corner of her eye and recognized Ben's form and stride a few feet away from her. She knew instantly Ben would believe his eyes and assume she and Cade were in a romantic clutch. And if nothing else, he'd be disappointed in what he would consider her bad judgment in continuing a relationship with Cade.

"Hey!" Katie called to Ben who was already staring at her with something like disbelief in his expression. She had moved her head away from Cade's and was trying to inch her body away from his in an unobtrusive way.

"Hey, Kate," Ben replied, stopping in front of her. His tone did not betray the obvious disapproval in eyes. "Fancy meeting you here. I thought after the long night last night and all your running around today, you'd be at home soaking in the tub."

Katie could see Cade eying Ben, no doubt wondering how Ben knew so much about her recent activities. "Ben, have you met Cade Ware?" Katie said.

"As a matter of fact I have. Some time back, though," Ben replied.

Cade nodded at Ben. "If I'm not mistaken, you own the golf cart monopoly here."

It was clear to Katie—and Ben, Katie could see—that Cade's barb was intentional.

"And you're buying up every available property in Potoma. What do you plan to do with them all?" Ben asked directly.

"I'm a preservationist. I'm just trying to save the architectural history of Potoma," Cade countered. "It's quite obvious that none of the Potoma natives have made any effort in that direction."

Katie watched Ben grimace. She'd never seen Ben angry but she was sure that if things went much further with Cade, she would see that side of him tonight.

"I'm sure if the people of Potoma had the financial resources you appear to have, they'd spare no expense in restoring every building here," Ben said. "Unfortunately, that's not the case."

"I'm sure you're not hurting too much in that area, seeing you're the only golf cart game in town. Correct me if

I'm wrong but you gain revenue from not only the vacationers you rent to all season but also the Potoma residents with sales, repairs, parts and modifications, and you have exclusive contracts for all the golf courses, too," Cade said, narrowing his eyes in challenge. "Certainly, you could afford to restore a few historic structures."

"How I spend my income is none of your business. However, for your information, I contribute to a number of charities and foundations, some of which do use the money for restoring and maintaining local historic structures," Ben replied, his eyes flashing.

"Then you should have no objection to my restoration projects," Cade postulated.

"On the contrary," Ben answered. "I appreciate your preservation work. It's how you intend to profit from it that bothers me."

"You're a businessman and an obviously very successful one at that. I can't believe you would have the audacity to criticize me for wanting to have a lucrative enterprise, too," Cade complained, his face tinged red with ire. "Or are you afraid I'll become top dog in town and topple you from your rooftop perch?"

"Not in the least," Ben argued. "What I'm afraid of is that you'll make it impossible for the regular Joe to live, work or vacation here."

Katie was becoming increasingly uncomfortable. She knew she should switch over to her policewoman persona to handle the confrontation but this was personal and she was finding it difficult to be objective. Both men were now standing on opposite sides of the picnic table, Katie leaning against the end, between them. Fortunately, both Ben and Cade had controlled the volume of their voices and hadn't created a scene. At least not yet.

"Why would that bother you in the least? Wealthier clients mean higher profits. And higher profits mean more money in your pocket. That's what business is all about ," Cade pronounced, his face ripe with real confusion.

"My business is about providing the best possible

service for the lowest possible cost to the customer. Most of the other business owners in Potoma operate on the same philosophy," Ben retorted. "Conscientious business owners can still make a good profit without putting their customers in the poor house or running them out of town."

"Well, that philosophy is why Potoma has struggled for the last hundred years to stay on the map. It needs an influx of capital if it's going to survive," Cade debated.

"No, it needs community in order to survive. And that's what it has. That's why the depression and the repression and two major hurricanes couldn't destroy it," Ben disputed.

Cade seemed to be enjoying baiting Ben, extracting a negative reaction, and it made Katie's blood boil.

"Towns run on money not warm, fuzzy feelings of community," Cade said mockingly. "Money provides services and personnel. The more money, the better the services and personnel."

"What you don't seem to understand, Mr. Ware, is that the town is the community, just like a church is its people, not the building that houses them," Ben replied.

It was apparent that Ben had bested Cade with his allegory and Katie could now see that Cade was no longer playing a game to see how much he could provoke Ben.

"If Potoma had more money, they could afford to hire more experienced public servants to run the town and protect its interests. For instance, they'd have the salary power to draw real police investigators here instead of relying on traffic cops to solve crime," Cade contended, giving Ben a wink full of meaning, then turning toward Katie and adding "No offense, honey."

Katie was flabbergasted at Cade's blatant insult. Katie looked at Ben and saw him clench his fists, his jaw become rigid. Before Katie could think of how to reply to Cade's belittlement, Ben stepped around Katie so that he was standing between her and Cade. Ben gently took Katie's hand in his and said to Cade, "I think Katie's heard all she needs to hear from you."

Katie regained her voice and said a little louder than

necessary, "Look around you Cade. See those people everywhere? They are the people that make up the town of Potoma. And make no mistake, they heard every word you said even though they were polite enough to pretend they weren't listening. You see, that's what happens when you live in a small town. Everyone knows everyone else's business and things get around quicker than the speed of light. Be sure, that by tomorrow morning, everyone in town will know exactly who and what you are. And no one will even speak to you, much less do business with you."

Without waiting for a reply, Katie, still holding onto Ben, turned and walked away. Katie didn't look back and walked quickly, wanting to get as far away from Cade as quickly as possible. Ben continued to hold her hand and they moved toward the entrance to the boardwalk in comfortable silence. When they reached Katie's golf cart, Ben offered to follow her home. Katie had liked the feel of Ben's hand over hers and was reluctant to break the connection when Ben left her to retrieve his own cart. Soon the two arrived at Katie's bungalow.

Instead of entering the house, they sauntered down to the beach and strolled along the river's edge then climbed the levee to amble above the water as the sun continued to wan and darkness tinted the sky a blue-gray. The moon was nearly full and it pierced the gathering dusk with warm, ambient light.

"I wasn't planning on having dinner with Cade," Katie said breaking the silence. "In fact, I had actually forgotten all about it by the time I left work."

"You don't have to explain yourself," Ben interrupted.

"I know that but I want to. When he called I didn't bother to look at the caller ID. If I had I wouldn't have answered. I would have just called him later and told him I was too wiped out for dinner. But then I made the mistake of telling him I was on my way home and he just presumed we were having dinner together," Katie explained. "I felt like I was sort of painted into a corner because I didn't really have a good excuse to beg off."

"It's really OK," Ben insisted.

"I guess I'm just too polite and honest, sometimes," Katie said, reproaching herself.

"Those are good qualities to have. I wish more people were like you. Cade took advantage of your natural niceness," Ben soothed. "I'm just glad you were able to see for yourself his true nature. It would have killed me to watch you being deceived over and over again."

"I'm not quite that naïve," Katie smirked as she gave Ben a playful slap on the arm.

"Are you sure about that?" Ben teased.

"Well, I *am* just a traffic cop," Katie laughed, mocking the earlier insult from Cade.

After several minutes of good-natured jibes, Ben became serious. "I assume you haven't found Jessie Ashton."

"Not yet. But we have been able to rule out several persons of interest. Unfortunately, though, we now have no strong suspects," Katie replied.

"What's your next move, then?" Ben asked.

"We've decided that we need to look outside of Jessie's neighborhood. We've never investigated anyone she works with or comes in contact with outside her immediate circle of friends," Katie answered.

"You've never mentioned that Jessie had a job," Ben mused.

"It's just part time as a park monitor," Katie replied. "Her mother mentioned it during the course of our interview with her at the hospital last Thursday. It was just an offhand comment actually and quite honestly, I didn't remember it until today."

"So she opens and closes the playground gates and makes sure kids are playing safely?" Ben inquired.

"Exactly. She alternates between morning and afternoon shifts every Saturday and does it a couple evenings during the week, too," Katie explained. By this time, Katie and Ben had turned around and were retracing their steps back toward Katie's house.

"I take it you haven't been able to find Alex Watson either," Ben remarked.

"No. Anna called his parents after they arrived home from work but they said that he was not at home and they actually hadn't seen him or spoken to him since dinner time last night," Katie reported.

"So in reality, you have two missing teenagers, not just one. Did Alex's parents file a *Missing Persons* report?" Ben inquired.

"I don't know. Anna encouraged them to do so but from what Alex's mother said, they weren't particularly worried about it. She told Anna that he's free to come and go as he pleases and since he's never been in any trouble, they don't really monitor him," Katie answered. "Sounds like to me they just don't really want to make the effort to keep track of him."

"Me, too," Ben concurred, nodding. "Sounds like another case of new husband, new life and children from the previous relationship being an inconvenience."

"That could be," Katie agreed. "But it could also be that Alex is just really independent—and I get the impression that he is, not to mention mature beyond his years compared to most kids his age—and his mother just gives him his space."

"Possibly," Ben conceded. "But knowing that Jessie Ashton is missing and that Alex is considered a suspect in helping her disappear...considering that Jessie was the victim of an attempted murder and the person who tried to kill her is still out there somewhere...I think I'd be very interested in where my son is."

"I have to agree with you there," Katie said. "I'm just hoping that they are, in fact, together, and out of danger...at least right at this moment, anyway."

Katie and Ben had reached Katie's driveway. Ogilvie was circling the yard with yelps of joy. "I'm going to let you get some rest," Ben said before he turned to climb onto his golf cart. "Call me if you need anything...or you could just send Ogilvie over."

Katie returned Ben's grin. They had a running joke that if you let Ogilvie loose anywhere in Potoma except the beach, he'd run, not home to Katie's house, but straight to Ben's to his "true love" Betsy. Katie had actually put that theory to the test, albeit unintentionally, on several occasions, and without exception Ogilvie was found sitting patiently on Ben's porch waiting for Katie to show up.

As Ben drove off, Katie entered the yard and gave Ogilvie a big hug, then walked up to her front door with every intent of sinking into her soft bed for a nice long sleep. At the moment, she'd forgotten all about her disastrous second dinner with Cade and the heated exchange between him and Ben. She wasn't even thinking about Jessie Ashton. She was just tired and enjoying the feeling of euphoria she always felt after spending time, no matter how brief, with Ben.

# CHAPTER 60

**Mick peeked out** of his window at the activity in the cul-de-sac. He was hiding now, embarrassed that his neighbors had seen him hauled away by the police earlier in the day. He knew that they'd all assume that he'd been peeping, probably at Jessie Ashton. No, they'd have all assumed he had something to do with what happened to Jessie last week and the fact that she was missing right now. Mick had made sure to take his medicine as soon as he'd run into his house and locked the door.

People were coming and going from the Ashton house, most of them carrying in dishes of food or flowers. No one stayed long; only the black sedan Mick knew belonged to the pastor of the church the Ashtons' attended had remained in front of the Ashtons' house for any length of time. It had shown up several hours ago. Mick also noticed that Casey Bailey had made several trips back and forth between her house and the Ashtons' house, often with food parcels. Mick assumed the Ashtons' refrigerator had gotten full and Casey was now making room in hers for the overflow. It reminded Mick of how people always brought food to the family when someone died. Surely, they hadn't found Jessie dead! Mick wanted to ask but he knew he wouldn't be welcome.

Ted Bailey had come home briefly, then left again. That was nothing unusual. He did that quite often and spent very few evenings at home. Mick had always suspected that Ted was having an affair and that's why he was rarely around. Casey Bailey, so petite, wasn't Mick's type but she was very pretty in an exotic way and Mick wondered who could tempt Ted to cheat on his young cherry of a wife. Of course, Mick didn't really understand marriage or any type of romantic relationship between a man and a woman and that's why his few weak attempts at dating had been fruitless and disappointing. Mick knew that his impulses made the possibility of ever having a normal relationship with a woman slim-to-none.

Mick realized he hadn't seen the Ashtons' other daughter around at all in the last week. Mick wondered where she was but figured she'd been shipped off to friends or relatives for the time being. The Ashtons were the sort of people that would automatically think that it was better for their other daughter to be removed from the scene so she wouldn't be distressed by the absence of her older sister.

Grace was holed up in her house like usual. Mick had observed that Grace seemed angry and agitated when she'd arrived at home. She'd left her car in the driveway instead of pulling into the garage as was her typical custom. She'd slammed the door way harder than necessary and had dropped her keys twice on her way to the front door. Then she kicked a pot of something green and leafy clean off her porch, its contents spilling down the steps and onto the brick path that wound across her front lawn. A few minutes after entering her house, she came back out, having changed from her smart suit into shorts and a tank top, and cleaned up the broken pot and debris. Despite feeling guilty about it, Mick had watched mesmerized as Grace worked on the mess. When she'd finished, she threw the broom against the garage where it lodged against the corner and stomped back inside her house. Mick hadn't seen her since.

Aster had left a long time ago and Mick didn't expect to see her again tonight. Most likely she'd come home in the middle of the night—or middle of the morning, to be more precise—like she always did on the days she worked. Mick knew she was supposed to be a waitress at some club casino across the river but he was convinced that she did more than serve drinks and cocktails. Aster might have been his type if her upper torso and legs weren't so muscular. Mick liked soft curves not carved ones. He also like naturally large breasts and it always looked to him like Aster was stuffing her push-up bra to create assets she didn't really have. Suddenly, Mick remembered something. The police had picked Aster up tonight. They'd come to her house and after about fifteen minutes inside had escorted Aster out. They hadn't made her wear handcuffs like they did Mick when they'd taken him this morning. *That's not fair*, Mick thought. Mick wondered if Aster leaving with the police meant that they now suspected her of doing something to Jessie. *Or maybe they found out she was doing more than waitressing*, Mick decided.

A little while ago, Ping had roared into the cul-de-sac in his beat-up truck. Strangely, he had sat in the truck for a while before getting out and going into his house. For some reason, Mick remembered that Ping had arrived just after Ted Bailey had gotten home and Ping hadn't gotten out of his truck until Ted had left. It seemed like to Mick that Ping was watching Ted. And then after Ted's car was out of sight and Ping got out of his truck, Ping just stood there in his driveway staring at the Bailey house, like he was trying to make up his mind about something. He stood there for a long time before he finally turned and went into his house. Mick thought Ping was a little odd anyway. Ping was a good-looking guy with a nice smile and he obviously worked out yet Mick had never seen Ping bring a woman to his house after his fiancée moved out. Occasionally, he'd have a group of guys over and sometimes there would be a few women in the group, too, but it was always evident that the women were already paired up. Mick was pretty sure that Ping had a thing for Casey Bailey—he'd noticed Ping giving Casey sidelong glances—but he'd rarely seen Ping interact with Casey outside of polite conversation at the cul-de-sac barbeques. If Casey returned Ping's admiration, Mick couldn't tell. She flitted around her husband and sons and showed little interest in anyone else in the cul-de-sac other than Ellen Ashton and her daughters.

Suddenly something occurred to Mick. Ted didn't usually leave on Wednesday evenings. Wednesday evenings and Saturday evenings he always stayed at home. Changes in people's routines bothered Mick because Mick had to rely on routines. At least he did before he promised Jessie Ashton that he wouldn't do anymore peeping. Well, Mick thought, it wasn't like he was going to be watching Ted Bailey or even Casey Bailey for that matter. So it shouldn't bother him. But it did. He couldn't help it. And then something that had fallen through the cracks of his memory, somewhere way back in his brain began to inch its way forward. Something about Ted Bailey. Something about Ted Bailey's regular routine. Mick squeezed his eyes shut, willing the thought to fight through the constant fog of his mind and emerge front and center. Mick concentrated, rubbing both temples with the heels of his hands. Slowly an image began to form. It was shadowy, without clear edges but Mick could make it out. It was last Thursday night, and Mick hadn't been able to sleep. Usually, Mick would cure his insomnia by lurking around someone's house, peeping in their windows even if all he saw was someone sleeping. But Mick had made that promise to Jessie Ashton and he was trying hard to keep it and so instead of sneaking around someone else's backyard, Mick was pacing around his own. And that's when he'd discovered another sudden and distressing change in Ted Bailey's normal routine. That's when he'd seen Ted Bailey, who should have been sound asleep thanks to his nightly pill, standing in the Ashtons' back yard.

# CHAPTER 61

**Casey didn't even** know Ted had left. She'd been so busy helping Ellen and Justin receive visitors she hadn't seen him leave. Of course, he'd waited until she was next door to slip away. If Sebastian hadn't told her he was gone, the truth is Casey would have just assumed Ted was still in his office with the door shut.

The pastor at Ellen and Justin's church had set up a prayer feast after learning of Jessie's disappearance. He'd installed himself in their living room to pray with each of the church members for Jessie's safe return. As a symbol of faith and hope and the old-fashioned link to comfort for the grieved, church members brought food and flowers as a gift for the Ashton family. Casey liked their modern Christian church with its contemporary music and unconventional church services but sometimes its New Age ways left Casey empty or even disturbed. This prayer feast was one of those things that Casey couldn't quite get her head around. It was too much like the traditional religious funeral rite. It didn't inspire faith or hope or comfort in her at all.

Ellen had confided in Casey, which was surprising to Casey given the fact that they'd been all but estranged for almost a year, that she wasn't comfortable with the prayer feast either but she hadn't known how to turn the pastor down when he'd all but insisted on it. So Casey, glad to have her closest friend warming up to her again, immediately offered to help her through it. And for the last hour, after Ellen's refrigerator couldn't hold another pot roast or bowl of banana pudding and every air pocket in her freezer chest had been filled with containers of chicken soup and packages of sweet rolls, Casey had been showing her support and love for the Ashtons by cramming her own appliances with fried chicken platters, bacon soaked green beans, apple pies, whole sliced hams, pound cakes and Jello rainbows. And she'd loaned Ellen her entire cupboard of vases to hold the flowers that now filled the living room and made it look like a funeral parlor.

Ted hadn't even spoken to Casey when he came in. He'd just headed straight for his study and shut the door. Casey had observed, as she passed him in the hall, that his hair seemed to be a little windblown and his suit was wrinkled. Casey went up to their bedroom and was stunned to see the pieces of his suit flung carelessly over the bed instead of folded neatly on the cedar valet. The master bathroom was also in disarray, with several puddles of water on the floor and a towel crumpled next to the shower stall. Ted's golf clothes were balled up on top of the hamper. Casey went back into the bedroom and crossed to the enormous closet where Ted kept all of his clothing, arranged in groups of suits, shirts, casual pants, ties and jackets hanging next to shelves of neatly folded sweaters and precisely placed shoes, and drawers of meticulously ordered underwear, t-shirts, and socks. Casey was pretty sure Ted had taken a pair of khakis, a casual collared shirt and penny loafers from the closet as evidenced by the gaping holes and the disordered condition of the clothing that would have been next to those items. Ted had clearly been in a hurry and Casey began to wonder why.

Casey went back downstairs and found Sebastian marveling at all the food that filled their refrigerator. "Can we eat any of this stuff?" Sebastian asked, his eyes darting around like fireflies.

"Ellen said we could have anything that caught our fancy. She said they'd never eat it all in a year," Casey replied with a chuckle.

As Sebastian grabbed a plate towering with ham biscuits and a casserole bowl filled to the brim with orangey-crisp macaroni and cheese, Casey asked him "Did you happen to talk to your dad before he left?"

"For a minute. Why?" Sebastian asked, transferring heaping spoonfuls of the macaroni onto a microwave plate.

"Did he say where he was going? He doesn't usually go out on Wednesdays," Casey questioned.

"He said if you asked to tell you he was meeting a client for dinner," Sebastian replied, his mouth full of ham biscuit.

"Did he say who or where?" Casey implored watching her son simultaneously stuff another biscuit in his mouth while punching up the time on the microwave to heat the large helping of macaroni sitting on the plate inside.

"No. He said it would probably run long so not to wait up for him," Sebastian answered, then changed his mind. "Oh, he did say something about going across the river for dinner."

A sick feeling crept into Casey's stomach. She had been right. He was seeing someone. Maybe it wasn't that snooty secretary of his but he was definitely having an affair. *What else could it be?* Sneaking out of here without even a word and giving their son vague information about his plans to pass on to her. Casey felt indignant but only for a moment. Never mind, it would just make it easier for Casey to leave at the end of the summer when Sebastian went off to Wyoming to college. In truth, Casey didn't really care if Ted was seeing someone else. She just didn't like Ted thinking that he was getting away with something behind her back.

Casey left Sebastian in the kitchen planning his next raid on the refrigerator and started to go back next door. Then she changed her mind. She called Ellen on her cell phone and told her that she needed to take care of something but she'd be back in a little while. Then Casey quickly left through the front door and circled around the side of her house. She was glad that the cul-de-sac was crawling with people and vehicles. That way no one would notice where she was going.

# CHAPTER 62

**Grace was getting** annoyed by all the traffic crawling by her house on their way to the Ashtons'. Cars were parked all over the cul-de-sac, in front of every house and there was even two rows queued up in the middle. Almost as many golf carts were scattered among the cars and parked three and four deep on the lawns of the Ashton and Bailey homes. Grace wondered what all the fuss was about. She recognized that all these people were carrying platters and bowls and boxes of food into the Ashton house and she speculated that perhaps they'd found Jessie Ashton and, poor girl, she was dead. It did look like the food fest most people had when a family member passed away.

Grace stood by the window and looked out. The cul-de-sac looked like a beehive with a hundred little insects crawling all over it, going in and out of the Queen's chamber. Grace laughed as she thought about the comparison between the Queen Bee and the Ashtons, especially Miss Perfect Mother, Ellen Ashton. Grace watched the people, trance-like, as they pulled up in a car or on a golf cart, alighted, moved casually or quickly toward the front door of the Ashton house and disappeared inside. As soon as one or two people would disappear through the door, other people would re-appear, retracing their original steps back to their mode of transportation, backing up, pulling forward, turning sharply, then retreating out of the cul-de-sac. Grace imagined it as a silent film accompanied by eerie symphonic music.

As Grace watched, she found it amusing that every container taken in through the front door of the Ashton house by a visitor would, just a few minutes later, be carried out through the back yard and next door by Casey Bailey. Grace had watched the monotony for fifteen minutes when she became aware that Casey was no longer moving back and forth between the houses. Maybe Casey's larders are full now, too, Grace thought dismissively just before she witnessed Casey Bailey exit her front door and walk quickly down the side of her house toward the rear. Grace refocused her attention and could observe as clear as day, even though by now the sun had set and darkness was moving in, that Casey Bailey had darted behind the house next to hers that belonged to weekenders. Grace raced through her house and out of the back, crouching down beside the neatly pruned boxwood that separated her yard from the house next to it. From her position she could clearly view Casey's movements and she watched in fascination as Casey reached the back patio of Danny Ping's house, knocked on one of the French doors, and then a moment later slipped inside.

# CHAPTER 63

**Katie hadn't eaten** much of her pizza when Ben had interrupted her dinner with Cade and suddenly her stomach was complaining to her about it. Katie opened the refrigerator and looked in. Ogilvie was also poking his nose in as if he too, was trying to decide what he wanted to eat. Katie laughed at him which just made him wag his tail even harder.

"OK, buddy. What kind of sandwich can I make for you?" Katie teased. "Roast beef with turkey or ham with hotdogs?"

Ogilvie gave her a look that seemed to say, "I'll take both, thank you."

Katie finally settled on heating up week-old lasagna and a small salad. It was the closest she could get to the pizza she'd forfeited without going back out. Katie made sure to scoop some into a separate bowl for Ogilvie before zapping the rest in the microwave. Ogilvie had no preference when it came to hot or cold. He liked his food any temperature as long as he got it as quickly as possible. While the lasagna was heating, Katie threw some lettuce and shredded carrots in a bowl, tossing them with a little honey-mustard dressing and a sprinkling of bacon bits. When everything was ready, Katie sat on her sofa to eat it, flipping to a reality cop show.

Ogilvie had slurped his lasagna down long before the microwave had beeped and had quickly fallen into snooze mode on the floor under her feet. Just as Katie finished the last bite of the lasagna, which had been even better after a week of "percolating" as her mother always said, her cell phone rang.

"I didn't disturb your date with Cade did I?" Anna said in a conspiratorial tone.

"No. Cade messed that up all by himself," Katie said with slight bitterness.

"Oh, so you did have dinner with him after all?" Anna replied. "Do tell."

"First of all, I was manipulated into dinner which was pizza on the boardwalk at a picnic table," Katie began. "And then all hell broke loose."

"What happened?" Anna said excitedly as if she had a room full of old ladies on speakerphone just waiting to spread the latest gossip.

"Well, Ben happened , actually," Katie replied, taking a breath. "Everything was going fine, Cade asked me about the case, we talked about me painting the murals in his bungalows, then Ben showed up."

"What? Is Ben stalking you now?" Anna half-teased.

"I take it Ben was on his way home from work, saw me and decided to stop and say hello," Katie answered. "I wouldn't doubt it though, now that I think about it, if he also wasn't trying to make some passive statement to Cade."

"Like *"Katie's my woman, hands off!"* That kind of statement?" Anna laughed.

"No, more like, *"I'm on to you so you better watch out."* That kind." Katie replied. "Anyway, things got really heated between them very quickly. At first it seemed like Cade was just being a jerk for the heck of it but then something Ben said must have hit home because he started insulting me, too. That's when I grabbed Ben and left."

"Did you tell him off first, I hope?" Anna inquired.

"Yeah, I think I told him off pretty good. The thing is, he said some pretty damning stuff that definitely did not endear him to all the people that could overhear the conversation between him and Ben. I think he'll have quite a bit of trouble making friends and winning clients after this," Katie said a little ruefully.

Anna had picked up the hint of regret in Katie's voice and admonished her for it. "Don't feel sorry for him. He did it to himself."

"I don't feel sorry for him. I just feel sorry for the town because despite what his motives might have been, he was actively preserving some great old houses that might never get renovated now," Katie explained.

"I see your point but I'm glad you saw him for who he was," Anna replied.

"So is this the sole purpose for your phone call. To interrogate me about my love life?" Katie asked, changing the subject.

"No, I called you about police business," Anna clarified taking on her professional persona. "I got an interesting call from the station a few minutes ago. They received a phone call from a nurse who works at the hospital and was on duty during the time Jessie disappeared last night. She's been asleep all day and had just been told by a neighbor about what happened.

This nurse claims that she saw a very strange looking golf cart parked in the far corner of the parking lot last night when she went outside during her break to grab a granola bar from her car. She couldn't really see it all that well because it was so dark but she says that it definitely had strange pipes sticking out from it. What does that sound like to you?"

"It sounds like the contraption I saw under the tarp in Alex Watson's workshop," Katie replied. "You know I did a little research on what they call "steampunk" and one of the main themes of the movement or lifestyle or whatever you want to call it is the actual use of steam-powered mechanisms. Aesthetically, it's a sort of mix-and-match of old and new that produces vintage looking machines that have a modern technological edge or vice versa."

"Well, that would fit Alex Watson to a tee. I would say that we now have undeniable proof that Alex Watson was Jessie's accomplice. Given the fact that they both have been missing since last night, I don't think there can be any doubt about it now," Anna concluded.

"I agree. I'm just wondering where Alex could hide such a fantastic-looking machine. It would stick out like a sore thumb anywhere and people would notice it. If any of our elderly set who are sticklers for regulation--and that's about a third of Potoma--saw Alex's contraption, they'd call the police immediately. I'm at a loss for why we haven't received even one report of a sighting," Katie sighed.

"That is very strange," Anna agreed. "Anyway, just thought you'd want to know. Apparently, Alex's parents still haven't filed a *Missing Persons* report on him. If nothing develops tonight, I think we should pay them a visit in the morning."

Katie concurred and said goodbye. Katie's yawns were coming in fast succession now and her eyelids were starting to feel heavy so Katie washed her face, brushed her teeth and, stripping down to her underwear, crawled into bed.

# CHAPTER 64

**Charles was still** in disguise as Aster. He'd have to remain so for another day or two until he could slip unobtrusively out of Potoma. He 'd be gone for at least a week or more before his neighbors in Versailles Court would realize he had moved away without saying goodbye. Not that they would actually care since he'd not really made friends with anyone in the cul-de-sac and they'd always looked on him with a combination of suspicion and confusion. He checked his makeup in the rear view mirror to make sure it wasn't slipping or fading or smudging too much. It still looked close to perfect but that really wasn't much of a surprise. The end of the operation had gone very smoothly without any real bumps. They'd apprehended Bobbo, whom they'd dubbed "Big Drug" without incidence, not even one shot was fired and all of his associates had been rounded up with one big, well-organized net. Well, almost all of them. One had gotten away but that was a necessary loss. They'd gotten Big Drug and the rest and that was what was important.

Charles had talked to Janice about one that had gotten away. He'd been an important link to Big Drug's operation but he wasn't that significant for prosecution on their bust. However, his ongoing activities, his other associations, made him dangerous man to certain people and his other crimes, if he was collared for them, could put him away for life. Charles had already convinced George, Janice's closest advisor, that revealing his identity to the Potoma police was essential. It had taken him a little longer to talk Janice into it. Janice didn't want to take any chances of blowing their own case which had been a year in the making and had eaten up hundreds of thousands of dollars in man-power and equipment. The truth was that even if Janice hadn't agreed to let Charles release the information to the Potoma police department, he would have done it anyway. There was a young girl's life at stake and Charles wasn't about to let her get hurt, now that that they had completed their mission and Big Drug and his cohorts were safely on their way to long lives in a maximum security prison. Charles had a teenage daughter of his own, after all.

Charles drove into the cul-de-sac taking note of the unusual number of cars parked there. He wondered what sort of event he'd missed but he didn't really care. By the time Charles had showered and re-applied his feminine face, most of the cars and golf carts that had been there earlier were gone. After throwing a frozen pizza into the oven and cracking open a Coke, Charles reached for his cell phone and dialed the direct line to the Potoma police department.

# CHAPTER 65

**Ping had been** relieved to see Casey at his back door. He'd been imagining the worst ever since he'd found the note on his windshield and the fact that he'd witnessed Ted leaving had done nothing to calm his worst fears. After taking Casey in his arms and sharing a long, passionate kiss, he'd lead her into the living room and showed her the note. She'd been shocked. Neither of them had thought that Ted had any clue about their relationship.

"How do you think he found out?" Ping had asked. "You don't think your son told him, do you?"

"I know my son and if he'd told Ted about us, he would have let me know," Casey had avowed. "For all I know, Ted could have had a private investigator following me or you or both of us."

Casey hadn't seemed all that concerned, really. "I think Ted is seeing someone else, anyway. That's probably why he wrote the part about being done with me a long time ago," Casey had suggested.

"Do you really think he'll just let you walk away?" Ping had asked. "Why would he do that, even if he is cheating on you?"

"One of two things," Casey had replied with a hint of melancholy. "Because he really, truly still loves me and he wants me to be happy or he hates me so much he can't stand the sight of me anymore."

"He's a rich, powerful man and people like that are possessive, even with things they don't want anymore. Even more so with things that they do. What makes your husband any different?" Ping had asked.

"A lot of things that happened in his past," Casey had answered with a note of wistfulness. "But mostly because of the pre-nup we signed. There's some pretty iron-clad stuff in there that protects me."

"OK," Ping had shrugged not needing or wanting to know more. He was looking toward the future and planning to leave the past behind him for good once he was gone from Potoma. It truly saddened him that at one time he had thought that Potoma was his new beginning, the place where he was going to start over. He really liked Potoma and he wished there was a way he could stay but then part of him knew that a new beginning meant everything had to be new including the place he would call home.

"What happened tonight?" Ping asked. He and Casey had been sitting for a while in silence as the darkness of the night closed around them. Casey had taken time out to call Ellen Ashton to check on her and tell her that things were taking longer than she'd expected. According to Casey, Ellen had told her not to worry. Everyone would be gone soon and she didn't need Casey to come back.

"With Ellen?" Casey replied.

"No, with your husband," Ping corrected her.

"Nothing. Absolutely nothing. When he came home he didn't say a word to me. Then he left without even telling me he was going. I found out from Bastian two hours later," Casey answered.

"Do you know where he was going?" Ping asked. He wasn't yet convinced that Ted wouldn't retaliate against Casey or himself. He worried about what would happen if Ted came home and found Casey gone. There was no doubt in his mind that Ted would come to his house first if he went looking for her.

"No. He mentioned something to Bastian about meeting a client across the river for dinner but I don't believe it. He didn't wear the right clothes for that," Casey pointed out.

"What do you mean?" Ping questioned.

"From what I could tell he was wearing casual clothing when he left. Ted always wears a suit or dress pants and a sports coat when he meets clients. He always wears a tie, too," Casey detailed.

"Then where do you think he went?" Ping asked still nervous, expecting Ted to start pounding on his front door at any minute.

"I don't know. He wears stuff like that when he's playing cards or going bowling but tonight wasn't his night to do either of those activities," Casey shrugged seeming unconcerned. "I suspect he was going to meet his lover."

"You don't seem to care much about that," Ping said.

"I don't. I'm here with you. This is what I care about," Casey replied looking deeply into Ping's eyes. "I wish I never had to leave this house or go back to mine ever again."

"Me, too," Ping murmured, pulling Casey to him and pressing his lips gently against hers.

# CHAPTER 66

**Katie turned her** head to look at the clock on her nightstand. It was only 11:45 pm. Katie had fallen asleep so quickly when she'd climbed into bed just a few hours ago that she was sure she must being reading the clock face wrong. Katie propped herself up on one elbow and stared at the numbers. Now it read 11:46. Katie could hear Ogilvie snoring softly on the floor next to her. Katie flopped back down on her back staring up into the darkness above her. She closed her eyes, willing herself to fall asleep again. Katie rolled over on her side, then on her stomach, then on her back again. The facts of the Jessie Ashton case crashed into each other in Katie's brain and they whirred through her mind so fast, Katie felt like her head was spinning. Katie slid out of the bed and walked to the bathroom. She felt wide awake although her head was beginning to ache. Katie quietly went out into the hall and opened the door to the roof deck. Suddenly, Ogilvie was beside her, the soft padding of his paws startling her. Out on the deck, Katie stood, breathing in the cool spring air and listening to crickets and the wash of the river as it flowed past. The moon was almost full and so bright Katie could make out the clear image of objects in the distance by its light. The longer Katie stayed on the deck, the more alert she became. Katie knew the only way to ward off her restlessness was do something to get rid of her nervous energy and make herself sleepy again.

Katie left the roof deck and went back to her bedroom, followed closely by Ogilvie. He could sense something was about to change and was becoming energetic, his tail wagging faster and faster. Katie pulled on a pair of jeans, her favorite over-sized sweatshirt and slipped her feet into some flip-flops. In the bathroom, she splashed cold water on her face; she noticed she'd neglected to remove her eyeliner and mascara before but it wasn't smudged so she let it be. Then she pulled her hair back into a ponytail and, since her mouth felt cottony and dry, she brushed her teeth. Downstairs, Katie clipped Ogilvie's leash on and grabbing a can of Coke from the refrigerator as an afterthought, led him out the back door. Then she remembered her cell phone. *Just in case.* Katie went back in the house to her bedroom. It wasn't on the nightstand where she usually left it, plugged in to recharge overnight. After a brief search, Katie found it on the coffee table downstairs. Katie slid the keyboard out to turn it on and noticed the battery was at 35%. It was getting low. Katie hoped it would last a little while longer and slipped it into her jeans pocket. Ogilvie had seemed confused with Katie going in and out of the house but when he saw Katie headed toward her golf cart, he dashed ahead, stopping just before the leash snapped taut.

Katie pulled out of her driveway, her electric golf cart silent in the quiet night. Katie really had no destination but she turned in the direction of town. As expected, no one else was out that late on a Wednesday night and very few homes still had lights burning inside. Katie's headlights made strange shapes of luminosity as they cut through the heavily shaded areas of her neighborhood where the illumination of the moon could not reach. Soon Katie reached the commercial district where the streets were vacant and single bulbs lit up the fronts of buildings. The only things open in Potoma after nine o'clock on a weeknight were the police station and the all-night convenience store at the end of the main street. The Potoma police department cruised the residential areas in electric golf carts like Katie's at night so as not to wake any occupants. A police car was used to patrol the commercial area but they only did a few sweeps each night and mainly waited, almost always in vain, for a crime to be called in. The truth of the matter was that nothing really happened in Potoma that required police assistance in the middle of the night other than the occasional domestic dispute or a drunk and disorderly on the weekends.

Although the town seemed almost abandoned without a soul in sight or any movement whatsoever, Katie didn't feel alone or in the least bit wary. Potoma was as safe at night as it was during the day. Criminals just didn't live or wage war in Potoma. Katie almost choked on the thought. Not usually, anyway, she corrected herself. Someone *had* tried to kill a teenage girl in her own bed in the middle of the night. And now that girl was missing, apparently frightened into disappearing to avoid an assumed second attempt on her life.

Katie reached over and petted Ogilvie. He was delirious with excitement, sitting easily on the seat, his tail in non-stop wag mode, his mouth open, nose wiggling frantically as he inhaled every scent that floated on the crisp air. Katie had tied his leash to the cart's hardtop bar with just enough slack so that if Ogilvie decided to jump off, he wouldn't hang himself before Katie had time to stop. Ogilvie had actually never even attempted to jump off while the cart was in motion but Katie couldn't help but be cautious. She'd seen too many accidents involving dogs and carts where the dogs had been injured, sometimes seriously, when they'd taken a flying leap and the owner hadn't stopped quickly enough to avoid disaster.

Katie had cruised down the main drag and was now on Riverside Drive. She slowed down a little as she passed the big Victorian cottages, standing like monoliths over the river, the moon reflecting off of their sparkling windows. Even before Katie could see Ben's house, Ogilvie began to wag his tale fervently and kept looking over at Katie as if to say *"Are we gonna stop? Are we gonna stop?"* "Not tonight, buddy. It's way too late," Katie said out loud.

When Katie caught her first glimpse of Ben's Queen Anne, her heart seemed to skip a beat. As always, she wondered what it would be like to live there and she felt a little jealous of the mysterious woman Ben was now pursuing. *What if Ben married her?* Katie's heart pounded a little harder. *Would this woman insist that Ben break off his friendship with Katie?* Katie really didn't want to think about it. Anna was Katie's best girlfriend but she wouldn't go so far as to say they were best friends. Although, they sometimes carried on like school girls at work and occasionally socialized outside of work, they rarely did best friend things like going shopping together or chatting for hours on the phone or seeing a movie together. Outside of work, Anna devoted her time and energy and emotion to her husband and two little girls. No, Ben was Katie's best friend and it terrified Katie to even consider the possibility of losing that relationship. When Katie passed Ben's house without even slowing down, Ogilvie seemed to deflate, flopping down in the seat with his head on Katie's lap.

"Sorry, Buddy," Katie said, rubbing Ogilvie's head.

Katie continued along Riverside Drive, flying past the strange Victorian configurations that at times seemed to defy gravity and the principals of balance. A little further up Riverside Drive around a wide, gradual curve that followed the river bend, The Tower suddenly sprouted awkwardly out of the ground. Despite its unusual design and the appearance that if not for the two-story addition on the back to anchor it securely, it would topple over in a strong wind, it had always been Katie's favorite cottage.

Katie decided to ride by Cade's bungalow court. All of the trees in the court had been removed by lightening or previous owners years ago and the brilliant radiance from the moon would make it easy to view the newly painted houses without a flashlight. Katie knew that after what had happened with Cade on the boardwalk earlier, she shouldn't even consider going anywhere near Cade's house but her curiosity was getting the best of her. *Besides,* she convinced herself, *Cade will be sound asleep.* Nevertheless, Katie was cautious as she approached the bungalow court. Thankful for the silence of her electric golf cart, Katie slowly pulled into the U-shaped driveway rimmed by quaint one-and-a-half story houses. She rolled past Cade's house which was dark without even the porch light turned on. She noted that two vehicles sat next to it; one of them was Cade's truck and the other was a car that looked vaguely familiar but she couldn't place it. Katie drove along the newly paved drive at a snail's pace looking appreciatively at the color palettes she had chosen for each house. Everything had turned out just the way she'd imagined.

Katie had been nervous enough to keep glancing at Cade's house as she rounded the drive but she'd detected no movement, no light, no noise. Despite the confrontation with Ben about Cade's motivations and intentions, Katie still couldn't help but admire the beautiful work Cade had done on the bungalows. She just wished he could beautify and preserve the rest of Potoma without changing it so much and without being such a money-hungry jerk. Katie saw dark shapes in the moonlight behind the bungalows. She knew they were the tarp-draped pieces of equipment and neatly stacked materials that Cade kept as much out of sight as possible when he wasn't actively using them. It was a quirk that had been a part of Katie's initial attraction to Cade. She had liked the fact that even in the midst of destruction and reconstruction, Cade had strived to keep the work site as pleasant-looking and uncluttered as possible.

Despite her slight uneasiness about being on Cade's property in the middle of the night, Katie gave into her impulse to make another circle around the court before heading back home. Still keeping one eye on Cade's house, Katie began another circuit of the houses. Having been completely focused on the bungalows the first time, she hadn't taken in anything else. This time, besides once again seeing how well the color schemes tied each house to the next, Katie's eye was also drawn to what was around the houses. She saw that Cade had begun to plant small trees and shrubs between the houses and she could also make out posts, sunk into the ground at regular intervals, around the rear yards of the structures. The posts were short and Katie wondered if they were the beginnings of traditional picket fences. She also tried to guess what was specifically under each tarp by its shape.

Suddenly, Katie's attention was drawn to a particular shadowy form that was sitting at the far rear of the property in almost complete darkness. In fact, Katie wouldn't have seen it if the beam from her golf cart headlights hadn't bounced off of the metal pieces sticking out of the tarp. Katie sucked in her breath and looked around. Cade's house was still quiet with no signs of life inside or outside. Katie quickly maneuvered her golf cart off of the driveway and between two of the bungalows. Narrowly avoiding a young sapling, Katie drove to the rear of the property, training her headlights on the bulky machine under the canvas tarp.

"Stay, Ogilvie", Katie whispered, as she hopped off the golf cart. Ogilvie perked up his ears but stayed put. Warily, Katie pulled up a corner of the shiny tarp. Just as she had suspected, it was a golf cart. But it was no ordinary golf cart.

From what Katie could see, it appeared to be styled like a Model T and there were several pipes extending from the body. Katie knew without a doubt that this was Alex Watson's missing contraption. Just as Katie fumbled her cell phone from her pocket and turned it on to call Anna, it rang, piercing the stillness of the night with the sound of old fashioned church bells.

# THURSDAY
## CHAPTER 67

**When the doorbell** rang, at first Casey thought it was part of the dream she was having and she didn't know why there were bells going off when she and Danny were sunbathing on a deserted beach on some exotic island somewhere. When the bell rang again, Casey was quickly pulled from sleep into consciousness. Still, she didn't get up, assuming Ted would go down and find out what was going on. Then Casey noticed that Ted wasn't in the bed next to her and given the fact the double pillows on his side were still stacked neatly, she realized Ted hadn't ever come to bed. Casey immediately wondered if Ted had even come home. Casey heard footsteps go down the staircase and then heard voices. Casey scrambled out of bed forgetting to grab her robe.

Sebastian was at the front door. It was flung open all the way and Casey could see Aster on the front porch. Sebastian must have heard Casey behind him because he turned around and said, "Go get Dad."

Casey didn't answer. "I'll take care of this. You can go back to bed."

Sebastian turned toward her, shrugging his shoulders. "Then why didn't you get the door in the first place? I wouldn't have had to interrupt my sleep," Sebastian said grumpily.

As Sebastian stalked past her, Casey looked at Aster. "Something about Ted?"

"Yes. I know it's terribly late and I'm so sorry to bother you but I have a problem and I didn't want to trouble Mr. Ashton with it with his worries over his daughter and all," Aster babbled.

Casey looked past Aster at the driveway. Ted's car was not in it. It was obvious to Casey that Ted was not at the house.

"I'm afraid my husband isn't here," Casey replied.

"He's not? Are you sure?" Aster asked.

"I'm sure," Casey answered sleepily.

"You don't expect him home, then?" Aster said, looking at Casey curiously.

Casey yawned, covering her mouth with the back of

her hand. "I didn't expect him to stay out all night."

"I see," Aster said. After a moment, she continued, "So I guess you have no idea when he might be home?"

Casey shook her head. Her brain was just beginning to dust the cobwebs and she realized she was glad that Ted hadn't come home. She wondered where he was, who he was with, but she didn't truly care. And she didn't care if he ever came home.

"Is there something I can help you with?" Casey asked, suddenly surprised that Aster would come to her or her husband for help. Especially in the middle of the night.

"No. I need a man", Aster replied.

"I could get Sebastian to help you," Casey offered. "He's just grumpy when he first wakes up."

Aster gave Casey a crooked grin. "No, he's a little young."

*Certainly, Aster hadn't wanted Ted for THAT*, Casey thought wryly. Even if she was the one he was having an affair with, there's no way she'd be bold enough to wake him up in the middle of the night when Casey was home, much less flaunt their relationship right in Casey's face.

"OK, well, I'm sorry I can't help you," Casey replied for lack of any witty response.

"Perhaps, I can ask Mr. Ping," Aster suggested.

Casey narrowed her eyes at Aster. "Mr. Ping has already assisted a damsel in distress tonight. I'm sure he's not up to rescuing any more right now."

Aster grinned, a knowing look in her eyes. Casey didn't care that Aster now knew about her and Danny. She was just glad she'd gotten her message across to Aster loud and clear.

"OK, I see," Aster replied. "Oh, just one more thing. Doesn't your husband drive a gold Mercedes?"

Casey made sure her expression spelled out annoyance but she nodded her confirmation. "If there's nothing else…" Casey said.

"No, nothing else. Again, I'm sorry I woke you up," Aster answered, then turned and retreated across the cul-de-sac in the direction of her house.

Casey closed the door but watched Aster through the

glass sidelites. Aster stopped in the middle of the court and pulled her cell phone out of her pants pocket. After a brief conversation, Aster went into her house.

Casey was now fully awake and so she went to the kitchen for a cup of tea. She turned off the kitchen light and walked in the darkness to her living room. Deep in thought, she stood by the window, sipping the sweet, milky liquid and looking out blankly at the other houses. She was bewildered by Ted's sudden departure from routine. She was confused by his seemingly benign acceptance of her relationship with Danny Ping. She had thought she knew everything about her husband worth knowing but now she questioned that knowledge. Ted had never been gone overnight unless he was away on business, much less stayed out all night on a whim. He didn't do things like that. He was responsible and reliable and at the very least, courteous. Casey just couldn't believe that Ted hadn't called to tell her he was going to be gone. Casey wondered briefly if Ted was in trouble. *Had he been in an accident?* But she knew the police would have been at her door immediately if that had been the case. Mostly Casey was annoyed. If she had stayed out all night, Ted would never have let her live it down and the accusations would have kept coming for months. She never dared stay out more than a few hours even when she knew that Ted would be out cold from his sleeping pills until morning.

Casey began to think about sneaking over to Danny's house again. Sebastian would be snoring again by now and never know she was gone. Casey looked at the glowing clock face on the mantel. It was a little after one-thirty in the morning. Casey was tempted to walk out the house right now and go to Danny's *but what if Ted did come home? How would she explain her absence?* Casey had finished the tea but she still held the mug, watching absolutely nothing going on outside. Then she saw the light flicker on in Aster's garage. As the overhead door began to rise, the light went out and within seconds Aster was pulling out into the cul-de-sac. Casey blinked several times, trying to flush out the sleepiness that was beginning to overtake her and blur her vision. Casey was sure she couldn't be seeing what she was seeing. *There was a man driving away in Aster's car!*

Casey wasn't sure what to do. *Was someone stealing Aster's car? Was this man the reason Aster had come over and wanted Ted to help her? Is that why she said she needed a man's help and wouldn't accept Casey's offer to get Sebastian to assist her? Was Aster in trouble?* She pulled her cell phone out and dialed 911.

## CHAPTER 68

**Katie nearly dropped** the phone as she tried to answer it and quell the noise echoing through the night.

"Hello," Katie whispered, looking around fervently. She crept along the side of the bungalow to the front, peering around to see if any lights or movements were perceptible at Cade's bungalow.

"Katie?" the male voice on the other end responded. Katie recognized Officer Darren's deep southern drawl.

"Yes," Katie replied, still craning her neck to see if the ringing of her telephone had garnered any attention.

"I hope I didn't wake you but you said to call if we got any kind of info that was related to the Jessie Ashton case," Darren began.

"Yes," Katie said impatiently. If she hadn't been riding around on her golf cart, she would have been asleep at this time of night, so of course Darren would have woken her up. *What a ditz!*

"I just received a call from someone named Charles. He said you'd know who he was. Anyway, he said that you need to look into Ted Bailey," Darren continued. "Oh, hold on, I've got another call."

Katie paced nervously in the shadows, glancing toward Cade's bungalow, waiting for Darren to come back on the line.

"Sorry about that," Darren apologized. "It was a good thing, I answered it. That was Charles again. He said Bailey is not at home and his wife has no idea where he is. He said to give you his number and for you to call him immediately."

Katie punched the number Darren gave her into her phone, then disconnecting with the police station, hit the "send" button to call Charles.

Charles answered on the first ring.

"When our bust went down tonight, Ted Bailey wasn't there. He was our guy's accountant and so he doesn't mean a whole lot to us as far as convictions. We were taking down the drug lord and his sellers. He was just the connection we followed. However, he's still dangerous to certain people and I think your teenage girl might be one of those people," Charles said.

"How so?" Katie asked.

"It appears from our surveillance that she was present during a rendezvous between Mr. Bailey and another one of his shady clients," Charles replied.

"So she saw or heard something she shouldn't have?" Katie surmised.

"Exactly," Charles confirmed. "Mr. Bailey met a particular client in one of the parks in Potoma. It looks like your girl was working at the time and saw Mr. Bailey and his client together."

"Do you know the identity of the client?" Katie inquired.

"Not yet. I'm working on it," Charles answered. "You have to understand, we were working our own case and the bulk of the action was outside of Potoma. We were focused on our own guy and didn't have the time or manpower to look into Bailey's other operations."

"I understand," Katie said, disappointed. "Any idea when you might get a lead on the client?"

"All I know right now is that from what the surveillance shows the client appeared to be residing in Potoma," Charles replied. "The day Miss Ashton witnessed the meeting was last Tuesday evening."

"OK. Thanks for the information," Katie said. "Let me know as soon as you get anything else."

"Will do," Charles promised before hanging up.

Katie immediately called Anna. It took four rings for Anna to pick up.

"I've got news," Katie blurted out. Without waiting for Anna to comment, Katie relayed the information she'd just received from Charles, alias Aster Bancroft. Then she told Anna what she had found at Cade's bungalow court.

"Did it occur to you that Alex and Jessie might be hiding in one of the bungalows?" Anna suggested.

Katie felt like punching herself. Why hadn't she thought of that possibility?

"I need to go back," Katie replied.

"I'll meet you there. Wait for me," Anna commanded and cut the connection.

Katie sat still for a minute, then calculating that it would take Anna at least thirty minutes, decided to go back by herself. Katie had nothing to be afraid of. It wasn't like Cade was going to ask to see her badge or question why she was back on duty after working all day. Everybody knew that if you were working a case, sometimes you worked a lot of overtime. At least that's what Katie had seen on TV, backed up by what Anna had told her. If Cade did find her there, she had cause to be there. Alex's missing contraption was in plain sight and that was reason enough to search the houses. Katie knew that was stretching the truth. It was under a tarp at the very back of the property and she wouldn't have been able to see it in the dark if she hadn't been trespassing in the first place and her headlights hadn't picked up a tiny reflection of chrome. But Katie didn't care about all that right now. Right now, she had to see if Alex and Jessie were there, if they were alright.

Katie pressed the pedal to the floor. When she arrived at the bungalow court, everything was as quiet and dark as before. The two vehicles next to Cade's house hadn't moved. Katie dialed Anna's cell phone.

"I'm at the bungalow court. I'm going to start looking around," Katie announced in a whisper.

"I told you to wait," Anna scolded. "I'm on my way."

Katie hung up before Anna could say more. Katie untied Ogilvie's leash and put her wrist through the loop on the end.

"Come on, buddy," Katie whispered to the black lab.

Katie started with the house opposite Cade's. The door was unlocked and as soon as Katie entered she was sure the two teens weren't inside. The entire interior had been gutted and only studs and floor joists remained on both floors. Even the stair case had been removed. The house next to it was in much the same condition. The third house was just the opposite, almost completely intact.

Katie cautiously stepped into the house letting Ogilvie lead. His nose was to the floor and his body quaked. Katie shined her flashlight around the large living room. It was empty but fairly clean. Katie walked through the living room into an adjacent room she supposed to be a dining room. This room, too, was empty. Carefully, Katie pushed open a door at the far end. Another empty room that was obviously a gutted kitchen with pipes sticking up from the floor and patches of old linoleum that hadn't yet been removed. Katie crossed the room and shined her flashlight into the hall. Opposite the kitchen was another large, vacant room; probably a bedroom at one time, Katie surmised. Katie took the staircase at the end of the short hall. Slowly she made her way up to the second floor, each step emitting a soft squeak, with Ogilvie tugging at the leash as he snuffed up a hundred different scents. At the top of the stairs was a bathroom containing a clawfoot tub and a large porcelain sink. The toilet had been removed and the linoleum was cracked and peeling. To either side of the staircase were closed doors. Katie tested the door to her right with her foot. It resisted any pressure so Katie gingerly turned the knob. As Katie waved her flashlight around she could see stained floral paper covering the walls and a blackened wood floor in need of sanding and refinishing. Like the rest of the house so far, the room had nothing in it, not even a scrap of trash. Katie crossed the small landing and opened the door to the other room. The striped wallpaper in this room was in surprisingly unmarred condition and the wood floors looked as if they'd been polished recently.

Ogilvie leaned away from the leash, his nose to the floor. He began to whine, pulling hard, trying to cross the room. Katie let go of the leash and Ogilvie ran to the opposite wall. His nose seemed to be stuck to the floor and his back end was skittering back and forth. Katie knelt down beside the dog and trained the flashlight on the area where his nose was glued. Katie could see red splotches. Some looked like drops and others appeared to be smeared. Blood, Katie thought and she knew she was correct. She swung the flashlight in a larger arc. She saw more tiny red spots on the wall, as if they'd been sprayed there in one short burst,  Her flashlight also picked up a glint of something shiny against the wall. Katie dropped down on her hands and crawled over to take a closer look. The baseboard had been removed from the wall and there was a space about half an inch wide between the floorboard and the plaster. Wedged in the space was an old-fashioned pocket knife. Using the bottom of her tank top as a barrier for fingerprints, Katie picked the knife up. She could see blood on the blade. It was already congealing and turning dark. Katie laid the knife on the floor. The handle was some sort of polished wood. She turned it over and saw the letters "C A W". *Cade A. Ware?* Katie wondered. *Or C. Alexander Watson?*

Katie noticed that Ogilvie had lost his enthusiasm over the blood and found a new interest. He was now prancing around with something dangling from his mouth.

"Come here, buddy," Katie called in a whisper, gesturing with her hands. Ogilvie obeyed, sitting down next to her and dropping the object in front of her. Katie pointed the flashlight at his prize. It was a pocket watch like her grandfather used to carry. Katie had seen Alex Watson wearing one when she'd questioned him at his house. She hadn't actually seen the watch face but she'd noticed the chain running from his vest pocket to his trousers. Katie pulled her cell phone out and pushed the "send" button twice. She hoped the battery would hold up.

"Where are you?" Anna asked.

"I'm in one of the bungalows. I'm sure Jessie and Alex were here, too," Katie said in a rush. Katie told Anna about the blood, the pocket knife and the watch.

"Don't go anywhere!" Anna yelled.

"Where are you?" Katie asked, already on her way down the stairs with Ogilvie pulling her along.

"I got hung up. Couldn't find the keys," Anna said. "I just left a few minutes ago."

"OK," Katie said, signifying nothing.

"I'm calling the station and getting you some back-up," Anna warned. "Stay put until somebody gets there!"

"I'm not on official business," Katie replied. "I don't even have my badge."

"Why not?" Anna demanded, sounding breathless as if she was running.

"I was just out riding around. I couldn't sleep," Katie answered. "I wasn't even looking for Jessie."

"Great!" Anna sighed. "All the more reason to stay put. But don't go into any more houses. And stay away from Cade's bungalow!"

There was no doubt that Jessie and Alex had been in that bungalow. It appeared that one or both of them was injured and bleeding. Now the question was whether they'd been hiding there or kept prisoner there. Either way, they were now gone and Katie was sure they'd been taken against their will. *Otherwise, why would Alex leave his machine here? Did Cade have something to do with it? Was he capable of harming a couple of kids? Was he capable of trying to kill someone?* Then it dawned on her who owned the car parked just across the court at Cade's house. *It belonged to Ted Bailey.*

# CHAPTER 69

**When the Potoma** police cruiser arrived, Casey rushed out of her house.

"You're the one that reported suspicious activity here?" the male police officer asked. His name tag said "R. Davis".

"Yes. It's my neighbor, Aster Bancroft," Casey began, pointing at Aster's house. "She came over earlier tonight and asked for my husband. She said she had a situation and needed some help. Anyway, when I told her that my husband wasn't here, she went back to her house. Then, maybe fifteen, twenty minutes later, I was still up and I noticed her garage light come on. Then her car came out but there was a man driving the car. I've never seen him before. She's never had any guests at her house."

Officer Davis looked at Casey quizzically. "How do you know she doesn't have visitors?"

"She's only been living here a few months. She leaves around dinner time or maybe a little before most days and doesn't come home until the wee hours of the morning," Casey explained. "She's a waitress, I think. I don't work so I'm home most of the time and I've never seen anyone there during the day or leaving in the morning."

"Can you describe the man you saw driving her car?" Officer Davis queried.

"I didn't really see him all that clearly. I think he was bald and he was wearing a dark shirt or jacket," Casey answered feeling hopeless.

"OK, Ms. Bailey. Go back to your house and we'll investigate," Officer Davis instructed. His partner had remained silent, taking notes on his tablet.

"Investigate what?" Sebastian asked, sleepily. Casey hadn't realized he was there.

"I think something may have happened to Aster," Casey answered, touching Sebastian's shoulder.

"She was just at our house like an hour ago," Sebastian offered running his hand through his hair, trying to flatten it against his head.

"So you saw her?" Officer Davis said. "Did she seem

to be in distress?"

"Not really. She was asking for Dad," Sebastian answered.

"Will you let me know if you find something?" Casey asked, pushing against Sebastian, moving sideways toward their front door.

"I will if I can," Officer Davis replied somewhat cryptically. "Please wait inside your house for now, though."

Casey turned, and followed by Sebastian, walked into her house. "Why don't you go back to bed. You have school tomorrow," Casey suggested to Sebastian.

"I haven't really been asleep. Just dozing on and off," Sebastian said, moving toward the kitchen. "I'm going to get something to drink."

Casey didn't argue. She sat down in the dark living room without turning on any lights after pulling the curtains aside so that she could keep an eye on what was going on at Aster's house. The moon was so bright it was almost like there were streetlights on outside.

"Where's dad anyway?" Sebastian asked, having appeared in the living room with a cup in his hand.

"I don't know, honey," Casey said, suddenly feeling tired.

"Dad never stays out all night," Sebastian remarked, then said weakly "Does he?"

"Not usually," Casey replied soothingly. She could tell that Sebastian was worried.

"Has he called?" Sebastian inquired hopefully.

"No," Casey answered.

About fifteen minutes later when the police knocked on Casey's door, it was apparent from the looks on their faces which seemed to be a combination of annoyance and confusion.

"There's no one in the house, Ms. Bailey," Officer Davis reported. "Do you think Ms. Bancroft could have been in the car with the man?"

"There was no one else in the car," Casey replied. "Not unless they were lying down on the backseat or in the trunk or something."

"Why are you looking for Aster?" Sebastian asked.

"There was a man at her house," Casey replied.

"So what?" Sebastian said.

"He drove away in Aster's car," Casey replied. "And now Aster has disappeared."

"What did he look like?" Sebastian asked.

"He was bald. That's all I could see," Casey said irritably. Sebastian coughed, unsuccessfully trying to cover up a chuckle.

"What's so funny?" Casey asked, spinning around to face her son.

"That was Aster," Sebastian replied, his expression clearly telling her she was incredibly stupid.

"What do you mean?" Casey asked, echoed by Officer Davis.

"Aster is a dude," Sebastian answered. "Like it wasn't obvious anyway."

"What?" Casey and Officer Davis said in unison.

"Come on, Mom. You never figured it out?" Sebastian said in genuine disbelief. "It was so right in your face. But then Jessie saw it for herself. She saw him one night. He was just standing out on his porch, bald head shining, no shirt on, no make-up. Dude's obviously a cross-dresser or a transvestite or something."

"Jessie knew this?" Casey asked, suddenly panicked.

"Yeah. She told me a while back," Sebastian replied. It was clear he wasn't connecting the dots like Casey was.

"Oh, my Lord!" Casey exclaimed. "She—he could be the one that tried to kill Jessie!"

"Jessie Ashton?" Officer Davis interrupted.

"Yes. She lives next door," Casey answered. "Now you've really got to find Aster Bancroft or whoever she—he is."

"I seriously doubt Aster did anything to Jessie," Sebastian scoffed. "This was a long time ago. Like a few weeks after she moved here. If she—he was going to hurt Jessie, wouldn't he have done it a long back then?"

Sebastian had a point.

"Anyway, why would Aster try to kill Jessie just

because she discovered her—his secret. It's not like anyone cares nowadays anyway if some dude wants to dress like a 'ho," Sebastian commented, shrugging. Casey gave him a warning look for his language.

"If Aster Bancroft was hiding her true gender, she might have been hiding other things, too," Officer Davis offered.

"Well, it's obvious what *things* he was hiding," Sebastian laughed.

"Sebastian!" Casey scolded although she couldn't help hiding the smile that crept onto her face.

"We still need to find Ms. Bancroft or whoever is posing as Aster Bancroft," Officer Davis said to his partner. Then he turned to Casey. "We'll follow up on this. Regardless of the circumstances with Ms. Bancroft's identity, we still need to confirm that she is in no danger. And we need to make sure she does not pose any danger to Miss Ashton and is also not involved in Miss Ashton's disappearance."

As the police officers walked briskly to their vehicle, Sebastian, who had contained his laughter in their presence, could hold back no more. "I really can't believe you didn't know, or at least suspect," Sebastian said to Casey.

"You should have told me," Casey rebuked him. "I probably just made a huge fool of myself."

"I promised Jessie. She'd promised Aster or whoever he is that she wouldn't tell any of the neighbors," Sebastian replied.

"Then why did she tell you?"

"Because she had to tell someone. And she knew she could trust me to keep my mouth shut," Sebastian replied, looking at Casey pointedly and reminding her that he was keeping her secret, too.

# CHAPTER 70

**Katie had turned** her phone on vibrate and returned it to her pocket. She was creeping across the court toward Cade's bungalow with Ogilvie pulled up short on the leash despite his constant straining to follow his nose. When the phone went off, pulsating against her thigh, it startled Katie and she jumped. Katie dug the phone out of her pants and looked at the caller ID. It was Anna again. Katie wasn't going to stand in the middle of the bungalow court and argue with Anna. Besides, she didn't have much battery left. Katie needed to determine if anyone was inside Cade's house. Katie let the phone go to voicemail.

After the screen confirmed a message was waiting, Katie went through the process of retrieving it. Anna reported that Katie's back-up was delayed. Davis and Miles were out on a call and Otis was in the middle of a traffic accident just outside of Potoma. Katie was on her own until Anna arrived and that would be at least another fifteen or twenty minutes.

Katie moved stealthily toward Cade's bungalow, her flashlight off, using the bright moonlight to see by. When she'd reached the house, she crouched down beside Ted Bailey's car, duck-walking along the length of it, popping up briefly to peek into the windows. The car was empty. Katie did the same with Cade's truck. Then Katie ran silently to the side of the bungalow. It was dark, silent, almost foreboding. Katie sensed that no one was inside but she needed to be sure. Most of the windows were uncovered and Katie cautiously glanced through them, straining to see any sign of life or movement. Ogilvie moved with Katie, no longer pulling at the leash but walking next to Katie, matching her stride, looking up at her periodically, as if he knew he was supposed to be her security guard and was waiting for her next command. When Katie was sure that the first floor was clear of anything living or breathing, she paused, pondering the best method for checking the second story. She knew she had no choice but to get inside and go up the stairs.

Katie moved around to the back of the house where three sets of double French doors spanned the large family room addition. Katie tested the levers on the middle set and was almost unsurprised to find them unlocked. Such was the pleasure of living in a small town with no crime. People rarely bothered to lock their back or side doors. Once inside the house, Katie moved quickly, praying that Ogilvie would remain quiet and just follow her lead. Except for the addition, Cade's house was laid out similarly to the bungalow where Katie had found evidence of Jessie and Alex. She went directly to the rear hall that held the staircase and slowly made her way up the steps, stopping at every other one to listen. Katie checked each of the rooms, finding them all empty. Cade had built a modest master suite over the family room addition and Katie curiously surveyed the décor, tastefully rendered in an arts and crafts style. She found it odd that his bed was unmade and clothes were scattered on the floor given his penchant for such neatness and cleanliness outside on his construction site.

Katie felt a strong desire to look around, to try and find some clue that might prove or even disprove Cade's involvement in the attempted murder or disappearance of Jessie Ashton but she didn't have a search warrant and anything she might find would be inadmissible in court. In fact, she herself could be charged with trespassing or breaking and entering for being in Cade's house. Katie reluctantly exited, deep in thought.

She looked at her cell phone; Anna was still a good ten minutes away. She also noted that she still had one bar left on her battery. She knew the phone wasn't going to last much longer. Katie pondered her next move. She was feeling anxious waiting for Anna and her mind was whirring with questions. *If Cade was involved and had taken Jessie and Alex from the other bungalow, where would he have taken them? And why was Ted Bailey's car at Cade's house? Was Cade Ted Bailey's mysterious client, the one that Jessie had seen him with in the park? And what nefarious business could Bailey and Cade be into together? So what if Bailey was Cade's accountant? That didn't mean that Cade was dirty.* Katie ran the facts through her brain trying to reason it all through, trying to find justifications, explanations. Katie wasn't trying to make Cade a good guy, he'd already proved himself to be sort of a bad one. She just didn't want to be wrong.

*Where could Cade and Ted, if indeed they were together as their vehicles seemed to indicate, have taken Jessie and Alex at this time of night?* Most likely they'd traveled via golf cart since the vehicles were parked and no one was at Cade's house. Almost instantaneously the answer was clear. *Cade's boat. No one would be at the marina at two-thirty in the morning and what better place to hide someone?* But did that mean Cade *and Ted intended to transport the two teenagers somewhere by boat?* Then a darker thought crossed Katie's mind. *Had they killed them and were now planning to dump the bodies in the river?* Katie knew that the amount of blood she'd found in the bungalow wasn't nearly enough to indicate that one person had been killed, much less two, but that didn't mean they couldn't have done something less gory to Jessie and Alex. They could have strangled them or used poison, something much more potent and fast-acting than they tried on Jessie before. They could also take them to a secluded stretch of the river and just shoot them right there before tossing them over the side. The possibilities began to mount and Katie's adrenalin began to surge. She had to get to Cade's boat.

# CHAPTER 71

Charles drove slowly through the dead streets of Potoma toward the pocket park where surveillance had picked up the images of Ted Bailey, his client, and Jessie Ashton. Charles reasoned that the client probably lived nearby. Charles hadn't told Officer Bell everything he knew about that meeting. He was used to telling only half the truth and keeping information on a need-to-know basis. And quite frankly, he wasn't so sure that Bell had enough police training to follow a sensible procedure for using the information. Charles sensed that Bell's outward girl-next-door appearance belied a far more complex and daring person that might take risky chances.

The meeting between Bailey and the mystery man had been about Big Drug's operation. It didn't appear that the client was being set up as a dealer but more of an enabler. Thus far, Potoma hadn't had a large drug culture; just the random teenager or out-of-town hippie looking to score. As far as Charles' associates could ascertain there was no one selling inside the town limits. They'd busted a few rednecks living in shacks about ten miles from town who grew weed in ramshackle greenhouses they'd pieced together from crates and pallets and junkyard windows but they'd stayed outside of Potoma and their clients had come to them. As for the hard drugs, there was no sign of any dealer within fifty miles. For Big Drug, Potoma had been the next big thing. When he'd discovered Potoma and its lack of illegal drug activity, he'd been like a chocoholic touring Willy Wonka's factory, allowed to take all the samples he wanted. And Potoma was an easy target. There was no competition and hundreds of kids just waiting to be tempted and seduced into the wonderful world of being high and carefree. There was plenty of money to be made in Potoma, that was certain.

Thanks to the success of the operation tonight, Big Drug had been taken out and there was no possibility he'd be back to victimize Potoma with his grand plans for a new drug colony. But Bailey still posed a threat, especially if his client decided to proceed without Big Drug's backing. Charles knew that wasn't a problem, unfortunately. For every Big Drug they took out, there were at least twenty Little Drugs just waiting for their chance to expand and take over the vacated territory. Bailey and his client wouldn't have any trouble finding a replacement for Big Drug in short order. And that meant that if Jessie Ashton knew anything, she was still a big threat.

Charles arrived at the little green space and surveyed the area around it. It was situated at the eastern corner of a crossroads. All the roads in this part of Potoma—the section called Riverside—were built in a precise grid pattern with the exception of Riverside Drive which wound along the river, looped over at the marina and then proceeded back down along the harbor so that on a map it appeared to outline the perimeter of the original residential peninsula-shaped section of Potoma. Charles reasoned that with Big Drug's takedown tonight, Bailey might have called an emergency meeting with his Potoma connection. It was a hunch that Charles was hoping was correct. It was obvious that Bailey wasn't at the park but this late at night, he might have felt safe enough to go to his client's home. Charles took a right and began to scour the houses for any sign of Bailey's ostentatious gold Mercedes.

# CHAPTER 72

**Katie ran across** the bungalow court to where she'd hidden her golf cart with Ogilvie loping along beside her. Without even tying Ogilvie's leash to the roof support, she mashed the pedal and flew across the court to the street. Although she was frustrated with the slow feel of the golf cart she knew it was going considerably faster than she could run on her own two feet. Ogilvie seemed to sense her excitement and he sat forward on the seat, his head jutting way out in front of him, his tongue hanging out of his half-opened snout.

The moon lit the streets, shining down through the trees in a soft haze. Aside from those with porch lights turned on, the houses were mostly hidden in shadow making the neighborhood look like an undeveloped landscape of crisscrossed grass blocks. Katie didn't use her headlights, peering through the dark like a cat stalking unseen prey.

When Katie reached the end of the road which ran into Riverside Drive, she took a sharp left, cruising noiselessly past a few small frame houses, then a boat shop that had been there since the thirties. A boatyard was behind the shop and beyond that a small privately-owned slip where Ben kept his small fishing cruiser. Katie loved Ben's boat with its beautiful teak built-ins that provided a tiny kitchenette complete with refrigerator, sink and freezer and a dinette that could be reconfigured into a full-size bed. There was also a miniscule half-bath that featured the same kind of toilet-sink combination found in the cheap Amtrak sleeper berths. Ben had bought the fixture on e-bay and installed it himself after Katie had complained about having to jump ship every time she had to pee. Katie reminisced about the times she and Ben took the boat out. They'd go out for the whole day and while Ben fished, Katie would sketch and they would have long conversations, usually about nothing of real importance. Katie napped in the air-conditioned cabin during the hottest parts of the day and when Ben had tired of fishing, they'd cruise along the river with the cool breeze in their faces, searching the shoreline for the wildlife that often gathered there. At night, if Ben had been lucky that day, they baked the fish in the miniature oven and ate out on the deck, enjoying the sunset and watching the lights twinkling off the shores.

Katie pulled herself out of her reverie as she approached the entrance to the marina. Swiftly, she maneuvered the cart onto the driveway and willed the cart to go faster. Katie tried to remember exactly where Cade's boat was tied up. She hadn't really been paying attention the other night; she'd just followed Cade's lead, admiring the fancy boats along the way. Although Katie had refused to board Cade's boat that night because she was reluctant to be in such close quarters with him alone, she now wished she'd taken the opportunity. At least she would have known how the boat was layed out. But first she needed to find it and that might not be such an easy task.

Before Katie stepped onto the pier, she pulled her phone out. She would call Anna and tell her where she was; Anna was probably close to the bungalow court by now. Katie tapped her phone to turn it on but the face of the phone barely lit up. Katie squinted and discovered that she no longer had any bars; her battery was dead and she had no way of letting anyone know where she was. Just like a woman immediately intuits she's in imminent danger when she finds herself alone in a dark alley with no one around, Katie realized that no one knew where she was and wouldn't even know where to begin looking. She was pretty sure she hadn't mentioned Cade's boat to Anna and so Anna wouldn't even think to come to the marina once she saw that Katie had left the bungalow court. Katie stared at the blank phone for several seconds. Then she looked at Ogilvie.

"OK, Buddy," Katie said. "Guess what, O? You can go see Betsy tonight, OK?"

Ogilvie cocked his head to one side as if trying to decipher her human-speak. Katie gave him a kiss on the nose and he licked her in return. Then Katie unsnapped his leash from his collar.

"Go see Betsy, boy," Katie said, shooing at him with her arms. Ogilvie remained seated, cocking his head to the opposite side, his ears alert. Katie walked back a few steps, shooing at Ogilvie again. Ogilvie raised his head, his ears still pulled up and back. He stood up and walked toward Katie.

"No," Katie said. "Go to Betsy."

Ogilvie looked at Katie intently, then turned his head to look over his shoulder. Katie nodded at him "Go, boy."

Ogilvie bounded away a few feet, stopping to briefly sniff the ground, then looked back at Katie. "Yes, good boy," Katie soothed as she took a few more steps back.

Ogilvie ran back to Katie, wagging his tail and licking her hand.

"Ogilvie, git. Go to Betsy," Katie said, waving him away. "Go see Ben, boy."

Ogilvie's ears popped back up and his intelligent brown eyes studied Katie. It appeared he'd keyed in on Ben's name. "Go to Ben, go to Ben," Katie repeated.

Ogilvie licked Katie's hand again, then without looking back, began running down the driveway toward the entrance to the marina. Katie watched him until he'd disappeared into the darkness. Then she tied his leash to the pylon at the entrance to the pier. Katie prayed that Ogilvie would go to Ben's house. She didn't like the idea of him wandering the streets alone. Katie knew that eventually someone would pick him up and look at his collar which would lead back to her but if things went wrong, it might be too late. At least if he showed up at Ben's house, and could wake him up somehow, Ben would know something was wrong and she knew Ben would come looking for her. That's why she'd tied Ogilvie's leash to the pier; on the off chance that if Ben came to the marina, he'd know she was out on the docks somewhere.

Katie closed her eyes, trying to remember where Cade's boat was and what it looked like. It was painted red and yellow, very flashy, Katie thought. There couldn't be too many boats like that at the marina. Most of the boats had traditional paint schemes which involved a lot of white with blue or aqua trim and accents. Katie followed the main dock out to where it split into four adjoining boat slips. She'd bypassed the first few rows of slips where the smaller, more agile boats had been moored. Each of the larger docks had several rows of piers branching off of them. Katie was pretty sure she and Cade had taken the second main branch to the left. Katie pulled her sweatshirt over her head and tied the sleeves around the first pylon. If Ben got this far, he'd know the tattered gray sweatshirt belonged to her.

Katie stepped without a sound, alert for any sign of movement, any shadow of a human being. She strode cautiously along the wood deck, hoping the moonlight would be bright enough to pick out the rich colors of Cade's boat. Straining to picture the path she'd taken with Cade a few nights earlier, Katie walked slowly, craning her neck to look down each branching arm of the dock. Near the end, Katie finally spotted the vibrantly hued cruiser. It seemed larger than she remembered but she was sure it was Cade's. The brass rails and fittings sparkled in the low light and she could see it moving smoothly with the tide of the water that slapped softly against the dock. As Katie edged closer, she could detect the faint glow of light in the cabin area where the curtains had been drawn tightly over the windows.

Katie had taken off her flip-flops a long time ago so they wouldn't make any noise on the wood slats of the dock. She now put them down next to the pylon closest to Cade's boat. Another clue to her whereabouts, she hoped. Ben had seen her wear the pink bejeweled thongs a hundred times and had even teased her about them so she was sure he'd recognize them. Of course all of Katie's clues relied on Ogilvie actually going to Ben's house and somehow bringing him back. Ogilvie knew how to fetch a stick but fetching a person was a whole other concept.

Katie crouched down next to Cade's boat, trying to make herself as small as possible and disappear into the shadows. She was glad she'd put on jeans and was wearing a black tank top that would help her blend in. Katie watched the illuminated cabin, hoping to see some slight movement or hear voices. She knew she needed to ascertain where the occupants of the boat, if there were any, were located. Tired of waiting and hoping that if Cade and Bailey were aboard they'd be where the light was, Katie climbed onto the back deck of the boat. Straight ahead and up a couple of steps was the cabin. If she kept to the right, there was door she was sure led below-deck, probably to sleeping quarters. If Cade's boat was laid out like most of the same style, the cabin area held a lounge, a control deck and probably a kitchen area. It was designed for cruising and taking in the sights while relaxing and eating, inside away from bugs and humidity.

Katie crept along the side of the deck like a ghost, heading straight for the door to the belly of the boat. She reasoned that if Alex and Jessie were here, they were probably being kept out of sight where any noise they might make would be hard to hear from the docks. When Katie reached the small door that featured a clear, round porthole, she peered in but all she could see was blackness. Katie tried the door. Unbelievably, it was not locked. Katie eased it open just wide enough to squeeze inside. The moonlight leaked in through the narrow opening, illuminating the steps leading down. Katie pushed the door closed, holding her breath as it made a barely perceptible click when it shut. Katie thought she'd counted about eight steps in the fleeting moment she'd been able to see the inside. Warily, Katie felt for each step as she descended, praying she wouldn't stumble or trip. At the bottom, once Katie was sure she was on solid floor, she flicked on her flashlight, keeping her hand around the head of it so its beam didn't spread out and filter through the porthole in the door. Three small doors led off from the space. Katie figured two of them were sleeping berths and the third was probably a bathroom.

Katie switched off the flashlight, finding the door to her left by touch and memory. It opened easily and Katie felt around the wall. As she moved her hand down, her fingers swept a cool horizontal surface and then found the edge of the sink bowl. Katie lit up the room with her flashlight just for a moment. It was empty. Quietly, Katie shut the door and felt along the wall for the next opening. Her fingers touched metal hinges and then the cool smooth surface of a polished wood slab set into the wall. Moonlight shining through the porthole in the entry door bounced shadows off the wall and Katie could make out a doorknob. Guardedly, she turned the knob and the door swung inward as she held her breath, listening for any sound from the interior. She thought she heard a quick sob and in reflex, crouched down just inside the doorway. With the door open, the light from the deck created a soft haze in the darkness. Katie waited, allowing her eyes to adjust. Gradually, she began to make out a dark form in front of her. Katie stood up, flattening her back against the wall and slid along the perimeter of the room toward the shape.

When she got closer, she could see slight movement from the dark form and she began to hear what sounded like labored breathing. Her sight now crisper, Katie saw that the object was larger than it had originally appeared and was spread across what Katie realized was a full-size bed. Katie stopped, breathing as shallowly as she could, willing her eyes to tell her what she was looking at. When her vision ceased to improve, Katie knew she needed to make a choice. Either get out of there or turn on her flashlight, hoping she wouldn't find herself looking down on a sleeping Cade or Ted Bailey.

It only took a split second for Katie to make her decision. She quickly moved back toward the door, being careful to make no noise. She grabbed the door and silently closed it. Then, taking a deep breath she switched the flashlight on, her eyes glued to the shadowy form in front of her. The yellow light lit up the bed and Katie saw, huddled together, Jessie and Alex. Their hands were obviously bound behind them and they were gagged and blindfolded. A complicated system of knots ran along a rope that bound their ankles together and clearly prevented them from moving their legs more than an inch or so apart. Katie could see tear streaks on Jessie's cheeks as she leaned her head into Alex's chest.

Katie moved quickly to the bed and touched Jessie's shoulder. She shrank back, pushing against Alex and making a whimpering sound.

"It's OK, Jessie. It's me, Officer Katie Bell," Katie whispered. "I'm going to try to get you two out of here."

Jessie relaxed and nodded as Alex tried to speak through the gag in his mouth. Katie moved around to Alex's side and worked to untie the cloth behind his head. When she had removed it, Alex said "Jessie's neighbor, Bug's dad, helped the other guy bring us here."

"I figured that out when I went to the bungalows," Katie replied quickly. "Are either of you hurt?"

Before Alex could reply, Katie heard distinct footsteps coming down from the cabin. She listened as they moved along the deck. Katie switched on the flashlight and flicked it around the room. On one side were built in cupboards and closets, the only place Katie could hope to hide. She turned the flashlight off bolting for the nearest closet door. Then she remembered Alex's gag was off. She could hear the door at the top of the steps opening and then the distinct stomp of shoes on the stairs. Quickly, Katie ran back to Alex, sweeping the gag back into his mouth and hurriedly tying it on in a sloppy knot. The footsteps were now outside the door to the room and Katie flung herself at the open closet, shutting herself inside just as light burst into the room.

# CHAPTER 73

**Charles had driven** up and down the streets adjacent to the park for four blocks in each direction without seeing Bailey's car. Now he was approaching an anomaly in the grid pattern; bungalows situated in a U-shape around a central paved courtyard with a large oval of grass in the center. Charles slowed for the golf cart in front of him. When the golf cart reached the first leg of the bungalow court's driveway, it turned in, creeping along in front of each of the bungalows. Charles was curious: *who was out on a golf cart at this time of night and what were they looking for in this court?* As Charles cruised past the court his headlights focused on the gold Mercedes parked beside the corner bungalow. Charles squinted to read the license plate, then flipped open his cell phone. Within a few seconds, he'd confirmed that the car belonged to Ted Bailey.

Charles pulled his car into the driveway of a small cottage that was obviously uninhabited, then walked back toward the bungalow court. When he reached the house where Bailey's car sat, he noticed that the golf cart had stopped and the driver was gone. Keeping one eye on the golf cart, Charles moved around the bungalow, looking into the windows as he went. When Charles reached the rear of the house, he tried the French doors and finding one unlocked, he slipped inside. Drawing his Beretta from the holster hidden inside his jacket, Charles moved slowly from room to room. Satisfied that the first floor was clear, Charles located the staircase in the middle of the house and climbed to the top. Gun out in front of him, Charles entered each room, sweeping each space, confirming that no one was present. The moon shone through the uncovered windows and provided enough light for Charles to see clearly into each corner and crevice.

Charles went to a front window and flattening his body against the wall, peered out into the illuminated circle of houses. He could see the figure from the golf cart moving around behind one of the houses across the court. When it emerged, Charles could discern that it was a woman with long blonde hair pulled back at the nape of her neck. Charles recognized her to be Officer Madrid with the Potoma Police

Department.

Charles walked across the bungalow court, arms raised, palms showing. He'd returned his gun to its holster. Officer Madrid stood still beside her golf cart, her hand resting on the top of the Glock in her belt. Charles knew she didn't recognize him; when he'd been interrogated at the station he was still in drag as Aster. When Charles was about twenty feet from her, Officer Madrid identified herself and ordered him to stop. Charles complied, raising his hands a little higher.

"Officer Madrid. It's Charles. Aster Bancroft as you know me," Charles called in the loudest whisper he dared.

"Charles?" Officer Madrid questioned. "Are you armed?"

"Nine in my shoulder holster," Charles answered.

Officer Madrid, her hand still fingering her weapon, moved cautiously toward Charles. She flicked her flashlight toward him, moving the beam from his face down to his feet.

"Let me see the gun," Officer Madrid commanded.

Charles took one hand and pulled his jacket back to reveal the holstered gun. Officer Madrid moved in quickly, pulling the Beretta out and securing it behind her back, wedging it, barrel down into her belt. Then she moved back a few feet just as quickly, continuing to search Charles' body with the flashlight.

"What's in your pants?" Officer Madrid asked.

Charles could think of several crude responses but he knew what she was asking. "Mustang."

"On your ankle?" Officer Madrid said, nodding her head downwards.

"Yeah," Charles admitted.

"Give it to me slowly," Officer Madrid commanded, her fingers moving over the gun at her side.

Charles, keeping one hand raised above his head knelt down. Using his other hand he pulled up his pants leg and unbuckled the leg holster. Gingerly, he pulled out the small caliber back-up and put it on the ground, standing up slowly and backing away a few steps.

Officer Madrid stepped forward, her gaze still on

Charles, and kicked the weapon behind her.

"Why are you here?" Officer Madrid demanded.

"I was looking for Ted Bailey," Charles answered calmly. "He's not at home and his wife and son have no idea where he is."

"Katie told me about your phone call earlier," Officer Madrid replied. "What makes you think Ted would be here?"

"I had a hunch that his client probably lived near the park. After our bust tonight, I figured Bailey might try to meet with his client. Since the game had obviously changed now. I thought he might feel comfortable meeting at the client's house. I was out looking for his car."

"And you found it here?" Officer Madrid nodded.

"It's over there next to that bungalow," Charles answered, gesturing with his head. "The gold Mercedes."

"You didn't find anyone in the house," Officer Madrid said with certainty. Charles nodded.

"You know who lives there?" Officer Madrid continued. "Cade Ware. According to one of our upstanding and long-time residents, he's into some shady business practices. You think he's in league with your guy?"

"I do," Charles confirmed. "Seeing as Bailey's car is here at his house, it looks like he's the mysterious client Bailey met with in the park."

"That's what Anna had concluded, too. She was here earlier. Found blood in one of the bedrooms of that bungalow," Officer Madrid revealed, pointing behind her. "Also found some other items that indicated that Jessie Ashton and the boy we think is with her were in there. Maybe hiding, maybe being held prisoner."

Charles slowly lowered his hands. Officer Madrid gave him a half-smile, reaching behind her back to retrieve his gun. "I'm convinced you're a good guy," Officer Madrid joked, handing the Beretta to Charles. "Not a good woman, though."

Charles grinned, taking the weapon and putting back in its holster. Then he walked over and retrieved his Colt Mustang from the ground. Squatting down, he returned it to the ankle holster and quipped, "Good enough to fool a very savvy drug lord."

"No one ever said drug lords had good eyesight," Officer Madrid laughed.

Charles chuckled, moving his arms out in an I-give-up gesture. Then he turned serious. "Where is Officer Bell now?"

"No clue. The last time I spoke to her on the phone she was here. I told her to wait for back up," Officer Madrid replied.

"Do you think she would search Mr. Ware's house? One of the back doors was unlocked," Charles asked.

"Unlocked back doors are not a rarity in Potoma. Hardly anyone locks their doors around here," Officer Madrid replied. "But yes, I had the feeling she was on her way to do just that when we hung up the last time. She didn't answer the phone the last time I tried to call her."

"What did she know?" Charles inquired.

"I left her a message telling her that there were no police officers available for back up so she'd have to wait for me," Officer Madrid said. "At the time I was at least fifteen minutes out and Katie would have known that. I suspect she got impatient."

"Is she reckless?" Charles said with growing concern.

"No, I wouldn't say that but she's like a hunting dog with a scent. Once she's on to something, she can't let it go. I suspect she found some sort of lead and is following it," Officer Madrid commented.

"You don't think Ware or Bailey was here and did something to her?"

"I doubt it. She was pretty sure nobody was home."

"I didn't see anything inside or immediately outside of Ware's house that would indicate any kind of struggle or confrontation. I presume Officer Bell would put up a fight even if it was just a way to leave a clue for you," Charles remarked thoughtfully.

"You're right about that," Officer Madrid answered. "I didn't see anything out here either. Unfortunately, that means we don't have any idea where Katie is now."

"What do you suggest we do then?" Charles asked,

shaking his head in frustration.

Before Officer Madrid could answer her cell phone went off. She looked at the caller ID then immediately pushed the Send button.

"Hey!" Officer Madrid greeted the caller. "I'm so…" It was obvious to Charles that the person on the other end had interrupted her. Charles watched as Officer Madrid listened intently, concern and fear blooming in her expression. "I'm on my way," she said as she hung up.

"What are you driving?" Officer Madrid asked.

"My car," Charles answered. "What's the deal?"

"That was Ben. He's Katie's best friend. Katie's dog showed up at his house a few minutes ago. He was foaming at the mouth like he's been running full out and he didn't have a leash on. He was with Katie tonight. Ben thinks she let him go deliberately," Officer Madrid said hurriedly as they jogged toward Charles' car, pausing to take a deep breath. "Ben has this dog, Betsy, that Ogilvie—Katie's Lab—is in love with and Katie and Ben have this running joke that if you let Ogilvie loose anywhere in Potoma he'll make a beeline for Betsy. Anyway, Ogilvie was howling and whining and of course, Betsy woke Ben up and wouldn't leave him alone until he went to the front door. When Ben tried to pull Ogilvie into the house, Ogilvie resisted and twisted right out of Ben's grasp. That's totally unusual for Ogilive. Any other time, Ogilvie would knock Ben down just to get to Betsy. As soon as Ben stepped out onto his porch, Ogilvie took off down the street. I guess he saw that Ben wasn't following so he came back and kept running up and down Ben's front steps. So finally Ben grabbed his cell phone and got on his golf cart, following Ogilvie. Ben's sure Ogilvie is going after Katie."

Charles and Officer Madrid had reached Charles' car. "Where are we going?" Charles asked opening the driver's side door and indicating to Officer Madrid to get in on the passenger side.

"He's on Riverside Drive, going toward the marina. I suggest we try to cut him off there," Officer Madrid directed and Charles floored it, no longer concerned about keeping silent in the sleepy neighborhood.

## CHAPTER 74

**From inside the** tiny cramped closet Katie heard the footsteps stop, then shuffle across the floor. Katie was sure the person was standing right next to her hiding place. She tried to hold her breath, then when she thought she'd pass out from lack of oxygen she forced herself to breathe deeply and silently through her nose. Katie could smell a familiar aroma. As Katie remained motionless and listened, she could hear Jessie trying to hold back her sobs and Alex's angry ragged breaths. Katie could imagine how helpless both of them felt and at the moment, Katie was having similar emotions.

After what seemed an eternity, a familiar male voice said, "I'm really sorry, Jessie. I really am. I wish it hadn't come to this."

Katie heard a decidedly feminine guttural sound in response to the man's words and he spoke again. "You put me in a terrible position. But I know you didn't do it on purpose." The man's voice was full of remorse and Katie was sure he was acting in some measure against his will. "I'm so sorry."

Then Katie heard footsteps retreating from the room, the door banging shut and the distant sound of shoes on the staircase, ascending toward the deck. Katie waited until the footsteps had banged up the steps to the cabin before she emerged from the closet. She switched her flashlight on and sat down on the bed beside Jessie, putting her arm around her and giving her a quick squeeze.

"OK, it's time to get you two out of here before he comes back," Katie said as she pulled the blindfolds off of each of the teenagers.

Katie made quick work of each gag and then set to work on the zip-ties that bound Alex and Jessie's wrists. Katie looked around the room, quietly opening drawers looking for something to cut the plastic ties. Not finding anything sharp, Katie turned off the flashlight, then cautiously opened the door to the room. She slipped into the small hall and went to the bathroom. Shutting the door and turning on her flashlight, Katie opened the top drawer along the side of the sink cabinet. There she found a pair of nail clippers. Pocketing them, Katie turned off the flashlight and returned to the sleeping berth. She quickly cut the zip-ties, freeing Alex and Jessie's hands. It took a little longer and some maneuvering to cut the thick ropes around their ankles.

While Alex remained seated, flexing his hands and rubbing his ankles, Katie helped Jessie to her feet, steadying her as she swayed back and forth.

"Maybe you should sit back down for a minute," Katie suggested in a whisper.

It was then, as Jessie sank back down on the bed, that Katie heard the rumble of the boat motors revving up. "Oh, no," Katie said under her breath.

"What do we do now?" Alex asked in a whisper.

"They're going to kill us, aren't they," Jessie said fearfully.

Katie didn't see any reason to lie. "That's probably their intention," Katie nodded.

"Maybe we can get off the boat first without them knowing," Alex suggested.

"Maybe," Katie said thoughtfully. "Can you both swim?"

Alex and Jessie nodded. Katie observed the two teenagers in the glow of her flashlight. They were sitting close together and Alex now had his arm around Jessie's shoulders protectively. Alex still wore the scrubs he'd had on when he walked out of the hospital and Jessie was in the oversized dark clothing she'd been wearing on the security tape. It was obvious that they had been abducted soon after they'd left the hospital last night.

"Do you have a plan?" Alex asked anxiously.

"Not yet but I'm working on it. If we're contemplating jumping ship, we'll need to see where they are on the boat," Katie replied. "Is there anyone else other than Ted Bailey and Cade Ware?"

"If there are more, we didn't see them," Jessie replied. "It was just Bug's dad and another man. I don't know his name, but I saw him in the park with Mr. Bailey last week."

Katie tried to evaluate Jessie's state of mind. Now

that she was unbound, she seemed to be gaining resolve. "Did you hear what they were talking about?"

"I didn't get that close," Jessie answered.

"Well, I think they were afraid that you did," Katie said.

"And that's why someone tried to kill me?" Jessie surmised.

"Looks that way. Are you sure you don't know who came into your room that night?" Katie said.

"I really don't remember," Jessie replied. "I just can't believe it could be Bug's dad."

Katie could see the distress in Jessie's expression. "Maybe it wasn't," Katie said soothingly but she was pretty sure now that it had been Ted Bailey. He would have been comfortable and familiar enough with the Ashton house to carry out the poisoning. It just made sense.

"It feels like we're moving," Alex commented. "We'd better do something quick if we're going to get off."

Katie nodded. "I'll go up and see if I can determine where they are and make sure we're only up against two and not more."

Katie turned the flashlight off and handed it to Alex. "Just in case but keep it off for now."

"What do you think they plan to do?" Jessie asked tentatively, grabbing Katie's arm.

"The truth?" Katie asked.

"The truth," Jessie said.

"I think they plan to take you and Alex somewhere and get rid of you," Katie answered in her official police voice, devoid of emotion. "I think they believe that you know something that puts them or whatever business they're into in jeopardy. Unfortunately, Alex stood in the way of them getting to you alone and so now he has to be disposed of as well."

"I wonder why they've kept us alive, then," Jessie mused. "Why didn't they just kill us at the house?"

"Too messy would be my guess," Katie replied. "It's much cleaner to take you to some remote location. Then hide the evidence."

"You mean dump us in the river?" Alex injected

"Yes," Katie replied.

"I feel so bad for Bug," Jessie sighed. "Just thinking about what he's going to go through when his father is found out."

"If he's found out..." Alex said, his lack of conviction clear.

"Don't worry. I'm going to do everything in my power to get you two out of this alive," Katie said resolutely, and she meant it. "And if my dog and my best friend and my partner have anything to with it, we've got help coming."

"What do you mean?" Jessie asked, hope apparent in her tone.

"I've been in touch with my partner all night and she's on her way," Katie answered, avoiding the whole truth.

"You have a phone?" Alex said with excitement in his voice.

"I do but the battery went dead just before I got on board," Katie admitted, knowing without seeing his face that Alex had just deflated.

"But if the boat has left the marina, how will she know where you are...where we are going?" Jessie inquired.

"I left her some clues. Don't worry," Katie answered trying to sound encouraging. Katie hoped Ogilvie had gotten to Ben and Ben had gotten in touch with Anna.

"I'll take care of Jessie," Alex said.

"Just stay here until I get back," Katie said.

After leaving the berth, Katie tiptoed up the steps and slowly opened the door to the deck. When she was sure all was clear, she slipped through the door and retreated to the shadows along the side, craning her neck to look up at the cabin. She needed to discern whether the boat was being driven from the cabin or from up top. Silently, Katie edged around to the cabin steps and crawled up on her hands and feet, keeping her head down and body as close to the stairs as possible. At the top, Katie flattened herself against the door, hoping no one would decide to come through. The curtains across the windows had been opened and Katie could see clearly inside the spacious interior. Katie observed Bailey lounging on the built-in banquette, his back to her. Cade was at the wheel, looking out over the water in front of him. Satisfied that there were no others on the boat, Katie quickly scrambled back down the steps and hurried back to the room where Jessie and Alex were waiting.

# CHAPTER 75

**Charles saw the** black Lab first, illuminated in his headlights. A second later, a golf cart zoomed into view.

"There!" Officer Madrid cried, pointing, then rolled down the window and stuck her head out, waving at the driver of the golf cart.

The driver pointed to the dog and gestured for Charles to follow him. The dog had headed down the driveway into the marina. When they reached the docks, the dog continued onto the pier. The golf cart skidded to a stop and the driver began running after the dog. Charles slammed on the brakes and he and Officer Madrid bolted out of the car in close pursuit.

"Ogilvie's leash," Officer Madrid said as she and Charles hit the pier, pointing to the pylon. The golf cart driver was several lengths ahead of them gaining on the dog who had slowed, his nose to the deck boards.

Charles and Officer Madrid soon caught up and Officer Madrid hurriedly introduced Charles to Ben.

The dog was moving forward, running a few steps, then pausing to sniff the dock, the air, a pylon. Suddenly, the dog barked and they saw a sweatshirt wrapped around a pylon. The dog had bitten the sweatshirt and was trying to pull it off of the wood. Ben bent down, untying the sleeves and let the dog have it.

"She turned here," Ben said just as the dog darted off onto the branching pier. The dog trotted confidently, nose to the planks again with Charles, Ben and Anna right behind him. Suddenly, the dog pulled up, barking and whining. He was standing next to an empty slip, shaking a flip-flop he had in his mouth. Charles noticed the matching shoe laying on the deck.

"Those are Katie's," Ben and Anna said in unison.

"I'd say she was on whatever boat was docked here," Charles said, looking around and mentally determining that the surrounding boats were unoccupied.

"I'd bet you're right," Anna agreed. "Does Ted Bailey own a boat?"

"Not that we're aware of," Charles answered.

"Ted Bailey?" Ben questioned. "Isn't he Jessie

Ashton's neighbor?"

"Yes," Anna answered. "We just discovered he was involved with a big drug operation across the river. Jessie saw Bailey at one of the pocket parks with a client and we think she might have seen or heard something she shouldn't have. We're pretty sure that client was Cade Ware."

Charles noticed that Ben's jaw tightened at the mention of Ware.

"Should have known he was involved," Ben commented. "No wonder he was so intent on getting cozy with Katie."

"So if Bailey doesn't have a boat, maybe Cade Ware does," Anna suggested.

"He does. Katie mentioned it to me the other day," Ben confirmed. "We need to see the marina's log to see if it was tied up here."

"How do we do that at three o'clock in the morning?" Charles asked, pretty sure he already knew the answer. In the car, Anna had briefed him on Ben and his position in the community.

"Hang on," Ben said, hitting buttons on his cell phone. Within two minutes, Ben had hung up with affirmation that Cade Ware had moored his boat in that slip and a description of his fishing cruiser. "Now we just need to figure out which way they went."

"Taking your boat, then?" Anna said as she, Charles and Ben retraced their steps along the docks.

When they reached Charles' car, they piled in along with the dog and Ben gave Charles directions to the small slip on the harbor. Ignoring the twenty-five mile-an-hour speed limit, Charles sped through the narrow streets of Riverside, careening around turns and arriving in less than five minutes. While Ben started the engines, Charles and Anna untied the ropes and lifted the anchor. Charles was amused to see the dog at the front tip of the boat standing on the very edge, head stretched forward, as if re-enacting a scene from *Titanic*. He'd obviously been on this boat before.

"Up river or down?" Ben called to Charles and Anna.

"I'm betting that Bailey and Ware would be heading for a spot that's fairly remote. Logically, they'd want to get rid of any witnesses and they wouldn't want anyone to be around when they do," Charles offered and Anna nodded in agreement.

"There's a lot more wild shoreline upriver," Ben said matter-of-factly. "I'll head that way."

Charles and Anna moved into the small cabin and sat down in the comfortable captain's chairs behind where Ben stood at the wheel.

Without turning around, Ben asked, "So how much danger is Katie in?"

"Bailey was in pretty deep with the drug operation. He was the accountant but he also served as a liaison and kind of marketing rep, too. He never came off as the violent type though. You know, he wasn't a trigger man and he gave the violent action a wide berth," Charles replied. "He managed to keep his hands pretty spotless, actually. We discovered him by accident."

"What do you know about Ware?" Ben asked.

"Not much. He wasn't part of our specific investigation and so we didn't make any effort to check him out," Charles answered.

"I did a little checking on him when I discovered he was buying up real estate all over Potoma," Ben said. "No criminal background that I could find but several shady real estate deals up north."

"Let me guess," Charles interrupted. "Foreclosures and dumps for next to nothing. Then suddenly those properties are cleaned up, glammed up and the neighborhood is suddenly the next Beverly Hills except most of the houses have already been bought up by mysterious individuals or companies."

"Exactly," Ben replied. "You obviously did a *little* checking on Ware."

"It was something I just put together. Our guy liked to set up product distribution centers. Most of his activity is up north," Charles said.

"So you're saying that Ware was setting up these distribution centers, so to speak?" Anna said.

"It's what I suspect," Charles replied. "It all makes sense now that I have the missing pieces."

"That means that Ware was most likely trying to do the same thing in Potoma," Ben groaned. "And I just thought he was trying to run the regular Joe out of town and make a huge profit while doing it."

"Don't beat yourself up," Charles answered. "You didn't have all the information."

"So let me get this straight," Anna piped in. "Ware was buying up real estate here in Potoma on the pretense of historic preservation. But what he was really doing was setting up a huge drug distribution center. Dealers and other members of the syndicate would move in en masse and be able to gain control of town leadership. They'd be able to dominate town elections and appointments, putting their own candidates in office then hiring their own police force. Everyone would be under the syndicate's thumb and there would be nothing town residents could do about it except leave."

"That's what I'm thinking," Charles said nodding. "We have evidence of the exact same thing in two other communities. Unfortunately, not enough to make it a federal case but we have very strong suspicions."

"It sounds like if we take down Ware, with your guy's arrest, we'll put a huge crimp in the plan for world domination," Ben commented with a hint of sarcasm.

"Sounds like," Charles replied.

"All the more reason to find Ware and stop whatever he plans to do with those kids," Anna mused. "If Katie is indeed on his boat, I wonder if he knows it."

"Let's just hope he doesn't," Ben commented.

Charles stood up and squinted. He thought he could see a bobbing light in the distance, glowing through the darkness. Clouds had moved in and dimmed the moonlight that had been shining so brightly just moments before. Charles counted this a good thing—it would be more difficult for Ware to see them approach, especially when he probably had no idea he was being pursued.

"Think that's a boat up ahead?" Charles asked Ben,

pointing toward the bobbling beam.

"Most likely," Ben answered. "I'm going to speed up until we can make a determination. If it's another boat, I'll cut the engine and use the trolling motor to close in on it.

"Good idea," Charles said, patting Ben on the shoulder. Charles could tell from the concern and determination on Ben's face that his feelings for Officer Katie Bell went much deeper than friendship. Charles thought about his own wife, Ellie, whom he hadn't seen in weeks. Charles thanked God every day for her and her patience and understanding of how important his undercover work was to him. For a minute, he let himself miss her and think about how wonderful life would be when he held her in his arms again. Then he pictured his two sons, Hank and Charlie, Jr. and his sweet daughter, Hazel, with her red hair and freckles. Just imagining their smiling faces and unconditional trust in him made him more resolute to keep Alex Watson and Jessie Ashton from whatever harm Ware and Bailey intended to subject them to.

Ben was running his small fishing cruiser full out and Charles watched the wake churling behind them, foam topping the dark, cold water of the river. Anna sat slightly forward in her seat, straining her eyes to follow the blinking light ahead of them. Ben was rigid and Charles could see the impatience in his stance. The dog was still sitting on the front deck, leaning into the wind. Charles couldn't see the dog's face but he imagined his nose was working overtime and his eyes were glued to the light as well.

"Assuming that's Ware and Bailey up ahead, we should decide what action we're going to take once we catch up," Charles suggested after they'd traveled in silence for a good ten minutes. "We can probably sneak up pretty close but we'll only have a limited amount of time before they realize they have company."

"I'm thinking one of us needs to get onboard undetected to determine the situation," Anna replied.

"I agree," Charles nodded. "Ben should stay here on the boat. He'll need to be in place for a quick getaway or if things go badly, to radio for help, so that means one of us."

"I'll volunteer, Anna replied. "Does Katie keep a bathing suit here?"

"In the cupboard next to the W.C." Ben directed.

While Anna went below to change, Charles and Ben continued to mull over a course of action.

"Once Anna determines what we're up against, I'll probably need to get aboard Ware's boat as well," Charles said. "I can swim if necessary but I'm not exactly dressed for it."

"Don't worry about that. I can get you close enough to walk on," Ben said then gave a wry chuckle, "Assuming we're not dodging bullets."

"Well, let's hope that's not the case," Charles replied. "Best case scenario, we find the kids and Katie and get them off Ware's boat without him even knowing."

"And worse case?" Ben queried, looking worried.

"We can't get them off for some reason or Ware and Bailey discover our rescue attempt and it turns into all-out warfare," Charles replied.

"I presume you and Anna are armed?" Ben remarked.

Charles nodded, lifting his jacket to reveal the holstered Berretta. "I've also got a secondary on my ankle and Anna's packing her Glock."

"She can't swim over with it," Ben answered.

"You know how to handle a gun?" Charles asked.

"I have some experience," Ben replied. "My dad's a collector."

"Good. We'll leave Anna's gun with you," Charles decided. "Once I'm on board, I'll give her my second."

"You're assuming Ware and Bailey are armed," Ben commented.

"Of that, I'm certain," Charles replied. "Whether they've already offed the kids and are just looking for a place to dump them or they're saving the dirty work for the last minute, they're going to have insurance in case there are unexpected witnesses."

"Do you think Jessie and Alex are already dead?"

"According to Anna, Katie had found evidence that they were still alive at the bungalow. There was blood but not enough to indicate a fatal wound to either of them," Charles answered. "My guess would be that killing them in Potoma would be messy and trying to transport dead bodies from the bungalow to the boat would be way too cumbersome. It'd be easier to make them walk. Even in the dark, there'd be a chance of being seen lugging the bodies around. So I think they were alive at least until they got on the boat."

"So there's a chance they're dead already?" Ben asked, deep creases appearing in his forehead.

"Could be but I doubt Ware would be too eager to contaminate his boat with dead bodies. Even if they killed them in a non-bloody way, there'd still be bodily fluids to contend with," Charles predicted. "Ideally, I think he'd find the location for the dump, bring the kids up on deck, maybe tie on weights to make them sink. Depending on how evil he is, he might just push them off the deck alive and let them drown or if he's got a weak stomach, he'd shoot them in the back and watch them fall."

Charles could see Ben shudder at the thought.

"So if we can find Ware before he finds his remote location, we probably have a shot at rescuing Jessie and Alex?"

"I'd say we have a real good chance of it," Charles replied.

Ben was silent for a minute, then he said, "I'm thinking that we should let Ogilvie jump off with Anna. If Katie's on that boat, O will find her."

"How's he going to get up on deck?" Charles asked not believing Anna capable of crawling onto the boat with a sixty-pound canine under her arm.

"He'll get up there, believe me. Especially if he smells Katie," Ben assured Charles. "All he needs is a foothold and he'll climb and scramble like a monkey."

"Won't that be noisy?" Charles cautioned.

"Nothing the engines won't drown out," Ben replied

"Alright," Charles agreed. "But I want Anna to agree to it, too."

"She will," Ben grinned confidently.

"She will what?" Anna asked, emerging from the

cabin, clad in a black bikini with a tank top pulled over it.

"To Ogilvie going on board with you," Ben explained.

"Good idea," Anna replied. "He'll be the fastest route to Katie. And unless Katie's being held, she'll be with Jessie and Alex."

They were now close enough to the light they had been tracking to discern that it was indeed attached to a boat. Cade Ware's bright red and yellow cabin cruiser, just as the marina manager had described to Ben. As they had drawn closer, they had discovered that the light they'd seen from a distance was in fact several shafts of light shining through the cabin windows. Ben had cut the motor and they lay silent as Ben's boat floated on the mild current. From where they sat, they could see two figures in the cabin, one at the wheel and the head of another inside a window.

"Looks like Bailey and Ware are up top," Anna whispered. "That probably means that Katie and the kids are below."

"There's probably a sleeping berth or two and a head under the deck," Ben said. "When you get on deck, there will be a door with steps down, under the cabin."

"Gotcha," Anna said stepping out onto the front deck of Ben's boat. Ogilvie turned his head and looked at Anna inquisitively.

"We'll just follow at this distance until they get where they're going and hope they don't look backwards," Ben said.

Charles looked up at the moon still shadowed by clouds and crossed his fingers.

# CHAPTER 76

**Grace had finally** put two and two together and now she was pacing around her bedroom. In the wee hours of the morning, Grace had been lying in bed, sleepless, thinking about what she'd seen earlier. She'd been mulling over Casey Bailey's clandestine visit to Mr. Ping's house. It was obvious that hadn't been the first time Casey had sneaked over there. Grace was a bit put out with herself that she'd never noticed before.

At first, Grace had gloated over the fact that perfect Casey Bailey with her perfect family wasn't so perfect after all. *Casey Bailey, the poster child for good Christian wives wasn't such a good Christian wife, now, was she? Carrying on some sort of dalliance with Danny Ping. Casey Bailey, acting like she had such high morals and the perfect little life with her older husband and all his money.* She'd always reminded her of that stupid Jacqueline Kennedy who stood by JFK even though she knew he was always sleeping with other women and involved with the mob and doing who knows what other insidious things. Grace was sure that Jackie O was actually relieved when Johnny Boy was assassinated so she wouldn't have to live in his Hell anymore. Why she ended up marrying that fat, ugly, old Greek was beyond Grace's imagination but she figured Jackie just couldn't give up the money and celebrity in the end, no matter what it cost her. Grace had *always* pegged Casey Bailey as another Jackie Kennedy.

Grace didn't like to admit it now but there had been a time, in Grace's distant past, that she'd had a little crush on Ted Bailey. It was when she was still a teenager and although there was absolutely no physical resemblance, Ted had reminded her of Burt Reynolds. Most of the kids her age had no idea who Burt Reynolds was but back then, Grace had had thing for 1970's and 80's movies and he was in a lot of them. Her infatuation had only lasted about three months and Grace had chosen to forget about it. Until tonight.

The realization that Casey Bailey was involved with Danny Ping had brought it back to her because it made her remember the thing that had happened at the library last week.

Grace had thought it a bit odd but just like any other time a man showed interest in her, Grace made up excuses as to why he couldn't possibly really be interested and how it was all in her imagination. Grace had thought the same thing when Ted Bailey had showed up at the library and seemed to be flirting with her.

Grace had assumed that Ted Bailey was happily married to his young, pretty, exotic-looking wife and probably never gave another woman a second look. He certainly never looked in her direction when they had the monthly cul-de-sac barbeques. Yet, when he'd come to the library, he'd complimented her on her hair and her dress and how pretty she looked that day. He'd commented enthusiastically on how intelligent she was and what a great job she had. It had been very weird to say the least. But tonight as Grace pondered Casey Bailey's relationship with Danny Ping, it started to make sense. If Casey was neglecting Ted because of Ping, then understandably, Ted might be lonely. He might look for attention elsewhere. Like any man, he'd flirt with other women, maybe even try to hook up with someone.

But then Grace wondered why Ted would flirt with her of all people. She lived across the cul-de-sac from him. They socialized. She was only four years older than his oldest son. It was stupid. It didn't make sense. Something didn't add up.

And then that's when everything starting adding up for Grace. She'd been so enthralled by Ted Bailey's attention, his compliments, the way his eyes seemed to show appreciation for her; she was so caught up in the flirtation that she hadn't paid any mind to what else was happening. All the while, she had been clicking away on her computer, helping him find information. Helping him locate a rare and out-of-print book on natural poisons that they just happened to have in the archives at the library.

And then, in violation of library policy, she'd left him alone with the book. It was only fifteen minutes, and when she'd come back to the sterile archive room, Ted still had on the cotton gloves required for handling the book and there was no visible damage anywhere. Grace had checked each and every page of the thin volume after Ted had left just to be sure.

It all became clear for Grace in an instant. Jessie Ashton had been poisoned by some concoction made from plant materials. A concoction that Grace had no doubt Ted Bailey had found in the book she had given him.

Grace checked the clock. It read 3:15 but uncharacteristically, Grace was unconcerned by the hour. She needed to warn Casey Bailey about her husband. If Ted Bailey found out about Casey and Ping, he might try to do the same thing to her that he'd tried to do to Jessie Ashton. Grace hurriedly dressed and rushed out the front door.

# CHAPTER 77

**Casey realized she** must have dozed off on the sofa when she heard loud knocking on the front door. She quickly punched the button on her cell phone and when she saw the time she instinctively rushed to the front door. A jolt of annoyance hit her when she saw through the sidelites that Grace was standing on her porch.

Nevertheless, Casey opened the door and said graciously, "Is everything OK, Grace?"

"No, no it's not," Grace said, seeming somewhat flustered. "I did something stupid and Jessie almost got killed and now you might be in danger, too, if your husband finds out."

"Slow down, Grace," Casey said gesturing for Grace to come inside. "What's going on?"

Grace followed Casey into the living room and sat down next to Casey on the sofa.

"I saw you go to Danny Ping's house tonight," Grace began. "It's none of my business, I know, but it made me remember something about your husband."

"What are you talking about Grace?" Casey asked. She was alarmed that Grace had seen her at Danny's house. *What would Grace do with that kind of information?*

As if reading Casey's mind, Grace said, "Don't worry. I'm not going to say anything about you and Ping. Especially not now."

"Grace, what's wrong? Why are you here at three o'clock in the morning? And what does this have to do with my husband?" Casey asked perplexed and increasingly alarmed.

"Your husband came to the library where I work last week. On Thursday morning. He was looking for a book on poisons. More specifically how to make natural poisons from plants. He probably told me he was trying to find some information on natural insecticides or some such. I don't even remember. But I let him look at a book from the early 1700's we have in our archives," Grace said, looking at Casey expectantly.

"I don't understand where you're going with this,"

Casey replied, confused. "My husband doesn't garden."

"Duh!" Grace exclaimed. "The person who tried to kill Jessie Ashton used poison made from plants. Everyday plants everyone in the town has in their gardens. I looked at the book after he left."

Suddenly Casey's stomach began to flip-flop and she became nauseous. *Could Ted have possibly tried to kill Jessie? A girl that was like a daughter to him? Would he really do that?* Even though Casey couldn't get her head around it, something in her gut kept telling her that what Grace was saying was true.

"Did you tell the police about this when they questioned you?" Casey asked.

"I didn't think about it all until tonight," Grace answered, then added in a quiet voice. "Your husband was flirting with me and giving me all these lovely compliments and I was so flattered...well, I was so wrapped up in all that...it just didn't register what had really occurred until I saw you at Ping's house tonight."

Casey could see Grace's embarrassment and suddenly, she realized that Grace wasn't the strange, eclectic neighbor she'd always thought. Grace didn't think she was attractive and because of that, she felt awkward and intimidated by people who were.

"Listen, obviously, I don't care about Ted or what he does with other women. I do care what he tried to do to Jessie," Casey said, soothingly. "We need to call the police right now."

Grace nodded. "Ted hasn't come home has he?" Casey could see that it had just occurred to Grace that Ted might be in the house.

"No, and I don't know where he is either," Casey answered.

Grace was silent, biting her lip, deep in thought. "You don't think he might be involved in Jessie's disappearance do you?"

"I don't know. Ellen, Jessie's mom, did tell me that the police had proof that someone helped Jessie leave the hospital in disguise and they think it was one of her friends. A boy named Alex Watson," Casey confided.

"So if Jessie's with him, then she's probably safe?" Grace concluded.

"My son says that Alex is a bit weird but all in all a good guy. So Jessie is probably safe from Ted tonight," Casey answered.

"Good," Grace said. "I guess I'll call the police then."

"You can stay here until they come," Casey said, touching Grace's arm. "I'll make some tea."

# CHAPTER 78

**Katie started looking** through the drawers in the berth. When she was finished she'd found a pair of men's pajama shorts with an elastic waist, a small t-shirt she was sure didn't belong to Cade and a pair of men's swim trunks. She gave the clothes to Alex and Jessie and told them to change. If they had to swim, the bulky clothes the teens were wearing would bog them down in the river's current. Katie rummaged through the drawers again, finding another pair of men's swim shorts. Katie pulled off her jeans in the dark and put on the bathing suit. When everyone was re-dressed, Katie grabbed the cast-off clothing and stuffed it in a pull-out bin under the bed.

Katie went to the door and opened it, poking her head out to make sure the coast was clear. Alex and Jessie were leaning in close around her and she led them out and up the steps to the deck. Katie paused, listening for any sounds of movement on the deck. Just as she was about to push open the door, she detected a quiet scraping sound. The moon had gone almost dark and very little light leaked through the porthole in the door. Katie stretched up toward the porthole and staying flat against the door she peered out through the glass. Outside, it was almost pitch black and Katie couldn't see anything beyond the window.

"I hear something. It could just be the wind blowing ropes or debris but we can't go out there yet," Katie whispered, gently pushing Alex and Jessie back down the steps. "Stay here, and if anyone comes through door, get back in the berth and lock yourself in."

"Okay," Alex mumbled. "What are you going to do?"

"Right now, I'm just listening," Katie replied. "If it quiets down, I'll go out on deck and look around."

Katie could hear Alex and Jessie creeping down the steps. When she was sure they were ready to retreat into the berth if necessary, Katie opened the door and stepped out on deck, grateful for the darkness. She was standing in the blackest part of the deck and unless someone stood right beside her they'd never know she was there. Katie waited until her eyes adjusted. The boat was still moving forward at a good clip. This wasn't a good time for her or the teenagers to try to jump overboard. They'd have to wait until the boat slowed down a little or risk being pulled under.

Off to the right in the distance, Katie noticed a light that seemed to be gaining on them. She was sure it was a boat traveling behind them. *Maybe, we'll be able to flag them down if we jump,* Katie thought. *That is, if they continue on this course,* Katie said to herself. Katie looked toward the shore and saw nothing but emptiness. She knew that they were now in the twelve mile stretch of river that ran through a state forest and wildlife management area. No one inhabited this area on either side of the river and it was off limits to all land vehicles except for the park rangers' jeeps. Katie was sure that if the plan was to dispose of Jessie and Alex in the middle of nowhere they were only a few miles short of that location.

Katie tried to gauge the time. Without the clock on her cell phone, she had no idea how long it had been since they'd left the marina but she could try to figure out about where they were in the river. When she and Ben cruised for fun, it usually took them no more than twenty minutes to get to the wildlife management section. Ben's boat was much smaller than this one but Katie wasn't sure if that meant it was faster or slower. She was sure that Cade's boat had a bigger engine but she didn't know if the increased bulk evened it all out or not. Ben ran flat out when they cruised; Katie had no clue how fast Cade was going.

Katie glanced at the boat light in the distance. It was still moving toward them and seemed to be closer now. Katie began to hope it was Ben. She almost believed that Ogilvie had gone to his house and now he was racing to rescue her. Katie knew it was a long shot when she let Ogilvie go but he'd looked at her and taken off. He seemed to know what she wanted him to do and every instinct in her body said that he knew where he was going when he began to run. He hadn't even looked back. It was as if he was saying, *"I am going to see you again. I don't have to say goodbye."* Katie felt a tear slide down her cheek and she brushed it away. Until now, her adrenalin had kept her from thinking about the "what ifs". It had kept her from dwelling on whether that was the last time she'd ever see her beloved Ogilvie.

Katie slipped back in through the door and felt her way down the steps calling softly to Alex and Jessie.

"We're going too fast to jump right now," Katie informed them. "We'll have to wait until the boat slows down some. But when it does, we have to be ready. I'm pretty sure my theory was correct. We've entered a very remote stretch of river and I'll bet that we're going to be stopping soon."

"Shouldn't we be up on deck, then?" Jessie asked.

"As soon as the engines throttle down, we'll go up on deck," Katie instructed. "Until then, we're safer here."

"What if one of them comes down before then?" Alex asked.

"We'll deal with that if it happens," Katie said firmly. "They've already checked on you once. There's no reason to check again before we get to the destination. If they come down, it'll probably be to use the bathroom. We can just hide in the berth."

"That makes sense," Jessie said.

"I'm going back up on deck. If they come out of the cabin, I'll have plenty of time to get back in here or defend you, if need be," Katie said. "Just wait for my signal."

Katie opened the door and stepped back out on the deck. Katie knew Cade would be stopping the boat any time now. Clouds had covered up the moon but soon the sun would start to rise and Katie knew that what Cade and Ted Bailey were most likely planning to do needed to be done under cover of darkness. A cool breeze blew across the deck and reminded Katie of the evenings she and Ben spent on his boat, flying through the water, occasionally feeling the refreshing mist of the river across their faces.

# CHAPTER 79

**Ware's boat had** slowed and Ben cautiously cut his speed. Ben had also extinguished the light on the bow, using the cover of night to creep in. They were now trailing the other boat by less than a hundred feet. Anna was out on the front deck, poised to dive in as soon as Ware's boat stopped. Ben had figured he could get in about thirty feet without being immediately seen. They had the advantage at this point as Ware wasn't expecting any company. Anna would be able to cover the distance between the two boats easily and swiftly and if they were extremely lucky, she and the dog would be able to board Ware's boat without being detected.

Charles found himself holding his breath as Ben's boat closed the gap. Charles was keeping his eyes glued to the cabin of Ware's boat, willing the two men to stay put. When Ben gave the signal, Anna slipped silently into the river, the dog following her with a gentle plop. Making sure Ben had Anna's Glock next to him, Charles climbed onto the bow. He watched Anna and the dog as they moved silently and rapidly through the water toward Ware's boat.

The dog had moved ahead of Anna and when he reached the side of the boat he looked back at her as if to say, *"Hurry up!"* When Anna got to the dog, she reached under the water and found his back feet. Treading water, she took a big breath and grasping both paws in her hands, she pushed upward with all her strength. The dog seemed to spring out of the water, grasping the brass rail of the deck with his front paws. Then he walked up the side of the boat with his back feet, scrambling over the rail with a mighty bound.

"Rope," Anna called in a hoarse whisper. "Ogilvie, rope!"

A moment later, the dog was dragging a tie-on across the deck and dropping it off the side. Anna pulled the rope taut, testing it, then climbed on board. When she went over the railing, she dropped to the deck in a crouch, looking around her. The dog had trotted over into the dark abyss under the cabin. Anna followed the dog, disappearing from sight.

Charles kept his gaze focused on the cabin. He could

see Bailey and the other man moving around inside of it. They were talking and gesturing and seemed to be having some sort of disagreement. Charles saw the flash of metal and realized that Ware was waving around a pistol. Bailey was no longer standing, his head just visible in one of the cabin windows.

Charles looked down into the shadows where Anna and the dog had gone. He could make out several forms and as they moved further out onto the deck he recognized Jessie Ashton, accompanied closely by a teenage boy. Behind them were Anna and Officer Katie Bell.

"Come on, come on," Charles said under his breath. His adrenalin was pumping. Charles motioned to Ben to pull the boat alongside Ware's. With only a few feet separating Ben's boat from Ware's, Charles leaped and landed a little noisily on Ware's deck. Charles looked up at the cabin. Ware was moving toward the door. Charles waved Ben away who reversed the boat abruptly and silently dropped back into the surrounding darkness.

Charles ran across the deck, out of sight of the cabin.

"You're going to have to swim," Charles whispered to Jessie and Alex. "Our boat is right behind this one. Just head for the dark. OK?"

Jessie and Alex nodded. "OK, go. Now!" Charles commanded. The two teens rushed to the railing and dived into water, coming up quickly and stroking powerfully toward Ben's boat hidden from view by the black night.

# CHAPTER 80

**When the boat** had slowed down, Katie had gone back into the hold to get Jessie and Alex. Just as she'd opened the door to lead them out on deck, a wet and furry nose had nuzzled her leg.

"Good boy!" Katie had whispered. "Where'd you come from?"

"He's with me," Anna had said.

"Is Ben here?" Katie asked.

"And Charles. He should be on board any minute," Anna replied hustling Katie and the two teenagers out onto the deck. "Stay in the dark until we tell you to move."

When Charles had arrived a moment later, they'd sent Jessie and Alex overboard first. They could already hear footsteps exiting the cabin above. It wouldn't be long before they were seen, even in the dark recesses where they were standing, waiting.

Charles pulled his gun from its holster, then reached down and pulled a smaller weapon from under his pants leg. "You'll have to share," Charles said, a hint of humor in his comment as he passed the gun to Anna who stood directly behind him.

From their hiding place, Katie watched as Cade, gun hanging by his side casually, opened the door and disappeared below deck. Ted Bailey was apparently staying in the cabin for the moment. Katie knew that it would only be seconds before Cade discovered that the two teenagers were gone.

"Give me the gun, Anna," Katie demanded. "You go make sure the kids get to Ben's boat."

"And what are you going to do?" Anna asked.

"Charles and I are going to make sure you and Jessie and Alex get safely away," Katie replied.

"Charles can go. I'll stay," Anna protested.

"I'm not dressed to go swimming," Charles said.

Katie pushed Anna to the rail, snatching the little Mustang from her hands. "Go. And tell Ben to stay back. Do not let him try to save me."

Anna gave Katie a backward glance then dove

effortlessly into the water, using powerful strokes to gain on the two teenagers in front of her. Just as all three glided from sight into the murky beyond, Katie heard Cade running up the stairs. He flung open the door and stopped, gun drawn in front of him.

"All right, come out, come out wherever you are," Cade said in a sing-song voice. He pulled a flashlight from his belt, turning it on and emitting a powerful beam. Charles and Katie froze as he swept the light back and forth across the deck, its strong radiance coming closer and closer to where they hid in the darkness.

"Bailey, get down here," Cade shouted to the open door of the cabin. "Get down here, now!"

For the moment Cade was shining the flashlight in the opposite direction from where Charles and Katie stood. Katie watched as Bailey appeared in the cabin doorway.

"Why? What's going on?" Ted Bailey called down.

"Our guests have disappeared," Cade sneered. "Maybe you helped them when you came down before?"

"I did no such thing," Ted Bailey answered with vehemence.

"Then explain how they got free of those zip-ties and ropes," Cade demanded. "There's no way they could have done it without help."

"I swear, I had nothing to do with it," Ted insisted.

"I said get down here," Cade yelled.

"I'm coming," Ted replied, fear showing in his voice. Katie could see Ted Bailey's hands and legs shaking as he ascended the steps and came to stand in front of Cade.

"Oh, looky here," Cade said as his flashlight beam rested on the rope Ogilvie had dropped over the side for Anna. "Looks like someone has been on my boat without an invite."

"How do you know that's not how the kids got off?" Ted asked nervously.

"Really? They would have just jumped and swum to shore," Cade replied. "No, this looks like somebody was getting on, not off. The question now is, are they still here?"

"Why would they still be here? Wouldn't they have jumped off with the kids?" Ted asked, edging away from Cade.

"True," Cade said thoughtfully. "I guess we need to turn around and go back the way we came. I thought I saw a boat behind me earlier but then the light went out so I dismissed it."

The last thing Katie wanted to happen was for Cade to plow full-speed-ahead into Ben. She could hear pure evil in Cade's tone and she was sure that Cade would relish shooting Ben and wrecking his boat if given the chance.

"Cade, put the gun down. You're under arrest," Katie shouted, Charles' gun out in front of her, pointed at the sound of Cade's voice.

Suddenly, a shot rang out, the clang of metal-on-metal hitting to Katie's left. Katie ducked, hoping Charles had done the same. *Where is Ogilvie?* Katie thought. Charles pumped out a few rounds and Katie heard the ping of bullets bouncing around the deck. Cade returned the volley, making contact with the railing above Katie's head. Then another single shot and Katie heard Charles groan.

"I'm hit. Shoulder," Charles whispered.

"Get over the rail," Katie growled. "As soon as Anna heard the shots she was in the water. Trust me."

Katie heard the slide of metal on the wood deck and felt something hard ram into the side of her foot. "Trade ya," Charles said. Then Katie heard a gentle splash.

"Sounds like you hit something," Ted called out.

"Get up to the cabin and give me some lights down here," Cade ordered.

Katie had pocketed the Colt Mustang and was now fingering the Beretta. *Where is Ogilvie?* Katie wondered again.

"Katie come on out. The lights will be on in a minute and you won't be able to hide anymore, anyway," Cade called out. "I guess we won't be going to dinner again, huh? I mean I sort of figured that after how our picnic ended tonight with your boyfriend riding in on the white horse and everything but you know, I was still holding out hope."

Katie bit her tongue. She so wanted to tell him off but this was not the time. She couldn't afford to give herself away. *Keep talking Cade,* Katie thought to herself. She was following

Cade's voice with the gun. When the lights came on, she'd have one fleeting chance to shoot before Cade shot her.

"You're really too gullible to be a police officer, you know," Cade continued in a taunting voice. "You were so easy to con. I would have let you paint the murals. I honestly was looking forward to it. I really do have a soft spot for renovating old houses and bringing new life to them. That part was real, Katie."

Katie could tell that Cade was making his way around the deck. She wondered why he didn't just wave his flashlight around and find her instead of waiting for Ted to figure out the light switches.

"You are an exceptional artist, Katie. I don't know why you're wasting your time on police work. You're really not very good at the police stuff, you know," Cade went on. "I mean, just look at what's happening right now. You're all by yourself on a boat in the middle of nowhere with two criminals. What kind of chance do you really have? Do you really think you can arrest two armed men all by yourself?"

*Keep talking, Cade*, Katie muttered. *Keep talking. The longer I keep you here, the further away Ben can get with Jessie and Alex and Charles. Even if you shoot me, you'll have a hard time catching up with them. Besides, Ben's probably already called the Coast Guard and I'm sure they're on their way to apprehend you.*

"What's taking so long?" Cade yelled in the direction of the cabin.

He was met with silence. Katie held her breath. Then she heard Ted Bailey's voice.

"Hang on. I got it."

Abruptly, the boat was flooded with light and Katie could see Cade just a few feet away from her. As he lifted his pistol into the air, a black mass, Katie realized was Ogilvie, hit him in the knees and knocked him off-balance making his shot go wild. Katie fired the Beretta and watched as Cade's arm jerked back. Then Cade squeezed off another round barely missing Katie's head. Katie slammed her body down on the deck, aiming the Beretta at Cade's forehead and pulling the trigger. Cade crouched down just in time and the bullet plinked into the brass rail on the opposite side of the deck. Katie pulled the trigger again putting a bullet in Cade's knee. Blood spurting, Cade leaped to one leg and ran limping toward the cabin. Katie got off another shot, hitting Cade in the back. Cade fell to his side, screaming, blood rapidly pooling around him.

Katie had moved back against the side of the deck, next to the door of the hold. Now that Cade was down, Katie needed to find Ogilvie and get off the boat. Frantically, she scanned the deck, unable to see any sign of him. Katie opened the door and called out his name. She thought she heard him whine but couldn't ascertain where the sound came from.

Now Ted Bailey was coming down the steps toward Cade. "You idiot," Ted yelled as Cade continued to moan. "I could have taken her out from the cabin. It would have been an easy shot."

For a moment, Katie was taken aback. She'd thought Ted was being coerced by Cade. She'd figured that if she took out Cade, Ted would give up and cooperate. But now Ted was standing over Cade's body, looking directly at Katie, derangement dancing in his expression.

"I counted the shots, Katie. You might have one or two bullets left," Ted said. "Me on the other hand, I've got a whole clip just waiting to fire. And I'll bet I'm quicker on the trigger than you are."

Katie pushed the door to the hold open again and scrambled down onto the steps. She knew she was trapping herself but at least she could lock herself in if it came to that. She wished she could find Ogilvie.

"Cade was right about one thing. You're no detective. If you had been, you wouldn't have thought Cade was the one in charge," Ted said, shooting into the night air. "I'm wondering if I should just put him out of his misery."

Katie peered around the metal door, aiming at Ted who still stood over Cade. Katie couldn't get a good shot at him from where she was but maybe she could wound him. She had to incapacitate him long enough to find Ogilvie and get off the boat. Quickly, Katie stood up and shot, the bullet finding its mark in Ted's forearm.

"Wrong arm, Officer Bell," Ted said, his bold words belied by the pain apparent in his tone. "You really should have aimed for my head or my heart."

Katie stood up again, aiming higher but when she pulled the trigger she heard an empty click. She dropped back down behind the door.

"Oops! Sounds like you're out of ammunition," Ted laughed. "Time to surrender, honey."

Katie peered around the door and saw that Ted was moving toward her. She ducked back behind the door, on the verge of pulling it closed, when she realized Ted had stopped.

"Oh, there you are, you mangy mutt," Ted snarled. Katie knew instantaneously he'd found Ogilvie, even before she heard him growl. Then she heard Ogilvie's nails clicking rapidly across the deck in her direction. All of the sudden she heard the crack of the gun and heard Ogilvie squeal. His front legs and the tip of his nose were in her field of vision and he was just a few feet from her. She could hear him panting.

Rage welled up inside of Katie and she shouted "You did not just shoot my dog!"

"Afraid so, honey," Ted said sweetly. "Right now, I'm trying to decide whether to finish off the dog first or Mr. Ware here."

Katie slid her hand into her pocket, wrapping her fingers around the tiny pistol inside. *It's not going to be my O!* Katie thought with a swell of rage that resulted in a deafening banshee scream as she stood up and stepped away from the door, raising the gun with both hands and aiming straight at Ted Bailey's heart. She barely heard the pop of her gun as the smirk on Ted Bailey's face slid into a shocked frown and then his mouth opened in surprise. Katie watched with relief as Ted jerked forward, then back, his hand reaching for his chest as he slumped against the rail and slid down, sprawling on the deck.

Katie knelt down beside Ogilvie and was relieved to find that the bullet had just nicked him in his hip. He was already licking at his wound and struggling to stand up. "It's OK, boy,"

Katie comforted him, rubbing his head.

Katie stood up, waving both hands back and forth. Seconds later, Ben's boat pulled alongside Cade's cruiser and Ben leaped aboard. He wrapped Katie in his arms before kneeling down to scoop Ogilvie up and hand him over to Anna. Within minutes, a Coast Guard cutter had pulled up and the deck swarmed with activity. After giving the Coast Guard Captain brief statements, Katie, Ben, Anna, Charles, Alex and Jessie were allowed to leave the scene. The Coast Guard would secure the boat and tow it back to the marina. Jurisdiction would be determined later but since the incident involved two off-duty Potoma police officers and two men who resided in Potoma that the two police officers were actively investigating, it was assumed that everything would be handled by the Potoma police department. Unless Charles' organization wanted to take over, of course. Katie didn't really care either way. She'd stopped two would-be murderers and rescued two kids from the clutches of tragedy. Now, Ted Bailey was dead at the scene and Cade Ware was in critical condition, not expected to survive.

Ben had treated Ogilvie's hip and now he sat next to Katie, twining his fingers with hers, while Ogilvie lay on the bench beside her, his head cradled in her lap. Anna, feeling a little disappointed that she'd missed all the action, was working out her adrenalin driving Ben's boat. Charles was resting in the cabin below; Ben had cleaned and dressed the wound despite his distress over the sound of gunshots from Cade's boat. Jessie and Alex sat together on the bow, talking and laughing softly together. The clouds had lifted and a brilliant sunrise was just beginning to glow on the horizon.

# CHAPTER 81

**Casey and Grace** had just finished giving statements to the police officer when his cell phone rang. He excused himself and stepped out of the dining room. After a few minutes, he returned to where Casey and Grace were sitting at the dining room table, a grim look on his face.

"Ms. Bailey, I'm sorry to tell you this but your husband was shot and killed by police this morning," the officer reported.

Casey didn't feel any emotion at first. She knew she should be sad, angry, devastated even, but she didn't feel any of those things. The only sensation she could conjure was empathy for her two sons. She was already trying to figure out how to break it to them.

"He and another man abducted two teenagers and when police officers tried to apprehend them, they opened fire on the officers," the police officer continued.

"He had Jessie?" Casey asked, already knowing the answer.

"Yes, ma'am," the police officer replied. "It is my understanding that he and his partner planned to kill the two teenagers and dump their bodies in the river."

"Are you okay?" Grace asked, putting her hand over Casey's on the table.

"More than you know," Casey said with a small smile. She hoped the police officer wouldn't think less of her but joy was filling her heart bit by bit as the truth dawned on her and it sunk in that Ted was gone. Really gone. And now she was free and clear to be with Danny. No messy divorce, no awkward neighborhood scandals.

Casey decided she would savor the moment for a while before she woke Sebastian. First, she'd give him the good news that Jessie was alive and well and by that time, at home, next door. Then, as gently as possible, she'd tell him about his father and she'd tell him the whole story. How he'd been involved in a major drug empire and helped the kingpin set up drug dealers in dozens of small towns and cities. How he'd abducted Jessie and Alex Watson. How he and his partner had taken them out on the river and planned to kill them and dump their bodies so they'd never be found. She'd tell Sebastian the whole ugly truth and maybe, just maybe he'd find it a little bit easier to forgive her for letting Danny Ping steal her away from his father.

# CHAPTER 82

**After a mere** four hours of sleep, Katie and Anna were back at the station meeting with Charles and the police chief. They had convened in the interrogation room and were sitting around the conference table. The day shift had already searched Cade Ware's bungalow and found some pretty damning evidence that left no doubt that he had been a major player in the drug connection that Charles' team had taken down the night before. When Katie and Anna arrived, Charles had just been released from the hospital and was feeling no pain thanks to a healthy dose of Vicodin.

"Before you make out your reports," the Chief said, spreading his hands on the table around a sheet of paper, "I just want to go over everything again."

Katie was still feeling groggy from lack of sleep and she noticed Anna's bloodshot eyes indicating she was still half-asleep as well.

"Where do you want to start?" Katie asked, hoping for somewhere in the middle.

"At this point, I'm just interested in how Ted Bailey and Cade Ware were involved in a drug operation headquartered across the river and how Potoma became involved," the Chief directed, leaning back in his chair and gesturing for the others to begin. He made no move to write on the paper in front of him.

"In the course of our investigation into Big Drug, as we affectionately call him, we identified Ted Bailey as the accountant for the operation. He distributed all the money and even did some laundering when necessary," Charles said. "After a little surveillance we discovered that Big Drug liked a certain club and went there almost every night for dinner and whatever else he could procure, if you know what I mean." Charles grinned and tilted his head meaningfully.

"At first we were going to send in one of our female agents as a waitress but after a few of Big Drug's conquests ended up in the critical care unit, it was decided that it would be better to plant someone with a little more muscle. Big Drug definitely went for the voluptuous girls so I fit right in," Charles continued, cutting his eyes at Anna. "We lucked out when a house in the same cul-de-sac where Ted Bailey lived came up for rent and was available immediately. I was able to keep an eye on Bailey, follow his movements without him even suspecting."

"Didn't he ever see you at the club?" the Chief interrupted.

"Bailey never came to the club. He and Big Drug did most of their business over throw-away cell phones or through a courier. When Bailey moved money, it was through the accounts of fictional people, hard to trace," Charles answered. "Believe me, we did a lot of undercover work to find the connection. It wasn't easy but lucky for us, we've got some pretty good hackers on our side."

"What was Bailey's connection to Cade Ware?" the Chief asked, leaning forward now, intrigued. Katie had never seen the thousand-year old Chief so animated but then again this was the first major crime case that had come to Potoma since the famous love-triangle murder back in the Victorian era of the town.

"That's where it gets really interesting," Charles said, raising his eyebrow. "Ware, whose real name is probably Calvin Watts, set up drug distribution communities in unsuspecting areas. Small incorporated towns like Potoma with scores of houses in need of renovation and occupancy. Through Ware, Big Drug bought whole blocks of houses and fixed them up. Made those neighborhoods appear attractive and respectable. He'd recruit dealers and set them up in the houses with their families or, in some cases, various associates who posed as spouses, parents, siblings, whatever. The new residents would quickly become involved in town government and ultimately influence elections and appointments. The dealers themselves, or townspeople who could be bought, would gain positions of power and before you know it, Big Drug was able to do business in the town without any interference. Bailey controlled the money that Ware used to set up these operations."

"Bailey's lived here for years. Why would he want to bring drug trafficking to Potoma?" Anna asked.

"Bailey was getting ready to leave town. He'd already purchased a rather large estate in Florida and moved most of his own personal accounts to banks down there. A very young and very pretty blond is already residing in his new house, too. Looks like he might have been planning to retire," Charles shrugged.

"So how does this tie in with the murder attempt on Jessie Ashton?" the Chief inquired, tapping his pencil against the blank paper.

"Jessie Ashton was a part-time park monitor. You know, making sure kids were using park playgrounds safely, picking up trash, ensuring that gates were unlocked and locked at the right times," Katie replied. "According to Charles' group's surveillance, she was at one of the pocket parks near the bungalow court at the same time Ted Bailey met with Cade Ware there. We can only assume that they must have thought that Jessie saw or heard something and felt the need to silence her."

"I don't understand the weird plant concoction. Why not just strangle her or at least use a more conventional poison?" the Chief queried.

"We're sure Ted Bailey is the one that tried to kill Jessie. He'd have known the layout of the Ashton house and where Jessie's bedroom was. His family and the Ashton family were close and spent a lot of time together," Anna interjected. "We think Bailey was given the job of getting rid of Jessie but given their father-daughter-like relationship, he couldn't bring himself to cause her any pain. After doing some checking, it looks like the combination of chloroform and the plant poison was supposed to accomplish that. The chloroform would have knocked her out and the poison would have killed her while she was unconscious. She wouldn't have felt a thing. Using a poison made from natural materials had the added benefit of being virtually untraceable. It was made from common plants that you see in almost every yard in Potoma. Even if the doctors figured out what had been used, there'd be no way to connect it to one single person."

"Bailey sure went to a lot of trouble," the Chief mused.

"But Bailey was an accountant. Not the usual type to brew up poison."

"We suspect that Cade Ware actually made up the poison," Katie said. "Since his construction projects usually involved landscaping that he designed himself, he would have been more likely to understand the process."

The Chief nodded in understanding. "What about Jessie Ashton's disappearance from the hospital? What's the story with that?"

"When Jessie regained consciousness and was told that what happened she panicked. Her friends didn't help much because they panicked, too. They started talking about the person who tried to kill her coming to the hospital and trying again. When the hospital staff told everyone to leave, Jessie became terrified of staying there alone. Before Alex left, they hatched a plan for him to come back and get her out without anyone knowing. He was supposed to be back in an hour but his golf cart had mechanical problems and he didn't arrive until about four in the morning. Jessie had been given a sedative to calm her down so she fell asleep soon after her parents left the hospital about midnight," Katie filled in. She left out the part about Mick sneaking into Jessie's room.

"So this Alex Watson sneaks in via the back stairs, changes clothes with Jessie and she walks out without anyone knowing. Then he walks out the front door looking like any other orderly," the Chief said. "How did Bailey and Ware get to them?"

"According to Jessie and Alex, that was just luck on Bailey's part. The two kids had met up outside the hospital in the parking lot and driven away in Alex's golf cart. They hadn't planned what to do once Jessie was out so they drove around for a while trying to figure out where to go. They had finally decided to go to Jessie's house and had just entered the New Town neighborhood when they saw Ted Bailey driving out. They assumed he was on his way to work and when he stopped to talk to them they didn't think anything of it. After all, he was like a second dad to Jessie. Of course, they told him they were on their way to Jessie's house and apparently Bailey panicked," Katie reported. "He pulled a gun out from under his seat and ordered them to get in the car. Then with the gun sticking in Jessie's side, he drove to a nearby park and made them get in the trunk. At that point, we assume he called Ware and Ware drove over in one of his panel trucks to pick up Alex's golf cart."

"It's hard to believe no one saw any of this," the Chief said shaking his head. "You'd think someone would have seen Watson's golf cart, if you can call it that. It doesn't exactly blend in with all the others in Potoma."

The other nodded in agreement, picturing the odd, steam-powered contraption that resembled a Model T sitting on a golf cart chassis. "Anyway, Bailey took the kids to Ware's bungalow court and tied them up in one of the bungalows," Katie continued her narrative. "They gagged them so they couldn't make any noise and tied their legs together so they couldn't stand up or move around. After a while, Alex was able to work his pocket knife out of his pocket and cut off all the ropes that bound his and Jessie's arms and legs but the door to the room they were being held in was bolted from the outside so they were unable to get out. The windows had also been nailed shut. When Bailey and Ware came in later, Alex and Jessie attempted to escape and Alex succeeded in stabbing Ware in his shoulder. That was the blood that was found." Katie and Anna gave each other a meaningful look. "Alex's pocket watch must have fallen out of his pocket during the ensuing struggle."

"Unfortunately, Bailey was able to overpower Jessie and after he held a gun to her head, Alex gave up. Bailey and Ware tied them up again, this time with zip-ties around their wrists, and after it got dark took them out the back of the house," Anna carried on. "They took them to Ware's boat in his golf cart and stashed them in the berth."

"With the intention of killing them and dumping their bodies in the river," the Chief summed up. Katie and Anna nodded. The Chief looked at Charles. "How did you get involved with our investigation?"

"Obviously, I knew about the investigation Officer Bell and Officer Madrid were conducting because I was questioned several times," Charles answered. "Even though I was aware of Bailey's meeting with Ware and the fact that Jessie Ashton was present, I found it difficult at first, to believe that Bailey might be involved in her attempted murder. You know, given the families' longstanding relationship. But after a while, nothing else made sense. So I got a little more interested in Bailey's activities. We had bugged Bailey's office but pretty much ignored anything that wasn't directly tied to our investigation. However, after I reviewed some conversations Bailey had with Ware, it became apparent that he had something to do with the Jessie Ashton affair, after all. The fact that Jessie survived the poisoning and then regained consciousness really spooked him. Then he met with Big Drug last night—the first and only time he ever came to the club—on the orders of Big Drug himself. Big Drug was enraged over Bailey's failure to kill Jessie the first time. He became even angrier that Bailey hadn't already killed Jessie instead of keeping her and the boy alive all day. He threatened to kill Bailey's son and wife if Bailey didn't do the job last night."

"And so as soon as your team had taken down Big Drug, you decided to find Bailey and Ware, hoping to find Jessie Ashton and the Watson kid, too?" the Chief concluded.

"Exactly. That's when I ran into Officer Madrid and we joined forces," Charles added.

"Well, we certainly appreciate your assistance," the Chief said, standing and extending his hand to Charles.

"My pleasure, Chief," Charles replied, shaking hands. "Now, I really need to tie up some loose ends so that I can get home to my family."

Charles shook hands with Katie and Anna, too, then followed the Chief out of the room.

"How do you feel about the shooting?" Anna asked with concern.

"I'm good," Katie assured her. "It was necessary."

"You did good, Rookie," Anna said, putting her arm around Katie's shoulders and squeezing. "You saved some lives, too. Don't forget that. But next time, you better cool your heels and wait for me."

Katie rolled her eyes, grinning, then said, "I'm going home and sleep the rest of the day."

"Me, too. But first I need to tell you something," Anna said.

"What?" Katie asked, suddenly feeling anxious.

"You know that mysterious woman that Ben's been seeing and wanting to get more serious with?"

"Yes. You know who she is?" Katie replied, not really sure she wanted the answer.

"Well, we had a little talk on the boat last night on our way to rescue you," Anna replied. "And Ben was right when he told you that you knew her very well."

"And…" Katie urged, her curiosity overcoming her apprehension.

"All I can say is that I can't believe what a total idiot you are," Anna said grinning and shaking her head.

"What do you mean?" Katie said impatiently. "Stop messing with me. Tell me!"

"It's you, dummy," Anna laughed.

Katie felt her stomach leap and then do somersaults. Her heart began to beat rapidly and she couldn't stop the wide smile that spread across her face.

"Guess I won't be going home and going to bed just yet, after all," Katie exclaimed as she ran out of the room, down the hall and out the front door of the station. She intended to run all the way to Ben's house if she had to but Anna had followed her out the door and in no time caught up with her on her golf cart.

"Get on," Anna said, keeping pace with Katie.

When they reached Ben's house, Katie repeatedly hit the doorbell. Ben, obviously sleepy-headed came to the door in his shorts and a t-shirt but he was fresh-shaven and holding a cup of coffee. When he saw that it was Katie, he put the coffee cup down on the hall stand and held out his arms to her. As soon as Ben stepped out onto the porch, Katie wrapped her arms around his shoulders and jumped up, wrapping her legs around his waist. Taken by surprise, Ben gave her a perplexed look that was quickly replaced by a sexy, full-toothed smile when Katie murmured "Kiss me, already!"

# ACKNOWLEDGEMENTS

First, I have to thank my eternal cheerleader, my husband, Steve, for all of the encouragement and prodding to publish my writing. He always had the confidence I often lacked.

Secondly, I have to give credit to my three boys, Zachary, Hunter, and Zebulon, who generously gave me several lifetimes of insight into the complicated world of being a modern teenager. Love you guys!

Also, heartfelt gratitude to the late Anne Bolin, owner of the The Bell House Bed & Breakfast, an exquisite Victorian landmark in Colonial Beach, VA. Her enchanting historic house lured me there and Anne's sincere charm and hospitality kept me coming back. She was a dear friend. Along the way, this wonderful little river enclave inspired the fictional town of Potoma. Long-time Colonial Beach residents will recognize many of the places referenced in the book even though the names have been changed and I have used some artistic license in adding to, subtracting from, and re-designing the town to suit the narrative.

Thanks to my mama, Kent Snead and her partner in crime, Miss Betty (Newman) for plodding through the first edits. (And also to Mama, for reading everything I've ever written since I learned to write!)

As silly as it may sound, I also have to acknowledge and thank the many dogs I have had the pleasure of parenting, for teaching me about loyalty and unconditional love and making it possible for me to write dog scenes that are authentic and true.

# PLEASE WRITE A REVIEW!

Online reviews are so important to newly published authors like me. They give us credibility and are often the difference between someone purchasing our books or passing them over. They also give us the confidence and motivation to continue writing and pursuing our dreams of being published authors, and in the process, providing great books for you, our most cherished readers, to enjoy and live through vicariously. If you liked this story, I would be eternally grateful if you would take just a few minutes to write a positive, enthusiastic review that will encourage other readers to engross themselves in the adventure, too.

Thank you,
Susan

Please post your review at:     *amazon.com*
                                *goodreads.com*
                                *barnesandnoble.com*

Susan Carol Kent has been an avid reader and writer since childhood and a lifetime lover of history, mystery, old houses and horses. She has degrees in Historic Preservation, Museum Studies, and Rural & Urban Planning. She is also an award-winning artist and photographer.

*Bad Neighbors* is Ms. Kent's debut novel. As a recent empty-nester, she is pursuing her lifelong dream of being a full-time novelist and is currently working on an historical mystery series inspired by real people and events, and her travels to several historic places around the South. She has three adult sons and lives on a small farm in Buckingham, Virginia with her husband and an animal menagerie, mostly rescues, that includes eight dogs. When not writing, she continues renovations to her 18th century home and enjoys equestrian activities, hiking, kayaking, and costume design &needlework.

# PLEASE VISIT MY WEBSITE:

## susancarolkent.com

Get know me better, find information about this book and future novels, watch occasional promotional and personal videos, and read my weekly blogs that cover subjects like what I do "When I'm Not Writing Novels…" and "Authors I Like…Books I Like…"

# SEND ME A MESSAGE:

## wilddaffodilpress@susancarolkent.com